The Italian poet Petrarch is one of the  love poets of world literature. Born in 1304, Francesco Petrarca moved with l to Provence. On April 6, 1327, in a church in Avignon, Petrarch was smitten by the sight of a young woman named Laura. She did not return his love, but the love stayed with Petrarch even after Laura's early death. Love became a spiritual ideal, redolent in the natural world. Laura inspired the 366 poems that make up his *Canzoniere*, or *Rerum vulgarum fragmenta / Rime Sparse*, translated here as *Scattered Rhymes*. Petrarch lived till 1374, and was writing and revising his sonnets into his last years.

Born in Key West, Peter Thornton went to Regis High School in Manhattan, a Jesuit school for gifted students where the curriculum was based on Latin and Greek. After graduation from Boston College he earned his PhD from Stanford University. Peter was Professor of English at Bradley University, Illinois, before a career switch to the law, taking his J.D. from the University of Illinois where he was editor-in-chief of the Law Review. Scholarship became his private passion. Speaking French, Spanish, Latin, Greek, German, and Arabic, it was Italian that became the first language of his evenings and weekends when he worked on his translations. The deep range of footnotes to his translation of Dante's *Inferno* showed him at the cutting edge of renaissance scholarship. That same scholarship underpins his translation of Petrarch, alongside his determination to inhabit this classic of Italian literature as a poet and present the work in a voice that speaks directly to contemporary readers of English.

Petrarch's Canzoniere

Scattered Rhymes

Rerum Vulgarium Fragmenta
in a new verse translation by

PETER THORNTON

BARB
ICAN
PRESS

Published by Barbican Press in London and Los Angeles

Registered office: Kirkley House #5, Lowestoft, NR33 0DE, UK
www.barbicanpress.com
@barbicanpress1

Cover by Jason Anscomb
Text design and typesetting by Tetragon, London
Cover Painting: Laura, by Ken Hamilton

A CIP catalogue for this book is available from the British
Library

ISBN: 978-1-909954-33-5

For Catherine Thornton

Qui mai più no, ma rivedrenne altrove

For Catherine Thornton

Qui mai più no, ma rivedrenne altrove

Translator's Preface

Like most Anglophones of a certain age, I came to Petrarch in youth through sixteenth and seventeenth century English poetry – direct translations by Wyatt and Surrey, more generic imitations by many sonneteers. As years went on, I read other translations of Petrarch sonnets, but my sense of him derived largely from his general reputation as the poet unhappy in love. In middle age, when I finally began reading *Scattered Rhymes* in the Italian, my eyes were opened.

I discovered a poet who was new to me and I understood for the first time why his name still echoes almost 700 years after his death. I experienced a poet of intelligence, whose verse could be surprisingly vivid and evoke strong emotional reactions as it developed over hundreds of poems a subtle analysis of erotic desire and the poet's vain struggles against it, the ecstasy it brings, its inevitable frustration and resulting anguish, and the possibility of transforming the experience, including the anguish, into art. I was seduced by Petrarch's exquisite turns of phrase, his ability to combine strong emotion with delicate expression and his harmonies of sound that can transform what might otherwise be an ordinary verse into something memorable. Among other things, I had known only some sonnets before. It is true that sonnets predominate in the collection, but some of the canzoni – the extended, high-cultural form of lyric poetry at the time – are among Petrarch's best poems.

Not having found much like this in the bits of Petrarch I had read in English over the years, I thought of translating Petrarch the way he sounded to me. This has proved to be particularly challenging. Charles S. Singleton remarked in the 1940s that translating Petrarch was much more difficult than translating Dante's *Comedy* because the essence of Petrarch's poetry depends so largely on the "delicate interplay" of word and phrase and rhythm (*Italica* 24.2 (1947), pp. 177–79). Having published a verse translation of the *Inferno* several years ago, I definitely see Singleton's point, though I think his formulation rather slights Petrarch, whose greatness depends on more than exquisite phrasing. I could not, however, resist the challenge of seeing what I could do with these lyrics (preferably using off-rhyme in at least the sonnets), for which I set aside my draft *Purgatorio*.

Given the impossibility of reproducing Petrarch's verbal music in English, I decided that my goal was not to convey the matter of Petrarch's sonnets and canzoni in adequately carpentered English that closely followed his grammar, let alone his difficult Italian syntax, which the Italian commentators not infrequently feel they need to explain to Italian readers. My goal was rather to create modern English poems that made Petrarch present to a contemporary Anglophone reader, conveying emotional impact on their own, singing and weeping believably in the idiom of our day, the verses pulsing with a life of their own, so that to some extent the poems would constitute independent creations. In *Scattered Rhymes*, as opposed to the *Comedy*, one is forced to act more like a poet, not merely a translator, or one quickly drowns – because a word-by-word translation often results in a particularly prosy bundle of lines whose syllables have at least been carefully counted by the translator.

Licensing oneself to act as a poet, however, could all too quickly get out of hand, allowing the original Petrarch, with his complex and shifting personality, to escape. To cabin that tendency I imposed a boundary condition: my poems would remain translations, because they would not betray Petrarch's texts. They would remain recognizable. Admittedly betraying a text is a broad concept, one that applies to performance as much as translation. Does Laurence Olivier's *Richard III* betray Shakespeare's text? What about Ian McKellen's? This suggests at the least that a poem leaves room for different voicings of which a translator may take advantage – beyond that he must trust his conscience not to stray beyond what Petrarch is saying and feeling.

The above is simply my own naïve version of the millennial debate between close translation and free translation, intended to let the reader know where I stand in the matter. The reader will have to judge the extent to which I have succeeded in creating real modern English poems out of Petrarch's texts. One thing I notice is that my poems at least give voice to some of the varied moods in the Laura cycle not typically associated with Petrarch.

In 22.31–36 the poet's erotic fantasies grow warm:

> One night with her – farewell the setting sun,
> and no one there to see us but the stars –
> only one night and let there be no dawn!
> And let her not turn into green-leaf wood
> And so escape my arms, as on the day
> Apollo once pursued her here on earth.

In *RVF* 52 the poet sees Laura in a fictional guise:

> However much Diana may have pleased
> the lover who by like chance spied her bare
> amid the frigid water, I no less
> delighted in the shy hill shepherdess
> washing a wisp of veil to keep her hair,
> glinting with gold, protected from the breeze.
> And even now, when the sky burns above,
> she makes me shiver with a chill of love.

82.1–8 finds the poet in a rare mood of rebellion:

> My love for you has never lost its force,
> nor will it, Lady, while my life endures;
> but I am weary of my constant tears

and hatred for myself has run its course.
I'd rather mark my grave with a blank stone
than have your name, to tell my fate, inscribed
on marble where my flesh would lie, deprived
of soul with which it could have still been one.

In 90.1–8 he remembers seeing Laura in a moment that haunts him, returning in poem after poem:

Her golden hair, disheveled by the breeze,
was tangled in a thousand pretty knots;
innumerable lovely glinting lights
blazed, as they do no longer, in her eyes.
It seemed to me I saw her face become
colored by pity, whether true or not,
and since I had love's tinder in my heart
is it surprising that I soon caught flame?

In 126.40–52 he experiences ecstasy when he recalls seeing Laura in nature:

From lovely boughs rained down
(still sweet in memory)
showers of snowy blossoms in her lap;
and there she simply sat,
meek amid so much glory,
already smothered in a loving cloud.
This bud fell on her dress,
that one on her blond curls,
which that day looked no less
than gleaming gold and pearl;
some landed in the water, some on shore,
one in a graceful swirl
turning as is to say, *Love triumphs here.*

In 129.40–52 he is alone in nature and experiences ecstasy seeing her everywhere until the illusion dissipates:

Often I have (who will believe my tale?)
seen her alive in the transparent water,
the smooth trunk of a beech, on the green grass,
in a white cloud, so lovely she would force
Leda to see the beauty of her daughter
lost like a star the rising sun's rays veil.
The more remote the place
where I may be, the lonelier the shore,
the lovelier my mind imagines her;
when the truth dissipates
that sweet illusion, right there I sink down
cold, a dead stone upon the living stone,
shaped like a man who thinks and weeps and writes.

A glut of examples and we are still early in the collection. In 289.1–8
Laura has died, still young:

My quickening flame, fair beyond all the fair
to whom heaven was so generous and kind
has now returned – too early, to my mind –
to her own homeland and her proper star.
Now I awaken and I see she spurned
my ardor for my profit, not my loss,
adopting an expression sweet yet cross
to damp the youthful urge with which I burned.

In 311.1–8, the poet is lamenting Laura's death,

The nightingale that so melodiously
sobs for his young, perhaps, or his dear mate,
floods the dark fields with sweetness and the sky,
as skillful heartfelt notes keep pouring out;
all night it seems his sobs accompany
mine, stirring memories of my own hard fate;
for there is no one I can blame but me,
who thought no goddess subject to Death's might.

Here Petrarch has lifted the nightingale vignette whole from Virgil, but has made it completely his own. I hope in my smaller way to have done something similar with Petrarch.

As for whether I have betrayed Petrarch's texts in my effort to make them new, the main charge against me would be that I have often relied on paraphrase. Such reliance is inevitable because I chose to use off-rhyme at least in the sonnets, which I believe greatly enhances the ability of the verse to sing. In addition, however, I have often found paraphrase necessary to bring out my understanding of the meaning of a passage or my sense of its feeling.

To begin with the basics here: I have translated the text of the *Canzoniere* (the usual Italian title of the work) from the second edition of Marco Santagata (Mondadori 2004). Petrarch's poetry generally looks straightforward and amenable to word-by-word translation. I find that re-reading it, however, often reveals surprising ambiguities and uncertainties. This is confirmed when I turn to modern Italian commentaries, in which interpretations of passage after passage are contested.

Accordingly, my translation has been informed to an extent by Robert M. Durling's standard English prose translation; but by far my greatest influence has been the commentaries of Santagata in the volume cited above and of Ugo Dotti in *Canzoniere* (Donzelli 1996). In addition, I have reviewed and been influenced by the commentaries of Giovanni Ponte in *Rime Sparse* (Mursia 1976), Daniele Ponchiroli (in Gianfranco Contini's *Canzoniere*) (Einaudi 1974) and Ezio Chiòrboli in *Le Rime Sparse* (Trevisini 1925). All translation, including word-for-word translation, is interpretation; Santagata, Dotti and Ponte not infrequently differ from Durling's word-for-word interpretations and in such cases I have virtually always preferred their readings. Indeed I could often be accused of translating Petrarch's modern Italian commentators more than his text. When I do so, it is because I think that Petrarch's reticent style can make full understanding of many passages difficult.

In 338.12–14, a poem commemorating Laura's death, Petrarch ends by saying

> Nor did the world know her when she was here;
> I knew her, who to mourn her stay behind,
> and heaven, *che del mio pianto or si fa bello*
> [which from my weeping now is made beautiful].

I resisted this word-by-word translation of line 14 because it sounds like an inappropriate boast about Petrarch's poetry, but that left me puzzled about the meaning of the line. Then I saw that Santagata and Dotti agreed that Petrarch means heaven is beautified by the cause of the poet's weeping, which placed Laura there. Accordingly I translate:

> and heaven, which the tears' source makes beautiful.

Once you see this interpretation, you realize it is a commonplace of the poems lamenting Laura's death – her presence makes heaven beautiful – rather than the *lèse majesté* suggested by the word-for-word.

As with my *Inferno*, I have included a good many notes at the ends of poems. For the poems outside the Laura cycle, historical explanations are required. For poems in the cycle, there are often legendary details Petrarch drew from classical literature that need elucidation. The majority of the notes, however, are there simply because I do not find Petrarch an easy poet and wish to be helpful. If you do not find them helpful, by all means skip them.

I will stick to my translator's role and not attempt to offer critical perspectives on *Scattered Rhymes*. Critical sources that I have found enlightening are Marco Santagata, *L'Amoroso Pensiero* (Mondadori 2014); Teodolinda Barolini, "The Self in the Labyrinth of Time" in *Petrarch: A Critical Guide to the Complete Works,* Victoria Kirkham and Armando Maggi, eds., (University of Chicago Press 2009); Marco Santagata, *I Frammenti dell'Anima* (il Mulino 1992); Peter Hainsworth, *Petrarch the Poet: An Introduction to the Rerum Vulgarium Fragmenta* (Routledge 1988).

Abbreviations

Aen.	Virgil, *Aeneid*
Carm.	Horace, *Odes* in *Odes and Epodes*, C.E. Bennet, trans. LCL (Harvard University Press 1964).
Civ. Dei	Augustine, *The City of God*, Marcus Dodd, trans., Modern Library (Random House 1950).
D	Ugo Dotti
De Animal.	Albertus Magnus, *Man and the Beasts*, James J. Scanlan, trans. (State University of New York at Binghamton, 1987).
ED	*Enciclopedia Dantesca*, 2d ed. 6 vols. Umberto Bosco, director; Giorgio Petrocchi, editor-in-chief. Istituto della Enciclopedia Italiana 1984.
Etym.	Isidore of Seville, *Etymoligiarium sive Originum.* W.M. Lindsay, ed. 2 vols. (Oxford University Press 1911).
Fam.	Francesco Petrarch, Letters on Familiar Matters I–XXIV, Aldo S. Bernardo trans., 3 vol. (Italica Press 2005).
Golden Legend	Jacobus de Voragine, *The Golden Legend: readings on the saints.* 2 vol. William Granger Ryan, trans. (Princeton University Press 1993)
Inf.	Dante, *Inferno*
Lindberg	David C. Lindberg, *The Beginnings of Western Science* (University of Chicago Press 1992).
Metam.	Ovid, *Metamorphoses.* Frank Justus Miller, trans.; rev.

	G.P. Goold. 2 vols. LCL (Harvard University Press 1977, 1984).
My Secret	Petrarch, *My Secret Book,* trans. J.G. Nichols, foreword Germaine Greer (Hesperus Press 2002)
Nat. Hist.	Pliny the Elder, *Natural History*, H. Rackham et al. trans. 10 vols. LCL (Harvard University Press 1949 *et seq.*)
Par.	Dante, *Paradiso*
Purg.	Dante, *Purgatorio*
Rel. L.	Petrarch on Religious Leisure, Susan S. Schearer, ed. and trans; intro. Ronald G. Witt (Italica Press 2002)
S	Marco Santagata
Sen.	Francesco Petrarch, Letters of Old Age I-XVIII, Aldo S. Bernardo, Saul Levin & Reta A. Bernard trans., 2 vol. (Italica Press 2005).
TM2	Petrarch, Triumph of Death II in *Trionfi, Rime estravaganti, Codice degli Abozzi.* Vinicio Pacca and Laura Paolio, eds. *(Mondadori 1996).*
VE	Dante, *De Vulgari Eloquentia*

PART ONE

1 *Voi ch'ascoltate in rime sparsi il suono*

> You that will hear in scattered bits of rhyme
> the sound of sighs on which I fed my heart
> in my first youthful folly, when in part
> I was another man than who I am,
>
> the changing tones in which I speak and weep,
> between my empty hopes and useless pain,
> among those who know love through trial may gain
> forgiveness, even pity, I would hope.
>
> But now I see how long when I was young
> I was a byword upon every tongue,
> for which I frequently am filled with shame;
>
> this is the fruit of my crazed wandering,
> with penitence and a clear grasp of one thing:
> the pleasure of this world is a brief dream.

Probably written as an introduction to one of the drafts of *Scattered Rhymes* (*rime sparsi*, 1.1) after Laura's death, this sonnet tracks the opening paragraphs of Petrarch's Letter to Posterity, his brief account of his life. *Sen.* 18.1 (672–73). But the collection as a whole (on which he continued to work for a good many years) is not reducible to the simple arc described in these two passages. **12:** *wandering:* between empty hopes and useless pain.

2 *Per fare un leggiadra sua vendetta*

> To take his elegant revenge on me
> and punish in one day a thousand slights,
> Love took his bow and kept me in his sights,
> lying in wait and watching secretly.

My forces huddled in the heart's stronghold,
there and behind the eyes to mount my main
defenses, when the fatal stroke came down
where every arrow's point used to be dulled.

Thrown in confusion by that first attack,
they lacked the opportunity or power
to take up weapons in that desperate hour

or lead me wisely by the weary track
up the high mountainside above the rout
from which they would but cannot guide me out.

5–8: Love enters by the eyes and strikes the heart; see 3.9–10.   5: *forces*: the
poet's reason and will (S).   12: *mountainside*: the seat of reason in the head (S).

3 *Era il giorno ch'al sol si scoloraro*

It was Good Friday, when the sun's bright rays
in sorrow for their maker dim their light,
when I was taken captive without fight,
Lady, for I was snared by your bright gaze.

It seemed a time I did not need to don
armor against Love's shafts: I went my way
secure and unconcerned; and on that day
of general grief my suffering began.
Unarmed Love found me, for no watch was set
to guard the path that led from eyes to heart,
eyes that are open sluices for tears now.

I think his gain in honor was not great,
wounding me with an arrow in that state
while to you, armed, he never showed his bow.

Petrarch first sees Laura. He said elsewhere that he first saw her on April 6, 1327
in the church of St. Claire in Avignon. This fatal meeting sets the stage for the
Scattered Rhymes and will be recalled numerous times in the collection.

4 *Que' ch'infinita providentia et arte*

He whose design and boundless providence
in all his wondrous handiwork appear,
who rounded this and the other hemisphere
and tempered Mars with Jove's mild influence,

coming on earth to illuminate the truth
hidden in scripture for so many years,
called John and Peter from their fishing gear
and granted heavenly portions to them both.

It pleases him to raise the humble one
above the rest and so he chose to grace
Judea and not proud Rome with his birth,

and from a village gives us a new sun,
for which we must thank nature and the place
where such a beauty has appeared on earth.

4: *i.e.*, the astrological effects of Mars and Jupiter.   **5–6**: As illuminating a
manuscript illustrates its meaning, the incarnation of Jesus revealed the truth of
Old Testament prophecies.   **7–8**: *i.e.*, carried out his mission through humble
men.   **9–14**: Laura as a new sun (12) appears pervasively in *Scattered Rhymes*.
Sometimes this is playful (see 100–1-2), sometimes, as here, it makes her take
on a world-historical significance. Though line 13 is careful to note that her
birth is the work of nature, it is nonetheless compared to the birth of Jesus. A
similar world significance will attend the image in the poems after her death.

5 *Quando io movo i sospiri a chiamar voi*

When I invoke you, breathing out my sighs,
and call your name, which Love wrote on my heart,
the first sweet syllable with which it starts
in LAUdatory sound begins your praise.

Your REgal state, the next one that occurs,
doubles my strength for this great enterprise,

but then: "Cease TAlk; to praise her," the last cries,
"is weight for shoulders far more broad than yours."

Your very name thus teaches us to LAUd
and to REvere you each time anyone
calls upon you, who merit both from us –

unless it rouse the anger of the god
Apollo that too bold a mortal voice
dares speak about his boughs forever green.

The sonnet ascribes alternative made-up meanings (considered appropriate
to the subject) to the syllables of Laura's name (in the form Laureta), much as
The Golden Legend, the popular medieval collection of saints' lives, does with
saints' names.   **4**: The medieval etymology of "laurel" in Latin derived it
from "praise" (*Etym.* 17.7.2).   **12–14**: The reference is to the myth of Apollo
and Daphne, which underlies the collection's master image of Laura as laurel,
combining the elusiveness of the object of desire with the transmutation of the
desire into art. The nymph Daphne, vowed to virginity, was the daughter of
the river god Peneus. When she rejected the young Apollo's love, he pursued
her. As he was about to catch her, she prayed to her father, who turned her
into a laurel tree, her hair becoming leaves, her arms branches and her feet
rooted in the ground. Apollo still loved her as a tree and wore her leaves in
his hair and on his lyre; and he declared that the laurel would be evergreen,
always maintaining its loveliness. *Metam.* 1.452–527. The laurel wreath is the
official recognition granted to poets, of whom Apollo is the patron; its grant
to Petrarch was a highlight of his life.

6 *Sì travïato è 'l folle mi' desio*

My mad desire has run so far astray
in his pursuit of her who's turned in flight
and unencumbered by Love's snares is light
and flies before my lumbering delay,

that when I urge him most insistently
to the safe path, my lead he most disdains,

nor does it help to use the spurs or reins,
Love's made his nature so refractory.

And when he takes the bit between his teeth
he has me under his control and aims
against my will to carry me to death;

only to stop beneath the laurel tree,
where I pluck bitter fruit, whose taste inflames
my wounds instead of soothing them for me.

1 : *desire*: the image of a horse for sensual desire resisting the control of reason will reappear frequently in *Scattered Rhymes*. Dante had compared appetite to a horse and reason to its rider without which it cannot go right, no matter how noble its nature (*Conv.* 4.26.6), but the image was already common in classical texts.   **12–14**: With Laura as the laurel, we are already at the end of the Daphne myth; she has already become inaccessible by the time the poet pursues her. Or rather, the poet does not pursue her, but is carried away by a bolting horse against his will.

7 *La gola e 'l somno et l'otïose piume*

Gluttony, sleep and cushioned indolence
have banished virtue from the world today,
so that our nature's almost gone astray
from its own course through habit's dominance;

and so extinguished is the favoring light
of heaven, from which human life takes form,
one who'd make Helicon produce a stream
is pointed out as some astounding sight.

Who seeks the laurel or the myrtle now?
"Philosophy, you travel poor and bare,"
observes the crowd, intent on sordid gain.

Companions on your road will thus be rare;
all the more, noble soul, I beg of you,
hold to the great-souled task you entertain.

This humanistic poem is the first indication that the collection will not consist entirely of love lyrics. **2**: *virtue (vertù)*: has the primary sense of "strength, power, excellence," here a capacity for achievement exemplified by classical scholarship. **5–6**: *i.e.*, favorable astrological influences on life on earth. **7**: *i.e.*, one who would revive poetry, Helicon being the mountain where the spring sacred to the Muses rose. **9**: *i.e.*, Who seeks poetic glory? For laurel in this connection, see note to 5.12–14; myrtle, evergreen like laurel, was sacred to Venus and was also associated with poetry. **10–11**: Petrarch elsewhere complains that Cicero's works are neglected because greed turns men to other pursuits. *Fam.* 24.4. **12–14**: Santagata believes the poem is addressed to the Dominican friar Giovanni Colonna, whom Petrarch is urging to continue his Latin biographies of ancient writers.

8 *A pie' de' colli ove la bella vesta*

> Below the foothills where the lovely soft
> covering of her earthly limbs first dressed
> the lady who wakes weeping from his rest
> the one who sends us to you as a gift,
>
> free and at peace we passed along the way
> of mortal life, as all of living kind
> desire, without suspecting we should find
> an ambush in the path to make us stay.
>
> But for our present wretched situation,
> snatched from the life we led without a care,
> and for our death, we have one consolation:
>
> revenge on him responsible for our pain,
> who, near his end and in another's power,
> remains entangled in a heavier chain.

This is a note to accompany a present of game consisting of live doves; uniquely in *Scattered Rhymes*, they and not the poet are the speakers (S). Santagata regards this as the first of three occasional sonnets (but see also *RVF* 7) addressed to members of the Colonna family, a powerful clan of the Roman nobility. Several members of the family were Petrarch's friends, and Cardinal Giovanni Colonna was his patron. He would thus be invoking at the start of the collection not only Laura but also his protectors.

9 *Quando 'l pianeta che distingue l'ore*

When the bright planet that divides the hours
lodges within the Bull as the year turns,
the influence falling from its flaming horns
dresses the earth in a new change of colors;

not only do the first flowers decorate
the banks and hills spread out where we can see,
but underground, where it is never day,
earth's moisture is made pregnant by new heat;

then fruits like these are gathered. So the one
who among other women is a sun,
turning her eyes toward me, with their bright beams

creates in me love's thoughts and words and acts;
and yet no matter which way she directs
that gaze, for me the springtime never comes.

Note to accompany a present of truffles. **1–2**: When the sun (a planet in pre-Copernican astronomy) is in Taurus, from April 21 to May 21. **11**: In addition to the sun image, throughout these poems, Laura's eyes will be sparks and stars and are often simply called lights instead of eyes. The image is not merely poetic fancy but was consistent with a medieval optical theory deriving from Euclid and Ptolemy, which assumed the extramission of light from the eye. See Lindberg at 309.

10 *Glorïosa columna in cui s'appoggia*

Glorious column, on whom all our faith
and hope rests, as does Rome's immense renown,
who have not turned aside from the true path
despite the wrath of Jove in wind and rain:

there are no palaces or theaters here,
but firs instead and beeches and great pines,
between lush lawns and nearby foothills where
we amble up and down composing lines,

direct our minds from earth to heaven's vault;
and sweetly in the dark a nightingale,
lamenting every night sobs out her song,

filling our hearts with thoughts of love. In all
this pleasure the one defect is your fault,
my lord: you stay away from us too long.

Addressed to Stefano Colonna the Elder, head of the powerful Colonna clan.   **1**:
column: a play on the name Colonna.   **3–4**: The struggle referred to is either the
past war between the clan and Pope Boniface VIII, or, as Santagata thinks, their
recent siding with Pope John XXII against the emperor.   **4–8**: Petrarch was
staying with one of Stefano's sons, Giacomo Colonna, Bishop of Lombez, at his
estate in the foothills of the Pyrenees; in his Letter to Posterity, he still recalled
the stay as a "nearly heavenly summer." *Sen.* 18.1. The use of the first person
plural may indicate that this is an invitation to Stefano from the family there (S).

11 *Lassare il velo o per sole o per ombra*

Lady, I have not seen you put aside
your veil in sun or shade
since you first recognized in me the great
desire that chases others from my heart.
For while I kept my amorous thoughts concealed,
which through desiring have destroyed my mind,
the face you showed to me was always kind;
but since the day Love made my feelings known,
your blond hair has consistently been veiled
and your enchanting glance has been withdrawn.
Stolen is what I most desired of you:
the veil mistreats me so

it threatens death, because in heat or frost
the sweet light of your lovely eyes is lost.

One of the few ballatas in the collection.   **6**: *i.e.*, desire kills reason (S).

12   *Se la mia vita da l'aspro tormento*

If I withstand these bitter agonies
long enough, Lady, so my life endures
until I see the splendor of your eyes
dimmed by the progress of your final years,

your hair turned silver that is now pure gold
and your green gowns and garlands put away,
your face blanched that now keeps my pain untold
as diffidence makes my complaints delay,

then at last Love will make me bold to try
to tell what it's been like – the suffering
that one by one the years, days, hours bring;

if time precludes my sweet desires by then,
it may at least assist my sorrow when
it seeks some comfort from a tardy sigh.

13   *Quando fra l'altre donne ad ora ad ora*

When among other ladies now and then
Love shows his presence in her lovely face,
to the degree the others lack her grace,
by that extent my longing grows again.

I bless the place, the hour, the season when
I lifted up my gaze to such a height
and say, "My soul, you must be grateful that
you were accorded such an honor then.

"From her comes love's ennobling aspiration,
which guides your footsteps toward the highest good,
placing small value on what men desire;

"from her comes the bold, joyous disposition
that leads you up to heaven by a smooth road,
so now I walk in hope, my head held higher."

The idea of Laura as the poet's guide to heaven, so reminiscent of Dante, seems
out of place this early in the Laura sequence of *Scattered Rhymes*, where the focus
is on the pain of frustrated passion. It anticipates sentiments characteristic of
poems that come later in the collection, mainly after her death (S).

14 *Occhi miei lassi, mentre ch'io vi gira*

While I am turning you, my weary eyes,
upon her face who was your death before,
be wary, I implore,
for Love now threatens, which inspires my sighs.
  Nothing but death can close the loving route
that always takes my thoughts in the direction
of a safe anchorage in their sweet port;
  but a small obstacle can block your light,
your nature being endowed with less perfection
and your power being relatively slight.
  So, though already sad, before there come
the hours of weeping, now approaching fast,
seize the chance for a last
brief solace for your lengthy martyrdom.

This ballata is usually understood to mean that the poet is going on a journey.
He tells his eyes to take comfort in their last sight of Laura. **1–4**: Seeing her,
as well as not seeing her, causes suffering. **2**: *death*: Her splendor blinded
them. **4**: *threatens*: Seeing her is also dangerous to his heart. **5–10**: Distance
is no problem for the mind, unlike the vision.

15 *Io mi rivolgo indietro a ciascun passo*

With every step I turn back on the way,
dragging my weary body with much pain;
and then the air you breathe soothes me again,
which drives it further, crying "Misery!"

Then, thinking of the good I leave behind,
how short my life is and how long the road,
I halt my steps and stare, pale and dismayed,
and fix my weeping eyes upon the ground.

Sometimes while I am shedding tears, a doubt
strikes me: how is it that the body's members
survive, far from the soul that gives them form?

But Love replies: "How could you not remember
the privilege that no lover goes without:
freedom from all of human nature's norms?"

The poet is on a journey away from Laura. **3**: *air you breathe (vostr' aere)*:
carried on a breeze from where she lives in Avignon. **9–11**: The soul is the
animating principle that informs the body; and since Laura is his soul, how can
his body survive separated from her? **12–14**: The wry answer is that lovers
stand outside of nature.

16 *Movesi il vecchierel canuto et bianco*

The frail old man with reverend white hair
leaves the sweet place where his whole life was passed,
deserts his little family, all aghast
at seeing their dear father disappear.

Dragging his ancient carcass out of there
across his final days' remaining span,
he draws from his good will what strength he can,
tired by the road and broken by the years.

He comes at last to Rome, where he aspires
to look upon the image of the face
of him he hopes to see in heaven one day.

So, Lady, as I go from place to place,
sometimes, alas, I search as best I may
in others for your true form, my desire.

9–11: The old man goes to see the veil of Veronica, on which the image of
Jesus remained after she wiped his face on the way to Calvary. Preserved in St.
Peter's, the cloth was periodically displayed and revered by pilgrims. See *Par.*
31.103–08.   **12–14**: It is difficult to judge the effect of this profession of fidelity
couched in a confession of a roving eye, in which other women are the image
of beauty and Laura the reality.

17 *Piovonmi amare lagrime dal viso*

The rain of salt tears streaks my face, the wind
of anguished sighs blows through me every time
I chance to turn my eyes toward you, for whom
alone I'm separated from mankind.

It's true your sweet and gentle smile allays
the urgency of the pangs of my desire
and keeps me out of the tormenting fire
while, all absorbed, I hold you in my gaze,

but then my blood runs cold because I see,
when you depart, the two stars of my fate
turn their mild glance away from me again.

And finally liberated by love's key
my soul, to follow you, deserts my heart,
and tears itself away with rending pain.

9:   *my blood runs cold (gli spiriti miei s'aghiaccian)*: This is the first reference to
the poet's vital spirits, a term impossible to translate adequately and that will
be common in *Scattered Rhymes*. The usual translation, "spirits," is misleading

because in modern English it generally signifies simply one's disposition or mood. The vital spirits, derived from Gelenic medicine, are fundamental to late medieval physiology. They are subtle invisible vapors formed in the heart as part of the process of respiration and carried by the blood through the arteries, where they create the pulse and support the life of the organism. See *ED* 5.387. The poet's vital spirits freezing here is thus a change in his physical condition threatening death not merely a darkening of his mood.   **10**: *stars*: her eyes.   **13–14**: The image suggests death.

18 *Quand'io son tutto vòlto in quella parte*

When all my thoughts are centered on the place
in which my lady's beautiful face shines
with splendor that my memory retains
to burn and melt my insides piece by piece,

I fear my heart is breaking and begin
to see the coming failure of my light
and I go off like one who's lost his sight
and knows not where he goes but blunders on.

I flee this way before the strokes of death,
yet not so rapidly that my desire
cannot keep up as it has always done.

I go in silence, for my talk of death
would soon make people weep, and I desire,
when I shed tears, to shed my tears alone.

6: *failure . . . light*: death.   **9, 10, 12, 14**: *death, desire*: Petrarch's poem uses *rime riche* exclusively.

19 *Son animali al mondo de sì altera*

Some animals have such proud piercing sight
that they can gaze unharmed upon the sun,

while others, whom the glare of day would stun,
only come forth at the failing of the light;

still others, with the foolish reckless hope
they can enjoy the fire because it shines,
experience its other power, which burns;
and my place is, alas, with this last group.

I am not strong enough to face the rays
this lady shoots and cannot use as screens
late hours or spots where day-long shadow lies;

but notwithstanding my weak tearful eyes
my fate draws me to where she can be seen,
quite conscious I am heading toward the blaze.

Santagata notes that while in 18 the poet was fleeing from Laura's splendor, here
he is drawn back to it irresistibly by the desire that he said never left him.   **1–2**:
some animals: eagles.   **3–4**: *others*: nocturnal birds like owls.   **5**: *still others*:
moths.   **9**: *rays*: from her eyes; see note to 9.11.

20 *Vergognando talor ch'ancor si taccia*

Sometimes when I feel shame that I have not
sung of your beauty, Lady, yet in rhyme,
I think of when I saw you that first time,
knowing no other could so please my sight.

For such a weight I find my arms too weak;
this needs too fine a finish for my file;
and so my talent, measuring its skill,
finds itself frozen if it sets to work.

Often my lips have moved to utter speech
and then my voice remained inside, held back:
but to your height what voice could ever reach?

I start to write some verses now and then
only to find my brain, my hand, my pen
completely vanquished in the first attack.

21 *Mille fiate, o dolce mia guerrera*

To make peace with your splendid eyes, I know
a thousand times, O my sweet warrior,
I have surrendered up my heart, but your
high spirit does not deign to look so low;

and should another lady want him more,
she nourishes a false and feeble dream;
yet since I scorn what you do not esteem,
he can be mine no longer, as before.

If I disown him and he cannot find
shelter with you to ease his sad exile,
nor live alone nor go where others call,

I fear his natural course might meet its end –
a great fault on the part of both of us,
but since he loves you more, on your part worse.

5: *him*: *he, his* and *him* refer to the poet's personified heart. In the courtly love
trope the lover's heart leaves his body to go to the beloved.

22 *A qualunque animal alberga in terra*

For every creature dwelling on the earth,
except for some of them that hate the sun,
the time of toil is while it is still day;
and when the sky illuminates its stars
some return home, some nest within the wood   5
to take some rest at least until the dawn.

But I find, from the time the rosy dawn
begins to shake the shadows from the earth,
waking the animals in every wood,
no respite from my sighs beneath the sun;   10
then when I see the flaming of the stars
I go in tears, now longing for the day.

And when the evening chases the bright day
and our dusk sets the stage for others' dawn,
I gaze with heavy heart at the cruel stars   15
that molded me a frame of feeling earth
and curse the day that I first saw the sun,
which makes me seem a wild man from the wood.

I do not think that ever in a wood
so cruel a beast has fed by night or day,   20
as she for whom I weep in shade and sun;
first sleep does not abate my tears nor dawn,
for though I am a mortal body of earth
my unwavering desire is from the stars.

Before I travel back to you, bright stars,   25
or plunge amid the hopeless lovers' wood,
letting my body turn to crumbling earth,
if I once felt her pity me, one day
would compensate for years and till the dawn
bring me contentment in the dark of the sun.   30

One night with her – farewell the setting sun,
and no one there to see us but the stars –
only one night and let there be no dawn!
And let her not turn into green-leaf wood
and so escape my arms, as on the day   35
Apollo once pursued her here on earth.

But I will be in dry wood under earth
and day will be aswarm with little stars
before the sun arrives at that sweet dawn.

18: *wild man*: from roaming the woods in his grief. **24**: *from the stars*: fated by astrological influence at his birth. **25–26**: *i.e.*, go either to heaven or hell after death. **26**: When Virgil's Aeneas visits the underworld, he sees in a myrtle grove the shades of those whom unrequited love consumed with wasting. *Aen.* 6.440–44. **28–33**: Lovers' regret for the dawn is a standard theme of love poetry from the troubadours through *Romeo and Juliet*. **28**: *pity*: this key concept of courtly love originally, as here, means the lady takes pity on the lover's suffering by surrendering to his sexual desires. Often in poetry as in most of the *Scattered Rhymes*, it has a sublimated meaning. **37–39**: Before the wish of 31–36 happens, the poet will be dead and the stars will shine in the daytime. **37**: *dry wood*: uncertain meaning; Leopardi thought it referred to the coffin, but Santagata suggests that, reinforcing the trope of impossibility, it contrasts with the lovers' greenwood of 26, meaning a place where the poet would no longer love Laura.

23 *Nel dolce tempo de la prima etade*

Because the pain is softened when I sing
I first will tell of how I lived in freedom
while my heart still regarded Love with scorn
   in the sweet season of my youth, my spring
when, as it were a green shoot, there was born   5
the fierce desire whose growth would injure me.
   I will continue with how thoroughly
that angered him and how he took revenge,
making me an example among men;
   although by now my torment   10
is written elsewhere, till a thousand pens
have been worn out and almost every valley
still echoes with the sound of heavy sighs
that testify to my life full of pain.
And if my memory fails to aid me here   15
as in the past, my sufferings must excuse it,
and the obsessive thought that tortures me,
making me turn my back on every other,
forgetting all else and myself as well;
it governs what's inside me, I the shell.   20

Quite a few years had slipped by since the day
when Love had tried me with his first attack
and so my adolescent looks had changed;
    and all around my heart my frozen thoughts
had formed a crust now, thick and diamond-hard,   25
which never let my stern intentions slacken.
    Tears never yet had bathed my chest nor broken
my sleep, and what I did not feel inside
appeared to me astonishing in others.
Ah, what am I? What was I?   30
Praise a life at its end, a day at night.
For the cruel god of whom I speak could see
that his shafts had as yet not injured me,
piercing no deeper than my outer dress,
and sought help from a lady of great power   35
toward whom I found and find of little use
cunning, entreaty or decisiveness.
Those two transformed me into what I am:
a laurel tree, no more a living man,
that sheds no leaves in winter, staying green.   40

    Ah, how I felt when I was first aware
of the new shape transfigured from my own,
seeing my hair transform into the leaves
    that at one time I hoped would form my crown,
the feet on which I stood and walked and ran,   45
responding to my changing soul, change now
    into two roots beside the rippling waves,
not of Peneus but a prouder river,
and my arms turn themselves into two boughs!
No less does fear still freeze me,   50
remembering I was covered with white feathers
afterwards when my hope lay dead, struck down
by thunder when it mounted up too high.
For since I was not sure of where or when
I might recover it, I went alone,   55

weeping, by day and night where it was lost,
searching along the banks and in the stream;
my tongue would not cease mourning that sad fall
while it could still form words, but I took on
the voice and then the color of a swan.   60

  And so along the well-loved banks I went;
trying to speak, I sang continually,
crying for mercy in my alien voice;
    nor could I tune my amorous lament
to such a sweet melodious harmony   65
that her fierce heart might soften even once.
  What were my sufferings? Just the memory
burns me – but less than a memory of her,
my sweet and bitter enemy, which here
I am obliged to tell,
though she surpasses any words by far.   70
She, who with just a glance abducts men's souls,
opened my chest and took my heart in hand,
saying to me, "Tell no one about this."
I saw her later in another guise
that I did not – ah, blindness – recognize   75
and, trembling, told the truth at her demand.
Quickly resuming then, to my surprise,
her usual look, she turned me – here I groan –
into a stunned and scarcely living stone.   80

  She spoke with so much anger on her brow
she made me quake with fear inside the stone,
hearing, "I may not be what you believe."
  I thought: "If she depetrifies me now
no kind of life will make me groan or grieve;   85
come back, my lord, and make me weep again."
  I don't know how, but my feet moved, I went
from there and blamed no one except myself,
hovering all day between death and life.

But since the time is short,   90
my pen cannot keep pace with my intent,
so many things inscribed in memory
must be passed over; I will only speak
of some I think will make a listener gasp.
Death's hand had tightened all around my heart,   95
nor could my silence snatch it from his grasp
nor strengthen my now ebbing vital force.
Since speaking out had been forbidden me,
with pen and ink I cried in a loud voice:
"I am not mine; my death would be your loss."   100

   I'd thought that, though unworthy, I could make
myself seem worthy of her pardon and
this hope had made me bold enough to speak;
   but though humility can quench disdain,
it can inflame it, as I later learned   105
when I remained long muffled in the dark,
   for at those prayers my light had disappeared.
And I, not finding any trace of her,
even a print her foot had left somewhere,
like one who sleeps beside   110
the road, fell weary on the grass one day.
While there, reproaching her retreating ray,
I loosed the rein on my sad tears, to run
and fall as copiously as they would.
Snow never disappeared beneath the sun   115
as I could feel myself all melt away,
until beneath a beech a fountain flowed.
I spent a good long time on that wet road.
A living man from whom a fountain springs?
And yet I speak of open, well-known things.   120

   A noble soul, the work of God alone,
for from no other could such grace derive,
retains a nature like its maker's own,

and so is always ready to forgive
one who with meek face and contrite in heart   125
seeks pardon for however many affronts.
    And when against her custom she permits
the begging to drag on, she mirrors him,
doing it so backsliding is more feared;
for he does not repent   130
truly who is prepared to sin again.
My lady finally, moved by pity, deigned
to look at me and when she saw my sin
had now been equaled by my punishment,
kindly restored me to my human form.   135
A wise man, though, trusts nothing in this world;
for when I begged her once again, she turned
my sinews and my bones into hard flint;
and shaken from this burden, I became
just a voice calling Death and her by name.   140

    Like a sad ghost I can remember drifting
for many years through far-off vacant caves,
always lamenting my temerity;
    later I reached the end of that misfortune,
returning to my earthly limbs again,   145
only, I think, so I might feel more pain.
    One day, when following my own sweet will,
having as usual gone out to hunt,
I came where that wild creature, fair and cruel,
was naked in a spring   150
while the hot sun of noon was beating down.
Because no other sight can satisfy me,
I stood there gazing, at which she, ashamed,
whether to take revenge on me or hide,
splashed water in my face with both her hands.   155
Now hear the truth, though it may seem a lie:
I felt myself dragged out of my own shape
and instantly transformed into a stag,

roaming alone from wood to wood, spellbound;
and still I flee the baying of my hounds.   160

My song, I never was the golden cloud
that once descended in a precious rain,
partially dampening the fire of Jove;
but sparked by a bright glance I was a flame,
and I the eagle that soars high above,   165
lifting the one my tongue acclaims aloud;
nor for whatever new shape could I part
from that first one, the laurel, whose sweet shade
sweeps every lesser pleasure from my heart.

This canzone, the first and longest in *Scattered Rhymes*, tells of the poet's love for
Laura in six episodes, in each of which he is transformed in the manner of Ovid's
Metamorphoses. Although the changes (tree, swan, stone, fountain, voice, stag)
can all be found in Ovid, Petrarch's treatment of them is fluid and elusive, since
unlike Ovid's they are metaphorical and transient; and he adapts them with wit
to the conventions of courtly love.   **8**: *him*: Love.   **38–49**: *First transformation*:
Following the principle that the lover identifies with his beloved, the poet is trans-
formed into the laurel.   **48**: *Peneus*: the river in the Ovidian myth of Daphne;
the prouder river here is likely the Rhone, which flows past Avignon, where
Laura lives.   **50–66**: *Second transformation*. When Phaeton drove the chariot of
the sun off course, Jove struck him with a thunderbolt and his charred body
fell near the Po. His uncle Cygnus went along the banks weeping until he was
turned into a swan. *Metam.* 2.367–80. Here the poet's hopes are Phaeton and
his grieving in song turns him into a swan.   **71–86**: *Third transformation*. When
Battus saw Mercury steal the herd of Phoebus, Mercury bought his silence with
a cow. Coming back in disguise, Mercury promised him a cow and a bull if he
would reveal where the herd was. When Battus blabbed, Mercury turned him
into the stone whose silence he had promised to equal. *Metam.* 2.676–707.   **86**:
my lord: Love.   **101–20**: *Fourth transformation*. Byblis fell in love with her twin
brother. When he rejected her advances and fled, she wept until she was changed
into a fountain flowing at the foot of an ilex tree. *Metam.* 9.656–65.   **136–46**:
Fifth transformation. The nymph Echo loved Narcissus and when he died she
pined until her body turned to stone and she remained only a voice. *Metam.*
3.370–400.   **147–60**: *Sixth transformation*. Out hunting, Actaeon saw the goddess
Diana bathing naked in a forest pool. To avenge her blush she splashed water

in his face and turned him into a stag; he was hunted and killed by his hounds. *Metam.* 3.155–252. **161–66**: The poet contrasts his transformations, mainly punishments for his love, with those of Jove, which the god used to possess mortals he desired. **161–63**: He never achieved consummation of his desire, as Jove did when he satisfied his passion with Danae, to whom he appeared in a shower of gold. *Metam.* 4.610–11. **164**: He did, however, burn with passion, as Jove became a flame to deceive Aegina. *Metam.* 7.615–18. **165–66**: As Jove became an eagle to lift Ganymede up to Olympus (*Metam.* 10.155–61), the poet has lifted Laura with the honor his poems bring her. **167–69**: The poet clings to his first transformation, in which his soul merges with Laura's and in which he wins the poetic immortality recognized by the laurel crown.

24 *Se l'onorata fronde che prescrive*

If the much-honored bough that holds at bay
the wrath of heaven when Jove thunders down
had not refused to wreathe me with the crown
reserved for those who write true poetry,

your goddesses, whom our age shamefully
abandons, would be my friends at this hour;
but that injustice drives me now too far
from her who introduced the olive tree;

for Ethiopia's desert sands could burn
beneath the hottest sun no more than I,
losing what I so love, which should be mine.

Seek then another fountain more tranquil;
mine has evaporated and is dry,
save for the trickle that my eyes distill.

Response to a sonnet asking Petrarch to participate with the author in the fount of the Muses, source of inspiration. Here the two primary meanings of the laurel are in conflict. Laura, by inspiring the passion that spills over into the poet's vernacular love lyrics, has prevented him from attaining the studious wisdom embodied in Latin verse, for which he is suited and which alone is worthy of the laurel crown recognizing poetic genius. **1–2**: *bough*: the laurel, supposed to be immune from lightning. *Nat. Hist.* 2.56.146.   **5**: *goddesses*: the Muses.   **8**: *her*: Minerva, goddess of wisdom, the basis of true poetry, gave the olive to men. *Georg.* 1.18–19.   **12–14**: Unlike the fount of the Muses, the poet's has dried up except for his tears, which trickle out in sonnets.

25 *Amor piangeva, et io con lui talvolta*

Love, from whose side I've never wandered far,
wept when he saw – and I with him as well –
how, in the wake of a strange, bitter trial,
your soul had been unfastened from his snare.

Now God has turned you back to the right way,
for which I lift my heart and both hands high
to thank him that he listens graciously
in his great mercy when we justly pray.

And if, returning to the amorous life,
to make you turn your back on it again
you've found your path more hill and ditch than plain,

it was to show you what a thorny road
it is, how mountainous the climb and hard,
by which a man gains true worth for himself.

This and 26 are addressed to an unidentified poet who abjured love and love poetry but has now returned to them.   **3**: *wake . . . trial (per gli effecti acerbi et strani)*: as a result of the unexpected pain of an unhappy love (Bellorini).   **13–14**: As in *RVF* 13, Love ennobles his servant, making him leave the common herd; but the identification of erotic love with religion in this and the next poem is a transvaluation of conventional imagery.

26 *Più di me lieta non si vede a terra*

More glad than I am no ship reaches land,
having been battered by a furious gale,

26

while its crew, painted pitifully pale,
fall to their knees in thanks upon the ground;

nor happier one released from prison ward,
whose neck the rope already coiled around,
than I, who see the sword sheathed in the end
that made war for so long upon my lord.

Now all you poets who praise Love in rhyme,
honor this man, who skillfully will spin
amorous verses though he strayed one time;

in heaven there is greater joy for one
converted soul, and he finds more esteem,
than for the other righteous ninety-nine.

7–8: The poet of *RVF* 25 had attacked in his verse Petrarch's lord, Love, and has now returned to writing love poetry.   **12–14**: Petrarch audaciously applies the words of Luke 15:7 about the lost sheep to a convert in the religion of love.

27 *Il successor di Karlo, che la chioma*

The heir of Charlemagne, who now adorns
his brow with his ancestral diadem,
has sworn to take up arms to break the horns
of Babylon and all who bear her name;

at the same time Christ's vicar, with the weight
of keys and mantle, turns again toward home
and will, unless turned back by some ill fate,
first see Bologna and then noble Rome.

Your noble, gentle lamb has just laid low
the savage wolves, and let that be the doom
of all who'd split a lawful bond in two.

Comfort her, therefore, for she waits for you,
and Rome, who mourns the absence of her groom;
and buckle on your sword for Jesus now.

This sonnet urges Orso dell'Anguillara, who married Angese Colonna, sister of Petrarch's patrons, to join the (abortive) crusade of Philip VI of France, which Petrarch parallels with Pope John XXII's (abortive) intent to move the seat of the papacy from Avignon back to Rome. **1–2**: Philip succeeded his uncle Charles IV (*Karlo*), but Petrarch suggests that he is the heir of Charlemagne, supporter of the papacy and crusader in *The Song of Roland*. (In 28.25 he will be "the second Charlemagne.") **6–7**: *keys and mantle*: symbols of papal authority. **9–11**: *Lamb* plays on Agnese's Colonna's name. The specific reference is unclear, but the wolves are enemies of the Colonna. **13**: *groom*: the pope.

28 *O aspeƈata in ciel beata et bella*

Blessed and beautiful soul, whom heaven awaits
and who go clothed in our humanity,
not, like most others, burdened by its weight;
    in order that the road may be less hard
for you, obedient servant loved by God,   5
that crosses to his kingdom from down here,
    look – there has risen lately for your ship,
its back already turned upon this blind
world toward a better port,
the gentle comfort of a western wind;   10
this will propel it, freed from the old snares,
through this dark valley ringing with the tears
we shed for our own and another's sins
along a straight course now
to the true East toward which it turns its prow.   15

Perhaps all the devout and loving prayers
of mortals, mingled with their holy tears,
have finally reached the seat of highest pity;
    or it may be they never were so strong
or numerous their merit served to bend   20
eternal justice one bit from its course;
    but heaven's merciful ruler, in his grace,
has turned his eyes upon
the sacred place where he was crucified

and breathes into the second Charlemagne's breast   25
the vengeance whose delay has brought us loss,
loss for which Europe down the years has sighed;
and so he comforts his beloved bride,
for merely at his voice
Babylon trembles and remains distressed.   30

All those between the Alps and the Garonne,
between the Rhone and Rhine and the salt seas,
follow in the most Christian banner's wake;
  all who are zealous for true glory's sake
leave Spain as desolate as Aragon   35
from farthest land's end to the Pyrenees.
  The love of Christ makes England undertake
great things, with all the islands Ocean bathes
between the Wain and the Pillars of Hercules
– as far as the words reach   40
of the teaching of most sacred Helicon –
varied in arms, in costume and in speech.
What love, however admirable and right,
for ladies or for sons
was grounds for anger so legitimate?   45

There is a region of the world that lies
forever frozen under snow and ice,
far distant from the pathway of the sun;
  and there beneath the overcast short days
is born a people unafraid to die,   50
inimical by temperament to peace.
  If, more devout now than before, this race
buckles its swords on with Teutonic rage,
you should be able to assess the odds
on Arabs, Chaldees, Turks   55
and all who put their faith in pagan gods
on this side of the sea of blood-red waves –
a people naked, timorous and slow,

who never grasp the sword
but let the wind deliver all their blows.   60

  The time has come, then, to remove our necks
from under the old yoke and tear in two
the veil that has been wrapped around our eyes;
    now let the noble mind bestowed on you
by heaven through immortal Apollo's grace   65
and your rare eloquence display their force,
    now with your tongue, now your applauded pen.
If you are not amazed to read about
Orpheus or Amphion,
you should be less at sons of Italy when   70
they waken at the clarion of your voice
and rush to take their lances up for Christ;
for if this ancient mother face the truth,
in battles of the past
she had no rationale of such high worth.   75

  You who enrich yourself with a great treasure
turning the ancient and the modern pages,
and whose mind soars despite the body's load,
    know that from Mars's son's reign through the ages
down to the great Augustus, on whose head   80
a laurel crown was placed three times in triumph,
    how often Rome was generous with her blood
to others who had suffered injury.
Why would she now not be,
not generous, simply grateful and devout   85
in punishing the impious offenses
received by Mary's glorious son, our Lord?
What hope could any enemy still nurse
of mere human defenses,
if Christ should stand with the opposing force?   90

  Consider Xerxes' rash temerity,
who, that our shores might tremble at his tread,

devised strange bridges to enslave the sea;
    and you will see the women robed in black
in Persia for the husbands who are dead   95
and all the sea at Salamis dyed red.
    And not alone this miserable wrack
of the unlucky people of the East
promises victory,
but also Marathon and the fatal track   100
defended by the Lion with few men,
and many others you have heard and read.
It is most fitting therefore that you should
bend knees and mind to God,
that he reserved your years for so much good.   105

    You will see Italy and the storied banks
of Tiber, Song, not hidden from my sight
by sea or mountain range,
but only Love, who with his noble light
most makes me yearn where he inflames me most,   110
for habit slowly makes our nature change.
Go now with your companions; join the rest,
for not beneath some furbelows alone
does Love reside, who makes us laugh and groan.

Addressed to Petrarch's friend, the Dominican friar Giovanni Colonna (or else Bishop Giacomo Colonna), urging him to preach the crusade announced by Philip VI of France (see 27).   **1–15**: Petrarch begins by paralleling Colonna's having turned his back on the world to reach heaven and the crusader's turning his back on Europe to reach the Holy Land.   **10**: *western wind*: the promise of a crusade coming from France.   **13**: *another's*: Adam's sin, which wounded human nature.   **15**: *true East*: the heavenly Jerusalem.   **16–27**: Jesus looks at Jerusalem, now under Muslim control, and inspires a crusade in the king of France, heir of Charlemagne.   **28**: *bride*: the Church.   **31–42**: All of western Europe is emptied by enthusiasm for the crusade.   **39**: *the Wain . . . Hercules*: from north to south.   **40–41**: *farthest . . . Helicon*: i.e., Christendom; Petrarch treats his religion in classicizing terms by reference to the mountain sacred to Apollo and the Muses (see 65).   **46–60**: If Petrarch's characterization of 14th century northern Europe and the Near East appears naïve, it is because it is over a millennium out of date, drawn largely from Lucan's *Pharsalia*. **56–57**: Those on this side of the Red Sea are the peoples of north Africa. **60**: *i.e.*, they are archers. **61–70**: Petrarch urges the addressee to preach the crusade in Italy, not yet roused like the lands catalogued in the third stanza. **65**: *Apollo*: Christ. **69**: Orpheus made trees and mountains bow to his music. Amphion's music made boulders dance into the shape of the walls of Troy. **73**: *ancient mother*: Italy. **79**: *Mars's son*: Romulus, legendary founder of Rome. **91–105**: Xerxes of Persia invaded Greece by constructing across the Hellespont the first pontoon bridge, consisting of boats topped with planks and earth. His navy was wiped out at Salamis. His father Darius had been defeated at Marathon, and the Spartan Leonidas (*the Lion*) and his few men held off the Persian host for a time at the mountain pass of Thermopylae. **106–10**: Song, I am sending you to Giovanni Colonna in Rome, but Love keeps me here in Provence. **111**: See 7.3–4 (D). **112–14**: Go join my poems of love, Song; they are your companions, for you are about love of God and country (S).

29 *Verdi panni, sanguigni, oscuri o persi*

Never was any lady dressed in green
or dark red, black or violet,
with blond hair twisted in a golden braid,
as beautiful as this one is, who strips
my will from me and pulls me from the path   5
of freedom, till I find I cannot bear
any less heavy yoke.

And if my soul in protest takes up arms
because it lacks all judgment
at times when suffering drives to despair,   10
the sudden sight of her will call it back
from heedless frenzy and will wipe my heart
clean of all raving schemes; seeing her face
softens all indignation.

For all I've suffered on account of love   15
and have to suffer yet

until she heals the heart that she has bitten
– still pity's enemy, who still inflames it –
there shall be vengeance, if her pride and anger
do not close off to my humility   20
my lovely path to her.

  The day and hour in which my eyes first opened
on lovely black and white,
which chased me from the place where Love rushed in,
were the first root of this tormented life;   25
the other she, the mirror of our age,
whom one must be composed of lead or wood
to gaze on without wonder.

  No tears my eyes are shedding on account
of arrows that my heart, which felt them first   30
upon my left side, drenches in its blood
dissuade me from pursuing my desire,
because the sentence falls where it is due:
my eyes have caused my soul great pain, and justice
requires they wash its wounds.   35

  My thoughts and I are now become as strangers;
a queen, worn out like me,
once turned her lover's sword against herself;
I do not ask, however, to be freed,
for other paths to heaven are less direct,   40
nor could one hope to reach the realm of glory
in any safer ship.

  Favoring stars, gathered to be companions
to the most fortunate womb
when the fair child descended to the world,   45
herself a star on earth! As laurel leaves
are evergreen, so her prized chastity;
no lightning ever strikes her, no unworthy
wind ever bends her down.

I know that trying to enshrine her praises   50
in verse would overcome
whoever set the worthiest hand to pen:
what store-room of the memory could contain
the wealth of beauty and virtue that he sees
who gazes in her eyes where they shine forth,   55
the sure key to my heart?

In the sun's circuit, Love has not a treasure
more precious, Lady, than you.

This canzone is written in a difficult stanza form of a type seen in troubadour poetry. There are no rhymes within a stanza, but each line in a stanza rhymes with the corresponding lines in every other stanza (as do the do the half-lines that occur at lines 4 and 6 of each stanza). Thus all nine rhymes are repeated eight times, and the last three are repeated a ninth time in the congedo. **19**: *vengeance*: Laura's finally taking pity on the poet. **21**: *path (passo)*: her eyes (S). **23**: *black and white*: her eyes. **24**: *the place*: his heart, no longer his own. **36**: The warring thoughts and feelings are described in the rest of the stanza. **37–38**: Virgil's Queen Dido kills herself with the sword of Aeneas, the lover who has abandoned her. **40–42**: Here the idea of Laura as the poet's spiritual salvation (see 13) co-exists with, if it does not actually emerge from, the pain of frustrated passion, anticipating poems late in the sequence when he is glad that she refused him. **48**: *no lightning*: the laurel was believed immune from lightning.

30 *Giovane donna sotto un verde lauro*

I saw a maiden under a green laurel,
whiter and colder, as it seemed, than snow
no sun had struck for many and many years;
the way she spoke, her lovely face, her hair
so pleased me they shall be before my eyes   5
wherever I may go, on hill or shore.

When my desires shall finally come to shore
no green leaves will be left upon the laurel;
the day I calm my heart and dry my eyes

we shall see freezing fire and burning snow;   10
and numberless as are my strands of hair,
for that day I'd wait gladly still more years.

But since time flies through all the fleeing years
so in a moment we all reach death's shore,
whether it is with dark or whitened hair,   15
I shall seek out the shade of that sweet laurel
through the most burning heat and through the snow
until the final day has closed these eyes.

Never have there been seen such splendid eyes,
either in our age or the antique years,   20
which melt me as the sun's heat melts the snow,
forming a stream of tears along the shore
that Love leads to the foot of the hard laurel
with diamond branches and with golden hair.

I fear my face will change, as will my hair,   25
before I see real pity in her eyes,
my idol sculpted out of living laurel;
for by my count, today marks seven years
since sighing, I have gone from shore to shore
both night and day, in heat and in the snow.   30

Still fire within and outside white as snow,
left with these same desires and graying hair,
I still shall go in tears on every shore,
perhaps arousing pity in the eyes
of one not born yet for a thousand years,   35
could culture so extend the life of laurel.

Topaz and gold in the sun beside the snow
are conquered by blond hair beside the eyes
that lead my years so swiftly to the shore.

Seventh anniversary (28): the first in an irregular series of poems commemo-
rating the day on which Petrarch first saw Laura.   **1–3**: She is now an ice

35

princess, alluring but forbidding.   **8**: *no green leaves*: the first of three impossibility commonplaces; in contrast to 29.46–47, her chastity is not now being praised.   **23–24**: Reinforcing the opening verses, she is beautiful but hard, now metallic and mineral.   **27**: Most striking of all, the laurel image for Laura is transformed: she is an idol carved out of living wood, conveying the poet's unease at having made her into a false god.   **35–36**: The laurel is now not Laura but his poems about his unhappy love for her.   **37**: *gold (l'auro)*: The rhyme scheme calls for laurel in this line; by substituting the homonym, Petrarch evokes Ps. 118:127: "for I have loved thy commandments above gold and the topaz (*super aurum et topazion*)." The poet loves her hair and eyes, rather than God's commandments, more than gold and topaz.   **39**: *shore*: see 14.

31   *Questa anima gentil che si diparte*

The noble soul departing from us here,
called to the other life too hastily,
if she is valued there as she should be
will soon inhabit heaven's most blessed sphere.

If she remains between the third great light
and Mars, the sun's resplendent face will dim
as worthy spirits, clustering round her, come
to gaze on boundless beauty with delight.

If she stops rising under the fourth nest
each of the other three will be less fair,
for fame will cry that she alone is best.

She will not dwell in the fifth sphere of Mars,
but if she flies still higher, I feel sure
she'll outshine Jupiter and all the stars.

This poem appears to commemorate a serious illness of Laura's, but as Santagata notes, it sounds like a literary exercise. It plays with the convention that Dante observed in the *Paradiso*, where the souls of the blessed appear in the sphere of the planet whose character suits them. Laura's nature would suit her to many of the spheres.   **5**. In the geocentric universe the third light is Venus; between Venus and Mars is the sun, the fourth planet in that scheme.   **6**: *dim*: by comparison with her, as in lines 10–11.   **9–11**: The three lower spheres (in which the planets nest) are those of the Moon, Mercury and Venus.   **12**: The one sphere obviously unsuited to Laura is that of Mars, the war god.   **14**: Her outward progress would take her to Jupiter and ultimately the sphere of the fixed stars.

32 *Quanto più m'avicino al giorno extremo*

The more my final day comes into sight,
which serves to shorten human misery's span,
the more I see how time runs swift and light,
my hope for it illusory and vain.

I tell my thoughts: "We have not far to go
speaking of love, for now the heaviest,
most solid earthly burden, like fresh snow
is melting, which will finally bring us rest:

"for with that weight the empty hope will fall
that kept us raving for so many years
and all our laughter, weeping, anger, fears;

"then we shall clearly recognize how all
mortals are striving for a doubtful prize
and ah, how often we heave useless sighs."

7: *burden*: the body.

33 *Già fiammeggiava l'amorosa stella*

Already in the eastern sky there burned
the star of love, while in the frozen north
those others, cause of Juno's jealous wrath,
were wheeling their resplendent spokes around;

the poor old woman, getting up to spin,
half-dressed and barefoot, stirred the drowsing fire;
lovers were being prodded by the hour
that makes them all habitually complain;

when my hope, guttered to its stub, no more,
entered my heart, not by the usual way,
which sleep was keeping closed and sorrow wet –

how changed, alas, from what she was before!
"Why does your courage fail?" she seemed to say.
"Seeing these eyes is not denied you yet."

This sonnet appears connected with 31 on Laura's illness; as the poet grieves in his sleep, she appears to him in a dream to comfort him.   **2**: *star of love*: Venus as the morning star.   **3**: *those others*: the stars of the Great Bear. This constellation, which turns around the pole without sinking below the horizon (see *Georg.* 1.245–46), was once Callisto, a nymph loved by Jupiter, turned into a bear by jealous Juno and into a constellation by Jupiter. See *Metam.* 2.401–530.   **7–8**: Lovers feel grief at having to part at dawn, a common motif in troubadour poetry.   **9–10**: *hope*: Laura, wasted by sickness, like a candle almost burnt out.

34   *Apollo, s'anchor vive il bel desio*

Apollo, if the sweet desire endures
that burned in you by the Thessalian wave,
and if those cherished golden tresses have
not been forgotten with the turning years,

protect the illustrious and sacred bough
where I was snared like you, who were the first,
from the cruel season with its sluggish frost
that lasts as long as you conceal your brow.

By the sustaining power with which love's hope
amid your hard times kept your spirits up,
now clear the atmosphere of this rough weather;

so shall we see a miracle together:
our lady seated in a grassy glade
creating with her own arms her own shade.

Whether or not connected to the previous poems, this appears to deal with an illness of Laura's under the image of wintry weather, against which the poet invokes Apollo not only as sun god but also as god of healing (S). **2**: The Daphne/Apollo story takes place in Thessaly. **5–6**: The poet addresses Apollo as a partner in the love of the laurel (Daphne/Laura). **9–10**: Hope sustained Apollo in the pains of love, as it does the poet.

35 *Solo et pensoso i più deserti campi*

> Slowly I measure tracts of empty land
> with halting steps, alone and racked by care,
> and ever poised for flight I train my stare
> where any human print may mark the sand.
>
> I find no other cover to evade
> people's frank recognition should they look
> at my expression – all joy dead, a book
> that tells how I am burning up inside;
>
> so I can well believe by now the kind
> of life I lead is known to plains and hills,
> rivers and woods, although concealed from men.
>
> Yet I can never find such wild rough trails
> as might cause Love to lag and fall behind,
> so our interminable talk goes on.

36 *S'io credesse per morte essere scarco*

> If I believed that I could liberate
> myself from love's oppression by my death,
> with my own hands I would have laid in earth
> by now this hateful body and its weight;
>
> but since I fear that this would be to go
> only from tears to tears, from war to war,

on this side of the pass that still is barred
I half remain, alas, and half pass through.

By now I should have felt – it is high time –
the final shaft loosed from the heartless cord,
already dripping red with others' blood;

for that I beg Love and that deaf one too
who left me painted with his pallid hue
and now forgets to summon me to him.

1–8: The poet contemplates suicide to escape the slings and arrows of love, but fears the punishment of hell that would result.　**12**: *deaf one*: Death, who is deaf to those who suffer.　**13**: *pallid sign*: pallor is characteristic of both lovers and corpses. See note to 63.1.

37 *Sì è debile il filo a cui s'attene*

My life grown heavy hangs by a mere strand
that has become so weak
unless relief is quick
it very soon will reach its course's end.
For ever since I had to take cruel leave   5
of her I hold most dear,
a lone hope and no more
has up to now supplied a cause to live,
whispering, "Though deprived
of your most cherished sight,   10
sad soul, you must stand firm.
It may be better days will come at last
and a far happier time,
and you may yet regain the good you lost."
This hope sustained me once, but now much less,   15
and I grow old as I indulge in this.

Time passes and the hours all run so fast
to finish the day's course,
I have not time enough

even to think of how I rush toward death;
    the sun has barely risen in the east
before you see it reach
a distant western peak,
along the great length of its twisting path.
    So short the lives, so heavy
the bodies and so frail
of all our mortal race,
that when I find myself so far away
from that enchanting face
(desire not giving me the power to fly),
my usual comfort is of no avail.
How long can I keep living in this way?

    I grow sad everywhere I cannot see
those clear and gentle eyes,
which carried off the keys
that opened me to sweet thoughts while God willed;
    so exile might more heavily weigh on me,
whether I sleep or wake
there's nothing else I seek,
and all I've seen since them has left me cold.
    What mountains, how much sea
how many rushing rivers
hide from me those twin lights
that changed the darkness of my life to bright
and cloudless midday sky,
only so that remembering might destroy
me more and by my present misery
teach how my former life was filled with joy.

    Since speaking of it just revives, I find,
the burning of desire
born on the fatal day
I left the better part of me behind,
    and since love fades through long oblivion,

who draws me to the bait
that makes my pain increase? 55
Why have I not in silence turned to stone?
    Crystal and glass do not
allow the hues they hide
to show through from inside
more limpidly than my despondent mind 60
reveals my troubled thought
and all the savage sweetness in my heart
through eyes that, prone to weeping, never cease
to search for her in whom they find their peace.

    What perverse pleasure often can be found 65
within the human mind,
to love whatever strange
object provokes the thickest swarm of sighs!
    And I am one of those who like to weep;
it seems that I arrange 70
for tears to brim my eyes
as all the sorrow in my heart wells up;
    and since when speaking of
her eyes I'm moved to tears
– for nothing stirs me so 75
nor reaches where my feelings lie so deep –
I frequently return
to them to make my sorrow overflow
and with my heart punish my eyes besides,
for on the road of Love they were my guides. 80

    The golden hair that ought to make the sun
go filled with jealousy,
the beautiful clear gaze
from which Love's beams blaze out so ardently
    they take my life before its days are done, 85
and the considered speech,
so rare, if not unique,

that she bestowed upon me graciously
   – all taken from me, gone;
and I more easily   90
forgive all other wrongs
than being denied her kind angelic greeting,
which would awaken in
my heart a goodness kindled by desire.
I think I shall hear nothing from now on   95
that moves me to do anything but groan.

   And so that I might weep with more delight,
her lovely slender white
hands and her graceful arms,
the way she moves, so sweetly dignified,   100
   her sweet disdain, humble for all its pride,
her beautiful young breast,
fortress of her high mind,
are hidden from me by this steep wild land.
   My hope is faint at best   105
to see her once again
before death; now and then
hope rises up yet cannot make a stand,
and falling back confirms
I've seen my last of her whom heaven acclaims,   110
in whom both courtesy and virtue dwell
and where I pray that I may live as well.

   My song, if you should see
our lady in her sweet land,
you must think when you meet   115
she will extend to you her lovely hand,
which is so far from me;
but do not take it; reverent at her feet
tell her I will make all haste to arrive,
either bare spirit or a man alive.   120

A canzone of separation, in which the poet has taken leave of Laura and is living at a distance from her, no doubt on one of Petrarch's sojourns in Italy. **24**: The twisting path along which the sun moves is the zodiac. The image appears to conflate the sun's apparent diurnal and annual courses, making a year pass in a day; but Petrarch is probably simply thinking of the sun's apparent path through the sky on a given day. **49–56**: *i.e.*, why must I write these verses, which only make me miss her more? **65–68**: In four lines Petrarch anticipates the theme of Proust's "Un amour de Swann."

38 *Orso, e' non furon mai fiumi né stagni*

Orso, there never was a river or pond,
nor, where all streams discharge themselves, a sea,
no shadow of a wall or hill or tree
nor cloud that veils the sky and showers the land,

nor other obstacle that interferes
with sight that has so roused my plaintive cries
as does a veil that shades two lovely eyes
and seems to say, "Now spend yourself in tears."

And how those eyes extinguish, when cast down
from modesty or pride, all of my joys
will be the cause I die before my time.

And of a white hand also I complain,
which always has been quick to do me harm,
making itself a barrier to my eyes.

Orso: Orso dell'Anguillara (see 27), with whom Petrarch stayed in Italy on his way to Rome in 1337.

39 *Io temo sì de' begli occhi l'assalto*

I tremble so when those bright eyes attack,
for Love dwells with my death there, side by side,
I run away as boys do from the rod
and my first flight was now a long time back.

I'd scale the highest peak, fatigue and pain
not mattering, in order not to meet
with her who would confound my mind and heart,
leaving me frozen, as she does, in stone.

If I return so late to see you, then,
to keep from meeting her who breaks me down,
it is a failing you should pardon me.

In fact, returning to the place I fled
and having freed my heart from so much dread
is no small proof of my fidelity.

Apparently written to a friend (perhaps Cardinal Giovanni Colonna) in Avignon,
where Petrarch is returning from Italy and where Laura lives.

40 *S'Amore o Morte non dà qualche stroppio*

If the new cloth whose warps are on my loom
is not first ripped in two by Love or Death
and I get free of the tenacious lime
while I am joining one with the other truth,

I may create a work of double merit,
combining modern style with ancient tongue,
so that, although I tremble as I say it,
as far away as Rome you'll hear the bang.

But since I lack, in order to complete
my work, a little of the reverend thread
my well-loved father spun so plentifully,

why do you close your hands to me so tight?
It's not like you. Please open them instead
and great things will result, as you shall see.

Petrarch addresses a friend in Rome, likely Friar Giovanni Colonna or Bishop Giacomo Colonna, whom he asks for the loan of a manuscript, probably of Livy's history of Rome, to help him complete one of his Latin works, likely *Africa* or *De Viris Illustribus* (Lives of Eminent Men). **2–3**: *Love . . . lime*: Petrarch's amorous passion, reflected in his vernacular lyrics, is not compatible with the serious work of Latin erudition. Birdlime is his frequent image of being captured by the laurel. **11**: *father*: probably Livy.

41 *Quando dal proprio sito si rimove*

When the tree Phoebus loved in human form
moves from its settled place and takes its leave,
Vulcan perspires and pants as work grows warm,
replenishing the piercing bolts of Jove,

who now unleashes thunder, rain and snow,
acting like January in July;
earth weeps and having seen his favorite go
from here, the sun as well stays far away.

Saturn and Mars, stars that are pitiless,
grow bold and armed Orion overwhelms
unlucky sailors, smashing shrouds and helms.

Aeolus, raging, makes the sea and air
feel, the way we do, how that lovely face
for which the angels wait has gone elsewhere.

In this and the two following poems, Laura departs from her home in Avignon, throwing the whole of nature out of balance, turning summer into winter. **1**: *tree . . . Phoebus*: the laurel, Apollo. **3**: Vulcan, the blacksmith god, forges Jove's thunderbolts. **6**: literally, "respecting Caesar('s month) no more than Janus('s month)." **8**: *the sun*: Apollo as sun god. **9**: *pitiless*: of malign astrological influence. **10**: The winter constellation Orion, the armed hunter, was associated with storms. **12**: *Aeolus*: god of the winds; *sea and air*: literally, "Neptune and Juno."

42 *Ma poi che 'l dolce riso humile et piano*

But when her smile, sweet in its modesty,
no longer hides its beautiful rare charm,
the ancient blacksmith known in Sicily
at the black forge now vainly swings his arm,

for the weapons forged in Mongibello's blaze
to stand all trials are fallen from Jove's rude
grasp and beneath Apollo's shining gaze
Jove's sister, bit by bit, appears renewed.

A breeze that freshens from the western shore
keeps sailors safe without seafaring skill
and in the fields wakes flowers amid the grass.

The baleful stars are fleeing everywhere,
scattered at once by that beloved face
on whose account so many tears were spilled.

In this companion piece, Laura returns and sets all right, in a point-by-point contrast with 41. **3, 6**: Vulcan's forge was the volcano Mongibello (Mt. Etna) in Sicily. **7**: *Apollo*: the sun. **8**: *Jove's sister*: Juno, identified with the air, now free of winter storms. **9–11**: The western wind is Zephyr, friend of sailors and associated with the generative powers of spring.

43 *Il figliuol di Latona avea già nove*

Latona's son already had looked down
nine times to search from his high balcony
for her who once had made him sigh in vain
and who now causes someone else to sigh;

when, tired of looking for the one he sought,
not knowing if she sheltered far or near,
he showed himself to us like one distraught
with grief at losing what he holds most dear.

And gone off in his sorrow by himself,
he failed to see the face return whose praise,
if I survive, will fill a thousand poems;

and she seemed changed by sorrow now herself:
her eyes were full of tears when she came home;
and so the sky remained the way it was.

The third sonnet reworks the theme in a different manner, with Laura return-
ing home changed.   **1**: *Latona's son*: Apollo, the sun.   **3**: *her*: Laura as new
Daphne.   **7**: *distraught*: his face is covered with clouds.   **12**: We are left to
guess at the source of Laura's grief.   **14**: The sky remains cloudy, unlike the
resolution of 42, reflecting Apollo's distress but also Laura's.

44 *Que' che 'n Tesaglia ebbe le man' sì pronte*

The man whose hands were so prompt to imbrue
the soil of Thessaly with civil blood
shed tears to see his daughter's husband dead,
presented with the features he well knew.

The shepherd boy who smashed Goliath's brow
wept for his rebel son's fatal mischance
and at the good Saul's death changed countenance,
which still gives the cruel mountain cause for woe.

But you, whom pity never has turned pale,
always alert to have your shields disposed
against the bow Love draws on you in vain,

though you observe a thousand deaths' travail
rack me, not one tear ever falls from those
bright eyes, but only anger and disdain.

1–4: In the civil war between Julius Caesar and his son-in-law Pompey, Caesar
decisively defeated him in Thessaly in Greece. When Pompey fled to his ally
Ptolemy of Egypt, Ptolemy had him killed and sent his head to Caesar, who
wept when it was presented to him. (In 102 Petrarch says Caesar pretended to

weep.)   **5–6**: David, who as a boy had slain Goliath, became king after the death of King Saul. David's son Absalom later rebelled against him, and when he was killed, David raised a great lament. 2 Sam. (2 Kings) 18.33.   **7–8**: When David heard of Saul's death, he cursed the mountain where it happened: "let neither dew nor rain come upon you." Id. 1.21.

45   *Il mio adversario in cui veder solete*

My enemy, in whom you often find
your eyes, which heaven and Love heap praises on,
seduces you with beauties not his own,
happy and sweet beyond our mortal kind.

On his advice you've driven me outside
the shelter that was once my cherished spot:
miserable banishment, though I may not
be fit to live where you alone reside.

Had I been firmly fastened there with nails,
no looking glass, to my harm, would have turned
you hard and haughty with that self-pleased stare.

Surely, if you recall Narcissus' tale,
your course and his will lead to the same end,
although the grass deserves no flower so fair.

1: *enemy*: Laura's mirror.   **6**: *shelter*: her heart.   **12–14**: Narcissus fell in love with his reflection in a pool and wasted away because he could not tear himself from this phantom lover, and was turned into the flower that bears his name.

46   *L'oro et le perle e i fior' vermigli e i bianchi*

The gold and pearls, the white flowers and the red
that wintertime must wither and then dry
have turned to sharp and poisoned thorns for me;
I feel their punctures in my breast and side.

49

This by itself will shorten my sad days,
for such deep sorrow seldom long endures;
but more I blame that murderous glass of yours
that you have wearied with your loving gaze.

It made my lord's words seem but empty sound
when he would plead my case, so he fell still,
for you yourself were your desire's sole end.

That glass was fused upon the deep of hell
and dipped in the eternal oblivion
where the beginning of my death was born.

This companion poem to 45 grows even more bitter about her mirror.   **1**: *i.e.*,
her hair, teeth, complexion and lips.   **2**: *wintertime*: age; the suggestion is that
the mirror not only reflects beauty but also the advancing years, allusion to her
narcissism (Fenzi). In Jean Cocteau's typically narcissistic image, death enters
through mirrors.   **9**: *my lord*: Love.   **12**: The image is of a weapon forged
in hell and then tempered in Lethe, the river of forgetfulness in Hades, which
suggests Laura forgetting all else in contemplating herself (S).

47 *Io sentia dentr'al cor già venir meno*

I felt the flow of life within my heart
grow weak, for it depends on you to thrive;
since living creatures of whatever sort
by nature fend off threats to stay alive,

I gave desire his head, now reined in tight,
and sent him down the half-forgotten road,
(for though he pulls me that way day and night,
against his will I make him turn aside).

He brought me, shrinking from a sense of shame,
to see once more those dazzling eyes that I
stay far from to avoid annoying them.

Now I shall live a while, for only one
glance from you strengthens me; then I shall die
unless I listen to desire again.

1: *flow of life*: the vital spirits, for which note to 17.9.   5: *desire*: to see her
again.   6: *road*: that leads to her.

48 *Se mai foco per foco non si spense*

If fire has never served to quench a fire
and rain has never yet dried up a river,
but adding like to like results in more,
while opposites may reinforce each other,

why is it, Love, who leave our thoughts no choice,
who form a single soul two bodies share,
that contrary to nature you reduce,
through passionate desiring, my desire?

It may be, as the Nile's cascade resounds
loudly and deafens those who live nearby
and as the sun dazzles the staring eye,

so the desire that goes beyond all bounds
falters from straining so toward its delight
and spurring harder only slows the flight.

12–14: These lines are difficult and are variously interpreted.

49 *Perch'io t'abbia guardato di menzogna*

Though I have brought you honorable fame
and kept you out of lies as best I could,
ungrateful tongue, this honor you've repaid
by angering me because you've brought me shame:

when my need for your help is most extreme
– to beg for pity – you appear to fail,
frozen in place; if you form words at all,
they break off, as if I were in a dream.

And you, sad tears, who all night do not cease
to wait on me when I would be alone,
then disappear in presence of my peace;

and you, sighs, quick to make my torment smart
but then too slow and faint to make it known;
only my face speaks what is in my heart.

11: *peace*: Laura, who would pity him on seeing his tears. 13: *then*: when she appears.

50 *Ne la stagion che 'l ciel rapido inchina*

At the hour when the swift heavens bend their race
into the west and soon our day has flown
to those who may await it over there,
  the tired old pilgrim woman, well aware
of being in a distant land alone,   5
hastens the more by quickening her pace;
  and lonely in that place,
the day's long tramp now past
she sometimes finds relief
in slumber where she can forget, a brief   10
while, the fatigue of all the miles she's crossed.
But all the grief day brings to me, alas,
the dusk serves to increase
as the eternal light takes leave of us.

  And when the sun propels his flaming wheels   15
to make way for the night, and deeper gloom
of shadows reaches out from the high hills,

the thrifty farmer gathers up his tools
and with the words of some old mountain tune
lightens his heart of the fatigue of toil;   20
    and then he loads his board
with poor and simple fare
like acorns, famous food
that everybody loves to praise and shun.
Let all who wish be cheerful when they can;   25
but as for me, I've known no hour of ease,
much less a happy one,
for any turning of the sun or skies.

    And when the shepherd sees the slanting rays
of the great planet sinking to its nest   30
as all the landscape darkens to the east,
    he rises up and with his trusty crook
slowly and gently moves his little flock,
leaving behind the beeches, springs and grass;
    and far from people there   35
he strews a grotto or hut
with green boughs, stretches out
on them and falls asleep without a care.
But ah, cruel Love, it's then you spur me most
to chase the voice, steps, prints of a wild beast   40
who is destroying me,
nor do you catch her as she hides and flees.

    Sailors at anchor in some sheltered cove,
after the sun has hid, throw themselves down
to sleep in their coarse clothes on the hard deck.   45
    But I, although it plunge beneath the waves,
leaving Granada and Spain behind its back,
Morocco and the Pillars of Hercules,
    though men and women gain,
and even animals,   50
some respite from their ills,
I find no end for my persistent pain;

and each day, to my grief, my losses grow,
for this desire has still increased in me
for nearly ten years now,   55
nor can I figure who could set me free.

  Since words ease pain, let me continue now:
at evening I see oxen that return,
unyoked, from fields they've furrowed with the plow.
  Why are these sighs not lifted then from me?   60
Why must this heavy yoke still press me down?
Why must my eyes be wet by night and day?
  Ah wretch, what was I thinking
when I beheld that face
for the first time, not blinking,   65
sculpting it with my fancy in a place
from which no force or art can draw it forth
until the moment I become the prey
of all-dividing Death!
And if he could himself, I cannot say.   70

  Song, if my company
through all these nights and days
has made you think like me,
you will not be too eager to be seen;
and you will care so little for men's praise   75
you only need reflect, in travelling on,
how I am crisped by flame
out of the living rock on which I lean.

3: St. Augustine had denied that people could live on the other side of the globe;
Petrarch leaves it open.   15: The sun god crosses the sky in his chariot.   24:
Petrarch works satire into his amorous lament: in the golden age men ate the
fruits of the earth, such as acorns, without hunting or farming. *Metam.* 1.89–150;
Consol. Phil. 2.5.5.   30: The sun is a planet in medieval astronomy.   47–48:
Sinking in the ocean, the sun leaves the western confines of the known world: the
Moorish kingdom of Granada, Spain, Morocco, and Hercules's Pillars (Gibraltar
and the Atlas Mountains).   66: *place*: memory, seated in the heart.   77–78:

Santagata notes the double oxymoron: she is a living rock and she is cold as stone but emits fire. But there was also a tradition of fire rocks in the medieval bestiary literature, associated with the power of sexual desire. See Debra Hassig, *Medieval Bestiaries: Text, Image, Ideology.* Cambridge (Cambridge University Press, 1995), 116–28.

51 *Poco era ad appressarsi agli occhi miei*

> Had it come any closer to my eyes,
> the light that from a distance dazzles them,
> as Thessaly saw her change in far-off days
> I would have altogether changed in form.
>
> And since I cannot, more than I yet have,
> change into her (not that it wins me grace)
> I'd now be made of some stone hard to carve,
> the anxious look still frozen on my face,
>
> sculpted in diamond or fine marble, white
> from fear perhaps, or jasper to be then
> valued by people's foolishness and greed;
>
> and I'd be free of this yoke's heavy weight,
> which makes me envy that old weary man
> whose shoulders cast Morocco into shade.

2: *light*: Laura.   **3**: *her*: Daphne.   **5–8**: The lyric trope is that the lover becomes the beloved, but the poet cannot do that more thoroughly than he already has. For the lover petrified by fear, see 23.79–80, 39.8; here Laura's transforming power associates her with Medusa, who is indirectly referred to at 13–14 (S).   **13–14**: The titan Atlas was turned to stone by seeing the face of Medusa and now, as a mountain range in Morocco, he bears the sky on his shoulders.

52 *Non al suo amante più Dïana piacque*

> However much Diana may have pleased
> the lover who by like chance spied her bare
> amid the frigid water, I no less

delighted in the shy hill shepherdess
washing a wisp of veil to keep her hair,
glinting with gold, protected from the breeze.

And even now, when the sky burns above,
she makes me shiver with a chill of love.

One of four madrigals in the collection (see also Nos. 54, 106, 121).   In each
of them the poet sees Laura in a different fictional guise; Santagata, however,
summarizes reasons for believing that this poem was originally independent of
the Laura sequence.   **2**: *lover*: Actaeon, for whom see note to 23.149–60.   **7–8**:
In keeping with the *galant* charm of the genre, this benign ending takes the place
of the more obvious one: as Actaeon's encounter ended in his being torn by
his own hounds, the poet's ended in his being torn by his unappeased desires.

53   *Spirto gentil, che quelle membra reggi*

O noble spirit who control the limbs
within which a brave lord, both shrewd and wise,
dwells while upon his earthly pilgrimage,
   now that you have attained the honored staff
with which you govern Rome and her strayed children   5
and call her back to her true ancient path,
   I speak to you, for elsewhere I can see
no gleam of virtue in a world gone dark,
nor anyone ashamed of doing wrong.
I do not know what Italy wants or waits for;   10
lazy and old and slow, she does not seem
to feel her injuries.
Will no one wake her, will she sleep forever?
I wish that I could grasp her by the hair!

   I do not hope that she will raise her head   15
from her long torpid sleep for any shouts,
given the burden that oppresses her;
   but now, in what I see as destiny,
our Rome, our capital, has been entrusted

to your arms, which have power to rouse and raise her.   20
    Be resolute – stretch forth your hand and seize
her locks, so reverend but now so disheveled,
and make the sluggard rise up from the mud.
I who lament her torment day and night
place the best part of all my hopes in you,   25
for if the stock of Mars
should recognize once more their glorious goal,
I think it would be only in your day.

    The ancient walls the world still fears and loves
and trembles at whenever it looks back   30
and calls to mind the ages that are gone,
    the tombs in which the bodies were enclosed
of men that will not be without renown
until the universe shall first dissolve,
    and all that lies thrown down in one great ruin   35
hope that through you their damage will be healed.
O faithful Brutus, O great Scipios,
how it must please you, if the word has spread
down there: the right man holds high office now!
And I am sure Fabricius   40
rejoices when he hears the news and says,
"My Rome will once again be beautiful!"

    If heaven cares about what happens here,
the souls that now are citizens up there,
having abandoned their remains on earth,   45
    beg you to end the lengthy civil strife
that makes the populace unsafe and fearful,
shutting off pilgrims' routes to the saints' churches,
    once venerated shrines but now in time
of war changed almost into dens of thieves   50
whose doors are only barred to the devout,
where, with the altars and the statues stripped,
bloody conspiracies are instigated.

What infamous behavior!
And no attack begins without a peal   55
of bells once hung above to thank the Lord.

    The weeping women, the defenseless mass
of children, the exhausted elderly,
who hate themselves for having lived too long,
    the Black Friars and the Grey Friars and the White,   60
the legions of the weak and the oppressed
cry out to you with one voice, "Help, lord, help!"
    The wretched populace, dismayed and dazed,
thousands and thousands of them, show you wounds
that would move Hannibal himself to pity.   65
If you examine why the house of God
is all in flames today, it will be clear
that quenching a few sparks
would calm the passions that are now so heated,
earning the praise of heaven for your works.   70

    Lions and bears, eagles and wolves and snakes
often commit offenses – harming themselves
as well – against a towering marble column.
    That is what has distressed the noble lady
who called you so you might eradicate   75
from her soil noxious weeds that cannot flower.
    More than a thousand years have now gone by
since the long line of noble spirits failed
whose exploits raised her to her former height.
Ah, the new men are haughty beyond measure,   80
lacking all reverence for so great a mother!
You be her spouse, her father:
all succor is expected from your hands;
the greater father tends to other work.

    It seldom happens that injurious Fortune   85
fails to oppose a noble enterprise,
for she consents with bad grace to bold deeds.

Now that she's cleared the path by which you entered,
she makes me pardon many other wrongs,
since here at last she contradicts herself,   90
    for never in the memory of the world
was the way open to a mortal man,
as now to you, to live in fame forever –
you that unless my foresight plays me false
can raise the noblest empire to her feet.   95
What glory when they say,
"Others gave aid when she was young and strong,
but this man saved her in old age from death."

    On the Tarpeian Mount, Song, you will find
a knight to whom all Italy renders honor,   100
more full of care for others than himself.
Say to him: "One that has not seen you yet,
but knows and loves you from your reputation,
tells you that Rome, her eyes
continually wet with brimming sorrow,   105
cries for your mercy from her seven hills."

1: *noble spirit*: traditionally supposed to be Cola di Rienzo, a commoner who seized power in Rome in 1347 and whom Petrarch initially supported. The poem is now believed to date from ten years earlier and to be addressed to Bosone da Gubbio, named a Roman senator by Pope Benedict XII in 1337. Petrarch begs Bosone to end the protracted civil strife among the baronial clans in Rome while the pope is absent in Avignon. As stanza six will make clear, he is really asking Bosone to aid one of the clans – his protectors, the Colonna – from their enemies. Santagata notes that this request could hardly be addressed to Cola, who opposed the Colonna.   4: *staff*: the scepter carried by a Roman senator.   26: *stock of Mars*: the Romans, Mars being the father of Romulus.   35: *all . . . ruin*: the monuments of ancient Rome.   37, 40: *Brutus*: instrumental in the founding of the Roman republic. *Scipios, Fabricius*: military heroes of later republican times.   44: *souls . . . up there*: the saints of Christian Rome.   60: three orders of Catholic religious.   65: *Hannibal*: the great enemy of Rome.   66: *house of God*: Rome itself, "the seat of Christ's bride," as Dante called it. *Epist.* 8.   71: The animals are emblems that appear in the arms of the warring clans; the bears are the Orsini, the chief rivals of the Colonna for power in Rome. **73**: *column*: the emblem of the Colonna. Ten years after this poem, which advances the interests of the Colonna, Petrarch would turn on his protectors by supporting their enemy Cola. **74**: *noble lady*: Rome. **77–79**: Just over a thousand years ago Constantine moved the seat of empire to Constantinople. **84**: *greater father*: the pope. **99**: *Tarpeian Mount*: the Capitoline hill, ancient seat of the Roman senate.

54 *Perch'al viso d'Amor portava insegna*

Because she bore Love's sign upon her face
a stranger stirred my vacillating heart,
for others seemed to merit honor less.

But as across the lush green grass I chased
that one, I heard a distant voice cry out:
"Ah, in the wood how many steps you waste!"

Then I drew up beneath a beech's shade
in doubt, and peering out I now could see

great perils on the path that lay ahead,
and I turned back when it was near midday.

Here Petrarch uses the madrigal, usually a light amorous lyric, as a vehicle for allegory. **5–6**: The voice is that of God (or conscience), and the wood is similar to the wood of error from the beginning of Dante's *Inferno*. **9–10**: The path is our journey through life and noon is the middle of it.

55 *Quel foco ch'i' pensai che fosse spento*

The fire I thought reduced to burnt-out coals
with winter overtaking my green years
flares up and once more devastates my soul.

Those embers never cooled, from what I see,
but under ashes smoldered secretly;

and my new folly may be worse, I fear.
With all the never-ending tears I scatter
the burning pain is leaking through my eyes
from my heart, with its store of sparks and tinder,
where what was flame is now a spreading blaze.

What fire would not have met a watery death
in the continual waves my eyes pour forth?
Love, as I realized only recently,
wants to destroy me between flood and fire,
and sets his traps in such variety
that when I hope my heart may struggle free,
her face as quickly tightens the next snare.

56 *Se col cieco desir che 'l cor distrugge*

Unless the blind desire that eats my heart
leads me, in counting up the hours, astray,
now while I speak the time is running out,
time promised both to pity and to me.

What shade is cruel enough to blight with cold
the seed when fruit was just about to swell?
What wild beast's roaring comes from my sheepfold?
Between the hand and harvest why that wall?

I do not know, alas, but I know well
Love lured me into hope's exultant state
only to make my life more sorrowful;

and something I have read I now recall:
that no man must be reckoned fortunate
before his ultimate departure date.

3–4: *time . . . promised*: a promised meeting that would offer the poet comfort
(S).   13–14: a frequent maxim of the ancients. See *Metam.* 3.135–37.

57 *Mie venture al venir son tarde et pigre*

My good luck, when it comes, comes slow and late,
my hope of it unsure, while longing grows,
vexing me whether I give up or wait;
then swifter than a tiger, off it goes.

Pitch-black, alas, and warm will be the snows,
the sea without a wave, the fish on mountains,
the sun will set beyond where water flows
to Tigris and Euphrates from one fountain

before I find in this some truce or peace,
or she or Love learn some new ways at last –
their wrongful plots against me never cease.

And so much bitter comes before the sweet
that irritation makes me lose the taste;
with other grace of theirs I never meet.

7: *beyond where*: in the east.   7–8: The Tigris and Euphrates were believed to
be two of the four rivers that flowed from one source in the garden of Eden.
Gen. 2:10, 14.

58 *La guancia che fu già piangendo stancha*

Rest on the first, my dearest lord, your cheek,
wearied by tears you shed for a long while,
and now more sparing of yourself, hold back
from the cruel one who makes his followers pale.

The next will help you close, on your left side,
the route by which his emissaries came;
because the time is short for the long road,
in every season show yourself the same.

Drink from the third an herbal remedy
to purge the trouble that afflicts your heart,
sweet in the end though bitter at the start.

Keep me where pleasures have been stored away
so Styx's pilot may not make me fear,
unless this is presumptuous in a prayer.

A manuscript note dedicates this sonnet "to my lord Agapito, together with several little gifts." Agapito Colonna was Bishop of Luni and had evidently been disappointed in love.   1: *the first (gift)*: a pillow.   4: *cruel one*: Love; *pale*: see note to 63.1.   5: *the next*: probably a religious book, to serve as a *remedia amoris*; *left side*: where the heart is.   6: *emissaries*: glances; see 3.   7: *road*: to heaven.   9: *the third*: a cup.   12–13: *me*: either the sonnet or the poet himself; in either case: keep me fondly in your heart, so I do not fear being forgotten.   13: *pilot*: Charon, who ferries souls across the Styx in the classical underworld.

59 *Perché quel che mi trasse ad amar prima*

Though her contrariness withdraws from me
what drew me first to love,
it does not shake me from my firm resolve.

Amid those golden locks Love hid the snare
he used to bind me fast;
and from those bright eyes came the icy cold
that passed straight to my heart
the way a sudden splendor lights the sky.
Remembering, even now,
still strips my soul of all desires but her.

Alas, it has been taken from me now,
the sight of that blond hair;
and those two bright chaste eyes that turn away
sadden me by their flight.
But since to die in a good cause wins honor,
though it brings grief and death
I would not have Love loose me from this knot.

60   *L'arbor gentil che forte omai molt'anni*

The noble tree I loved so long and well
while its slim boughs did not disdain me, made
my feeble talent flower in its shade
and, amid all my sufferings, grow tall.

But since it changed from sweet to heartless wood
when I was not expecting such a trick,
my thoughts all tend the same way and they speak
forever in sad tones of their lost good.

What would a youth who warmly sighs for love
say, if my youthful verses gave him hope
different from this that through her he has lost?

"Then let no poet gather it nor Jove
grant it immunity, and let a burst
of the Sun's anger dry its green leaves up."

1: *tree*: laurel/Daphne/Laura.   **12–14**: The poet distances himself from the curse by attributing it to a disillusioned lover, to be balanced in *RVF* 61 by a blessing in the poet's voice. For the features of the laurel alluded to: *poet*: for a wreath; *immunity*: from lightning; *Sun*: Apollo, who had made it evergreen).

61   *Benedetto sia 'l giorno, e 'l mese, e l'anno,*

I bless the year, the season and the day,
the morning, hour and minute on the dot,
the province and the place where I was caught
by the two eyes that have imprisoned me;

and blessed be the earliest sweet hurt
experienced when I encountered Love,

blessed the bow and pointed shafts that gave
me wounds that penetrated to my heart.

And blessed be the thousand phrases that
I scattered, calling on my lady's name,
and all the longing and the tears and groans;

and blessed be my pages for the fame
they win for her and every loving thought
where others have no part, but she alone.

1–3: the time and place of the poet's first meeting with Laura.   10: *scattered*:
see 1.1.

62 *Padre del ciel, dopo i perduti giorni*

Father in heaven, after the days lost,
after my frequent ravings in the night
from fierce desire, with my heart set alight
watching her fluid movements to my cost,

be pleased at last to guide me with your light
back to a life and tasks of higher aim,
so may my adversary burn with shame
at having spread in vain his cunning net.

It's now eleven years – that date again –
since I submitted to the ruthless yoke
that weighs most cruelly on a willing neck.

Have mercy, Lord, on my disgraceful pain,
direct my erring thoughts to a better place:
today, remind them, you were on the cross.

The eleventh anniversary of the poet's first seeing Laura, and thus Good Friday
(Petrarch would have been in his early thirties). This is the first poem since the
introductory sonnet that adopts the attitudes developed in *My Secret*, abjuring his
passion for Laura as sinful folly. The juxtaposition of this penitential sonnet with
61 is striking.   6: *tasks*: presumably his Latin works.   8: *adversary*: the devil.

63 *Volgendo gli occhi al mio novo colore*

You turned your eyes toward my unnatural
complexion, which for most brings death to mind,
and pity touched you; that inspired your kind
greeting, which kept my weak heart beating still.

The frail life that as yet survives in me
was, it is plain, a gift from your fine eyes
and the angelic voice I heard that day.
    I owe my being here, I recognize,
to them; a stick will prod an animal
that dawdles: so they roused my torpid soul.
    Lady, you hold within your hand both keys
that fit my heart, and I am glad you do;
I am prepared to sail on any breeze,
honored by anything that comes from you.

1: *unnatural*: The extreme pallor of the lover is a commonplace of medieval
poetry. See *Inf.* 5.131. Here and elsewhere (see 36), Petrarch suggests it is because
hopeless love brings the lover close to death.

64 *Se voi poteste per turbati segni*

Lady, if all your irritated airs —
dropping your eyes or lowering your head,
fleeing more promptly than another would,
turning your face from my respectful prayers —

or suchlike tricks enabled you to quit
my heart, where Love engrafts a thousand shoots
from the first laurel, I would not dispute
that your scorn would be justified by it.

A noble tree's not suited, to be sure,
to arid wasteland, and so naturally
it would be happier to depart from there;

66

but since you are forbidden by your fate
to go elsewhere, try at least not to be
confined forever in a place you hate.

3: *another*: *i.e.*, another lady.   **6–7**: *shoots . . . laurel*: memories of their first meeting have multiplied the poet's love many times over.   **12–14**: Petrarch plays on the rooted nature of the laurel, for the reverse of which see 41.

65   *Lasso, che mal accorto fui da prima*

Alas, how I was unaware at first,
the day when Love arrived and wounded me,
who step by step then gained the mastery
of my whole life, atop which he is perched.

I did not think that he could use his file
to make the courage or the steadiness
of my already toughened heart decrease,
but those who rate themselves too high must fall.

From now on all defense would come too late,
except to test the measure, small or great,
of Love's attention to our mortal prayers.

I do not pray, nor could it ever be,
my heart may burn in moderate degree,
but only that the fire may be shared.

66   *L'aere gravato, et l'importuna nebbia*

The heavy air and the oppressive cloud
condensed by pressure from the raging winds
are soon forced to convert themselves to rain;
almost like crystal now the frigid rivers
and now instead of grass throughout the valleys   5
there's nothing to be seen but frost and ice.

And in my heart, still colder than the ice,
I harbor heavy musings like a cloud,
the kind that sometimes rises from these valleys,
closed as they are against love-bearing winds   10
and hemmed in by no longer running rivers,
while the dull sky is drizzling a fine rain.

A short time sees the end of heavy rain
and growing warmth dissolves the snow and ice,
swelling the proud appearance of the rivers;   15
however thick the sky-concealing cloud,
when ambushed by the fury of the winds
it flees in wisps above the hills and valleys.

I, alas, get no help from flowering valleys,
but weep beneath clear skies and in the rain   20
and in the soft as in the freezing winds;
for on the day my lady's inward ice
thaws and she sheds her usual outward cloud,
the sea will dry, as will the lakes and rivers.

As long as seas receive the flow of rivers   25
and wild beasts love to haunt the shady valleys,
before her brilliant eyes will hang the cloud
that makes my own give birth to constant rain,
and in her breast will linger the hard ice
that draws forth from my own such doleful winds.   30

And yet I well should pardon all the winds
for love of one breeze that between two rivers
enclosed me in fresh verdure and sweet ice,
so that I limned then in a thousand valleys
the shade I'd sheltered in, nor cared for rain   35
nor heat nor crack of thunder tearing cloud.

But no cloud ever fled before the winds
as on that day, nor rivers rush with rain,
nor ice melt as sun opens the cold valleys.

1–10: The landscape suggests that of Vaucluse, the rural valley to which Petrarch moved in 1337. **10**: *love-bearing winds*: that come from Avignon, where Laura lives. See 15.3. **31–36**: After five straightforward stanzas, the sixth is difficult and has given rise to various interpretations; one is suggested here. **32**: *one (breeze)*: the usual pun *Laura/l'aura* is implied rather than stated. **32–33**: Either Laura in Avignon or the poet in Vaucluse would be between two rivers. The ice continues to be her coldness, which he finds sweet. The verdure (*bel verde*) I take to be that of the laurel (Laura's other form), whose shade (*ombra*, 35) encloses him. **34–35**: His widely scattered verses (see 23.11–13) paint her image. **36**: He is indifferent to thunder because the laurel is immune from lightning. **37**: *that day*: nothing fled as quickly as the day he fell in love with her (or perhaps, as in some later poems, the day he parted from her).

67 *Del mar Tirreno a la sinistra riva*

On the left shore of the Tyrrhenian sea
on which rough winds cause waves to break and weep,
I suddenly caught sight of the proud tree
that makes me fill so many pages up.

Love, which inside my soul at that point boiled
as I went on remembering golden locks,
pushed me, and in a stream the grass concealed
I fell, now scarcely living from the shock.

I was alone with woods and hills and yet
I felt shame; for a noble heart the mere
fact is enough, it needs no other spur.

I'm pleased that I could change my style at least
from eyes to feet, if by their being wet
a gentler April now may dry the first.

Commentators associate this sonnet and the next two with Petrarch's first voyage from Provence to Italy in 1337. On such a journey the left shore would be the west coast of Italy (or the coast of Provence). **3**: *tree*: the laurel. **5–11**: The incident recalls the philosopher Thales falling into a well while gazing at the stars; but while Thales was praised for prizing wisdom above practicality (see

ED 5.512), the poet is ashamed at his loss of self-control.   **12–14**: The incident leads to a witty wish for a saner attitude.   **14**: *gentler*: than the April in which he fell in love.

68 *L'aspetto sacro de la terra vostra*

> Your holy city, now before my eyes,
> makes me recall my bad past and lament.
> "Why are you losing heart? Be strong!" it cries
> and shows the path to heaven that I should mount.
>
> A second thought then launches an attack,
> admonishing, "What's this? Why must you flee?
> If you recall, the time for turning back
> to see our lady soon will pass us by."
>
> Listening to these contradictory words
> I turn to ice inside, like one who's heard
> some news that suddenly has made him wince.
>
> Then the first thought returns and puts its foe
> to flight; which one will win I do not know.
> They've fought for a long time, not just this once.

1: *Your city*: Rome; perhaps addressed to Orso dell'Anguillara (see Nos. 27 and 38).   **3**: The voice is that of Rome, internalized as the poet's thought (Bettarini).   **13–14**: The unresolved struggle between religion and passion is developed at length in 264.

69 *Ben sapeva io che natural consiglio*

> Mere human cleverness, I plainly saw,
> provided no defense, Love, against you;
> your traps, your empty promises I knew
> and had too often felt your savage claw.

But recently, and it still surprises me
(I tell it as the one it happened to
sailing upon salt water while in view,
near the islands, of the coast of Tuscany),

I'd slipped your clutches and was on my way,
wind, wave and sky all hastening me there,
and as an unknown foreigner, I roamed free;

when look! your ministers, from who knows where,
arrived to show me that it does not pay
to hide from or to fight one's destiny.

This concludes the three sonnets inspired by Petrarch's first trip to Rome. **4–8**: The poet is sailing from Provence to Italy, away from Laura. **8**: *islands*: Petrarch mentions Elba and Giglio, the two largest islands in the Tuscan Archipelago. **12**: *ministers*: thoughts and memories of Laura, which come seemingly out of nowhere like gulls after his ship.

70 *Lasso me, ch'i' non so in qual parte pieghi*

I do not know where I can point my hope,
it has been dashed so many times by now;
if no one listens to me with compassion,
why scatter prayers so thickly to the sky?
But if it happens that before I die   5
I still may be allowed
to cease these poor laments,
let my lord not be vexed if I still beg
that I might say amid flowers and grass one day:
I have good cause to sing and to be gay.   10

It's only fair that I should sing some time,
for I have sighed so long that I could never,
if I began now, even up the score
and equal all my sorrows with new joys.

And could I ever give those holy eyes   15
reason to take delight
in some sweet words of mine,
how happy I would be beyond all lovers!
But ah, to boast with more than idle talk:
a lady bids me, so I wish to speak.   20

Enticing thoughts that step by step like this
have led me on to speak so loftily,
you see my lady has a stony heart
into which on my own I cannot go.
   She would not condescend to look so low   25
that she might hear our words,
for the stars are opposed
and fighting their design has worn me out.
And as my own heart hardens and grows tough,
now in my speech I wish to be as rough.   30

What did I say? Where am I? Who deceives me
if not myself and my excessive yearning?
If I ran through the sky from sphere to sphere,
I'd find no planet sentence me to weep.
   If the veil of body clouds my vision up,   35
are the stars then to blame,
or beauties of the earth?
In me she lives who day and night afflicts me
since I was filled with pleasure all at once
seeing her lovely face and gentle glance.   40

Everything that brings beauty to the world
comes good from the eternal craftsman's hand;
but dazzled by the splendors that surround me,
I cannot penetrate beyond their shine.
   If I see sometimes the true light within,   45
my eye cannot hold steady,
it has become so sick
only through its own fault, and not the day

on which I turned toward her angelic charm
in the sweet season of my youthful time. 50

Instead of the variations on the theme of frustrated love of canzoni like Nos. 23 and 50, this poem presents a more serious introspective meditation that develops consecutively from one stanza to the next. Santagata believes that this canzone rejects the idea of love expressed in 23 (the "canzone of metamorphoses") and many other preceding poems and announces a new theme, developed in the three following "canzoni of the eyes." He suggests that the shift is from a sensual and pessimistic conception of love to a sublimated, stilnovist conception, with a changed perception of Laura.   **10**: The final line of each stanza quotes a line from an earlier poet, beginning here with one erroneously attributed to the troubadour Arnaut Daniel; subsequent stanzas work through Petrarch's Italian predecessors to end with his own 23.   **20**: A verse from Guido Cavalcanti's most famous poem; as repurposed here, Petrarch imagines Laura not only being pleased by his love poems, but asking him for more.   **30**: The verse is from one of Dante's *rime petrose*.   **33**: *sphere (cerchio)*: the planets were believed to be stars embedded in revolving crystalline spheres.   **35**: *veil:* seen as occluding the soul's perception of the essence of things.   **40**: a verse by Cino da Pistoia (for whom see 92).   **50**: the first verse of 23 (the fourth in this translation).

71 *Perché la vita è breve*

Given that life is short
and my powers cringe before so great a task,
I do not place much confidence in either;
    but still I hope my pain,
crying out silently, may be understood 5
where it must, where I need it to be most.
    Enchanting eyes in which Love makes his nest,
it is to you I turn my flat bare verse,
limping itself but spurred by great delight;
and one who speaks of you 10
gains from his theme a noble frame of mind,
which, lifting him on wings
of love, takes him far distant from low thoughts.

Borne on them, I now come to speak of what
I long have carried hidden in my heart.   15

   I am of course aware
how much my praise must do you injury;
but I cannot resist the great desire
   within me since I saw
what beggars words, another's or my own,   20
and renders thought itself inadequate.
   Origin of my sweet tormenting state,
I know that only you can understand me.
Beneath your burning rays I turn to snow
and my unworthiness   25
may then provoke your flash of noble anger.
Ah, if the fear of that
did not damp down the fire in which I burn,
what bliss to melt away! for I'd prefer
to die in front of them than live elsewhere.   30

   If I do not dissolve,
a thing so fragile in so fierce a fire,
the credit for surviving is not mine;
   rather my fear, which freezes
the blood that courses through my veins, renews   35
my heart's resistance so it still may burn.
   O hills, fields, woods, O rivers rushing on,
all witnesses of my unhappy life,
how often have you heard me call on death!
Ah, most unhappy fate: 40
staying destroys me and fleeing does not help me.
But soon a short quick road
would bring an end to this harsh suffering
if I were not restrained by a greater fear;
and all the fault is hers who does not care.   45

   Why do you draw me, pain,
out of my path to speak against my purpose?

Let me proceed where inclination urges.
 I don't mean to complain
of you, eyes more serene than those of mortals,   50
nor yet of him who keeps me bound like this.
 Observe how frequently Love paints my face
with many different colors and you may
imagine what he does to me inside,
where day and night he stands   55
above me with the power he draws from you,
blessed and joyful lights,
in all except the power to see yourselves;
but what you are you easily can see
in someone else each time you turn toward me.   60

 If you could know as fully
as those of us who see it the divine
beauty beyond belief of which I speak,
 excessive joy would flood
her heart — perhaps why nature keeps that beauty   65
far from the power that directs your sight.
 The soul that sighs for you is fortunate,
celestial lights, for whom I offer thanks
to life, which does not please me otherwise.
But ah, why give so seldom   70
what I could never have a surfeit of?
Why do you not more often
notice how Love is tearing me apart?
Why must you always quickly snatch from me
the joy my soul may feel occasionally?   75

 I mean that on some rare
occasions thanks to you in my soul's depth
I feel a strange and unfamiliar sweetness
 that suddenly relieves me
from all the burden of my troubling thoughts,   80
so of a thousand one remains with me,

the only thing in life that brings me joy.
And if this bliss would last a while, no other
happiness in the world could equal mine.
Perhaps, though, so much honor   85
would stir up others' envy and my pride;
so, alas, it must be
that at its limit laughter turns to tears,
and breaking off that rapture, I sink down
into myself and my concerns again.   90

    The loving disposition
within her is revealed to me through you,
displacing from my heart all other joy;
    and that inspires in me
actions and words that may in time, I hope,   95
make me immortal though my body die.
    When you appear my pain and trouble flee,
and they return together when you go;
but since my memory, now filled with love,
closes the door on them,   100
they can obtain no access to my heart.
So if some wholesome fruit
springs from me, it is you who sowed the seed;
for I myself am arid land, no more:
you till me, so the credit is all yours.   105

You do not calm me, Song, but make me burn
to speak about what steals me from myself;
make sure, then, you do not remain alone.

This canzone and the two following form a suite in praise of Laura's eyes.   **1**:
task: speaking about her eyes.   **7–9**: This direct address to her eyes, will be
carried consistently through the poem.   **17**, 23, et seq.. : *you*: It can be difficult
to remember throughout the poem that *you* and *your* refer not to Laura but to
her eyes.   **17**: *praise . . . injury*: because it will be inadequate.   **24**: *rays*: see
note to 9.11.   **30**: *them*: the eyes, referred to in the third person because here
the poet is speaking to himself.   **42–44**: his urge to suicide is forestalled by

fear of damnation.   **45**: *hers*: Laura's.   **46–47**: These lines echo 70.31–34: the poet rebukes himself because his suffering has unjustly made him blame his lady. The theme is no longer complaint but praise.   **51**: *him*: Love.   **58–66**: The fact that her eyes cannot see themselves becomes the ground for ingenious conceits: the inability is seen first as detracting from their happiness, then as necessary to preserve Laura's health.   **71**: *what*: the sight of you.   **81**: *one*: the thought of you.   **91–92**: See 72.4–6.   **96–97**: As often in Petrarch, there is ambiguity between heavenly and literary immortality, but here the context appears primarily literary.   **107**: *what*: the eyes (106–08 being addressed to the Song itself).

72   *Gentil mia donna, i' veggio*

I see, my noble lady,
a glimmer in the movement of your eyes
that lets me visualize the way to heaven;
    and as it always does,
within there, where I live alone with Love,   5
I almost see your heart come shining through.

    This vision is what moves me most to do
good and what guides me to the glorious goal;
this alone separates me from the crowd.
No human tongue could tell   10
the half of what those two celestial lights
inspire me to feel,
both when the winter strews the frost around
and when the year rejuvenates in spring,
as in the time of my first suffering.   15

    I think: if up above
whence the eternal mover of the stars
sent down to earth a sample of his art
    the others are as lovely,
then open up the prison that confines me   20
and bars me from the path to such a life!
    Then I turn back to my habitual strife,

thankful to Nature and my day of birth
that have reserved me for so great a good,
and her who raised me up   25
to such a hope – for until then I lay,
a burden to myself,
since then am satisfied with who I am –
filling with one high sweet thought instantly
the heart to which her bright eyes hold the key.   30

   There is no happiness
Love or inconstant Fortune ever gave
to those who were in life their favorites
   that I would not exchange
for one glance of those eyes, from which my peace   35
emerges as the tree does from the root.
   Beautiful sparks, angelic, the complete
blessedness of my life, igniting pleasure
that sweetly melts me till I am consumed,
as every other light   40
grows faint and vanishes before your splendor,
within my heart I feel,
each time such sweetness settles down upon it,
how all else, every other thought will leave
till none remains in there with you but Love.   45

   The sweetness until now
felt in the hearts of happy lovers, gathered
all in one place, pales before what I feel
   when every now and then
you sweetly toss a shining glance my way   50
in which Love plays between the black and white.
   I think for my defects and Fortune's slights
ever since I lay swaddled in the cradle
heaven has given me this remedy.
Yet there's the veil that wrongs me   55
as does the hand so often interposed

between what most delights me
and my eyes, where my passion overflows
continually to give my heart release
as it adapts to changes in her face.   60

Because, to my chagrin,
I see my natural gifts are not enough
to make me worthy of that precious glance,
    I strain to make myself
equal to the exalted hope I cherish   65
and to the noble fire in which I burn.
    If by persistent effort I can learn
promptly do to the right, avoid the wrong
and scorn the vanities the world desires,
perhaps then word of mouth   70
would help me win her favorable opinion.
The end of all my tears,
which my sad heart seeks nowhere else, will be
to see at last her sweetly trembling eyes,
where noble lovers' ultimate hope lies.   75

    Just before you, my Song, goes your first sister
and now I sense the other getting ready
in the same room, so I will rule more paper.

7–9: The idea that love raises the lover's soul to a higher moral level appeared
in 13 and was a common stilnovist theme. See *Inf.* 2.104–05. **8**: *glorious goal*:
not fame this time but heaven. **15**: *first suffering*: see 3. **20**: *prison*: the poet's
body. **50**: *you*: her eyes. **51**: *black and white*: the pupil and white of the eyes (see
29.23). **60**: Dotti cites Book 3 of *My Secret*, where Augustine blames Francesco
for becoming happy or sad depending on Laura's attitude. **74**: *trembling eyes*:
a sign that she is at last in love, showing an anxious emotion in his presence; so
Dante speaks of "the trembling of my eyes" in *VN* 11.2. **76–77**: *first sister . . .
the other*: Nos. 71 and 73. **78**: *room*: the poet's mind.

Since by my destiny
this burning passion forces me to speak
as it has forced me for so long to sigh,
    Love, who inspire these words,
you be my guide and show me how to make   5
my verse express my longing suitably;
    but not so much my heart will melt away
in floods of sweetness, as I fear could happen
from what I feel where no one's eyes can reach;
for my words burn and goad me,   10
nor does this mental effort make the fire
that fills my mind die down
as once it used to, so I quake in fear.
Hearing my words, in fact, I melt and run
as though I were a snowman in the sun.   15

    I thought in the beginning
that when I spoke about my ardent longing
I might find some brief respite, even truce.
    This hope emboldened me
to give expression to my inmost feelings;   20
now it abandons me in time of need.
    Yet my great task must nonetheless proceed,
further developing this song of love,
such a strong impulse carries me away;
and reason, which once grasped   25
the reins, is dead and cannot hold it back.
So teach me, Love, at least
to speak the kind of words that will, if ever
they strike the ears of my sweet enemy,
make her a friend to pity if not me.   30

    I say: in ancient times
when souls were zealous to attain true honor,
diligent men went travelling far and wide

through different lands, traversing
mountains and stormy seas, in search of things   35
that bring renown, whose finest flowers they culled;
    but now, when Nature, God, and Love have willed
that the whole range of virtues should be gathered
in those clear lights that make my life a joy,
I have no need to cross   40
from shore to shore, change one land for another.
To them I always turn
once more as to the fount of my salvation;
when driven by desire I almost die
only the sight of them can comfort me.

    Just as the weary helmsman
battered by winds lifts up his head at night
toward the two lights that always hug our pole,
    so in the storm of love
that I am weathering, those shining eyes   50
are my sole comfort and my own North Star.
    Ah, but I steal much more from them by far,
now here, now there, as Love suggests to me,
than what is offered as a gracious gift.
The little that I am   55
depends on making them my constant norm;
since the first time I saw them
I've made no move toward living right without them,
so I have placed them high up over me:
they deserve credit for my worth, not I.   60

    I never could describe,
much less explain, the wonderful effects
that those mild eyes produce within my heart;
    all of the other pleasures
in this life seem to me inferior,   65
all other beauties trail in second place.
    Perfect tranquility, untroubled peace
like the eternal peace that reigns in heaven

emanates from their love-inspiring smile.
Ah, could I steadily   70
gaze at how Love controls their gentle motions
up close for just one day,
while the celestial spheres would cease to turn,
thinking of others and myself no more –
and let the blinking of my eyes be rare!   75

   Ah, but I keep desiring
something that cannot be in any way
and live on longing while bereft of hope;
   if only the tight knot
Love ties around my tongue when the excessive   80
light overpowers my weak mortal sight
   were loosened, I would pluck up courage right
then to write verses so remarkable
they would make everyone who heard them weep.
But wounds imprinted deeply   85
compel my injured heart to turn away,
and I grow pale because
my blood is hiding, where I cannot tell,
nor am I still what I was; and I know
this is how Love has struck the fatal blow.   90

   By now my pen begins to tire, Song,
for the sweet talk it's joined in has been long;
my thoughts, though, go on whispering to me.

10–15: See Nos. 50–57, where the poet found that making verses about his pas-
sion gave it relief; now he finds that his verses exacerbate it.   **33–36**: Petrarch is
thinking of the travels of Greek philosophers, mentioned in his letters (D).   **48**:
two lights: the Great and Little Bears.   **70–75**: The poet's wish closely echoes
22.31–33, but this time in the key of mystical contemplation rather than sensual
gratification (S).   **76–90**: After the shift from complaint praise to in the three
canzoni of the eyes, the series closes with a stanza on the pain of unrequited
love. It is typical of the sequence that developments are provisional and subject
to reversal.   **78**: So Dante describes the souls in limbo. *Inf.* 4.42.

74 *Io son già stanco di pensar sì come*

I now grow weary when I think about
how my thoughts never tire of circling you,
how I have not abandoned life by now
to shed my sighs' intolerable weight;

how, speaking of your face, your splendid eyes,
your hair – the themes on which I always speak –
my tongue and voice have never yet grown weak,
calling your name through all my nights and days;

and how I have not yet worn out my feet
although your footprints lead me where they will
and I lose all those steps to no avail;

and where the ink comes from and every sheet
I fill with you – and if those words fall short,
impute the fault to Love, not lack of art.

14: *the fault*: because Love ties his tongue, as in 73.79–81 (D).

75 *I begli occhi ond'i' fui percosso in guisa*

The eyes that wounded me in such a way
that only they themselves could heal the hurt,
and not the power of herbs or magic art
or stones from lands that lie beyond our sea,

from every other love so cut me off
my soul is soothed by only one sweet thought;
and if my tongue desires to follow that,
its guide and not itself should bear the scoff.

These are the splendid eyes that always make
my lord's campaigns assured of victory,
the one against my side the most of all;

these are the splendid eyes that always dwell
within my heart, each with a burning spark,
so speaking of them never wearies me.

This sonnet expresses a view opposed to the last one, as line 14 in particular makes clear. **1–2**: The lance of Achilles alone could heal the wound it made, an Ovidian motif used by the troubadours. **4**: *our sea*: *mare nostrum*, the Roman term for the Mediterranean **6**: *one . . . thought*: of her eyes. **8**: His tongue should not be mocked for attempting a task (expressing the thought her eyes inspire) beyond its skill; only its guide, Love, deserves mockery for leaving it no choice (S). **10**: *my lord*: Love. **11**: *my side*: his left side, where the heart is.

76 *Amor con sue promesse lusignando*

Love lured me once more into the same jail
with lying promises and gave the key
to her who long has been my enemy
and keeps me from myself in exile still.

I took no notice until suddenly
I was their captive. Now in great distress
(who will believe me though I swear to this?)
with deep sighs I regain my liberty.

Like a real prisoner marked by his affliction,
most of my chains I carry still, my heart
written upon my brow and in my eyes.

As soon as you have seen my pale complexion,
"From his looks," you will say, "if I am right,
this one did not have far to go to die."

77 *Per mirar Policleto a prova fiso*

If Polyclitus wished to test his eye
against the others famous in his art,

they would not see, if centuries went by,
half of the beauty that has won my heart.

My Simon must have been in heaven though,
before this noble lady left her place;
seeing her there he painted her, to show
the proof down here of such a lovely face.

A work like this only in paradise
could be imagined, not among us here
where flesh supplies a veil the soul must wear.

He could not have performed that gracious feat
once he descended to feel cold and heat
and found himself possessed of mortal eyes.

The Sienese master Simone Martini (best known for his magnificent Annunciation in the Uffizi) lived in Avignon in his later years, where Petrarch knew him. Simone did a portrait of Laura for him (now lost), the subject of this sonnet and the next. It appears to have been a miniature or a drawing touched up with watercolor (Contini) done on parchment.   1: *Polyclitus*: great sculptor of ancient Greece.   5–14: The poem turns on the idea that we fell from our home in heaven into our bodies, which occlude the beauty of the spirit and the ability to perceive it.

78 *Quando giunse a Simon l'alto concetto*

When Simon felt his inspiration warm
as he took up his pencil for my sake,
if he had given to the noble work
a voice and intellect as well as form

he would have caused my heavy sighs to cease,
sighs that make others' treasures dross to me,
for her appearance breathes humility
and her expression promises me peace.

And when I come to talk with her at need
she seems to listen to me tenderly,
but then she is unable to reply.

Pygmalion, how it must have made you glad
to have from your work time and time again
what I so long for only once from mine!

For the portrait of Laura with which this sonnet deals, see 77 and note. **6**: a variant on the ennobling effect of love; see 72.9 and note. **12–14**: Pygmalion fell in love with the statue of a beautiful woman he had carved and at his prayer Venus endowed it with life. *Metam.* 10.243–97.

79 *S'al principio risponde il fine e 'l mezzo*

If it predicts the way the rest will go,
the start of this, my fourteenth year of sighs,
no shade can save me anymore, nor breeze,
for I can feel my burning passion grow.

Love – for my thoughts are focused all on him
and his yoke never lets me breathe at ease –
so rules me I'm not half of what I was,
turning my eyes too often toward my harm.

So I grow weaker as the days slip past,
sapped from inside, with none but I aware
and she I gaze at, laying my heart waste.

I've barely brought my soul along this far,
nor know how long it will remain with me,
for death comes on and I can feel life flee.

Another commemoration of the anniversary of the poet's fatal meeting with Laura (see Nos. 30, 50, 62); the date indicated is April 1340, when Petrarch would have been in his mid-thirties. **3**: *shade . . . breeze*: The breeze (*l'aura*) is Laura, but the cool shade is that of the laurel, also her, suggesting that her current coolness cannot dampen his rising passion. Santagata notes that this line inaugurates the play on *l'aura* that will often be repeated.

He that has set a course to spend his life
upon the treacherous waves among the rocks,
kept from his death by only a small boat,
cannot be too far distant from his end
and therefore should attempt to make for port   5
now while his tiller still controls the sail.

The soft breeze to which I surrendered sail
and tiller entering the enamored life
and hoping I might reach a better port
soon carried me among a thousand rocks;   10
and yet the causes of my sorry end
were inside and not just around my boat.

Long shut within this blindly aimless boat
I drifted, never looking at the sail
bearing me prematurely to my end;   15
then it pleased him who brought me into life
to call me back some distance from the rocks
so that at least far off I saw the port.

Sometimes at night the lighthouse of some port
is sighted out at sea by ship or boat   20
unless it is obscured by storms or rocks;
so I could now, above the bellying sail,
make out the beacons of the other life;
and then I sighed with longing for my end.

Not that I yet am certain of my end: 25
wanting by fall of night to be in port
is a long voyage for so short a life;
fear grips me then, at being in this frail boat
where more than I would wish I see the sail
full of the wind that drove me to these rocks.   30

Could I come out from all these fearsome rocks
alive, my exile reaching a good end,
how happy I would be to furl my sail
and cast my anchor finally in some port!
But I am blazing like a fired boat,   35
it is so hard to leave my usual life.

Lord of my coming end and of my life,
before I smash my boat upon the rocks
direct my weary sail to a good port.

Petrarch repurposes the sestina, which usually expresses erotic desire (see 22),
using it here to depict his love for Laura as a spiritual danger from which he wants
to be saved. The lord invoked here is not Love but God. In this allegory the sea is
not the generic tempestuous sea of life but the sea of erotic infatuation, on which
the poet is dangerously adrift in a small sailboat, having surrendered his reason (the
tiller) and his passions (the sail) to the soft breeze (Laura), which becomes a wind
driving him toward the rocks of sin before he can reach the port of heaven.   **4**:
end: the initial meaning of this key word is a bad death; after the intervention of
God's grace in line 16, it will come to mean death leading to salvation.   **6**: *i.e.*,
while the passions still obey reason; but whatever the type of Petrarch's sail (most
likely lateen), it would not have been controlled by the tiller.   **7**: The soft breeze
(*l'aura soave*) is Laura via the pun introduced in 79.   **11–12**: The poet accepts
responsibility for his predicament.   **23**: *beacons* (*insigne*): I take the signs of the
other life to be the stars, but others think otherwise.

81 *Io son sì stanco sotto 'l fascio antico*

My old familiar load so wearies me,
weighed down by sins and evil habits still,
I fear I'll faint along the way and fall
into the clutches of my enemy.

A great friend came to gain my liberty,
supremely generous beyond all due;
then he rose up and passed beyond my view,
where now I strain my eyes in vain to see.

But here the echoes of his voice still last:
"You that are overburdened, here is the way;
come, if no other bars the path to me."

What grace, what destiny or, ah, what love
will fit me out with wings as of a dove
that I may rise from earth and be at rest?

A penitential sonnet placed after the sestina that identifies the poet's love for Laura as a moral danger. **4**: *enemy*: Satan. **5**: *friend*: Jesus. **10–11**: "Come to me, all you that labor and are burdened, and I will refresh you." Matt. 11:28. "I am the way, the truth and the life." John 14.6. **11**: *no other*: presumably the enemy, but the qualification is foreign to the gospel passages. **13–14**: "Who will give me wings like a dove, and I will fly and be at rest?" Ps. 54.7.

82 *Io non fu' d'amar voi lassato unquancho*

My love for you has never lost its force,
nor will it, Lady, while my life endures;
but I am weary of my constant tears
and hatred for myself has run its course.

I'd rather mark my grave with a blank stone
than have your name, to tell my fate, inscribed
on marble where my flesh would lie, deprived
of soul with which it could have still been one.

If you can let a faithful loving heart
content you without tearing it apart,
I ask for pity on this one's behalf;

but if your scorn seeks to be satisfied,
it reckons badly and will not succeed,
for which I greatly thank Love and myself.

Positioned thematically with the last two poems, this sonnet and the next take the novel tack of showing the poet's passion tempered by reason. **6**: *tell my* *fate*: as in "he died of unrequited love for Laura."   **8**: *still been one*: if her scorn had not caused his premature death (S).   **14**: *for which*: *i.e.*, that her scorn did not kill him; *Love*: who does not rule over the poet as he did (S).

83   *Se bianche non son prima ambe le tempie*

> Until my temples are as white as snow,
> which time is mingling slowly, streak by streak,
> I won't be safe, though now and then I take
> chances by going where Love draws his bow.
>
> But death and mayhem I no longer fear,
> nor, though he scratch its outside with his darts,
> each tipped with poison, can he pierce my heart,
> nor capture me although I trip his snare.
>
> Tears can escape no longer from my eyes,
> although they still remember their old track
> so well that I can scarcely hold them back;
>
> and though I may be warmed by her fierce rays
> they will not make me burn, while her cruel shape
> may trouble but not interrupt my sleep.

3–4: Although advancing years have not made the poet quite safe, he sometimes ventures into Laura's presence.   **12**: *fierce rays*: her glance.

84   — *Occhi, piangete: accompagnate il core*

> "Weep, eyes, commiserate with my sad heart,
> who through your fault is suffering death's pain."
> "So we do constantly, though we must mourn
> more for his error than our role in it."
>
> "Love gained his access first through you, my eyes,
> to where he still comes in as though at home."

"We only opened up the way for him
because hope stirred within the one who dies."

"The cases are not equal, as you claim:
for that first look your greed deserves the blame,
which was the cause of both your ruin and his."

"Here is what saddens us the most in this:
that perfect judgments rarely come along,
and one is censured for another's wrong."

A dialogue between the poet and his eyes. **4, 6, 8, 11**: *his . . . where . . . the one . . .
his*: the heart.   **12–14**: The eyes are reduced to a formulaic response, leaving
the better argument to the poet (D).

85 *Io amai sempre, et amo forte anchora*

I always loved, love passionately yet
and I will love still more from day to day
that sweet place to which I so frequently
return in tears when Love torments my heart.

I'm still resolved to love the hour I shed
forever every thought and wish that's base;
and love above all her whose lovely face
inspires me by example to do good.

Who would have thought, though, I would ever see
all these sweet enemies I so much love
attack my heart from all sides in a group?

Love, with what power you conquer me today!
And were it not that longing nurtures hope,
I would fall dead when I most want to live.

The details of the poet's first meeting with Laura (the place, the time, her face),
always present in memory, sometimes overwhelm him.

86 *Io avrò sempre in odio la fenestra*

That window always will arouse my hate
from which Love shot a thousand shafts at me,
for none of them has struck me fatally
and it is good to die while life is sweet.

Lingering here within this earth-bound jail
alas, results in endless woes for me,
which, worse yet, I will feel eternally,
for death will not untangle heart and soul.

My wretched soul, who by now should have known
from long experience that there is no way
to turn back time or even check its pace.

Often I have admonished her like this:
"Go, sad one, he does not depart too soon
who has already seen his happiest day."

1: The opening line contrasts with that of 85; *window*: an actual window at which Laura appeared, not a metaphor for her eyes (S).   5: *jail*: the body.   8: Cf. Dante's Francesca in *Inf.* 5.   12: *her*: his soul.

87 *Sì tosto come aven che l'arco scocchi*

As soon as he has loosed a shaft, the trained
archer can judge, though at a distance, just
which shot will miss, which other he can trust
to strike the target cleanly where he aimed.

Lady, it was in that same way you knew
the shot your eyes released that day was bound
to penetrate my vitals; through that wound
my heart's eternal tears must overflow.

"Poor lover, where will longing carry him?"
I'm sure you must have murmured at the time.
"With that shaft Love intended him to die."

Now, seeing how the pain disables me,
what my two foes are doing to me still
serves to increase my suffering, not to kill.

13: *foes*: her eyes.

88 *Poi che mia speme è lunga a venir troppo*

My hope has been deferred without a date
for its fulfillment, and since life is brief
I wish that sooner I had known enough
to make a headlong galloping retreat.

At least I'm fleeing now, though I've grown weak,
lame on the side that's twisted by desire;
although safe now, I still bear every scar
from love's encounters carved upon my cheeks.

My counsel: you embarking on Love's way
turn back, and you already touched by flame
do not delay – the heat will grow extreme.

Though I live, in a thousand none gets out;
no one was stronger than my enemy
and yet I saw her wounded in the heart.

6: *side*: the left, where the heart is.   **13–14**: Even Laura was subject to Love's power, in an episode here referred to only in general terms.

89 *Fuggendo la pregione ove Amor m'ebbe*

Escaping from where Love imprisoned me
for many years and used me at his will,
good ladies, it would take me long to tell
how irked I grew at that new liberty.

My heart was telling me that not one day
could it survive alone, when by the road

that traitor, cleverly disguised, appeared;
he would have fooled a wiser man than me.

And sighing often for my former state,
I said, "The chains in which I once was wrapped
were sweeter to me than this walking free."

Ah wretch, who saw what I had done too late –
with how much trouble I break free today
from that mistake in which I had been trapped!

76 already dealt with Love's prisoner feeling ambivalent about whether chains or freedom were preferable.   **7**: *traitor*: Love; Laura pulled this trick in 23.75– 76.   **10**: *chains*: Petrarch includes a yoke and shackles.

90   *Erano i capei d'oro a l'aura sparsi*

Her golden hair, disheveled by the breeze,
was tangled in a thousand pretty knots;
innumerable lovely glinting lights
blazed, as they do no longer, in her eyes.

It seemed to me I saw her face become
colored by pity, whether true or not;
and since I had love's tinder in my heart
is it surprising that I soon caught flame?

She moved not in the way that mortals walk,
but like an angel, and the words she spoke
sounded with other than mere human voice;

it was a spirit of heaven I saw, no less,
a living sun, and were she now not so
no wound is healed by slackening the bow.

1–2: This vision of Laura recalls Daphne, her hair streaming in the breeze (*Metam.* 1.529), and Venus letting her hair be scattered in the wind (*Aen* 1.318–19). It is one of Petrarch's favorite images of her (see Nos. 194, 196–98, 227 and many others). The vision would be captured in Botticelli's Venus rising from the sea.   **1**: *breeze (l'aura)*: the pun on her name again.   **4, 13**: The simplest explanation for her faded beauty is that the poet is recalling a moment from the distant past.   **9–11**: The description again recalls Venus (*Aen.* 1.327–29), with angel substituted for goddess.

91   *La bella donna che cotanto amavi*

> The lovely woman whom you loved so greatly
> has gone abruptly, leaving us below,
> and climbed to heaven, I should hope, by now,
> for all she did was gently done and sweetly.
>
> It's time to repossess both your heart's keys,
> which while she was alive were in her care,
> and with the straight path open, follow her,
> impeded by no further earthly ties.
>
> Unburdened of the greatest of your loads,
> you easily may lay the others down,
> and climb like a good pilgrim, carrying less.
>
> You see now how created things all run
> toward their deaths and how light the spirit needs
> to be when it confronts the perilous pass.

Commentators surmise this sonnet was written to Petrarch's brother Gerardo after the death of a woman he loved; in 1343 Gerardo became a monk. Writing to his brother in 1350, two years after Laura's death, Petrarch said it was fortunate for their souls that the two women for whom they had felt a sinful love had died young; but he complained that, unlike Gerardo's, his desire had not abated when his chains were broken. *Fam.* 10.3.   **6**: *both . . . keys*: one opens and one shuts. See 63.11 and note.

92   *Piangete, donne, et con voi pianga Amore*

> Weep all you ladies, and let Love weep too,
> and lovers from all lands, let your tears fall;

for he is dead who zealously used all
his talent, while he lived, to honor you.

As for myself, I beg my bitter grief
not to obstruct the tears that need to rise
and to be kind enough to let my sighs
vent when my heart has need of some relief.

Let poetry weep too, let every rhyme
acknowledge amorous Messer Cino's name,
for he has lately taken leave of us.

Pistoia and its wicked populace
should weep to lose a citizen so sweet;
and heaven, where he has gone, should celebrate.

On the death of the poet Cino da Pistoia (1270–1336/37). This tribute echoes
Dante's naming of his friend Cino as the illustrious love poet in Italian. *VE*
2.2.8.   **12**: *wicked*: Like Dante, Cino was exiled from his city because of
shifting political factions; but unlike Dante, he returned a few years later, after
another shift.

93 *Più volte Amor m'ave già detto: Scrivi*

Love has already often said to me:
"Write what you've seen in golden letters: all
the ways in which I turn my followers pale,
when in a single breath they live and die.

"Once you yourself experienced this, being
a member of the love-sick poets' choir;
then other work removed you from my power,
but I caught up with you as you were fleeing.

"And if those lovely eyes, which were the place
where I appeared to you and made my fort
when I broke through the hardness of your heart,

"return to me my all-destroying bow,
you may not always have so dry a face,
for tears are food to me, as you well know."

Love recaptures the poet after he has escaped (see also Nos. 69, 76, 89).   **3**: *pale*:
See note to 63.1.   **7**: *other work*: probably Petrarch's *Africa* and *De Viris Illustribus*,
Latin works that he considered more important than his Italian love poems (S).

94 *Quando giugne per gli occhi al cor profondo*

Entering the eyes, her image dominates
and drives all others from the inmost heart;
the vital powers the soul would portion out
desert the limbs, now left as inert weights.

And from this first a second miracle
is sometimes born: the part cast out of there,
fleeing its own abode, arrives somewhere
that brings revenge and gladdens its exile.

This makes two faces turn the color of death,
the force that showed vitality in both
in neither any more where it had been.

And I remembered this upon the day
I saw two lovers' faces change the way
that I have long been used to in my own.

Seeing two lovers, the poet analyzes the symptoms of mutual attraction, only
half of which (lines 1–4, not 5–8) he has experienced, since his love has not
been returned..   **3**: *powers*: the vital spirits (for which see note to 17.9), driven
from the heart, can no longer animate the limbs (*i.e.*, her beauty leaves him
stunned).   **5**: *miracle*: remaining alive when the vital spirits are banished.   **7**:
somewhere: sometimes the vital spirits ("the part cast out") migrate to the beloved's
heart, driving out her own spirits and leaving her similarly incapacitated.   **8**:
revenge: as often in Petrarch, the woman falling in love in turn.   **9**: *color of death*:
see note to 63.1.

95 Così potess'io ben chiudere in versi

If I could just enclose my thoughts in verse
the way I hold them close within my heart,
no one could ever be so heartless that
I would not make him pity my distress.

And yet, you blessed eyes that dealt me once
the blow no helmet and no shield could spare,
you see my inside and my outside bare
although my sorrow spills in no laments.

Your vision penetrates me thoroughly
the way a ray of sunlight shines through glass,
so my desire without words should suffice.

Peter and Mary Magdalen were not harmed
by faith, which seems adverse to none but me;
and no one else but you can understand.

11: *desire*: here, faithful love, as the next two lines indicate.   12–14: *i.e.,* You alone, eyes, see into me and so understand my faithfulness; but unlike the faith of Mary Magdalen and the apostle Peter, which saved them, mine actually harms me.

96 Io son de l'aspettar omai sì vinto

Waiting in vain has now so worn me out,
as has this unremitting war of sighs,
that my desires and hope I now despise
and every snare in which my heart is caught.

And yet the face depicted in my breast
and that I see no matter where I look,
compels me; though resisting, I fall back
into the same cruel torments as at first.

I went wrong when the road where long ago
I walked in freedom closed in front of me,
for it is wrong to chase what charms the glance;

my soul ran to its harm unbound and free,
but now it must take orders where to go
after committing that sin only once.

97 *Ahi bella libertà, come tu m'ài*

Ah, sweetest freedom, how you have revealed,
in taking leave of me, the way I left
my happiness behind when that first shaft
gave me the wound that never will be healed!

My eyes so doted then upon their hurt
they would no more respond to reason's rein,
for mortal things drew only their disdain –
alas, as I had trained them from the start!

I hear no talk except when anyone
speaks of my death; and with her name alone,
which has so sweet a sound, I fill the air.

Love spurs me nowhere else except toward her
and my feet know no other road, nor does
my hand know how to write another's praise.

7: *mortal things*: all but the divine Laura (S).   10: *death*: Laura, who causes his death (S).

98 *Orso, al vostro destrier si pò porre*

Orso, your charger wears a rein and bit
with which he can be turned back from his course;
but who can bind your heart from breaking loose
when he craves honor, hates its opposite?

Though you are kept from going, do not fear:
no glory can be taken from his name,
for by the general consent of fame
before the rest he is already there.

It is enough for him to take the field
on the appointed day, armed with such bold
weapons as courage, birth and love supply.

"I burn with noble ardor," he will cry,
"like my lord, who is kept from taking part,
for which he suffers and is sick at heart."

Addressed to Orso dell'Anguillaria (for whom see note to 27), evidently to
console him for being prevented from participating in a tournament.   **4**: *he*:
From here on, "he," "his" and "him" refer to Orso's personified heart.

99 *Poi che voi et io più volte abbiam provato*

Since you and I know from experience
how our hopes often prove illusory,
lift up your heart to a more certain joy
where the supreme good never disappoints.

This life on earth is like a meadow where
among the flowers and grass a serpent lies;
if any of its sights should please your eyes
it is to leave your soul the more ensnared.

If you desire, then, to attain at last
a tranquil mind before your final day,
desert the crowd and imitate the few.

"Brother, you go on showing," one might say,
"others the path along which you've been lost
often yourself, and never more than now."

A moral sonnet addressed to an unknown correspondent.   **4**: *supreme good
(sommo ben)*: as in Dante's *Purgatorio* and *Paradiso*, God.

100 *Quella feneſtra ove l'un sol si vide*

The window at which one sun shows her face
when she may please, the other around noon;
the window where the cold air plays its tune
when struck by Boreas during the short days;

the stone my lady sits on, deep in thought,
on long days, speaking with herself alone;
the places that her lovely form has thrown
in shadow or imprinted with her foot;

and the cruel pass where Love caught up with me
and springtime year by year, when once again
that day still makes my old wounds open up;

her face and words above all, which remain
deeply embedded in my heart today:
all of these make my eyes desire to weep.

1–4: *window . . . window*: presumably windows on different sides of Laura's house. **2**: *first sun*: Laura. **4**: *Boreas*: the personified north wind strikes the air with his breath, making it whistle. **6**: *long days*: in summer, in contrast to line 4. **9–11**: the memory of the day the poet fell in love (see 3).

101 *Lasso, ben so che dolorose prede*

I know too well to what extent the one
who spares none turns us into wincing prey
and how the world forsakes us in a day,
keeps faith with us for only a brief run.

I see a poor reward for all love's pain
and hear my last day thundering in my heart;
yet Love will not release me for all that,
demanding tribute from my eyes again.

I know how days and hours and minutes tick
our years away; I'm constantly assailed
by greater power than magic, but not tricked.

Desire and reason have battled in my head
twice seven years; the better will prevail
if souls on earth may presage future good.

This sonnet commemorates the fourteenth anniversary of the poet's unhappy passion, one year after 79.   1: *the one*: death.   8: *tribute*: tears.   11: *power*: the irrational force of passion.   14: Petrarch predicts the ultimate victory of his reason.

102   *Cesare, poi che 'l traditor d'Egitto*

When Caesar was presented by the Egyptian
traitor with his great rival's honored head,
he hid his obvious pleasure and instead
made show of shedding tears, as it is written;

and Hannibal, seeing Fortune so reverse
as to destroy his empire, laughed aloud
amid the tears of the lamenting crowd
so as to vent his sullen bitterness.

So everyone conceals as best he may
his real emotion with its opposite,
cloaked in a countenance now dark, now bright;

and therefore if at times I laugh and sing,
it is because I have no other way
to hide the bitter tears my anguish brings.

1–4: *See* 44 and notes for the historical details. There Petrarch treated Caesar's grief as genuine; here he adopts Lucan's anti-Caesar view. *See Phars.* 9.1038–41 (the writing referred to).   5–8: When there was general lamentation in Carthage at the indemnity to be paid to the Romans, Hannibal was seen laughing.

Rebuked, he answered that his laughter sprang from a mind beside itself with misfortune. Livy 30.44.4–6.

103 *Vinse Hanibàl, et non seppe usar poi*

Hannibal conquered, but then never knew
how to exploit that victory with his sword;
exercise caution, therefore, my dear lord,
so something similar does not fall to you.

The she-bear raging for her cubs, for whom
the pasturage of May turned bitter, gnaws
herself within and whets her teeth and claws
to take revenge on us for all her harm.

While she is grieving for this recent wound,
do not return your rapier to its sheath
but go straight on the path where fortune sounds

its call, which can immortalize your name,
bestowing on you even after death
thousands of years of honorable fame.

Addressed to Stefano Colonna the Younger, the victor in a skirmish with the rival Orsini family in May 1333, in which two leaders of the Orsini party were killed. Petrarch's advice to continue the struggle also appears in a letter to Stefano. *Fam.* 3.3.   **1–2**: As Petrarch points out in the letter, after virtually annihilating the Roman army at Cannae, Hannibal failed to take advantage of his victory by attacking Rome.   **5–6**: *she-bear*: The house of Orsini, chief rivals of the Colonna in Roman power struggles. The bear is a pun on the Orsini name; Dante had already made the crack about the bear and its cubs. *Inf.* 19.70–71.   **8**: *us*: Petrarch counts himself as a dependent of the Colonna family.

104 *L'aspeĉtata vertù che 'n voi fioriva*

The prowess we expected, whose first flower
came in the time you felt Love's battle start,

has now attained its ripeness in the fruit
matching buds and brought my hope to shore.

And so my heart commands me set down
words to ensure that your renown will live,
for in no other substance can one carve
a lasting monument to a living man.

Do you believe that Caesar or Marcellus,
Paulus or Africanus owes his name
to metal casting or to chisel blows?

No, my Pandolfo, such memorials fail us
in time's long course and only verse or prose
confers the immortality of fame.

Addressed to the young Pandolfo Malatesta, perhaps after he crushed a rebellion
against Malatesta rule in Fano in 1343. In contrast to 103, immortal military glory
can come only through Petrarch's verse. The sonnet is an elaboration of Horace's
"a monument more lasting than bronze." **2**: *time*: in adolescence. **9–10**:
Roman military heroes. **11**: *i.e.*, bronze or marble statues.

105 *Mai non vo' più cantar   com'io soleva*

I wish to sing no more in my old way –
she never listened, so it brought me scorn;
and in a pleasant place one may feel low.
It no good to sigh perpetually;
already all the hills are white with snow;   5
I lie awake because the day is close.
Sweet virtuous denial is dignified;
a love-inspiring lady pleases me
by going with head high and eyes that warn
but without stubborn pride: 10
Love rules his kingdom without force of arms.
He who has lost his way, let him turn back;
who has no shelter, let him sleep on grass;

he who has lost or lacks
a gold cup, let him quench his thirst from glass.   15

    I placed all in St. Peter's care – no more;
let him who can, construe me as I do.
Hard service is a heavy load to bear:
    I squirm free as I may and stand alone.
Phaeton, I hear, died and fell in the Po;   20
and now the blackbird's flown across the stream –
    come see it. Now I want no part of love:
no trifle is a reef among the waves
nor birdlime among leaves. I hate to see
a lovely woman hide   25
her qualities beneath excessive pride.
Some answer though not called, some in their place,
although implored, will disappear and flee,
    while others melt in ice
and others wish for death both night and day.   30

    The maxim "love who loves you" is antique.
I know whereof I speak – but let it be,
for everyone must learn at his own charge.
    A lady grieves her lover while looking meek;
a fig is hard to judge. It seems to me   35
prudent to undertake no task too large;
    good lodging may be found in any land.
Unbounded hope drives many a man to death
and that's a dance that I have sometimes joined.
The short life I have left   40
would not be shunned if offered as a gift.
I place my trust in Him who rules the earth
and gives his followers shelter in the wood,
    that with his gentle crook
He may at last lead me among his flock.   45

    Perhaps not all who read this comprehend:
some do not make a catch when nets are spread

and one who's splitting hairs may break his head.
  The law should not be lame while people wait.
To be secure, one often must descend;   50
beauty that's gaped at early on may late
  be sneered at; quiet beauty is the best.
I bless the key that turned inside my heart,
letting my soul go free, prying apart
links of my heavy chain   55
and stripping sighs past number from my breast!
Where I most grieved, another feels distress
and by that sorrow softens all my pain;
and I thank Love for this:
that I no longer feel what is no less.   60

  Silence that voices wise and careful thought,
sound that makes all except her fade away,
dark prison that contains the lovely light;
  midnight-dark violets in the fields of May,
wild animals at large within the walls,   65
her noble bearing and sweet modesty;
  a river with two sources, jealousy
and love, that flows, as I wish, toward its peace,
and pools at will – these have borne off my heart,
and in her face those stars   70
that lead me by a path of greater ease
toward my hope at the end of my distress.
My dearest treasure – and what comes of that,
now peace, now truce, now war –
never abandon me in this mortal dress.   75

  I weep and laugh for my past troubles, for
I place great confidence in what I hear.
Content at present, I expect yet more,
  am silent and cry out, counting the years.
I nest on a good branch in such a fashion   80
that I give thanks and praise her firm rebuff

106

that conquered in the end my stubborn passion
and wrote upon my soul: "Ah, when they hear,
how they will point at me," while scrubbing off
(now I am pushed so far   85
I can confess): "You were not bold enough."
It's she who pierced and heals my side and she,
inscribed more in my heart than in my rhymes,
who makes me live and die,
for whom I freeze and burn at the same time.   90

RVF 105 is written in a difficult form full of split lines (not printed as such here)
with internal rhymes, the outward shape of a hermetic poem. Petrarch's usual
sustained syntax is broken into a succession of proverbs and observations cast as
proverbs, the relation among which is not always clear. The best way into the
poem is to apply the maxims to the poet and Laura. Read in this way, the first
four stanzas suggest that the poet has given up his hopeless quest for Laura; they
thank Love for this change of heart; and they suggest a religious conversion.
The last two stanzas (where integrated syntax returns) suggest that he still loves
Laura but no longer seeks to possess her, having sublimated his passion. (The
following interpretations are selected from Ponte, S and D.)

5–6: The poet is awakened to his folly in old age, on the eve of his
death.   **12–15**: Given his failure to date, the poet renounces his hopes.   **16**:
Apparently a metaphor based on entrusting one's property to the Roman
church. The sense is: I placed myself in the service of Laura, but now no
more.   **18**: *hard service. Mal bauet* is the heavy feudal obligation owed to one's
lord; the relationship of vassalage is the paradigm of courtly love.   **20**: For
Phaeton, see note to 23.50–66; as in that poem, he is an emblem of the crash
of the poet's hopes.   **21–22**: The poet is the blackbird that has escaped the
hunter, an interpretation confirmed by the assertion that he does not wish to
be subject to love.   **27–30**: four different approaches to love.   **31–33**: The
poet knows this maxim is wise from his experience of the contrary, but does
not need to argue it.   **35–37**: *task too large*: like praising Laura; there are other
fish in the sea.   **50–52**: It may be more sensible to love a lesser beauty than
Laura.   **57–60**: In the preceding lines the poet is thankful to escape the chain
of passion; here Laura grieves that he has done so, which pleases him.   **61–72**:
The stanza gives a catalogue, in difficult images, of the things that make the
poet love Laura.   **63, 65**: The dark prison is the body that contains the light
of her soul, and the walls are again her body within which her fierce nature

rejects his advances.   **64**: dark purple flowers on a green dress.   **67–69**: The river of his passion flows to the sea of its sublimated satisfaction, gathering in pools according to its nature.   **70–72**: Passion spent, Laura's eyes once more (see 72.1–3) lead him to salvation.   **76–79**: The poet weeps for the past but laughs for the present and the future, in which he hopes for heaven, placing faith in the promises of religion.   **80**: The fine branch is of course on the laurel.   **83–86**: His illicit passion quenched, he fears becoming a byword to people, rather than telling himself he should have been more aggressive.

106 *Nova angeletta sovra l'ale accorta*

> A wondrous little angel winged straight down
> nimbly from heaven to the sprngtime shore
> where destiny had made me walk alone.
>
> Seeing I had no company or guide,
> she fashioned and spread out a silken snare
> upon the grass that greens the riverside.
>
> Then I was caught, and yet pleased at my plight,
> because her eyes poured forth so sweet a light.

The third of four madrigals in the collection (see Nos. 52 and 54), in each of which Laura appears in a different guise, though some critics doubt that this one (De Robertis) or all four (Fenzi) were originally about Laura.

107 *Non veggio ove scampar mi possa omai*

> By now I see no way of breaking loose:
> her bright eyes wage incessant war on me,
> making me fear protracted agony
> may waste my heart, which never knows a truce.
>
> I'd run away, but in my memory
> their love-inspiring splendor still shines on,
> daily and nightly, so in year fifteen
> they dazzle me even more than the first day;

Their images are strewn so far and wide
I cannot help but see on every side
their brightness or reflections that it lights.

So from one laurel such a forest grows
that through my adversary's magic arts
I wander where he leads among its boughs.

9–14: Seeing Laura's image in nature will be treated more extensively in canzoni 127 and 129.   **13**: *adversary*: the god of love.

108   *Aventuroso più d'altro terreno*

Fortunate ground beyond all others, where
Love brought her footsteps to a halt one day
and turned those blessed sparkling eyes toward me,
which make the air around them calm and clear,

sooner could time erode an image made
of solid diamond till it's worn away
than that sweet glance, with which my memory
and heart are overflowing still, could fade;

and even if I see you times past count
I still will stoop to find the phantom print
left in that gracious turn by her slim foot.

If Love is sleepless in a noble heart,
beg my Sennuccio, when he visits here,
for a small sigh or solitary tear.

This sonnet is addressed to the particular spot in Provence where Laura once turned and looked at the poet.   Nos. 108 and 109 deal with the persistent memory of encounters like those described in 110 and 111.   **2**: *Love*: this time Laura herself.   **12–14**: Sennuccio del Bene, a poet from Florence, became friends with Petrarch in Provence. Because of his noble heart, he will pity the poet's doomed love at this special spot.   **12**: *Love*: the god again.

109 *Lasso, quante fiate Amor m'assale*

Each day, when Love mounts his attacks on me
– thousands between the daylight and the dark –
my mind returns to where I saw those sparks
that keep my heart on fire eternally.

There I feel calm and I am brought to this:
at every dawn and noon and evening bell
I find them in my thoughts and feel their spell
and I forget all else, nor feel the loss.

The sweet breeze wafting from her radiant face
with her considered words, which lightens all
the atmosphere around her where it blows,

as if it were a breath of paradise,
seems always in that place to soothe my soul
and there my weary heart can find repose.

3: *i.e.*, to the place where the poet saw Laura (as in 108); *sparks*: her eyes.   **7**: *them*: the sparks.   **9–14**: The poem moves from her eyes to her breath when she greeted him; his memory has become so vivid he is now reliving the experience (Chiòrboli).   **9**: *breeze (l'aura)*: the usual pun on her name.   **12**: *breath (spirto)*: The root meaning of "spirit" is breath.

110 *Persequendomi Amor al luogo usato*

When Love pursued me to our former spot
I braced like one awaiting an attack
who shuts the passes to protect his back,
arming myself with my old modes of thought.

I turned and sidelong on the ground could see
a shadow the sun cast; at once I knew
her that unless my judgment is askew
was worthier far of immortality.

I murmured to my heart, "Why do you fear?"
But while the thought was taking shape, those rays
that always melt me had already come.

With lightning, thunder sounds at the same time:
so when the flash of those refulgent eyes
struck me, her greeting sounded in my ear.

1: *former spot*: where the poet has seen Laura before.   **4**: *old modes*: when he still
scorned love.   **8**: *i.e.*, like a goddess or an angel.   **10**: *rays*: from her eyes; see
note to 9.11.   **12**: *same time*: only when the storm is on top of you, underlining
her proximity.

III   *La donno che'l mio cor nel viso porta*

The one who bears my heart upon her face
appeared where I was sitting as I thought
of love's joy; to show reverence as I ought,
I stood up, pale and bowing, in my place.

As soon as she perceived my troubled state
she turned to me with features gone so white
Jove in his greatest fury at that sight
would be disarmed and let his wrath abate.

Recovering, I heard her speak as she
passed onward; at the time I could not bear
her words or the sweet sparkling of her eyes.

But now I find how pleasure multiplies
when I recall that greeting in my ear
and feel no pain, nor have I since that day.

1: Because the poet's moods change with Laura's expressions (Leopardi); see
72.60 and note.   **4**: *pale*: the lover's anxiety.   **6**: *white*: Seeing him shaken by
the encounter, she too turns pale, pitying his infatuation.   **9**: *Recovering (mi
riscossi)*: *i.e.*, from his fugue state; he comes back to himself.   **13**: The sacra-
mental status of the lady's greeting is a stilnovist convention, best known from

VN 3.1 (at the greeting of Beatrice, Dante says, "I seemed to see the furthest limits of blessedness.").

112 *Sennuccio, i' vo' che sapi in qual manera*

Sennuccio, I would like to have you know
how I am treated, how my life goes on.
I burn and melt as I have always done;
spun by the breeze, I'm still the same man now.

Here I once saw her humble and there proud;
now harsh, now mild; cruel, then compassionate;
now grave in her demeanor and now light;
now docile and now full of scorn and wild.

Here she sang sweetly, there she took a seat,
here she once turned toward me, here stayed her feet,
and there my heart was pierced by her bright gaze;

here she once smiled and said a few words there,
changed color here. In thoughts like these, my dear
friend, our lord, Love, consumes my nights and days.

1: For Sennuccio, see note to 108.   **2**: *treated*: by Love.   **4**: *breeze* (*l'aura*): the usual play on her name.   **13**: *changed color* (*cangiò 'l viso*): perhaps growing pale from love.

113 *Qui dove mezzo son, Sennuccio mio*

Sennuccio, here, though only half of me
(would I were whole with you content here, friend)
I came to flee the tempest and the wind
that turned the weather nasty suddenly.

Here I am safe and wish to make you see
why I don't fear the lightning as before

and why my passionate desire, so far
from being spent, has not cooled one degree.

I'd reached love's palace; when I gazed upon
the birthplace of the sweet pure breeze that clears
the air and drives the thunder from the sky,

Love lit the fire within my soul again,
where she rules, and extinguished all my fear:
How would I feel then looking in her eyes?

A missive to Petrarch's friend that tells of a journey to Vaucluse, in the course
of which he passed the town where Laura was born (see 4). **1–2**: *half*: because
his friend is his other half. **6**: Petrarch really was afraid of lightning, as
recorded in *My Secret*. **9**: *love's palace*: presumably the area he associates with
Laura. **10–11**: Laura is the breeze (*l'aura*) that chases the clouds, but also the
laurel, in ancient belief immune from lightning.

114 *De l'empia Babilonia, ond'è fuggita*

From wicked Babylon, where shame is dead,
a town abandoned now by all that's good,
a house of sorrow, nurse of error's brood,
I too, desiring to prolong my life, have fled.

Here I'm alone and at Love's invitation
I gather herbs and flowers or verse and rhymes;
I talk with him and think of better times
continually, my only consolation.

I do not care for Fortune or the crowd,
nor myself overmuch, nor worldly trash,
nor fires within nor turmoil from outside.

I only want two people and I wish
one had kind feelings toward me in her heart,
the other, as he once did, a sound foot.

: *Babylon*: Avignon, seat of the papal court. Comparisons of the worldly church to Babylon, with reference to the Apocalypse, had long been common in the writings of the Spiritual Franciscans and others. Petrarch's attacks on the Avignon papacy will culminate in Nos. 136–38.   **5**: *here*: Vaucluse.   **6**: *verse, rhymes*: as in 92.9, Latin and Italian verse.   **12–14**: The people are Laura and Petrarch's friend Friar Giovanni Colonna, who suffered from gout (the subject of *Fam.* 3.13).

115 *In mezzo di duo amanti honeŝta altera*

> I saw a lady placed between two lovers,
> she chaste and proud, and with her was the lord
> whose power is felt by every man and god;
> it was the Sun on one side, I the other.
>
> Feeling herself too dazzled in the sphere
> of her more radiant friend, she turned to me,
> her look so full of joy, I wish that she
> might never show me any look more fierce.
>
> At once the jealousy that reared its head
> within my heart at my first sight of such
> a noble rival turned into delight.
>
> And his sad tearful face, no longer bright,
> was covered over by a little cloud,
> for losing disappointed him so much.

The gentle humor of this fantasy is most evident in the "little cloud" (*nuviletto*) of line 13; see also Nos. 34, 41–43.   **2**: *the lord*: Love.   **4**: *the Sun*: Apollo; for his role as lover of Laura, see note to 5.12–14.   **5**: *dazzled*: Leopardi's interpretation of Petrarch's "enclosed (*chiusa*)."

116 *Pien di quella ineffabile dolcezza*

> Full of a sweetness words cannot express,
> drawn from her face by my attentive eyes

the day I would have gladly let them close
never to look on beauty that was less,

I left what I most long for; and I'd trained
my thoughts so much to dwell on her alone
they now see nothing else; to hate and scorn
what's not her is my settled frame of mind.

Here, to a valley closed all round by high
rock walls, a comfort for my weary sighs,
I came alone with Love, careworn and late.

I find no ladies here, but only rock
and fountainhead and everywhere I look
the image of that day my thoughts create.

Petrarch leaves Avignon, where Laura lives, to move to the country in Vaucluse,
some 25 km away.

117 *Se 'l sasso, ond'è più chiusa questa valle*

If the great cliff that hems this valley in
the most and gives it by that fact its name
should turn its craggy forehead south toward Rome,
turning its back on Babel in disdain,

the sighs I heave would have an easier trail
to follow, homing where their hope still lives;
now they take scattered paths, yet each arrives
where I direct it, so that not one fails.

The welcome they receive there must be sweet,
for none of them, as I observe, comes back,
such is the joy that causes them to stay.

It is my eyes that grieve; at break of day,
longing for the sweet places they now lack,
they bring me tears and steps to tire my feet.

If the cliff over the spring of Vaucluse, which blocks Petrarch's view toward Avignon, moved aside, his sighs would have a more direct route to Laura there; but they reach her by circuitous paths anyway. His eyes, though, unable to see around the crag, make him climb it every morning.   **2**: "Vaucluse (*Valchiusa*)" means enclosed valley.   **3–4**: The poet imagines that the crag, like him, scorns the papal court in Avignon, which he usually calls Babylon; see 114n.   **4**: *back*: its more sloping side.

118   *Rimansi a dietro il sestodecimo anno*

The sixteenth anniversary of my sighs
has come around, and still I make my way
toward the last one; yet it seems yesterday
I saw what made my suffering arise.

My loss has value, and I find bitter sweet;
though life is hard, I pray it will endure
longer than my cruel fortune; but I fear
Death may first close the eyes I celebrate.

Now I am here, but want to be elsewhere;
and want to want it more, but I do not
and do my best to fail at doing more;

and these new tears for old desire prove
that what I used to be once, I am yet
and though I turn and turn I have not moved.

On the sixteenth anniversary, the poet would be approaching 40.   **5**: *loss . . . value*: Laura's rejection of his culpable passion is good for his soul.   **9–11**: One part of him wishes he could free himself from his passion, but the stronger part conspires to frustrate the wish – the internal struggle described by Augustine in *Conf.* 8.5.   **9**: *here . . . elsewhere*: not physical locations but spiritual conditions.

119   *Una donna piú bella assai che 'l sole*

A lady more resplendent than the sun,
equally ancient and more beautiful,

with her famed loveliness
drew me still immature among her train.
     Being a precious rarity on earth   5
she captivated all my thoughts, words, deeds
and down a thousand roads
was there to lead me on, aloof, alluring.
     For her alone I changed from what I was,
once I could bear up close her dazzling eyes;   10
for her love I engaged
quite early in a strenuous enterprise:
so if I reach the port for which I'm bound
I hope through her to live
long after people think me in the ground.   15

     For many years this lady guided me,
full of the ardor of my youthful passion,
only, as I now see,
to have more certain proof of my devotion,
     showing me of herself at times her veil,   20
her shadow or robe, but hiding her face still;
and I alas believing
that I saw most of her, passed all my youth
     content, which is a memory I enjoy
now that I see more deeply into her.   25
Only quite recently
she showed herself to me as until then
I'd never seen her; ice began to form
within my heart, and will
remain there until I am in her arms.   30

     But neither fear nor chill prevented me
from pumping so much courage to my heart
that I embraced her feet
so I could draw more sweetness from her eyes;
     and she, who had by now removed the veil   35
before my own, said, "Friend, at last you see

117

how beautiful I am;
ask of me what you think will suit your years."
    And I replied, "My lady, I have long
reposed in you the love that now has grown   40
so ardent as to take
all wishes from me different from your own."
Then in a voice whose timbre thrilled my ear
she answered, with a look
that will forever make me hope and fear: 45

    "Rare is the man among the world's great crowd
who, when he hears at first about my splendor,
does not feel in his heart
some spark, if only for a little while;
    but then my enemy who disturbs all good   50
soon quenches it and noble striving dies,
and a lord rules instead
who promises a life of quiet ease.
    Love, who in youth first opened up your mind,
tells me the truth about you – I can see   55
the strength of your desire
will make you worthy of an honored end;
and as a sign that you are my rare friend
a lady will appear,
one whom your eyes will cherish even more."   60

 "That is not possible!" I would have cried,
but she: "Now see" (I looked up somewhat toward
a more secluded place)
"a lady who has shown herself to few."
    At once I bent my face down out of shame,   65
feeling inside a new and greater flame;
she took it laughingly:
"I see now where you stand," she said to me.
    "Just as the powerful radiance of the sun
causes all other stars to fade from sight,   70

you see my countenance
diminished in the blaze of greater light.
But I do not dismiss you from my suite,
for she and I came forth,
she first then I, from one seed at one birth." 75

    Instantly I could feel those words had snapped
the knot of shame that tightened round my tongue
when I was first abashed
to see she understood my new-found ardor;
    and I replied, "If what I hear is true, 80
I bless your father and I bless the day
when you both graced the earth,
and the years I've spent in contemplating you.
    If I have sometimes strayed from the straight path,
it stings my conscience far more than I show; 85
but if you find me worthy
to learn your nature more, I long to know."
Pensive she answered me, while her sweet gaze
held me so steadily
her face impressed her words upon my heart: 90

    "As our eternal father pleased, we two
were born immortal. Wretched race of men,
what good was that to you?
Better for you if we had never been.
    At one time, young and charming, we were loved; 95
now we have come to such a sorry end
my sister spreads her wings,
bent on returning to her home above;
    I am a shadow. Now I have explained
in brief as much as you can understand." 100
After she had withdrawn,
saying, "Do not fear I will leave you now,"
she gathered up a garland of green laurel
and placed it with her hands
upon my head, wreathed round about my brow. 105

Song, to whomever calls your sense obscure,
reply, "I do not care, for soon I hope
another message, spoken
more openly, will make the truth quite clear.
I only came to rouse men from their sleep, 110
if I was not deceived
by him who charged me when I left his side."

1–15: The lady is Glory; from an early age, the ambitious Petrarch becomes
her ardent lover, hoping for literary immortality. **12**: *enterprise*: probably
Petrarch's Latin verse epic *Africa*. **28–30**: Glory is treated as the lady the
poet loves; so he experiences the chill of awe before her beauty typical in lyric
convention. **50–52**: *enemy*: sensual pleasure, which makes men soft; *lord*:
some related personification, such as sloth. See 7. **59–60**: The second lady is
Virtue, understood primarily in the sense of "strength, power," here ability to
achieve great things (in Petrarch's case, his scholarly Latin poetry). See 7.2 and
note. Notably, Petrarch believes virtue was common in pagan antiquity but not
in the Christian present (95–98). Nonetheless, by making Virtue a daughter of
God, he merges this conception with the moral or religious understanding of
virtue. **84–85**: Consistent with both senses, he is sorry for his falling into
sensuality. **99**: *shadow*: Glory is the shadow of virtue; with Virtue leaving the
earth, her shadow must fade. (Santagata suggests as an alternative "a shadow
of my former self.") **103–05**: The culmination of the allegory is Petrarch's
receiving the laurel crown at Rome in 1341, something he had ardently desired
and lobbied for. **108–09**: *message*: That of another work, probably *Africa*,
which will make true glory clear in the person of its hero, the Roman general
Scipio Africanus.

120 *Quelle pietose rime in ch'io m'accorsi*

Your moving tribute made me understand
your wit and heartfelt generosity
and your lines seemed so powerful to me
that I immediately took pen in hand

to give you reassurance that the mortal
bite of him whom, like all men, I await,

I have not felt as yet, although of late
without fear I approached his very portal;

then I turned back because some writing said
above the threshold that the time prescribed
for my life's limit had not yet arrived,

although the day or hour could not be read.
Therefore allow your troubled heart some ease
and seek a man more worthy of your praise.

"Reports of my death have been greatly exaggerated." Written to Antonio Beccari, who had heard rumors of Petrarch's death in 1343 and written a lament for him. **6**: *him*: Death. **7–11**: These lines parallel Petrarch's account in *Fam.* 4.11 of a grave illness he suffered.

121 *Or vedi, Amor, che giovenetta donna*

Just see now, Love, the way a maiden scoffs
at all your power and shrugs my torment off,
quite safe between such enemies as we two.

While you are armed, she sits in a light dress,
with hair unbound and feet bare in the grass,
heartless toward me and arrogant toward you.

I am in jail; but if your steady bow
still has some mercy and an arrow or so,
take vengeance for yourself and for me too.

The fourth and last madrigal in the collection. Laura appears in the guise of a shepherdess. **4**: *armed*: with his bow.

122 *Dicesette anni à già rivolto il cielo*

Seventeen years the heavens now have wheeled
since I caught fire; it still has not gone out,

but now when I reflect upon my state
amid the flames I feel an icy cold.

The proverb puts it well: your hair turns white
before your vices fade, and slackening sense
leaves human passions still no less intense;
the heavy veil's deep shadow causes that.

Ah me, when will the day arrive on which,
looking at how my years have taken wing,
I leave the fire and my long suffering?

And will I see the day when just as much
and no more than I want, her sweet face would
delight these eyes, and only as it should?

4: *cold*: dismayed by the persistence of desire (S).   **8**: *heavy veil*: the body. which burdens and darkens the soul.

123 *Quel vago impallidir che 'l dolce riso*

The winning paleness that concealed her sweet
smile in a cloud of love with so much grace
and majesty appeared before my heart
that he went out to meet it in my face.

I knew then how in paradise they see
each other, for her tender thought was clear,
though it would not have been except to me,
I who have never fixed my gaze elsewhere.

Every angelic look, all humble ways
ever displayed by lady filled with love
would be but scorn beside what I speak of.

She bent toward earth her grave and noble gaze
and in her silence seemed to me to say,
"Who sends my dear and faithful friend away?"

The poet takes leave of Laura.   **1–4**: Her pallor is the sign of her regret at his departure; seeing it, his heart expands and his face reflects his emotional commotion (Ponte).   **5–6**: In heaven the angels and the blessed communicate without words, a frequent motif in Dante's *Paradiso* (De Robertis).

124 *Amor, Fortuna et la mia mente, schiva*

Love, Fortune and my mind, which turns aside
from what I see, intent upon the past,
afflict me so that sometimes, feeling lost,
I envy those upon the other side.

Love wastes my heart and Fortune takes away
all comfort, while my foolish mind in vain
weeps and is troubled; so in chronic pain
I'm forced to live embattled day by day.

Nor do I count on good times coming back,
for what remains will go from bad to worse;
and I have finished more than half my course.

I see my hopes slip from my hand, alas,
and since they are not adamant but glass
all of my fragile expectations break.

1–2: *mind . . . past*: the attitude of Petrarch the humanist, scornful of the corruption of his day and immersed in classical antiquity (D).   **4**: *other side*: the dead.

125 *Se 'l pensier che mi strugge*

If the strong sharp desire
consuming me could be
dressed in the colors suited to its shape,
    perhaps she, quick to flee
when she inflames, might share   5
the heat, and Love wake where he lies asleep.

The prints these tired feet trace
would not be so alone
on hills and in fields then;
tears would not wet my face   10
if she were ardent who is cold as ice
and does not leave a gram
of me untouched by flame.

But Love robs me of force
and strips away my skill,   15
and so my rhymes are harsh, their sweetness scarce.
    True, plants may not at all
display their native powers
upon their sheaths or in their leaves or flowers;
    and Love and those fine eyes   20
he makes his shady seat
see what is in my heart.
But if my sorrow vents
and overflows in weeping and laments,
the first hurts me, the other   25
her, for they should be smoother.

    You sweet and graceful rhymes
that in Love's first attack
I used because I had no other arms,
    what would it take to crack   30
this heart now cased in stone
and let my feelings find their old release?
    Inside it there is one
who paints my lady's face,
praising her constantly;   35
but drawing her on my own
exceeds my powers, which is killing me.
So I, poor wretch, have lost
my comfort of the past.

As a young child whose tongue   40
has not grown limber yet
cannot speak but insists on blabbering,
　　desire drives me to write
so my sweet enemy,
I hope, will hear my words before I die.   45
　　If she finds all her joy
in her own lovely face
recoiling from all else,
you green banks, hear my song
and lend my sighs a flight so high and far   50
it will be told for long
how great a friend you were.

　　You know so fair a foot
was never yet set down
as on the day when you were marked by hers;   55
　　and so my worn-out heart
and body racked with pain
return to share with you their hidden cares.
　　If only you had kept
her footsteps as she passed   60
among the flowers and grass,
so that my sad life might
find consolation, gazing while I wept!
Still, in such doubts as these,
searching, my soul finds peace.   65

And everywhere I look
I find soft radiance
and think: "Here fell the brightness of her glance."
　　The flowers or grass I pluck
are rooted in the ground   70
where I imagine that she used to walk
　　through meadows by the stream
and where she sometimes found

a seat, fresh, flowering and green.
So none of it is lost   75
and greater certainty would bear a cost.
Blest spirit, how is it you
make others feel so too?

Poor little song of mine, you are so crude!
I think you recognize it: 80
remain here in the wood.

Alone in Vaucluse, the poet meditates on his consuming passion. In the first
three stanzas he complains that the pains of love have deprived him of his former
skill so that his crude speech is unable to communicate properly with Laura or
even describe her. In stanza four he decides to speak anyway; but thinking she
will not hear, he asks the banks of the river Sorgue in Vaucluse as a consolation
to echo his voice through space and time. In the last two stanzas he is first
disconcerted that the rural landscape does not retain the prints that he imagi-
nes her feet having left (Wilkins at 18 asserts she once visited Vaucluse with a
touring party). Then, however, he realizes that this uncertainty gives him some
comfort, because knowing exactly where she trod would cramp his ability to
imagine her everywhere in nature. This train of thought will take him in 126 to
imagine in great detail time that she spent in the solitude of Vaucluse.   **3**: *colors*:
the expressive power of words.   **18**: *native powers*: *e.g.*, medicinal properties
(S).   **33**: *one*: Love or his imagination.

126 *Chiare, fresche et dolci acque*

Clear waters, cool and sweet
that bathed her slender arms,
she who alone is mistress of my heart;
    straight trunk that she was pleased
(as, sighing, I remember)   5
to make a column to support her side;
    blooms and grass gently pressed
by the light dress she wore
and her angelic breast;
air, blessed and pure air   10

126

here where Love pierced my heart with two bright eyes:
listen now, all together
to my lament, before I end forever.

   If it's to be my fate
effected by the stars   15
that Love shall shut these eyes still filled with tears,
   may fortune plant my poor
body among you here,
my soul returning naked to its home.
   Death would not be as cruel   20
if I could bear this hope
into that dreadful pass,
for my exhausted soul
could never leave my anguished flesh and bone
in a more tranquil tomb,   25
nor in a final harbor more serene.

   Perhaps a time will come
when that wild creature, fair
and gentle, will return to her old haunts;
   and toward the same spot where   30
she saw me, on the day
I bless, will turn her glad and eager glance,
   seeking me and – the pity! –
seeing me dust among
the stones, be moved by Love   35
to fill the air with sighs
so soft and sad that she takes heaven by force
and so procures me grace,
using her delicate veil to dry her eyes.

   From lovely boughs rained down   40
(still sweet in memory)
showers of snowy blossoms in her lap;
   and there she simply sat,
meek amid so much glory,

already smothered in a loving cloud.   45
    This bud fell on her dress,
that one on her blond curls,
which that day looked no less
than gleaming gold and pearl;
some landed in the water, some on shore,   50
one in a graceful swirl
turning as if to say, *Love triumphs here.*

    I kept repeating while
awe-struck I took this in,
"In paradise that one was surely born."   55
    Her bearing, half divine,
her face, her speech, her smile
had plunged me deeply in oblivion,
    so stealing me away
from how things really were,   60
I could but sigh and say,
"How, when did I come here?"
thinking myself in heaven, not where I was.
Since then this verdant place
so pleases me, elsewhere I find no peace.   65

If you had all the graces you desire,
Song, you could boldly leave
the woods and circulate where people are.

Wilkins at 21 suggests that this canzone is based on Laura's having once come
to Vaucluse with a party to view the Fountain of the Sorgue. Whether or not
that is so, it seems clear that the details of the poem, in which she came there
habitually – apparently alone – and met and spoke with the poet, are wholly
imagined. **1–13**: Features of Vaucluse that Petrarch imagines having come
into contact with her are called on to witness his sad words: the waters of
the Sorgue, a poplar tree that grew near its fountain, the ubiquitous grass and
flowers of pastoral lyric and the air made holy by her presence. **11**: There is
no need to think that this falling in love in Vaucluse replaces the first encounter
at the church in Avignon, which has become the foundation of the ongoing

story.   **31–32**: *the day / I bless*: the day described in stanza 4, which is apparently not the day described in stanza 1 (S).

127   *In quella parte dove Amore mi sprona*

It's clear I must direct my doleful rhymes,
faithful reflections of my mind's distress,
to the one theme toward which Love urges me.
    But which to put in first, which in last place?
When he advises me about my torment   5
I'm doubtful, for he speaks confusingly.
    So I will tell the story of my suffering
the way I find it written on my heart
by his own hand (which I go over often);
for speaking of my sighs   10
brings some relief and sorrow seems to soften.
I'll tell how though I gaze
intently at a thousand different things,
I only see one lady's lovely face.

Ever since my remorseless destiny,   15
forever hurtful, obdurate and proud,
drove me so far away from my great good,
    Love keeps me living only through memory.
So if I see the world when it looks young,
beginning to wear green again in spring,   20
    I seem to see in adolescent bloom
the lovely girl who is a woman now.
Then when the sun grows hot in summertime
I see her as a flame
of love that dominates a noble heart.   25
But when the day laments
the sun's retreating northward gradually,
I see her reaching full maturity.

Looking at violets or at leaves on boughs
during the season when the cold grows less
and strength increases in more gracious stars,
   I only see the violets and green dress
that Love, at the beginning of my war,
was so well armed with he still conquers me;
   and see the bark, so tender and so smooth,
that once enclosed the adolescent limbs
in which there now is housed the noble soul
who makes all other beauty
seem to me low and mean, for I recall
her modest look so well
that flowered then and grew before her time,
to cause and comfort all my suffering.

When upon distant hills I see soft snow
struck by the sun, Love acts on me the way
the sun does snow, as I start thinking of
   the more than human beauty of the face
that from a distance makes my eyes grow wet,
but up close blinds them and subdues my heart,
   where between white and gold there always shines
the inner beauty that no mortal eyes
have ever seen, I think, except for mine;
thinking of how she sighs
and smiles inflames me with desire so hot
it does not fear it might
fall in oblivion, but becomes eternal,
a flame no change of season can put out.

After an evening shower I never saw
the wandering stars wheel through the lucid air,
flaming amid the fall of frigid dew,
   but I have had before me those bright eyes,
the sole support that props my weary life,
as I once saw them shaded by a veil;

and as their beauty lighted up the skies
upon that day, so bathed in tears I still
can see them sparkle and am still afire.   65
Watching the sun arise
I feel the light appear that wins my heart;
as sunset ends the day
I seem to see her when she turns away,
leaving all dark behind as she departs.   70

   If ever I saw crimson roses mixed
with white ones, gathered in a golden vase,
roses a maiden's hand had freshly plucked,
   it seemed to me that I could see the face
of her who overtops all other wonders   75
by mingling in it three outstanding beauties:
   the golden tresses loose upon the neck
that would have put the whitest milk to shame,
the cheeks embellished with a subtle flame.
But if a breath of wind   80
ripples a field of white and yellow flowers
it brings before my mind
the day when I first saw her golden hair
wind-blown, which filled me suddenly with fire.

   I must have thought that I could count the stars   85
or bottle up the sea in a small jar,
when I came up with the audacious thought
   of mentioning each place on a few sheets
that she who is all beauty's choicest flower,
remaining herself still, illuminates,   90
   so that I never go away from her.
Nor shall I: even if I sometimes run,
she's closed to me the routes of earth and sky,
present to my tired eyes
everywhere, always, till I am undone.   95
She so remains with me

I see no other nor desire to see
and call no other name amid my sighs.

   Song, you know well that everything I say
is nothing to the secret thought of love   100
I carry in my mind both night and day,
the comfort that alone
keeps me from dying in this endless war;
my heart remaining far
away, tears would have finished me by now,   105
but with that thought I stave off death somehow.

127 develops further one of the main themes of this series of canzoni: separated
from Laura, the poet sees her everywhere in nature, kindling his passion anew.
Instead of being in Vaucluse, here and in 129 he is in Italy. In a metrical epistle
to Giacomo Colonna, Petrarch elaborates this theme in its most negative sense:
he fears and is dismayed by her appearance in nature (Wilkins at 20). **20**:
Green dresses were associated with young women (see 12.6). **26–27**: The
autumn day regrets its shortening. **32**: *violets . . . green (le violette e'l verde)*:
thought to refer to her green dress ornamented with violets (or to violets in
her hair), Love's weapon(s). **49**: *between white and gold*: her eyes, the windows
of her soul, between her face and hair. **52–56**: a difficult passage, variously
interpreted. **58**: *wandering stars*: the planets. **63–65**: "That day" is the Good
Friday when he first met Laura (3); her eyes were bathed in tears for Christ's
passion (Chiòrboli). **67**: *light*: not from her eyes, but Laura as another sun
(S). **83–83**: *hair / wind-blown*: see 90 and note. **89–90**: The most general
formulation of the theme: without diminishing her beauty, Laura transfigures
all of nature for him, as the sun illuminates the world without growing dim
itself. **97**: *other*: woman.

128 *Italia mia, benché 'l parlar sia indarno*

   Although mere words, my Italy, will not serve
to heal the numerous
and deadly wounds I see upon your body,
   I like to think my sighs will voice the hopes
of Tiber and of Arno   5

and Po, where I sit sad and serious.
    Ruler of heaven, I pray
the pity that once drew you down to earth
may turn you toward your well-loved noble land.
Generous Lord, you see   10
how trivial quarrels turn to savage wars;
the hearts that proud fierce Mars
has hardened and closed up,
open and soften, Father, set them free;
there let your truth be heard,   15
though I may be unworthy, through my words.

    You that by Fortune's favor hold the reins
in these fair, fruitful lands
for which, as it appears, you feel no pity,
    why are so many foreign swords among us?   20
Is it so our green plains
may turn the color of barbarian blood?
    You cherish an illusion:
myopic, you believe that you see far,
looking for loyalty in venal hearts.   25
He with the most hired swords
is most surrounded by his enemies.
O deluge harvested
from a dim northern waste
so as to inundate our smiling fields!   30
If we have brought this host
here by ourselves, who then can be our shield?

    Nature provided well for our protection,
erecting the great wall
of the Alps to keep us safe from German rage;   35
    but lust for power, blind to its own well-being,
has nonetheless contrived
to infect the healthy body with disease.
    Now in a single fold

the gentle flocks are penned with savage beasts,   40
so that the good are always made to groan;
and to deepen our disgrace,
these are the offspring of the lawless race
dealt such a deadly wound
by Marius, as we read,   45
whose deed survives in memory now as ever,
who thirsty then and tired
drank as much blood as water from the river.

   Why mention Caesar, who in every land
painted the grass dark red   50
by opening their veins with our good steel?
   But now, who knows through what bad stars, it seems
we bear the hate of heaven,
thanks to you lords to whom great power was given.
   Your quarrelsome ambitions   55
lay waste the fairest place in all the world.
What human flaw, divine decree or fate
makes you oppress your weak
neighbors, seize goods from the unfortunate,
and in the northlands seek   60
the sort of men you like
because they shed blood, sell their souls for coin?
For love of truth I speak,
not out of hate or scorn for anyone.

   Can you not recognize from experience   65
Bavarian trickery:
their hands held up to play a game with death?
   The loss brings less shame than the mockery;
yet your blood still rains freely,
because real hatred whips you on and wrath.   70
   Ponder your situation
an hour and you will understand how little
he values you who holds himself so cheap.

O noble Latin blood,
shake off this harmful burden; do not make   75
an idol of so false
and vacuous a fame;
for if this furious and stiff-necked race
surpasses us in cunning,
it is not natural – we are to blame.   80

   "Is this land not the ground that I touched first?
And is this not the nest
in which my childhood was so sweetly nursed?
 This not the fatherland in which I trust,
the kind and loving mother   85
that softly covers both my parents' dust?"
   In God's name let this thought
move you sometimes, and look with some compassion
upon your people's sorrow and distress,
whose only hope for peace   90
is, after God, in you.   At the first sign
of sympathy and concern,
firm strength will take up arms
against brute rage; the combat will be short,
for the ancestral courage   95
is not yet dead in the Italian heart.

   Consider, lords, how rapidly time flies
and with what speed life flees,
while death is always hanging over our backs.
   Now you are here, but think: when you are gone   100
how naked and alone
the soul must come to that dark dreadful track.
   While passing through this valley,
try to lay down your hatred and your anger,
winds that blow hard against a peaceful life;   105
and let the time you spend
in causing pain be turned to worthier ends

of hand or intellect,
some fine praiseworthy act
or noble occupation of the mind;   110
this will bring joy on earth
and open up the heaven-trending path.

　　I must advise you, Song,
to phrase your message very tactfully,
for you must go to lords puffed up with pride,   115
full of ill will, too used
to hearing customary flattery,
always truth's enemy.
Better to try your luck
among the few great souls goodness will please.   120
Ask, "Who will offer me
protection? I go crying: peace, peace, peace."

This canzone is addressed to the Italian lords and condemns their never-end-
ing struggles with each other for power and in particular their use of German
mercenaries to fight their battles, with disastrous results for Italy. Petrarch felt
the effects of this chaos himself. In 1344–45 he was staying in Parma when a
war for control of the city broke out among two powerful families and their
allies, with German mercenaries hired by both sides. He apparently wrote the
canzone during the siege of the city. Later he slipped out one evening with
companions, was pursued by hostile forces and spent a nightmarish night injured
by a fall from his horse, eventually making it to Bologna (*Fam.* 5.10). **6**: *Po*:
Parma is near the Po.　　**22**: *barbarian*: German; Petrarch had toured Germany,
which he found "surprisingly civilized for a barbarous land" (*Fam.* 1.5). In this
poem he characterizes the Germans of his time as though he were an ancient
Roman.　　**29**: *northern waste*: Germany.　　**40**: *flocks . . . beasts*: Italian civilians,
German soldiers.　　**44–48**: In 102 BC the Roman general Marius defeated a
German tribe in southern Gaul with vast slaughter. Petrarch takes the detail from
a Roman historian.　　**49–51**: Caesar's campaigns against German tribes.　　**58–59**:
seize . . . unfortunate: lit. "harry their damaged and dispersed goods," *i.e.*, confis-
cated possessions, *e.g.*, in the case of political exiles, as happened to Petrarch's
own family when he was a child.　　**65–67**: The mercenaries quickly surrender
when the battle goes against them. Petrarch says "hold up the finger," which

was the gesture of surrender of the gladiators.   **66**: Bavarians participated in the war for Parma (Ponchiroli).   **73**: *so cheap*: as to sell his loyalty.   **77**: *fame*: the reputation of German mercenaries for fighting bravely.   **93–96**: By this point in the argument, the lords' mercenaries have become an invading army, against which the lords are urged to raise the populace.   **103**: *valley*: this life.

129 *Di pensier in pensier, di monte in monte*

From thought to thought, mountain to mountain-top,
Love leads me on, for I find beaten tracks
inimical to my composure, while
   a stream or spring upon a lonely slope
or shady valley nestled between peaks   5
can bring some quiet to my troubled soul,
   which, answering Love's call,
now laughs, now weeps, now feels assured, now fears.
My face, in which the soul's moods are expressed,
grows clouded and then clears,   10
varying from one minute to the next.
Seeing me, one who knows love's ways would note:
"He seethes, and is unsure about his state."

On mountain heights and in thick woods I find
some rest, but any dwelling place of man   15
my eyes account a mortal enemy.
   At every step a new thought springs to mind
about my lady and they often turn
the pain I undergo for her to joy.
   And scarcely do I yearn   20
to change this sweet and bitter life, when now
a new thought, "Love may save you," soon appears,
"for better times; although
you may feel worthless, she may hold you dear."
Immediately, sighing, I think then: 25
"Really? Could that be true? But how? But when?"

Where a tall pine's or hill's cool shade is cast
I sometimes stop – at once in my mind's eye
I sketch upon the nearest stone her face.
   Returning to myself, I find my chest   30
wetted with pity for my state and cry,
"Look where you've come, so far from her, alas!"
   But while I hold in place,
firm in my wandering mind, that first clear vision,
lost to myself and gazing still at her,   35
I feel Love is so near,
my soul is satisfied with its illusion:
I see her in such beauty everywhere,
should the illusion last, I ask no more.

   Often I have (who will believe my tale?)   40
seen her alive in the transparent water,
the smooth trunk of a beech, on the green grass,
   in a white cloud, so lovely she would force
Leda to see the beauty of her daughter
lost like a star the rising sun's rays veil.   45
   The more remote the place
where I may be, the lonelier the shore,
the lovelier my mind imagines her;
when the truth dissipates
that sweet illusion, right there I sink down   50
cold, a dead stone upon the living stone,
shaped like a man who thinks and weeps and writes.

   Up where no other mountains' shadows pass,
upon the highest and most open ridge,
my deepest longing often urges me;   55
   up there my eyes can measure out my loss
and, raining all the while, my tears can purge
the doleful fog that swathes my heart each day,
   while lost in thought I see
how much air separates me from the face   60

always so close to me and yet so far.
Softly, "What do you know,
poor wretch?" I ask myself, "Perhaps out there
she may be sighing for your absence now."
And in this thought my soul can breathe anew.   65

   Beyond the Alps, my song,
under a sky far happier, more serene,
once more you'll see me by a running steam
where you can feel the breeze
scented by a fresh fragrant laurel tree.   70
There is my heart and she who steals it away;
here you see just a shape, the shell of me.

The poet wanders in the mountains of Italy and thinks about how far he is from
Laura. This canzone brings to a climax the theme of his seeing her everywhere in
nature. In view of the mountain setting, it is worth remembering that Petrarch
in fact climbed Mount Ventoux in Provence, something remarkable for the
period. But after taking in the view from its summit, he opened Augustine's
Confessions and was chagrined to read that men go to admire the summits of
mountains while they fail to look inside themselves. *Fam.* 4.1.   **13**: *unsure*:
Lines 22–26 suggest the uncertainty is about whether his love is returned.   **37**:
Love: not the god this time, but Laura herself.   **40–52**: In the visions of stanza
5, Laura becomes universal, the poet's muse (the visions in the wilderness never
lack for writing materials, 52).   **44**: *daughter*: Helen of Troy, the most beautiful
of women.   **51**: *living stone*: the stone that, as in line 29, he has imagined to be
Laura.   **53–65**: Climbing a ridge with a distant view, he looks toward Provence,
where she is.   **66–72**: He sends the poem to Provence, where it will find him
because his heart is there; only his body is in Italy.   **68**: *stream*: the Sorgue in
Petrarch's beloved Vaucluse, where he imagines Laura.

130   *Poi che 'l camin m'è chiuso di Mercede*

   Since pity's highway has been closed to me
   I've travelled far on a despairing route
   from those eyes where by some mysterious fate
   lies the reward for my fidelity.

I feed my heart, which asks no more, on sighs
and live on tears, born as I was to weep;
nor does that grieve me – in my present shape
weeping is sweeter than you would suppose.

And to one image only I hold tight,
made not by Zeuxis nor by Phidias
but by a master of a higher style.

What shield were Scythias or Numidias
if not content with my unjust exile
envy can find me here, so out of sight?

9–10: Laura's image created by Love in the poet's heart surpasses the art of the greatest ancient Greeks: the painter Zeuxis and the sculptor Phidias (Petrarch includes the sculptor Praxiteles). 11: Scythia and Numidia were held to be the northern and southern limits of the habitable world. 13: *exile*: far from Laura. 14: *envy*: apparently of fate or of other people for his love (see 172 and note).

131 *Io canterei d'amor sí novamente*

I wish to sing of love things so new-found
that they would force each day a thousand sighs
from her hard breast and finally arouse
a thousand deep desires in her cold mind;

I wish to see her face pale, her eyes wet
with pity for me as I watch her turn
them toward me, looking conscious of the pain
that she has caused me and too late regrets;

and see the scarlet roses in the snow
stir in the breeze, revealing ivory
that turns to marble those who gaze close by;

see change in all that lets me live with no
regret the brief life that remains to me,
and boast that I survived to see this day.

A fantasy of Petrarchan revenge, *i.e.*, his poetry finally making Laura fall in love with him.   **9–11**: Her red lips in her white face part with her breath, revealing her teeth.   **11**: She turns men to stone like Medusa (originally a beautiful girl).

132 *S'amor non è, dunque è quel ch'io sento?*

> If it's not love, what is it that I feel?
> But if it's love, in God's name what is that?
> If good, why does its cruelty almost kill?
> If bad, how can its torments be so sweet?
>
> If I burn willingly, then why complain?
> And if not, what good is it to lament?
> O death in life, O pleasurable pain,
> how can you rule me, lacking my consent?
>
> And if I give it, shame on my complaint.
> Lashed by conflicting winds in a frail craft
> I'm drifting rudderless on the high seas,
>
> laden with folly, with no prudence left,
> so I myself do not know what I want.
> I burn in winter and in summer freeze.

A classic statement of Petrarchan antithesis; for a more schematic and less analytic treatment, see 134.

133 *Amor m'à posto come segno a strale*

> Love set me as a mark at which to shoot,
> placed me like snow in sun, like wax in fire,
> mist in the wind; I've grown so hoarse I'm mute
> from begging mercy while you do not care.
>
> From your eyes, Lady, came the mortal blow
> no change of time or place can ever heal;

from you alone comes what seems small to you:
the sun, the fire, the wind that make me fail.

My thoughts the arrows and your face the sun,
longing the fire; with these, armed to the teeth,
Love blinds me, pierces me and melts me down;

your words, your angel's singing, your sweet breath,
against which I'm defenseless, are the breeze
before which what remains of my life flees.

134 *Pace non trovo, et non ò da far guerra*

I find no peace and have no arms for war;
I fear and hope; I burn and turn to ice;
I'm down aground and soaring past the stars,
grasp nothing, hold the world in my embrace.

She does not open nor yet lock my jail,
nor holds me for herself nor sets me free;
Love neither pulls his shafts nor seeks the kill,
wants me to live nor acts to rescue me.

Eyeless I see, without a tongue I cry;
although I call for help, I want to die;
I love another and myself I hate.

Weeping I laugh and sorrow is my food;
in life and death alike I see no good.
You alone, Lady, put me in this state.

This is perhaps the most thorough use of antithesis to express the Petrarchan
account of the lover's state. The technique did not originate with him, but in
later times became the emblem of the Petrarchan fashion in English love poetry,
the typical parody being "I freeze! I burn!"

Whatever is most strange
and marvelous in any far-off land,
if properly considered,
is most like me; to this, Love, have I come.
   Out where the day comes forth   5
a lone bird flies that, lacking any mate,
after its self-willed death
is born again, the same in its new life.
   So, equally alone,
when my desire has reached the very summit   10
of its high thoughts, it turns to face the sun
and is incinerated
in the same way, returning as it was;
it burns and dies and then, its strength renewed,
a fit match for the phoenix, it lives on.   15

   Out in the Indian Sea
is found a stone so strong it will by nature
draw iron to itself,
stealing the nails from wood, which makes ships founder.
   And I endure the like   20
on waves of bitter tears; for that fair rock
by its unyielding pride
has drawn my life to where it now must sink.
   A stone that's full of greed
for flesh, not iron, has disjoined my soul   25
(stealing my heart, which formerly was firm
and kept me integrated, who am now
sundered and scattered). Fortune, you are cruel –
flesh that I am, I see how I am pulled
by a sweet living magnet to the shore.   30

   And in the farthest west
there is an animal as tame and gentle

as any beast could be,
and yet her eyes hold tears and grief and death.
   You must be very wary 35
if ever your own eyes alight on her;
unless you meet that gaze
you may observe the rest of her in safety.
   But I, a reckless wretch,
run always toward my harm. I know how much 40
I've suffered and expect more; but desire,
insatiate, blind and deaf,
so carries me away, the sainted face
and the enchanting eyes of this angelic
and innocent wild thing will be my death. 45

   Far in the south there gushes
a spring they call the Fountain of the Sun,
which by its nature boils
at night-time, but at break of day turns cool;
   and it grows ever colder 50
as the sun mounts, approaching ever closer.
And so it is with me,
who am a never-ceasing spring of tears;
   for when the lovely light
that is my sun withdraws and leaves my eyes 55
bereft and downcast in the dark of night,
I burn; but when I see
rays of the living sun appear in gold,
I feel myself completely change at once
and I become so cold I turn to ice. 60

   Epirus has another
fountain, one that runs cold, of which we read
that it will quench a burning
torch and will light one that has been extinguished.
   My soul, which had as yet 65
not felt the scorching of the fire of love,

as soon as it approached
the cold one who forever makes me sigh,
   at once burst into flame;
such torment, never seen by star nor sun,   70
would have roused pity in a heart of stone;
after it was alight,
her perfect freezing virtue put it out.
How often she has lit and doused my heart
I know who feel it, and I chafe at it.   75

   Far beyond our sea's shores,
out in the legendary Fortunate Isles,
are two springs; he that drinks
from one dies laughing, but if from the other
   afterwards, he is saved.   80
The same fate marks my life: I could die laughing,
from the great joy I feel,
were it not tempered by my anguished cries.
   Ah Love, who guide me still
only in hidden shades obscure to fame,   85
we shall not speak of our spring, always full,
but which most surges up
when the sun is united with the Bull,
as my eyes always weep but weep the most
in the same month I saw my lady first.   90

   Whoever asks you, Song,
what I am doing, say: below a cliff
in a closed valley where the Sorgue pours forth,
he lives in solitude,
except for Love, who never leaves his side,   95
and for her image, she who utterly
destroys him; he shuns other company.

1–4: The canzone will be a set of variations on this theme, echoing the form of previous canzoni like 50. **6–15**: There is only one phoenix at a time; it builds its nest at the top of a palm tree, dies and is reborn. *Metam.* 15.393–407. Its death by fire is post-classical; Albert the Great explained that the bird exposes itself to the sun's rays and, with its resplendent feathers acting as a magnifying glass, bursts into flame. *De Animal.* 23.110. **10–11**: At the height of his thoughts about Laura (like the bird at the top of the palm), the poet is so close to her, his sun, that he is consumed in her radiance; but this is only a phase in the cycle of desire. **16–19**: Albert also described this supposed action of the magnet (D). **20–23**: The poet imagines Laura as a reef that attracts flesh as though magnetically; with his heart lost, which kept him safe from love, he falls apart like the ship. **31–38**: Pliny described an animal in west Africa called the catoblepas: "all who see its eyes expire immediately." *Nat. Hist.* 8.32. **46–51**: Pliny described a fountain in Africa that boils by night and is cold by day. *Nat. Hist.* 2.106.228. The poet burns with passion in her absence, but in her presence is frozen with fear. **58**: *living sun . . . gold*: her radiant gaze and golden hair. **61–64**: In the same passage Pliny described the fountain of Jupiter in Dodona that lighted spent torches; Augustine cited both fountains in defense of miracles. *Civ. Dei* 21.5. **76**: *shores*: of the Mediterranean. **77**: *Fortunate Isles*: the Canaries. **84–90**: Unlike all these phenomena famous in antiquity, Petrarch will not speak about his own unknown and retired fountain of the river Sorgue in Vaucluse. **88–90**: The Bull (Taurus) joins the sun in April, when Petrarch first saw Laura. **92–94**: In a letter Petrarch described how to find his retreat: following the Sorgue to the spring where it surges up from beneath a high cliff, you would see him on the right shore. *Fam.* 6.3.

136 *Fiamma dal ciel su te tue treccia piova*

May fire from heaven rain upon your hair,
wicked one, whom corruption pleases so,
once fed by acorns and the brook but now
grown rich and grand by making others poor,

you nest of treachery, the hatching place
from which the evils of today have spread,
slave of the bottle, groaning board and bed,
in whom lust has produced its masterpiece.

Young girls and old men frolic through your rooms
and in their midst Beelzebub attends,
with mirrors and with bellows for their flames.

You were not raised on cushions in the shade
but barefoot among thorns, bare to the winds.
May your new way of life's stench rise to God.

This and the next two attack the corruption of the papal court in the "Babylonian captivity" of Avignon. See note to 114.   **1**: *fire*: the punishment of Sodom in Gen. 19:24–25.   **2**: *wicked one (malvagia)*: Petrarch imagines the papal court as the whore of Babylon (Apoc. 17:1–5), as Dante had done in *Inf.* 19.106–11.   **3**: *acorns*: proverbial food of the golden age (see 50.23), here standing for the poverty of the early church.   **9**: *old men*: no doubt cardinals.   **11**: *mirrors*: as sexual stimulants. *bellows*: to fan the fading flames of lust.

137 *L'avara Babilonia à colmo il sacco*

Gluttonous Babylon has so stuffed the sack
with God's wrath and her impious, shameful vices
it now is bursting, and for gods has picked
carousing Bacchus, Venus who entices.

Waiting so long for justice I'm worn out,
I yet see a new sultan for her, still
to come, though not as soon as I would want,
who will make Bagdad the sole capital.

Her idols will lie smashed upon the ground
as will her proud towers, heaven's enemies,
the tower dwellers' souls and bodies burned.

Great spirits whom the paths of virtue please
will rule the world; and then the age of gold
will be restored and the great deeds of old.

A prophecy of the destruction of the corrupt papal court at Avignon, couched in the obscure terms of prophecies.   **5–8**: The ironies of this quatrain are difficult to parse. Most commentators think the sultan will be a new emperor or pope who will move the papacy back to Rome. Santagata suggests Petrarch means that with the papal courtiers behaving like infidels Avignon is really the second capital of the Muslim world, an anomaly that a future sultan will correct upon its destruction by restoring Muslim unity at Bagdad.   **10**: *towers*: The papal palace at Avignon, one of Europe's great medieval buildings, makes Petrarch think of the Tower of Babel that challenged heaven (S).

138 *Fontana di dolore, albergo d'ira*

> Springhead of sorrow, residence of rage,
> heresy's seminary, error's shrine,
> once Rome, now false and wicked Babylon,
> cause of the lamentations of our age;
>
> hell of the living, it would be a wonder
> – O horrid prison house, O forge of lies
> where evil breeds and grows and goodness dies –
> if Christ did not at last show you his anger.
>
> Founded in humble poverty and chaste,
> do you now, shameless whore, lift up your horns
> against your founders? Is your hope now placed
>
> in your adulterers or your vast ill-gotten
> treasure hoard? Constantine will not return
> from hell, where your wealth sinks him to the bottom.

The last of the Babylonian sonnets.   **2**: *heresy*: In *Fam.* 2.12 Petrarch referred to the heretical opinion of Pope John XXII that the souls of the saved do not see God face to face until the Last Judgment.   **10–11**: *horns*: The beast of the Apocalypse has ten horns (Apoc. 17:3); the Avignon papacy lifts them in rebellion against Christ and his apostles.   **10, 12**: *whore, adulterers*: The whore of Babylon (see note to 136.2) committed fornication with the kings of the earth. Apoc. 17:1–2.   **13–14**: The Donation of Constantine, a forged document believed genuine in Petrarch's time, purported to grant the popes temporal power in the West when the emperor moved the capital to Constantinople.

139 *Quanto più disiose l'ali spando*

The more I spread my wings to come your way,
sweet flock of friends with whom I would alight,
the more is Fortune sure to impede my flight
and make me wander far from you, astray.

In spite of her my heart, which travels free,
is always with you in that open place
where the land holds our sea in its embrace;
weeping, I let him go the other day.

I took the left-hand turn while he went right,
he led by Love, I forced elsewhere by fate,
he to Jerusalem, to Egypt I.

But patience is a comfort in all grief;
in the arrangement we are living by
our times together must be few and brief.

Probably addressed to Petrarch's brother Gerardo, a monk in the Charterhouse
of Montrieux, and to his fellow monks, after a visit there (S). Petrarch's *On
Religious Leisure* is addressed to them, and it begins by regretting that his recent
visit there was too brief.   **5**: *her*: Fortune.   **6–7**: *place*: the valley where the
monastery is located, near the Mediterranean coast where a broad bay and a chain
of islands partly encloses the sea.   **9**: Petrarch goes to Avignon while his heart
returns to Montrieux. (Others think Petrarch returns to Avignon from Italy
and addresses the poem to friends there.)   **10**: Jerusalem is the promised land,
Egypt the land of slavery (likely another attack on the papal court in Avignon,
as in Nos. 136–38).

140 *Amor, che nel penser mio vive et regna*

Love, who exerts his lordly rights upon
my thought and has his chief seat in my heart,
comes armed into my face at times to start
– camp pitched and banner planted – a campaign.

But she who bids us love with resignation
and wishes that shame, reason and respect
would hold desire and ardent hope in check
regards our impudence with indignation.

Then, terrified, Love beats a quick retreat,
quitting the field to run inside my heart,
where he hides, trembling, and does not appear.

What can I do when my lord shows such fear
but by his side until my last hour stand?
He that dies loving well makes a good end.

141   *Come talor al caldo tempo sòle*

As in the summer it is sometimes seen
a witless moth that seeks the light will fly,
in its erratic quest, in someone's eyes,
resulting in its death and the other's pain,

so to my fatal sun I'm always drawn,
the eyes from which such sweetness comes to me
that Love, despising reason's rein, breaks free
and what I long for trumps what I discern.

And how those eyes avoid me I know well
and know that it will be the death of me;
it so torments me that my strength will fail;

yet Love so dazzles me that I lament
for her annoyance, not my injury;
and my soul blindly goes to death content.

2–3: In medieval physiology, the eyes send out beams of light by which they
see things; see note to 9.11.

Into the grateful shade of the cool leaves
I ran, escaping the relentless light
that burned me as it fell from the third heaven;
already clearing snow-drifts from the hills,
the loving breeze by then renewed the time,   5
in meadows waking flowers in grass, on branches.

The world has never seen such graceful branches,
nor ever did the breeze stir such green leaves
as were revealed to me in that first time;
and so, in terror of the burning light,   10
I sought for shelter not the shade of hills
but of the one tree most esteemed by heaven.

A laurel then protected me from heaven
and often, filled with longing for its branches,
I since have walked through woods and over hills,   15
where I have found no other trunk or leaves
so privileged by the celestial light
they did not change appearance with the time.

And so more resolute with passing time,
following where I heard the call of heaven   20
and with the guidance of a soft clear light,
I've come back, always true to those first branches,
both when the ground is thick with scattered leaves
and when the sun brings fresh green to the hills.

Woods, rivers, rocks, the meadows and the hills,   25
all things are overthrown and changed by time:
and so I beg forgiveness of these leaves
if after many turnings of the heavens
I steeled myself to flee the baited branches
when I had just begun to see the light.   30

I was so pleased at first by the sweet light
that joyfully I crossed the highest hills
just to get close to my beloved branches;
but now life's brevity, the place and time
show me a different pathway to reach heaven   35
and to bear fruit, not only flowers and leaves.

A new love, other leaves and other light,
a different climb to heaven by other hills
I seek – it is high time – and different branches.

Like 80, this poem repurposes the sestina, here as an account of spiritual evolution. This is partly accomplished by the shifting meanings of key words. In particular, *cielo*, "heaven," shifts from the harmful influence of Venus (the third heaven of the geocentric universe) (3, 13) to the Christian heaven (35); *lume*, "light," from the burning light of Venus (2, 10) to the light of Laura's eyes (21, 31) to the light of reason or grace (30); *tempo*, "time," from the cycle of the seasons, ever renewed (5, 18), to the linear march that destroys all created things (26, perhaps 34). **1–12**: In the springtime of his life the poet seeks relief from the urgings of sensual passion and finds it in his (questionably) sublimated love for the laurel tree (whose branches are Laura's limbs and whose leaves are her hair). **12**: The laurel was believed immune from lightning. **18**: The laurel is evergreen. **25–30**: After many years of loving Laura (28), the poet's growing sense of his own mortality causes a spiritual awakening that makes him reject amorous involvement. **26**: Not only the poet but also the laurel must die. **29**: The branches are now baited with birdlime. **30–31**: *light*: the most startling change of meaning. **37–39**: The key words become even more unstable. The new love is love of God, the spiritual climb to the Christian heaven through difficulties (the other hills) is clear enough, and the other light is perhaps that of eternity. The other leaves and branches are a puzzle; commentators suggest Christ's crown of thorns and the arms of his cross.

143 *Quand'io v'odo parlar sí dolcemente*

Hearing you use the honeyed turns of phrase
that Love inspires in every devotee,

I feel the hot desire so spark in me
that it would set the coldest soul ablaze.

In all her beauty then my lady appears,
sweet to me as she ever was and calm
and with the look that wakes me from my dream
when my sighs are the only bell I hear.

I see her, her hair blowing in the breeze
as she looks back and in her loveliness
enters my heart as mistress of its keys.

But since my tongue is stopped by the excess
of pleasure, I lack courage to declare
in plain words what it's like when she is there.

This sonnet and the next two reverse the renunciation of love with which 142
closes and speak of the persistence of desire, continually reborn (Noferi).   **1**:
Probably addressed to a love poet, perhaps Sennuccio del Bene, to whom No
144 is addressed.

144   *Né così bello il sol già mai levarsi*

I never saw the sun come up so fair
when the clear sky had not a cloud to show,
nor after rain beheld the heavenly bow
diffuse such varied colors through the air

as on the day when I assumed love's cares
the range of flaming colors that transformed
the face – and here my words are not too warm –
with which no other mortal thing compares.

And I saw Love, who turned her shining gaze
so softly every other sight I saw
in later times seemed darkened to my eyes.

Sennuccio, I could see him, see him draw
his bow; and now my life is not secure
and yet I yearn to see that sight once more.

4–8: On the day when the poet falls in love, Laura blushes on noticing that he is staring at her.   **9**: The god of love lives in Laura's eyes.   **12**: For Sennuccio del Bene, see the note to 108.

145 *Ponmi ove 'l sole occide i fiori et l'erba*

Put me where grass is withered by the sun
or where his heat is quenched by ice and snows,
where his bright chariot temperately goes,
where he comes forth or where he rests when done;

set me in humble state of life or high,
or in maturity or youth's green phase,
or when the nights are longer or the days,
beneath a clear or dark and threatening sky;

put me in heaven, on earth, or in the pit,
in a deep bog or on a hill above,
out of this body or attached to it;

make my name celebrated or unknown:
I'll still be what I was, live as I have,
my fifteen years of sighing will go on.

A rhetorical amplification of a passage in one of Horace's odes. *Carm.* 1.22.17–24. The more cheerful ending of Horace's poem is imitated in 159.

146 *O d'ardente vertute ornata et calda*

O noble soul aglow with virtue's blaze,
who fill the pages you inspire in me;
O last unbroken home of chastity,
secure tower built on merit's deep-laid base;

O roses strewn on living snow, O flame
in which I see myself, but purged of dross;
O wings of joy that lift me toward the face
brighter than anything the sun's rays warm!

If people everywhere could understand
my verses, I would make your name resound
from Iceland to Gibraltar and the Nile;

but though I cannot make it heard in all
earth's corners, they shall hear it in the land
Apennines split and sea and Alps surround.

5: *roses . . . snow*: her face; *flame*: her eyes.   6: The poet sees himself mirrored
in Laura's bright eyes and the reverence he feels when he looks at her sublimates
his carnal desires.   11: Petrarch lists six places that made up the ends of the
earth for the ancients.

147 *Quando 'l voler che con duo sproni ardenti*

When my desire, which with two burning spurs
drives me and masters me with a hard bit,
blunders at times beyond where bounds are set
to keep me satisfied for a few hours,

he meets one who can read upon my face
my deepest heart's effrontery and fear
and sees Love, who arrests his wild career
with anger flashing from her stormy eyes.

At that, like one who fears the thunderbolt
of angry Jove, he draws back all at once,
for great fear reins in great desire's assault.

But cooling fire and hope beset by qualms
within my soul that show as if through glass
help to recover her sweet face's calm.

1–2: Unlike the traditional image of 6, where desire is the horse and the poet is the rider, here the poet is the horse and desire the rider, with the spurs of yearning and hope and the bit of fear (S). This will be the normal form of the image from now on. (The problem here is that fear is more properly the opposite of desire, Petrarch's usual formulation.)

148 *Non Tesin, Po, Varo, Adige et Tebro*

Neither the Rhine, the Danube nor the Don,
the Tiber nor the Arno nor the Po,
the Tigris, Indus, Ganges nor the flow
of the Euphrates, Nile or Loire or Rhone,

neither fir, beech nor juniper nor pine
could cool the fiery pain my sad heart bears
like the loved stream that always joins my tears
and the slim tree I celebrate in rhyme.

This is my help against the assaults of Love
amid which armed in readiness I need
to live this life that flees in such great bounds.

So on the fresh bank may the laurel thrive
and he who planted it, in its sweet shade
write wise and joyful thoughts near rippling sounds.

Petrarch has planted a laurel tree on the bank of the Sorgue in Vaucluse; his letters describe his planting trees. **1–6**: The trees might soothe the poet's burning with shade, as the rivers with water. **1–4**: Petrarch manages to get 24 rivers into these lines.

149 *Di tempo in tempo mi si fa men dura*

With time, the posture of her angel form
has grown less stiff toward me; her smiles become
less strained; the look is less
stern in her eyes and on her lovely face.

What business do these sighs still have with me?
Born as they were from grief,
they published openly
the anguished desperation of my life.
　　Now when it happens that I look at her
to pacify my heart,
it seems that Love is there,
lending me aid and arguing my case.
　　Still, I do not believe this ends the war
nor is my heart in any mood at peace;
the more hope reassures,
by just so much it makes desire burn more.

150 *Che fai, alma? che pensi? avrem mai pace?*

"What do you think, my soul, shall we have peace
or truce, or must it be eternal war?"
"I don't know, but from what I've seen so far,
her eyes are never pleased by our distress."

"What good is that, if with those eyes she makes
us burn in winter and in summer freeze?"
"Not she, but he whose power controls her eyes."
"So what, if knowing that, she never speaks?"

"Her tongue is silent, but her heart complains
aloud; and though her tearless face may smile,
she weeps where no one watching her can tell."

"No matter what, my mind is not at rest;
the sorrow that has pooled there never drains:
in high hopes wretched men can place no trust."

A dialogue between self and soul, as 84 was a dialogue between heart and
eyes.　**7**: *he*: Love, who displays Laura to advantage to inveigle the poet.　**8**:
i.e., if knowing the effect she has on us, she does nothing about it.

151 *Non d'atra et tempestosa onda marina*

No weary helmsman ever had to flee
to port when waves were battered by black air
as fast as I from swirling dark despair
to where desire most spurs and urges me.

Never was mortal vision overcome
by light from heaven as mine was by the light
shining in that sweet gentle black and white
in which Love gilds his shafts and sharpens them.

I see him with his quiver there, not blind,
naked except where shame requires him veiled,
a boy with wings – no picture, but alive.

He shows me what for most remains concealed,
for point by point within those eyes I find
all that I ever say or write of Love.

7: *black and white*: Laura's eyes (see 29.23 and 72.51), the port to which the poet fled in line 4.   **6**: *light from heaven*: The implication is that the effect of Laura's eyes on the poet surpasses a miraculous event. (St. Paul was converted when a light from heaven shone around him and he fell on the ground blinded. Acts 9:3–4, 8.)   **9–11**: This is the only time the love-god is described in *Scattered Rhymes*; he is in his traditional form, but not blind. In *Triumph of Cupid* 1.23–30 he appears on a triumphal car, naked and armed with his bow.   **9**: *there*: in her eyes.

152 *Questa humil fera, un cor di tigre o d'orsa*

This gentle beast with tiger's heart or bear's,
showing a human face, an angel's shape,
spins me so often between fear and hope
I cannot tell my laughter from my tears.

If she will not accept or free me soon
but keeps me hanging like this, in between,

till the sweet poison coursing through my veins
reaches my heart, then, Love, my life is done.

I cannot, with the weakened strength that's left,
tolerate changes that remain so swift:
to burn, to freeze; to blush and then turn pale.

Hoping to end these pains, I slip away
like someone who from hour to hour fails;
for he is powerless who cannot die.

153 *Ite, caldi sospiri, al freddo core*

Go, my warm sighs, to her cold heart again
and break the ice that locks her pity there;
if heaven then lends an ear to mortal prayer,
let death or favor terminate my pain.

Go, my sweet thoughts, speak openly about
what stirs within me where she cannot look;
then if her cruelty or my star should strike
we will at least be free from hope and doubt.

Tell her, though explanations may fall short,
that our condition is as turbulent
and dark as hers is full of peace and bright.

Love will go with you, so be confident;
and now our bad luck may be winding down,
if I can read the weather by my sun.

14: If by Laura's (my sun's) expressions I recognize that her state of mind
(weather) is turning favorable (Ponte).

154 *Le ſtelle, il cielo et gli elementi a prova*

The stars, the elements and heaven compare
their different arts until they have perfected
this living light where nature is reflected,
as is the sun, which finds no match elsewhere.

Their handiwork is so sublime a feat
no human eye can safely hold its gaze;
for Love rains grace and sweetness on the eyes
with which no earthly beauty can compete.

The air ignited by their gentle ray
burns with a purity that exceeds by far
our power to express or to conceive.

And there no base desires can survive,
but those of virtue and honor. When before
has peerless beauty cooled lust in this way?

1–4: Dotti cites *Conv.* 4.21, where Dante explains the forces that combine to generate a human soul and how their varying qualities (*e.g.*, the changing positions of the heavens) result in its being more or less pure. 1: *elements*: earth, water, fire and air. 3: *living light*: Laura and especially her eyes, which become the acme of creation.

155 *Non fur ma' Giove et Cesare sì mossi*

Caesar and Jove were never so worked up,
one to strike enemies and one to thunder,
that pity would not mollify their anger
and make them let their favored weapons drop.

My lady wept and spoke in plaintive tones
and my lord wanted me to see and hear
to fill me with enough grief and desire
to penetrate the marrow of my bones.

Love painted her amid those tears for me,
sculpted her rather, and inscribed those words
upon a diamond in my deep heart's core,

where he, with those sure, well-adapted keys,
often returns and draws from me, still stirred,
a storm of tears and heavy sighs once more.

Nos. 155 through 158 form a group dealing with the sorrow of Laura, for which
no motive is suggested (unlike the episode of Beatrice weeping for the death
of her father in *VN* 22).

156 *I' vidi in terra angelici costume*

Once on this earth I saw an angel's form,
heavenly beauty our world cannot show;
remembering it brings joy but sorrow too,
for all else now seems shadow, smoke and dream;

then from two radiant eyes I saw tears spill,
eyes that have made the sun feel jealousy,
and I heard words breathed out upon a sigh
that would make mountains move and streams stand still.

Love, wisdom, virtue, pity, all combined
with grief, turned weeping into a symphony
sweeter than any that the world had heard;

the heavens so hung upon that harmony
there was no leaf on any branch that stirred,
so great a sweetness filled the air and wind.

157 *Quel sempre acerbo et honorate giorno*

That always bitter yet still reverenced day
impressed its living image on my heart

more than can be described by skill or art,
but I return in memory frequently.

The bittersweet laments that I could hear,
her bearing, which expressed a noble pity,
left me to wonder if a mortal lady
or goddess caused the sky around to clear.

Her head was fine gold and her face warm snow,
her eyebrows ebony, her eyes two stars
from which in vain Love never drew his bow;

pearls and red roses where her sorrows passed
to words where they were ardently expressed;
her sighs were flame and crystal her pure tears.

1: *day*: the day the poet saw Laura weeping (see Nos. 155 and 156).   6: *noble pity*:
This is the most specific motive for Laura's sorrow that the poet can divine as he
observes; see 156.9–10; 158.5–6.   12: *pearls, roses*: her teeth and lips.

158 *Ove ch'i' posi gli occhi lassi o giri*

Wherever my tired eyes may rest or turn
to calm the restless prodding of desire,
I find a lady's image painted there
to make my passion stay forever green.

Graceful in grief, she breathes out, it appears,
deep pity such as grips a noble heart,
while throbbing words and blessed sighs join sight,
seeming to rise and fall upon my ears.

Love and the truth were with me when I said
that what I saw were beauties, every one,
such as were never seen beneath the stars.

Nor were such words of tender pity heard
ever before, nor the sun ever seen
such lovely eyes produce such shining tears.

This poem does not describe the poet's seeing Laura weep (see Nos. 155–157), but rather Love or his imagination representing that scene to him again and again.

159 *In qual parte del ciel, in quale ydea*

> In which of heaven's realms, in what Idea
> did Nature find the archetype for those
> lovely beguiling features when she chose
> to show down here what she can do up there?
>
> What fountain nymph or goddess of the wood
> loosed hair of such pure gold upon the wind?
> When in one heart were all these virtues found,
> though theirs will be the guilt when I am dead?
>
> For heavenly beauty he would search in vain
> who never gazed upon those peerless eyes
> or saw their gentle movement when they turn;
>
> he does not know the way Love heals or kills,
> who never heard the sweetness of her sighs
> or of her speech or how her laughter trills.

1–2: In a Christianized Platonism the Ideas, the archetypes of created things, pre-exist in the mind of God. **3–4**: Nature does not operate in heaven as on earth; rather down here she accepts the archetype from up there. **5–6**: Petrarch's beloved image of Laura's blond hair loose in the breeze now suggests a goddess (as in Virgil; see note to 90.1–2). **8**: *guilt . . . dead*: for resisting the poet's love, which killed him. **13–14**: Petrarch imitates the final lines of Horace's "Integer vitae" (*Carm.* 1.22), the previous passage of which he imitated in 145.

160 *Amor et io sí pien' di meraviglia*

> Love and I, marveling, stare at her together,
> like someone who cannot believe his eyes,
> and as she speaks and laughs feel new surprise,
> for she is like herself alone, no other.

Beneath her tranquil brow like a clear sky,
the sparkle of my faithful stars is bright,
kindling and guiding like no other light
an aspirant whose aim in love is high.

Ah, what a miracle, amid the grass
to see her sit as if a flower or press
her white breast on a cluster of green leaves!

How sweet in spring to see the way she strolls,
alone with her reflections, while she weaves
a garland for her gleaming golden curls!

161 *O passi sparsi, o pensier' vaghi et pronti*

O eager wandering thoughts, O aimless paces,
tenacious memory, fierce internal fire,
O feeble heart, O powerful desire,
O eyes of mine, no longer eyes but fountains!

O bough that crowns with honor famous faces,
the twin achievements' only decoration,
O wearying life and O sweet aberration
that send me searching across plains and mountains!

O face where Love has placed both rein and spur
with which he turns and pricks me as he will,
while all my kicking is of no avail!

O noble souls in love, if you exist
in this world still, and you, bare shades and dust,
ah, stay to see the pain that I endure.

5–6: The laurel is the crown of military as well as poetic glory.   **13**: *shades and dust*: deceased lovers.

162 *Lieti fiori et felici, et ben nate herbe*

You gay and happy flowers, fortunate grasses
on which my lady walks while deep in thought;
you bank that hear her sweet words as she passes
and keep some imprint of her shapely foot;

slim and straight saplings, leaves in spring's fresh green,
bunches of charming violets, small and pale;
deep shady woods invaded by the sun
whose rays are making you grow proud and tall;

O gentle countryside, O limpid stream
that bathe her face and eyes and replicate
the lucid splendor of their living light:

how her dear presence makes me envy you!
Nor is there any stone among you now
that has not learned to burn with my soft flame.

Petrarch envies the woods of Vaucluse and its river, the Sorgue, for their imagined contact with Laura.   **7–8**: The sun is Laura, its generative rays her glances.   **10–11**: Dotti suggests that the river bathes the reflection of her face and eyes. In any case it is by reflection that the water takes on her radiance.

163 *Amor, che vedi ogni pensero aperto*

Love, who know every thought as though expressed
and this rough path where you are my sole guide,
turn your eyes toward my heart, look deep inside,
open to you though hidden from the rest.

You know how I have suffered keeping up,
yet you climb higher hills from day to day
and higher still, not noticing the way
my strength wanes as I find the path too steep.

True, I can see from far off the sweet light
toward which you spur me by this rugged trail,
but unlike you I have no wings for flight.

Still, you will leave my longing satisfied
if I expend my life in loving well
and she is not displeased to know I sighed.

164 *Or che 'l ciel et la terra e 'l vento tace*

Now when the sky and earth and wind are still
and sleep is holding birds and beasts all bound,
the sea lies in its bed with a smooth swell
while Night's star-spangled chariot wheels around,

awake, thought-racked, I burn, I weep; my scourge
remains, to my sweet pain, before my face;
my life is warfare, full of grief and rage,
and only thoughts of her bring me some peace.

So from one spring of clear and living water
flows what I live on, both the sweet and bitter;
the hand that stabs and heals me is the same;

and that my suffering may never end
I die and am reborn time after time,
so far am I from having peace of mind.

Monteverdi's madrigal setting of this text is vividly atmospheric and expressive.

165 *Come 'l candido pie' per l'erba fresca*

Her white feet press the fresh grass as she strolls
with sweetly measured paces; and a power
that opens and revives surrounding flowers
appears to issue from their tender soles.

For noble hearts alone Love sets his snare,
scorning on lesser ones to test his might,
and makes her eyes shower such warm delight,
for other good or lure I cannot care.

Her bearing, poised and dignified, accords
with her walk and the softness of her gaze
and with the gentle sweetness of her words.

From these four sparks and not from them alone
is born the fire in which I live and blaze,
who have become a night bird in the sun.

14: *night bird*: dazed by Laura's beauty as an owl is by the sun.

166 *S'i' fussi stato fermo a la spelunca*

If I had only lingered in the cave
in which Apollo first became a prophet,
Florence today, perhaps, would have her poet,
as Mantua, Arunca and Verona have.

But lacking water from that rock, my ground
no longer puts forth rushes; I must trade
the star I follow and with curving blade
harvest the thorns and thistles on my land.

The olive tree is parched; the stream derived
from Mount Parnassus, causing it to grow
luxuriant in the past, turns elsewhere now.

So fortune or my fault leaves me deprived
of all good fruit, unless eternal Jove
showers his grace upon me from above.

Petrarch bemoans the fact that he has stopped writing Latin verse, the only serious
poetry, and is now frittering away his talent on Italian love rhymes. Compare 24.

167

1–2: The cave at Delphi, on a spur of Mt. Parnassus, where Apollo's oracle was.   **4**: Vergil was from Mantua, Lucilius (the founder of Roman satire) from Arunca, and Catullus from Verona. (Dante is not the poet of Florence because he wrote in Italian.)   **5**: The Castalian spring near Delphi (referred to again in lines 9–10), considered the source of poetic inspiration.   **6–7**: *trade . . . follow*: follow Venus and not Apollo's sun.   **8**:   *thorns and thistles*: Petrarch's Italian rhymes.   **9–11**: The olive symbolizes wisdom, necessary for a true poet (see notes to 24).

167   *Quando Amor i belli occhi a terra inclina*

When Love directs her gaze upon the ground
and with his hands forms from her breaths' caprice
a sigh he then releases in a voice
with a divine, soft, clear, angelic sound,

I feel my heart so sweetly stolen, with
desire and thought so rising to their best,
I say, "I have become her spoils at last
if heaven allows me such a happy death."

Yet the sweet notes that keep my senses bound
with longing to rejoice in listening yet
restrain my soul that's ready to depart.

So I keep living, as the thread is wound
and unwound of my life's allotted store
by the one heavenly siren among us here.

The poet listens to Laura singing.   **12–14**: Laura acts like the Fates: in a variation of the myth, her song is the spindle on which the thread of his life is first shortened and then lengthened. Then, because she acts through her song, she is a siren. However, to avoid the negative implications of that image – not only shipwreck, because Isidore of Seville said the sirens were an image of whores (*Etym.* 11.3.31) – she is a celestial siren.   **14**: As Durling notes, there are celestial sirens in book 10 of Plato's *Republic* (616b-617d); each one, stationed on one of the heavenly spheres, sings a single note which together blend in the music of the spheres. This myth was available to Petrarch through Macrobius's commentary on Cicero's "Dream of Scipio" (Stahl, 193–94). The Fates also appear in the passage from Plato, singing with the sirens; but they are omitted in Macrobius.

168 *Amor mi manda quel dolce pensero*

I hear the flattering thought that Love inspires
(it's been a go-between of ours forever);
he comforts me by saying he was never
more ready to advance what I desire.

I'm not sure what to think, for I have found
his words are sometimes false and sometimes true;
so my heart lives in doubt between the two,
for neither *yes* nor *no* has the right sound.

Meanwhile time passes; in my glass I see
I've reached the season with the smallest scope
for what he promises and what I hope.

Well, growing old is not reserved for me;
my longing does not change from year to year,
but our remaining lives are brief, I fear.

169 *Pien d'un vago penser che mi desvia*

Filled with a passionate thought that drives away
the rest of them and marks me as unique,
sometimes, escaping from myself, I seek
always and only her whom I should flee.

But when I see her, sweet and cruel, pass by,
my soul's so shaken it is poised to leave
my body, for this enemy of Love
and me leads a great legion of armed sighs.

Unless I'm wrong, though, I can see some rays
of pity pierce the clouds of that proud gaze,
which partly reassures my aching heart;

I gain possession of my soul again,
but when I go to tell her of my pain
I have so much to say I dare not start.

170 *Più volte già del bel sembiante humano*

Often I've seen her face in a kind mood
and plucked up courage with my trusted guides
to storm my enemy with proper words,
modest and humble in my attitude.

But then her eyes show my intention vain,
for Love, the only one who can, has placed
in her hands all my fortune and my fate,
my life, my death, my pleasure and my pain.

So I could never form a sound to speak
words that made sense to anyone but me,
for he has left me trembling, my voice weak.

I see now how devotion has the power
to tie the tongue and steal the breath; for he
who can describe it burns in a small fire.

2: *guides*: the poet's amorous thoughts.   12–14: *devotion (caritate)*: Deep affection
can leave him abashed like sensual passion.

171 *Giunto m'à Amor fra belle et crude braccia*

Love's put me in a lovely cruel embrace
that kills me without cause; if I complain
I can expect the doubling of my pain;
better to die in love and hold my peace.

Her eyes could cause the frozen Rhine to burn
or make the hardest rocks split open wide;
and equal to her beauty is her pride,
which faced with admiration turns to scorn.

No matter how I try I cannot scratch
the hardness of her heart's bright diamond core
within her living, breathing marble shape;

no more can she, despite her haughty stare
and the dark frown that she displays so much,
deprive me of my sweet sighs and my hope.

172 O Invidia nimica di vertute

O Envy, always virtue's enemy,
happy to turn a good beginning bad,
by what path did you silently invade
the white breast you convert so artfully?

From it you've torn my well-being by the root,
making me seem too fortunate a lover
to her who heard my poor chaste prayers with favor
but now rejects them, as it seems, with hate.

But though with this new cruelty she may weep
when I do well and laugh when I'm in tears,
she cannot alter the resolve I keep,

nor, though a thousand times a day I'm killed,
stop me from loving her and hoping still;
Love reassures me though she makes me fear.

Envy is a standard theme of love lyrics beginning with the troubadours, where bystanders envious of the lovers' happiness try to sabotage it. The backstory of this poem remains ambiguous. Either Laura's change of heart simply shows the envy of fate or an enemy has spread gossip about the poet's faithfulness or she thinks that he is becoming too familiar because she has been too accommodating. See 130 and note.

173 *Mirando 'l sol de' begli occhi sereno*

Gazing upon the light of those clear eyes
where he resides who makes mine red and wet,
my weary soul parts company with my heart
to enter its terrestrial paradise;

and finding bitter there as well as sweet,
sees the world's works are woven of no more
than cobwebs and complains of the hot spur
Love uses and the hardness of his bit.

Because of these opposed yet mixed extremes
and with desires that turn now hot, now cold,
it dangles between misery and bliss,

but with ten sad for each glad thought, it seems,
mainly regrets its venture as too bold;
such a root brings to birth a fruit like this.

2: *he*: Love, who lives in Laura's eyes.   **4**: *paradise*: her eyes.   **5–14**: The subject of these lines is the poet's soul.   **7**: *cobwebs*: see 294.12, "shadow and dust."   **9**: *extremes*: the sweet and bitter of line 5.   **13**: *venture*: looking into her eyes (Ponte).

174 *Fera stella (se 'l cielo à forza in noi*

Cruel was the star (if the stars rule our fate
as some believe) beneath which I was born,
cruel was the cradle where they laid me down
and cruel the earth where next I set my feet;

cruel she who with her eyes and with the bow
that found me pleasing only as a mark
made the wound, Love, of which you've heard me speak,
for with those weapons you can heal it now.

But you take pleasure in the pain I have;
she does not, wishing it were more severe:
the wound is from an arrow, not a spear.

Still, I take comfort – better to pine for her
than to enjoy another, so you swear
upon your golden shaft and I believe.

1–4: These lines find a modern echo in the blues lyric "Born under a bad sign,
I been down since I began to crawl . . . ." 8: For the lance of Achilles, see
75.1–2n.

175 *Quando mi vène inanzi il tempo e 'l loco*

When that time, that place come before my eyes
in which I lost myself, and that dear knot
Love used in binding me with so much art
that bitter became sweet and tears were joys,

I'm straw and sulfur, a fire in my heart
from those soft sighing words that echo on.
I burn within and I am glad to burn;
caring for nothing else, I live on that.

That sun, the only one that shines for me,
with her resplendent beams thus keeps me warm
at evening just as early in the day;

and from a distance sets me on fire still
so that the memory, ever fresh and whole,
shows me again that knot, that place, that time.

1, 14: *that time, that place*: The ever-recurring memory of the poet's first meeting
with Laura is emphasized by the repetition in the opening and closing lines.

176 *Per mezz'i boschi inhospiti et selvaggi*

Through these dark, dangerous wild woods where men,
even though armed, at great risk roam about,
I go secure, afraid of nothing but
the rays of living love beamed from my sun;

and I go singing (heedless whim of mine!)
of her whom destiny cannot keep from me,
who haunts my vision, whom I seem to see
with maids and ladies, which are beech and pine.

I hear her in the boughs the breeze has tossed,
the rustling leaves, the birds' laments, the murmur
of waters as they run through the green grass.

Seldom has silence or the lonely horror
of shadowy forests pleased me like this place,
except that here my sun is too much lost.

This sonnet and the next refer to a journey Petrarch made from Cologne to Provence in 1333, described in more detail in a letter to his patron, Cardinal Colonna. He passed through the Ardennes Forest ("dark and frightening"), where a local war was taking place. ("As the saying goes, however, God helps the heedless.") *Fam.* 1.5. **7–11**: See 129.40–52.

177 *Mille piagge in un giorno et mille rivi*

Love showed me in a single day, no more,
a thousand crags and streams in the Ardennes;
my heels and heart wore wings he gives his men
to fly, while still alive, to the third sphere.

I'm pleased that unarmed and alone I passed
where armed Mars might attack on any side,
a ship at sea without a helm or mast
I went, dejected and preoccupied.

And only now, with this dark journey over,
recalling where I've come from, on what wings,
rashness gives birth to apprehension's pangs.

The smiling land, though, and delightful river
with their bright welcome reassure my heart
heading now toward the dwelling of his light.

1–11: See note to 176. **4**: The third sphere of heaven is that of Venus, *i.e.*, Love lets the poet fly in imagination to Laura. **8**: *dejected*: because far from her; *preoccupied*: thinking of her. **10**: *wings*: Imagination would not have protected him against armed bands. **12–14**: After the dark and dangerous Ardennes, he will be happy, sailing down the Rhone, to see Provence once more, where she (his light) lives.

178 *Amor mi sprona in un tempo et affrena*

Love spurs me while he pulls back on the reins,
assures and frightens, burns me and then freezes,
welcomes me, spurns me, calls me and then chases,
now feeds my hopes and now doles out my pains;

he lifts my weary heart then lays it low
till wandering desire has lost its way
and seems displeased with its most cherished joy,
my mind confused from vacillating so.

A friendly thought points out a way to cross
(not through the copious water my eyes spill)
to where my mind hopes it will be content;

then pulled away, though, by a greater force
along another path, it must consent
to its slow death and mine against its will.

7: *joy*: Laura. **9–14**: The poet sees a way out of his destructive obsession but is inexorably pulled back into it. The nature of the way out is controversial (the interpretations varying from suicide to a journey to Rome). Dotti suggests it is a reformed spiritual life.

179 *Geri, quando talor meco s'adira*

Geri, when my sweet enemy in all
her pride at times grows furious with me,

my death is stayed by one small remedy,
the only thing that keeps me breathing still.

When wrathfully she turns away her eyes
(perhaps she hopes to take my light away?)
I show in mine such true humility
that of necessity her anger dies.

If it did not, approaching her would be
like gazing full upon Medusa's face,
the sight of which made people turn to stone.

You do the same; all other help I see
as a lost cause, and fleeing is no use
before the wings on which our lord swoops down.

A response to a sonnet by Geri Gianfigliazzi of Florence asking Petrarch for advice on dealing with the anger of the woman he loved. **14**: *our lord*: Love.

180 *Po, ben puo' tu portartene la scorza*

Po, on your powerful and rapid course
you bear away the outer shell of me;
the spirit hidden in it, though, is free
and does not care about your current's force;

not tacking either left or right, it soars
straight on the breeze that favors its desire,
and winging toward the gold leaves through the air
prevails against wind, water, sail and oars.

Monarch of rivers, haughtiest of streams,
who meet the sun escorting in the dawn
but leave a lovelier radiance in the west,

you bear my mortal part upon your horn;
my other part, arrayed in love's own plumes,
wheels on the wing to his sweet place of rest.

The poet sails eastward across Italy down the Po, but his spirit flies westward back toward Laura in Provence. **7**: *gold leaves (l'aurea fronde)*: the leaves are golden in order to pun on the laurel and also because they are Laura's blond hair. **11**: *radiance*: Laura, the poet's sun. **12**: *horn*: River gods were imagined with horns. The commentators cite *Georg.* 4.371–73, where the Po, "than which no stream more powerfully flows," is described "with gilded horns on a bull's countenance."

181 *Amor fra l'erbe una leggiadra rete*

Love spread upon the grass a pretty net
fashioned from gold and pearls beneath a branch
of the cool evergreen I love so much
although its shade more saddens than delights.

The seed he sows for harvest was his bait,
bitter and sweet, that I both crave and fear,
his call beguiling more than any lure
since Adam's eyes first opened, soft and sweet.

A light that made the sunlight disappear
flashed all around; and as it pulled the rope
a hand gleamed more than snow or ivory does.

I fell into the net, entangled there
by her angelic words, her charming ways
and my desire, my pleasure and my hope.

One of the most developed examples of Petrarch's favorite bird-catching metaphor, depending this time entirely on the net, not birdlime. **2**: *gold and pearls*: Laura with bejeweled hair beneath the laurel that is also her. **4–8**: After spreading his net, the bird-catcher scatters birdseed (her beauty) and gives a birdcall (her words). **5**: *harvest*: by catching the birds that eat it (the bird-catcher now being compared to a farmer). **9**: *light*: her eyes. **10**: *rope*: to close the net.

182 *Amor, che 'ncende il cor d'ardente zelo*

Love sets the heart afire with passion first,
then grips it with the icy hand of fear,
making the mind doubt which will dominere,
whether the hope or dread, the flame or frost.

It shivers in the heat, burns in the cold,
desiring but suspicious all the while,
as if beneath a lady's dress or veil
she had a man of flesh and blood concealed.

The first of these two pains is mine: both night
and day to burn; how strong this sweet disease,
no thought, much less a verse or rhyme, can seize;

the second no, for my flame treats all men
the same; and he will spread his wings in vain
who thinks to fly as high up as her light.

A sonnet about jealousy, not a typical Petrarchan theme. The octet describes the situation of lovers in general and the sestet that of the poet. **2, 6–8**: Passion inspires jealousy, even absurd suspicions. **4**: Here the dread/frost is not the usual Petrarchan fear of offending the lady and being rejected but the fear that she loves another. **9–14**: The poet is free of jealousy, convinced that Laura's virtue rejects other men as it does him.

183 *Se 'l dolce sguardo di costei m'ancide*

If her sweet glance toward me alone can kill
and those soft little words phrased skillfully,
and Love gives her such power over me
when I but hear her speak or see her smile,

what will become of me if hostile fate
or my own fault should cause her eyes to turn
from pity, so that she who is my screen
from death today would threaten me with it?

So if I tremble, with a heart of ice,
when I see changes pass across her face,
a long experience underlies my fear.

A woman is by nature changeable,
and in a woman's heart, as I know well,
a loving feeling cannot long endure.

12: *Femina è cosa mobil per natura*: see *Aen.* 4.569 (*mutabile semper femina*). Verdi's librettist Piave ironized the sentiment (*La donna è mobile*) by placing it in the mouth of a rake.

184 *Amor, Natura, et la bella alma humile*

Love, Nature, and her lovely gentle soul,
where every noble virtue lives and reigns,
conspire against me now; for Love lays plans
to make me die outright, as is his style;

and Nature holds her soul on such a slim
thread it cannot withstand the slightest strain;
and she so scorns this life she will not deign
to lengthen what is base and wearisome.

So hour by hour her vital spirits droop
in those dear beautiful chaste limbs that once
were the true mirror of her inner grace;

if heaven's pity does not rein death in,
I see, alas, the state of utter ruin
of what I used to live on – my vain hope.

Laura is ill (as in 31 and 33) and the poet fears for her life.   **1–3**: Love conspires against him in lines 3–4, Nature in 5–6 and Laura's soul in 7–8.   **6**: *thread*: holding her soul to her body.   **9**. For the vital spirits see note to 17.9.

185 *Questa fenice de l'aurata piuma*

This phoenix has a ruff of golden plumes
around her white neck, forming without art
a precious ornament that every heart
is softened by, but my heart it consumes;

she has a natural diadem that casts
light through the air, from which Love's silent steel
draws subtle liquid flame that keeps me still
burning today amid the coldest frosts.

A purple gown trimmed with a sky-blue border
sprinkled with roses veils her delicate shoulders –
unique dress, like her beauty in the world.

Legend would have it she remains concealed
in the rich perfumed hills of Araby,
yet she soars high and proud across our sky.

The first appearance of Laura as the phoenix, which will be repeated in 321 and
323 (but see 135.5–15, where the poet was the phoenix). Petrarch relies on Pliny,
who described the Arabian phoenix having a crest of feathers and gleaming with
gold around the neck, all the rest being purple save for a blue tail decorated with
roseate feathers. *Nat. Hist.* 10.2.3.   **1–3, 5**: Laura's blond hair forms a golden
crest and falls to wreathe her neck.   **14**: *proud*: because she does not mate (S).

186 *Se Virgilio et Homero avessin visto*

Virgil and Homer, had they gazed a while
upon that sun I see, and with my eyes,
would have strained all their powers to sing her praise,
mixing the lofty with the pleasant style,

leaving Aeneas troubled, others sad –
Achilles and the one Aegisthus killed,
him who for half a century ruled the world
so well, Ulysses, the odd demigod.

That ancient flower of virtue and of arms
was born to share a similar destiny
with this new flower of beauty and chastity:

Ennius praised him in unpolished terms,
I her. Oh, may my fancy not displease
and may she not be scornful of my praise!

4: To praise Laura (the poet's sun), Virgil and Homer would mix their "tragic" style (the one proper to epic) with the elegiac style (the one proper to love poetry) (Martellotti).   **4–8**: With Virgil and Homer diverted to Laura's praise, the heroes celebrated in their epics (and the emperor to whom the *Aeneid* was dedicated) would grow troubled and sad.   **6**: *the one . . . killed*: Agamemnon.   **7–8**: *him . . . so well*: the emperor Augustus.   **9**: *ancient . . . arms*: Scipio Africanus, who defeated Hannibal, and was Petrarch's favorite among the ancient great.   **10–14**: Scipio was, and Laura is, greater than the heroes sung by Virgil and Homer, but their fate is to be celebrated only by the second-rate poets Ennius and Petrarch.

187 *Giunto Alexandro a la famosa tomba*

When Alexander reached the famous tomb
of fierce Achilles, he exclaimed with sighs,
"Fortunate man, to celebrate your name
you found a trumpet that could soar so high!"

But this pure white dove, she whose counterpart
I do not think the world has ever seen,
resounds but little in my feeble art;
so each one's destiny is set in stone.

Though she deserves that Orpheus or one
like Homer or the shepherd Mantua still
honors should always sing of her alone,

a wayward star and fate cruel in one thing
leave her to one who loves her name too well
but scants her praise perhaps with his rude song.

A companion to 186, with Laura once more failing through an unjust fate to find a poet worthy of her. **1–4**: Alexander the Great envied Achilles, who had Homer to immortalize his deeds, a tale Petrarch told in *Fam.* 4.3. **10**: *the shepherd*: Virgil, a native of Mantua, called a shepherd as author of the *Eclogues*, his poems about shepherds.

188 *Almo Sol, quella fronde ch'io sola amo*

Life-giving Sun, you first loved that green bough,
my only love, alone among those here
green in this season, and without a peer
since Adam first laid eyes on our fair woe.

Sun, let us gaze at her and make it last,
I pray, I beg you, yet you run away;
as hills cast shade, you carry off the day
and fleeing take from me what I want most.

The shadow falling now from that low hill,
here where my gentle fire was once a spark,
the laurel a slim sapling at one time,

grows longer as I speak, until the dark
causes my sight of this glad place to fail
where my heart with his lady is at home.

The poet is at Laura's birthplace (see 4 and 113) on an autumn or winter afternoon. **1**: *Sun*: Apollo, with the usual Daphne/laurel/Laura connections. See 34 for a previous appeal to the common interest of the god and the poet, a theme repeated in 192. **3–4**: *fair woe*: beautiful Eve, who became the downfall of Adam and the human race. **10**: *fire*: Laura.

189 *Passa la nave mia colma d'oblio*

My vessel loaded with forgetfulness
sails on a winter's night in a rough sea

through Scylla and Charybdis, and what's worse
steered by my lord, in truth my enemy.

At each oar sits a reckless desperate thought
that seems to scorn the tempest and the end;
the sail is torn by a relentless wet
wind of desire and sighs and hopes too fond.

A rain of tears and fog of scorn, foul weather,
soak and stretch further every worn-out rope
twisted from strands of ignorance and error.

I cannot see my guiding stars at all,
drowned are my reason and my seamanship,
and now my hope of port begins to fail.

The lover is a frail craft driven by a storm of passion from the heavenly port.
This is a favorite image of Petrarch's, developed at greatest length in the sestina
80; but this sonnet has a condensed power that makes it his best treatment of
the theme. Sir Thomas Wyatt did a fine translation of this sonnet, "My galley,
chargèd with forgetfulness." 1: *forgetfulness*: Laura makes the poet forget his
destination, as the sirens did the ancient mariners (Picone). 3: The fabled
trial of passing between a rock and a whirlpool. 4: *lord*: Love. 5: *end*:
shipwreck. 10: *rope*: the stays that hold the mast up. 12: *stars*: Laura's eyes.

190 *Una candida cerva sopra l'erba*

Upon the green grass right before my eyes
a pure white doe with horns of gold appeared
between two rivers in a laurel's shade
in early springtime, just as the sun rose.

I found her look at once so proud and sweet,
to follow her I set aside all work,
just as a grasping miser out to seek
gold sweetens toil with visions of delight.

In diamond and in topaz round her neck
was written this: *Let none lay hands on me.*
My Caesar has been pleased to make me free.

The sun reached noon and still I stayed to look
when I fell, eyes not sated but now tired,
into the water and she disappeared.

2: The doe wears Laura's colors; here the white signifies not only her complexion
but her chastity, the gold horns her hair (sometimes a doe will have small stub
horns). **9–12**: In *Fam.* 18.8 Petrarch recounts the legend that in ancient times
a hunter caught a stag with a golden collar bearing the inscription "Let no one
capture me," and which Caesar ordered freed. Here Caesar is God, guarantee-
ing Laura's independence and chastity. The jewels repeat Laura's colors and are
associated with chastity. See *TP* 122 and note (Pacca/Paolino, 248–49). **13**:
fell: As in 67.7–8, reality intrudes on the poet's fancy.

191 *Sí come eterna vita è veder Dio*

Eternal life is seeing the face of God,
which renders wanting more impossible;
likewise in this life, Lady, brief and frail,
seeing you is the purest joy I've had.

Nor have I ever seen you look before
so beautiful, if eyes speak truth to heart –
sweet moment that beatifies my thought
surpassing every hope and all desire!

And if it did not slip away so fast
I'd ask no more; for just as some survive
on scents alone, in tales that pass for true,

and some on fire, on water, things deprived
of sweetness satisfying touch and taste,
why should I not on this life-giving view?

192 *Stiamo, Amor, a veder la gloria nostra*

Come, Love, and see our glory shining forth,
something sublime, exceeding nature's norm;
look how much sweetness showers on her form,
see the light showing heaven here on earth;

see what art gilds, stains carmine, studs with pearls
her soul's choice garment, elsewhere never seen,
and how her feet, her eyes glide through the green
and shady cloister of these wooded hills.

The thousand-colored flowers and tender grass
scattered beneath the old black holm oak tree
pray they may feel her slim foot touch or press;

and all around, with glittering sparks the skies
are lighted up, rejoicing visibly
at being made serene by such bright eyes.

The sestet of this sonnet was originally attached to the octet of 191.   **1**: *glory*: Laura.   **5**: The gold is her hair, the carmine her lips, the pearls her teeth.   **8**: The cloister is Vaucluse, the "enclosed valley," where Laura is imagined walking.   **10**: The holm oak, an evergreen oak of southern Europe, has blackish bark.   **12**: *sparks*: stars.

193 *Pasco la mente d'un sì nobil cibo*

My mind is nourished on such noble food
that I do not begrudge Jove his ambrosia;
looking at her, all else fades as amnesia
rains on my soul and I drink Lethe's flood.

I write upon my heart things that she says
so I can find a cause for sighing there,
and carried off by Love, I don't know where,
I drink a double sweetness from one face;

for pleasing even those in heaven, that voice
pronounces words so gracious and so dear
as one who has not heard could not conceive.

And all together, plainly it appears
how much in life, within a span or less,
art, wit and heaven and nature can achieve.

2: *ambrosia*: food of the gods.   **4**: *Lethe*: river of oblivion in Hades.   **8**: *double*:
through sight and hearing.   **12**: *span*: the size of her face.

194 *L'aura gentil, che rasserena i poggi*

This gentle breeze clears the hills as it blows
and in this shady wood stirs flowers to wake;
I recognize its soft breath, for whose sake
my fame must spread the more my suffering grows.

To find some place my weary heart may lean,
I've left my native sweet Italian air;
to dissipate my somber, turbid cares
I seek my sun and hope to see her soon.

She makes me know delight in all its shapes,
so Love compels me to return to her,
and then so blinds me fleeing is too late.

I would need wings, not weapons, to escape;
but heaven will have me perish from this light:
tormented when afar, I burn when near.

Petrarch is returning from Italy to Provence, where Laura is. This sonnet and
Nos. 196–98 form a group whose theme is Laura as the breeze.   **1–4**: *L'aura,*

the breeze, is her breath, her spirit, which will re-ignite his amorous torment and make him court poetic fame again by singing about her. (The latter also alludes to Laura as the poet's laurel crown.)   1: *clear*: of clouds.   8: *sun*: also Laura.   11: *blinds me (m'abbaglia)*: by bringing me too close to my sun.

195 *Di dí in dí vo cangiando il viso e 'l pelo*

My face and hair are changing day by day
but still I bite the hook's sweet bait and clutch
with no less ardor at the birdlimed branch
of the green tree no sun or frost dismays.

The sky will be without its stars, the sea
run dry before I cease to fear and crave
that tree's shade or no longer hate and love
love's deep wound, which I hide unskillfully.

In my affliction I expect no pause
till I am sinew-stripped, unfleshed, deboned,
or till my enemy begins to care.

What cannot happen will occur before
one besides Death or her could heal the wound
Love opened in my heart with her bright eyes.

4: *tree*: the laurel, which is evergreen.   11: *enemy*: Laura.

196 *L'aura serena che fra verdi fronde*

The breeze that clears the clouds comes murmuring
through the green leaves and strikes against my face,
making me recollect the time and place
Love gave me the deep sweet wound that first spring,

making me see the face she now withholds,
which anger or else jealousy conceals,

and the hair, twisted now with gems and pearls,
which then was loose, more blond than shining gold

and which I saw the breeze so gently strew
and gather up again so prettily,
recalling it, my mind is quaking now.

Time later twined that hair in a tight knot
and with a sturdy cord secured my heart
so fast that only Death can set it free.

Nos. 196–198 form, with 194, the group whose theme is *L'aura*, the breeze.   **7–14**:
The loose tresses of a maiden, contrasting with the formal hairstyle of a married
woman (perhaps a cap studded with jewels), become a metaphor for the way
that love has bound the poet ever more strongly over the years (S).

197 *L'aura celeste che 'n quel verde lauro*

The breeze of heaven blowing through the green
laurel, where Love first pierced Apollo's chest
and placed a sweet yoke on my neck at last
from which I seek my freedom now in vain,

controls me as Medusa did the old
Moroccan giant whom she changed to flint;
nor can I slip from this entanglement,
brighter than sunlight even, much less gold,

by which I mean the strands of her blond hair
that bind so softly in a curling snare
my soul armed with humility alone.

Her very shadow turns my heart to ice
and washes fear's pale tint across my face,
but her eyes can transform them both to stone.

Laura is both the breeze and the laurel it blows through.   **5–6**: When the giant
Atlas refused hospitality, Perseus showed him the head of Medusa, which turned
the giant into the Atlas mountains of north Africa. *Metam.* 4.621–62.

198 *L'aura soave al sole spiega et vibra*

> The soft breeze in the sunlight stirs that hair,
> beside bright eyes, whose gold Love spins by hand;
> it binds my weary heart with those same strands
> while scattering my light spirits in the air.
>
> All of the marrow in my bones and all
> the blood in my veins shudders if my path
> encounters her who often weighs my death
> and life upon an unforgiving scale,
>
> seeing the eyes that set me afire burn,
> seeing the curls that hold me captive shine
> on her left shoulder now and now her right.
>
> Words fail me, for I cannot comprehend;
> my mind is overwhelmed by those two lights,
> wearied by so much sweetness it is stunned.

This time Petrarch's beloved scene of Laura's hair blowing in the breeze (identified with her) introduces an image of her as a fearsome goddess, with the poet her trembling votary. **4**: *scattering . . . air (lievi spirti cribra)*: The breeze disperses the poet's vital spirits (for which see note to 17.9), as if winnowing chaff from threshed grain. **13**: *two lights*: her eyes (9) and her hair (10).

199 *O bella man, che mi destringi 'l core*

> You shapely hand clasped tight around my heart,
> keeping my life enclosed in a small space,
> hand in which heaven and nature both have placed,
> for their own honor, all their care and art;
>
> and you, like five matched orient pearls in hue,
> smooth and soft fingers, only cruel and hard
> in my wounds, Love consents to make me glad
> leaving your nakedness a while on view.

Dear little glove, so delicate and white,
for ivory and fresh roses once a home,
who in the world ever saw such sweet spoil?

Might I be just as lucky with her veil!
But, ah, how mutable our human state!
This itself is a theft she will reclaim.

This sonnet artfully reveals the poet's situation bit by bit, so that only in the last
line is it fully clear.   **9–14**: This is the first of three sonnets on Laura's glove.

200 *Non pur quell'una bella ignuda mano*

Not that one shapely naked hand alone,
which now is clothed once more to my great loss,
but both of them and those arms quickly press
my meek and unresisting heart again.

Among the beauties never before seen
that grace her heavenly person in in a way
no style, no gift for language, could convey,
Love sets a thousand snares and none in vain,

some in her clear eyes beneath starry brows;
and some in her angelic lips, which brim
with roses, pearls and sweet words that can make

you tremble with the wonder they arouse;
some in her forehead and her hair, which seem
to make the sun at noon in summer dark.

12: *tremble*: the typical effect of the lady's greeting in stilnovist poetry (S).

201 *Mia ventura et Amor m'avean sí adorno*

I was so favored by my luck and Love
with a fine silk and gold embroidery

that I was almost at the height of joy,
thinking whose hand had been inside that glove.

Nor does the memory of that day return,
which brought me wealth then quickly poverty,
but I feel wrath and sorrow rise in me
and I am filled with shame and love's self-scorn,

I that did not keep gripping my prize tight
when necessary, and could not resist
the force of one small angel's mere request,

or fleeing, did not add wings to my feet
to take at least some vengeance on the hand
that makes my eyes discharge tears without end.

4: *thinking*: This reading follows Chiòrboli; the poet is thrilled because it is
Laura's glove. The modern reading (Santagata and others) suggests that the poet
is asking himself whose glove it is. This would imply he is thrilled at envisioning
a choice of beauties, unusual for *Scattered Rhymes* and to that extent less plausi-
ble.   9–11: The poet is ashamed of himself for giving the glove back to Laura at
her request. The modern reading implies that he had found it, rather than stolen
it as in 199.   13–14: *tears*: because Laura's hand often hides her face from him.

202   *D'un bel chiaro polito et vivo ghiaccio*

A smooth transparent piece of living ice
sends out the flame whose fierce heat melts me down,
licking my heart and drying every vein
so I am dying, though it leaves no trace.

Death, with his arm already raised to strike,
as angry heavens thunder and lions roar,
hotly pursues my life, which flees before,
as, terrified, I make no sound and quake.

Pity and love together might well yet
protect me, as two bulwarks put in place
between my spent soul and the mortal blow;

I doubt it though, nor see it in the face
my lady, my sweet enemy, lets show,
for which I do not blame her, but my fate.

1: *living ice*: Laura.

203 *Lasso, ch'i' ardo, et altri non me 'l crede*

I burn and, sadly, she does not believe it;
my state is obvious to everyone
but her for whose belief I care alone;
she seems mistrustful, yet she must perceive it.

So little faith, for all your boundless beauty,
do my eyes not reveal my heart and mind?
If not for my adverse star I should find
sympathy, surely, at the fount of pity.

My ardor, which you think of little worth,
and your praise, which I spread with all my works,
may yet make thousands burn for you like me;

for in my thoughts, my sweet fire, I foresee
a cold tongue and two bright eyes closed in death,
long after us remaining full of sparks.

8: *fount of pity*: Laura – an (optimistic) theme that will recur in nearby poems;
see 206.40, 207.25, 210.7, 216.13.   14: *sparks (faville)*: his poetry celebrating her
beauty will start new fires in others (11).

204 *Anima, che diverse cose tante*

My soul, who think and speak and read and write
and see and hear so many different things,
my yearning eyes, and you, the sense that brings
her noble blessed words to touch my heart,

be glad you did not reach, before her date
or after it, this road we stumble on,
to find those two lights not yet lit or gone
and no prints left by those beloved feet.

Now with such signs and such a shining light
we must not, on this brief trip, lose our way,
which readies us for an eternal home.

Strive on, my weary heart, toward heaven's gate,
following, through the sweet clouds of her scorn,
her upward-trending feet, her divine ray.

3: *sense*: hearing.   6: *road*: of this life.   7: *two lights*: her eyes.   9: *signs, light*:
her footprints, her eyes (repeated at 14).   13–14: *i.e.*, do not be discouraged by
her rejection, which is ultimately for your own good; and follow the example
of her life.   14: *ray*: gaze (see Gen Notes, *eyes*).

205   *Dolci ire, dolce sdegni et dolci paci*

Sweet anger, sweet disdain, sweet times of ease,
sweet hurt, sweet suffering of a pleasing weight,
sweet words I cherish in sweet spells of thought,
now full of fire and now a cooling breeze!

Soul, do not groan but bear up quietly,
allay our bitter pains, sweet though they are,
with the sweet honor brought by loving her
to whom I said, "None but you pleases me."

Someone perhaps will sigh at this and say,
pale with sweet envy, "In his day this man
endured, for a consummate love, much pain."

Another: "Fate, my eyes' worst enemy!
I never saw her. Why did she not come
later or I much earlier in time?"

If ever I said it, let me feel the hate
of her whose love I need, or else I'd die.
If I said that, make my days few and sad,
my soul reduced to some base slavery;
    and let there league against me all the stars,   5
with no one on my side
but fear and jealousy,
and with my enemy
more beautiful and toward me still more fierce.

    If I said that, let Love use all his shafts   10
of gold on me and on her those of lead;
let earth and heaven, every man and god
all turn against me, she grow still more cruel.
    Let her, who with desire's sightless flame
sends me to death, remain   15
always as usual
and may she never seem
more kind to me in word or attitude.

 If ever I said it, let my short harsh way
be filled with everything I least desire;   20
may the fierce heat that makes me go astray
increase to match the hardened ice in her.
    If I said that, let my eyes never see
bright sun or sister moon,
ladies or maids, but gaze   25
upon the grim cyclone
that Pharaoh saw when he pursued the Jews.

    If I said that, may every sigh I spent
be vain and all compassion dead for me;
and may her speech be harsh, which on the day   30
I yielded myself, vanquished, sounded sweet;

If I said that, may I bear all the hate
of her I could adore
alone in a dark cell
from infancy until   35
my soul was plucked out – and I really might.

But if I did not, may she who so sweetly
opened my heart to hope at a young age
still, at the helm of her inherent mercy,
steer my small weary boat; nor let her change,   40
    but still be only what she was before,
when I could not resist
her pull till I was lost
(nor should I now lose more).
One should not soon forget such loyalty.   45

    I never said it and I never could,
even for cities, castles, heaps of gold.
So let the truth, victorious, sit its saddle
while the lie, vanquished, tumbles in the mud.
    Love, you know all of me; if she should ask,   50
tell of me what you should.
Three, four and seven times
would I call happy him
who, faced with languishing, dies first instead.

    I served my time for Rachel, not for Leah,   55
and with no other could
I live; and I could bear,
when heaven shall call us home,
to share Elijah's chariot with her.

This canzone refutes a false accusation, which is never specified, but hinted at:
that the poet said he loved another woman. Like 29, it is an exercise in technical
virtuosity in the manner of the troubadours. In particular, all 59 lines share
only three rhymes (*-ella, -ei, -ia*). As befits this form, the sense is sometimes
elusive.   **4**: *base slavery*: passion for an unworthy woman.   **10–11**: Love has

two arrows: the golden inspires love, the leaden hatred. *Metam*. 1.468–71.   **24**: Diana the moon goddess is the sister of Apollo the sun god.   **26–27**: Petrarch imagines Pharaoh seeing the pillar of fire and of cloud before the Red Sea closes over the Egyptians. Ex. 14:23–28.   **44**: *more*: her mercy (Ponte).   **45**: *i.e.*, she should not forget our history because of this slanderous accusation.   **48–49**: The image is that of a joust between two champions, Truth and Falsehood (S).   **55**: Jacob served Laban for seven years to earn Rachel and Laban instead gave him her elder sister Leah; Jacob protested. Gen. 29:21–26.   **59**: Elijah was taken up to heaven in a fiery chariot. 4 Kings 2:11.

207 *Ben mi credea passar mio tempo omai*

I thought by now that I could live my life
as I have lived it during these past years,
without more effort, learning no new tricks;
   but with my lady offering me no longer
her usual help, you see, Love, what a state   5
you've brought me to in teaching me such skills.
   Perhaps I should be angry
that at my age you make me turn a thief
of her resplendent glance,
without which I could not survive this pain.   10
I should have in my youth
picked up the habit that I now must learn,
for failings in one's youth bring far less shame.

The gentle eyes that for so long have kept
me living were so generous to me   15
in the beginning with their noble beauties,
   I lived the way a man does who survives
in poverty on secret gifts from someone,
without annoying either them or her.
   Now, though it troubles me,   20
I have become unjust, importunate,
for a poor starving man
sometimes does things that in a better state

he would have blamed in others.
If envy causes pity's hand to close,   25
love-hungry helplessness is my excuse.

    In fact by now I've tried a thousand ways
to see if any mortal creature could
make my life last one day without those eyes.
    My soul, though, when it finds no rest elsewhere,   30
keeps running back to those angelic sparks
and I, though made of wax, approach the fire.
    I spy the time at which
what I desire is least kept under guard,
and as a bird on a branch   35
is soonest caught when it is least afraid,
so from her lovely face
I steal one glance and then one more again;
and these both nourish me and make me burn.

    I feed upon my death and live in flames –   40
strange food, and a prodigious salamander,
but not a wonder, for it's Love who wills it.
    I lay a while, a happy lamb among
his pining flock; now in my last days he
and fortune treat me in their usual way: 45
    roses and violets come
in springtime and in winter ice and snow.
And so if I procure
from here and there some food for my short life,
though she may call it theft,   50
so rich a lady should accept the loss
if I can live on what she does not miss.

    Who does not know that I have always lived,
since I first saw them, on those lovely eyes,
which made me change my habits and my life?   55
    Who can know all the human temperaments
although he visits many distant shores?

Out near the Ganges there's a tribe that lives
    on scents; here I with fire
and light appease my weak and famished spirits.   60
But Love, I have to tell you
this stinginess does not become a lord.
You have a bow and arrows –
finish me, so I do not waste from yearning,
for a fine death sheds honor on a life.   65

    A covered fire burns hotter, and if it still
grows, then in no way can it be concealed;
I know this, Love, from having felt your power.
    You saw how though at first I burned in silence,
by now my cries – not even I can stand them –   70
make me a nuisance to those far and near.
    O world, O useless thoughts,
O my cruel fate, what you have led me to!
Ah, what enthralling light
made my poor heart give birth to stubborn hope   75
with which she shackles it,
she who with your power leads me to my end!
Yours is the wrong and mine the loss and pain.

    And so for loving well I suffer torment
and seek forgiveness, but for others' sins –   80
or rather mine, who should have turned my eyes
    from too much light and stopped my ears against
the siren song; still I do not repent,
although sweet poison overflows my heart.
    I only wait for him   85
to loose the final shaft who shot the first;
and it will be, I think,
an act of mercy if he kills me quickly,
for he is not inclined
to treat me other than the usual way   90
and one dies well whom dying frees from pain.

Song, I shall hold the field,
for being killed while fleeing brings disgrace;
and I reproach myself
for these laments, because my fate is sweet –   95
my tears, my sighs, my death.
Servant of Love who read these verses, know
the world has no joy that can match my woe.

1–13: The poet speaks as a mature man comparing his early experience in love to the present. Petrarch's manuscript indicates that it was written over a period of 22 years.   **3**: *effort, tricks*: to obtain Laura's glances.   **25**: *envy*: characteristic of the jealous bystanders of romance tradition, *e.g.*, those who spread the lie of 206 (S).   **32–42**: The poet unveils the other side of the paradox: what prolongs his life also kills him by setting him afire; the food he steals is his death.   **33–39**: The snared bird is usually the poet, one of the commonest images in *Scattered Rhymes*. Here the bird is Laura, best glimpsed when unaware, as a birdwatcher knows; but line 39 shows that the poet is caught in his own trap.   **40**: *death*: in her eyes.   **41**: The salamander was believed to live in fire.   **43**: *flock*: unhappy lovers.   **58**: *lives ... scents*: see 191.10–11 and note.   **56–57**: *Who ... shores*: *i.e.*, You think that's not possible? Let me explain.   **60**: *spirits*: the vital spirits, for which see note to 17.9.   **61–65**:   **74, 82**: *light*: from her eyes.   **78, 80**: *yours (vostra) ... others' (altrui)*: both Love's and Laura's.   **85**: *him*: Love is no longer being addressed.   **92**: *hold the field*: a military image: go on loving and suffering (Ponte).   **94–98**: This congedo is a palinode and gives a concise statement of the paradox at the heart of *Scattered Rhymes* (though it is not original with Petrarch but consistent with troubadour and stilnovist tradition (D)).

208 *Rapido fiume che d'alpestra vena*

Swift river, rushing from your Alpine source,
gnawing (from which your name comes) through the land,
night and day you, with me who yearn, descend
where Love leads me, you only nature's force.

Race on ahead, not hindered by the rein
of weariness or sleep; and yet before
you pay the sea your debt, look closely where
the air is purer and the grass more green.

There can our gentle living sun be found,
who graces your left bank and makes it bloom,
perhaps (fond hope?) grieved I have not yet come.

Kiss her slim foot or beautiful white hand;
tell her (in place of words, let the kiss speak):
the spirit is eager but the flesh is weak.

This sonnet, addressed to the Rhone, may follow on Nos. 176–177 (see the notes to same). If so, Petrarch is returning from Germany; in any case, he is traveling along the Rhone toward Avignon.   **2**: A false etymology derived "Rhone" (*Rhodano*) from "gnawing" (*rodendo*).   **10**: Avignon, where Laura lived, is on the east bank of the Rhone (the left in the direction of flow).   **14**: *weak*: Unlike the river, he needs sleep; Petrarch translates Matt. 26:41.

209 *I dolci colli ov'io lasciai me stesso*

The sweet hills where I left myself behind,
leaving the spot that I can never leave,
are always in my eyes, and when I move
I still bear the dear weight that Love assigned.

I often marvel at myself: although
I now have travelled far, I've yet to doff
the yoke I've often vainly shaken off;
it presses more the further off I go.

And as a stag in whom an arrow sank,
the poisoned barb still buried in its flank,
flees, and its pain increases with its speed,

so I, with that shaft stuck in my left side
destroying me while bringing me delight,
am wracked by grief and worn out by my flight.

The poet is again traveling far from Laura.   **1–8**: The classic formulation is by Horace: those who hurry across the sea change their sky, not their cast of mind. Epistles 1.11.27.   **1**: *hills*: of Provence.   **12**: *left side*: where the heart is.

Though you search every seacoast carefully,
from India's Ganges to the Ebro in Spain,
and from the Caspian waves to the Red Sea,
you'll find earth holds no phoenix but the one.

What left-side raven or what right-side crow
croaks out my fortune, what Fate winds the skein?
My hoped-for happiness is misery now
with Pity deaf as an asp to me alone.

I would not speak of her; but at the sight
of her, at once new love and sweetness fill
all hearts, she has so much of them to share;

and yet for me she turns this sweetness cruel
by seeming not to know or not to care
my temples prematurely bloom with white.

A sonnet of complaint couched in obscure terms.   **1**: The relevance of the phoenix's unique status is unclear.   **2**: *i.e.*, from east to west (to indicate the east, Petrarch names a more obscure river than the usual Ganges).   **3**: *i.e.*, from north to south.   **5–6**: *What . . . fortune*: In ancient Rome, these birds croaking in these positions relative to the observer were good omens, ones the poet does not expect. (Petrarch is echoing a phrase in Cicero's *De Divinatione* 1.39.)   **6**: *Fate*: There were three Fates in ancient mythology. He fears the second Fate has stopped winding the thread of his life, ready for the third Fate to cut it.   **8**: *Pity*: Laura personified. For the asp, see note to 239.29; Laura refuses to listen to him.

211 *Voglia mi sprona, Amor mi guida et scorge*

My passion spurs me while Love scouts the road;
where pleasure pulls me, habit holds the course;
hope whispers to encourage and entice,
offers my weary heart a helping hand.

The poor wretch grasps it, being unaware
of just how blind and faithless is our guide;
the senses are in charge with reason dead;
restless desire gives birth to more desire.

Her virtue, beauty, sweet words, gracious bearing
ensured that in these boughs I would be caught,
and still my heart remains there, sweetly fixed.

In thirteen twenty-seven, April the sixth,
exactly at the first hour of the morning,
I entered this maze; I see no way out.

10: *boughs*: of the laurel/Laura, where the poet's heart is the bird stuck to the branch with birdlime. **12–14**: The date and time the poet first saw Laura. **13**: *first hour*: 6 am.

212 *Beato in sogno et di languir contento*

Happy to dream, content to be consumed,
to grasp at shadows, chase the summer breeze,
I swim through bottomless and shoreless seas,
plow water, build on sand and write on wind.

I've stared hard at the sun so long a time
the radiance has by now put out my sight;
I hunt a wandering doe that's swift in flight,
my hound a lumbering ox that's sick and lame.

Too blind and tired for all else but my hurt,
which I chase, panting, every day and night,
I call on Love, my lady and Death alone.

So for the troubles of these twenty years
sighs, tears and sorrow are my only gain.
I took the baited hook beneath bad stars.

1: *be consumed (languir)*: by my hopeless passion.   2: *breeze*: In the usual pun, the breeze is *l'aura*.   5, 8: *sun, doe*: Laura.

213   *Gratie ch'a pochi il ciel largo destina*

Graces that heaven freely grants to few,
rare virtue of a more than human kind
and underneath blond hair a gray-haired mind,
beauty still modest though arousing awe,

a natural charm unparalleled and new
and, raising echoes in the soul, her song,
a heavenly walk, an ardent spirit strong
to break recalcitrance and make pride bow;

then lovely eyes that could turn hearts to stone,
that could illuminate hell's gaping night
and draw men's souls forth, making them her own;

and last, speech full of sweet and lofty thought
mingled with softly interrupted sighs.
I've been enchanted by these sorceries.

1: The first line summarizes the qualities of Laura itemized in lines 2–13; the way they affect the poet is described at line 14.   9: *stone*: not emotionally hardened but stunned by her beauty. The Medusa-like power of Laura's eyes is a recurrent theme (see 23.79–80, 131.11); the Medusa reference is explicit in 179.9, 366.III.   11: *draw . . . own (tôrre l'alme a' corpi, et darle altrui)*: her eyes transfer the lover's soul to the beloved (S); or "draw souls forth and give them back again" (Ponchiroli).

214   *Anzi tre dì creata era alma in parte*

A soul was made, three days since, in its place,
fit to attend to matters high and new
and feel contempt for what most people prize.

While yet uncertain of its fated course,
unformed in thought, still innocent and free,   5
it came in springtime to a blooming wood.

A tender flower had opened in that wood
the day before, its roots in such a place
that no soul could approach it and be free;
for snares lay there of a design so new,   10
toward which its beauty so allured one's course,
that losing freedom was a thing to prize.

Ah, how that precious, noble, difficult prize
caused me at once to enter the green wood
that often makes men detour in mid-course!   15
I later searched the world from place to place
to try if spells or stones or juice of new
herbs could restore my mind and make it free.

But now I see my body will be free
from the dear knot that is its greatest prize   20
before exotic remedies, old or new,
can cure the wounds I suffered in that wood,
so thick with thorns, that put me in such a place
I limp out lame, who entered in full course.

And now I must complete this dangerous course,   25
snare- and thorn-filled, for which a light and free
foot would be needed, sound in every place.
But you, Lord, you who take compassion's prize,
stretch out to me your right hand in this wood;
let your sun pierce my shadows strange and new.   30

Look at the state I'm in from wondrous new
beauty that has diverted my life's course
and made me a resident of the shadowed wood;
return to me, if possible, once more free,
my erring consort; let yours be the prize   35
if we both meet you in a better place.

Each in its place, here are my doubts anew:
What am I worth now? Have I run my course?
Is my soul free? Still prisoner in the wood?

This sestina, in which the poet deplores his love for Laura and turns to God, is more difficult than previous ones because the meanings of the key words repeated at line endings (especially "place," *parte* and "prize," *pregio*) keep shifting. **1**: *A soul . . . in its place*: The poet's soul was created in his body; *three days since*: He had reached adolescence, the third of the traditional six ages of human life. See *Etym.* 11.2.1. **6**: *wood*: at first glance an ideal setting for young love. **7**: *flower*: Laura's soul. **8**: *day before*: earlier adolescence; *place*: her body. **13–15**: The wood by now has become the forest of this life, full of snares and dangers (see *Conf.* 10.35; *Inf.* 1). Because the amorous prize is its chief temptation, it is probably also the despairing lovers' wood that Aeneas sees in the underworld (see note to 22.26). **17–18**: *stones . . . new herbs*: amulets or rare plants with occult properties. **20**: *knot*: with the soul, from which the body receives its life. **21**: *remedies*: see 17–18. **23**: *thorns*: the pains of love; *place*: condition. **24**: The poet is lame from the wound of concupiscence. **25**: *course*: the journey of life. **27**: *place*: part. **30–31**: *new*: as often, extraordinary. **35**: *consort*: the poet's soul, imagined as the bride of the body; *prize*: honor.

215 *In nobil sangue vita humile et queta*

A noble birth, a humble, quiet life,
a high intelligence, a simple heart,
in time of flowering youth, mature ripe fruit,
behind a thoughtful look a cheerful self,

united in this lady by her planet
 – rather the ruler of the starry dome –
with her true honor and deserved esteem
are such as to defeat the greatest poet.

Love has combined in her with chastity,
a natural beauty with a studied poise,
gestures that silently are eloquent,

and something in her eyes that suddenly
can brighten night and darken daytime skies,
turn honey bitter and make wormwood sweet.

Another litany of praise for Laura, the rhetorical hook here being that nearly
every item is a combination of opposites.   **5–6**: *planet . . .ruler*: by the controlling
astrological influence at her birth, but really by God, who controls the stars.

216 *Tutto'l dì piango; et poi la notte, quando*

I weep all day and then when night appears
and weary mortals take their rest again,
I feel my cheeks wet from redoubled pain;
and so I use up all my time with tears.

Salt moisture goes on wearing out my eyes
as sorrow does my heart; I am the most
wretched of creatures, kept from any rest
by love's barbed arrows all my nights and days.

Ah, as today's sun follows the last sun,
this dark the last dark, I by now have run
most of the way through this death we call life.

More than my pain her fault inspires my grief:
Pity herself, on whose help I relied,
watches me burn in the fire and gives no aid.

11: *death we call life*: a favorite quotation of Petrarch's; *e.g.*, in a letter to his
brother: "what we call our life is death, according to Cicero. . . ." *Fam.* 10.5. In
TM 2.22, when the spirit of the dead Laura comes to Petrarch, she says, "I am
alive and you are still dead now. . . " (see Appendix).   **13**: *Pity*: Laura.

217 *Già desiai con sì giusta querela*

Once I resolved to make my feelings heard
by justified complaint in fervent verse

to light a flame of pity with my words
in that heart, which in summer's heat is ice,

and make the veil of cloud that keeps it cold
disperse with a warm breeze of poetry;
or make men hate the one who keeps concealed
from me the eyes that are destroying me.

I seek no hatred for her now, nor pity
from her for myself – one I do not wish,
the other is denied me by cruel fate.

Instead I sing about her heavenly beauty
so that when I have shaken off this flesh
the world may understand my death was sweet.

4: *summer's heat*: youth, when the heart should be susceptible.   5: *cloud*: her scorn.

218 *Tra quantunque leggiadre donne et belle*

Among whichever beauties she appears,
the one who has no peer from east to west,
the beauty of her face does to the rest
what morning does to all the lesser stars.

Love seems to me to whisper in my ear,
saying, "As long as she is in the world
life will be good, but later dark and cold;
virtue will die, my kingdom disappear.

"Should sun and moon be taken from the skies,
the grass and leaves from earth, the winds from air
and from man his intelligence and speech,

"the sea denuded of its waves and fish:
so will the world be desolate and more,
should Death forever close and veil her eyes."

219 *Il cantar ovo e 'l pianger delli augelli*

The sobbing song of birds as the day breaks,
renewed each morning, makes the valleys ring,
as does the liquid crystal, murmuring
as it descends in clear, cool, rapid brooks.

She of the golden hair and snowy face,
whose love knew no deceit nor variance,
wakens me as I hear the love-filled dance
as she combs out her ancient's whitened fleece.

So I awaken to salute the dawn,
the sun it brings and the other sun still more,
which dazzled me in youth and does so yet.

Sometimes I've seen the two of them peep out
together; then at once as I gazed on,
he made the stars and she him disappear.

5–8: Aurora, goddess of the dawn, loved a mortal for whom she obtained
immortality but forgot to ask for eternal youth; despite his resulting decrepi-
tude, she remains faithful to him (see 291.9–11 and Tennyson's "Tithonus"). **7**:
love-filled dance (amorosi balli): the celebratory sounds of waking nature (1–4), in
harmony with Aurora's love (Ponte). **10–11**: *other sun*: Laura. **14**: Outshining
the real sun improves on her usual feat of eclipsing the stars (other beauties),
as in *RVF* 218.

220 *Onde tolse Amor l'oro, et di qual vena*

Where did Love mine the gold, from what rich vein,
to make those blond braids? From what thorny stem
gather those roses, from what meadow glean
fresh, tender frost? give pulse and breath to them?

Where did he find the pearls to break and rein
sweet decorous phrases, never commonplace?

Where all the beauties, many and divine,
shown in the cloudless heaven of that face?

From what angelic choir came, what sphere,
the heavenly singing that destroys me so
there's not much to destroy of me by now?

And what sun birthed the vivifying light
of those eyes that declare my peace and war
and that with fire and ice torment my heart?

3–4: *roses, frosts*: her cheeks among her pale complexion.　**5–6**: *pearls*: her teeth; *break and rein*: divide and articulate her words.　**10**: *destroys*: with intense emotion.

221　*Qual mio destin, qual forza o qual inganno*

Is it my fate, deception or duress
that brings me to the field again, unarmed,
where I lose every time? I would be stunned
to come out whole; if I die, it's my loss.

Not loss but gain, because my heart finds all
the sparks and flashes it encounters sweet;
they dazzle as they slay and set alight
the fire that in this twentieth year burns still.

I sense the messengers of Death appear
when those eyes flash like lightning from afar;
then, if they turn my way at her approach,

Love soothes and wounds me with intense sweet pain
I cannot quite recall, much less explain:
the truth escapes my tongue's, my reason's reach.

Another anniversary sonnet; in the fiction, Petrarch would be in his early forties. After all these years, seeing Laura again remains a field of battle where loss of life is sweet.　**12**: *soothes and wounds*: the reversal of the natural order suggests simultaneity, conveying the piercing sweetness the poet feels.

222 *Liete et pensose, accompagnate et sole*

"Gay yet distressed, together yet alone,
ladies who stroll in talk along the path,
where is the one who is my life, my death?
Why of you all is she the missing one?"

"We're happy in our memory of that sun,
but sad that now we miss her company,
which envy took from us and jealousy
that think the good of others harms their own."

"Who can hold lovers back or give them laws?"
"The soul, none; but bad temper can the body,
as now it does with her, at times with us.

"Often the heart is written on the face:
so we have seen her beauty darkened lately
and seen the dewdrops moistening her eyes."

The poet inquiring of a group of ladies about his love is a common motif in the
poetic tradition Petrarch inherits (*e.g.*, the two sonnets in *VN* 22).   **7, 10–11**: It
is tempting to see the jealous husband of courtly convention lurking here; but
because the sequence otherwise avoids the jealous husband scenario, the refer-
ence is better taken as a generic courtly commonplace about obstacles to love.

223 *Quando 'l sol bagna in mar l' aurato carro*

When the sun dips his chariot in the sea
my mind grows darker like our hemisphere
and with the sky and moon and all the stars
I set out on a night of agony.

And then to one who, sadly, does not hear
I tell my troubles, one by one recalled,
complain about blind fortune and the world,
Love and myself and her whom I hold dear.

Sleep is exiled and no repose remains;
until dawn nothing but laments and sighs
and tears my soul sends up to flood my eyes.

Then dawn arrives and turns the dark air bright,
not me: the sun that burns and yet delights
my heart, and that alone, can soothe my pains.

13: *sun*: Laura, already referred to in lines 5 and 8, appears in her guise as sun, contrasted favorably with the real sun, as in 219.9–14.

224 *S'una fede amorosa, un cor non finto*

If faithful love from a straightforward heart,
sweet pining, properly restrained desire;
if virtuous longing warm with noble fire,
long wandering in a maze with no way out;

if showing every thought upon the face
or else in stuttered phrases that appear
senseless, impeded now by shame, now fear;
if pallor tinged with violet, love's own trace;

if holding someone more than one's self dear,
sighing and shedding tears unceasingly,
feeding on sorrow, anger and distress;

if burning from afar, freezing when near
are means by which love puts an end to me,
it will be your fault, Lady, and my loss.

8: *pallor . . violet*: The commentators cite Horace, "the violet-tinged pallor of lovers" (*Odes* 3.10.14).   13: *are means*: *i.e.*, all the preceding

225 *Dodici donne honestamente lasse*

Twelve ladies lounging decorously I saw,
rather twelve stars, and in their midst a sun,
all lively in a little boat alone;
I doubt its like had plowed the waves before.

Jason had not its equal when he sailed
to find the fleece all want to wear today,
nor did the shepherd whose theft still grieves Troy,
both of whom stir such talk throughout the world.

I saw them next in a triumphal car,
my Laurel looking saintly and demure,
sitting apart and singing dulcetly.

No merely mortal vision this appeared—
fortunate pilot, happy charioteer,
who guided this delightful company!

2: *sun*: Laura (see Apoc. 12:1: "A woman clothed with the sun . . . and on her head a crown of twelve stars.")   **3**: *alone*: i.e., without men.   **5–6**: Jason sailed the Argo to find the golden fleece.   **7**: *shepherd*: Paris, who sailed to Greece and seduced Helen, starting the Trojan War.   **10**: *Laurel (Laurëa)*: her name in its Latin form.   **13**: Petrarch names the helmsman of the Argo and Achilles's charioteer, expecting his audience to understand the learned references.

226 *Passer mai solitario in alcun tetto*

No sparrow on a roof is more alone
than I, nor a wild beast in any wood;
her face, my eyes' sole cynosure, is hid
and I do not know any other sun.

My endless weeping is my one delight,
laughter is grief, poison and gall my food,
my nights exhausting, clear skies dark, my bed
become a field where battles are hard fought.

Sleep, as the saying has it, is indeed
death's relative, removing from the heart
what keeps it tied to life, that one sweet thought.

Fortunate land, unique in all the world,
green banks in flower, shady countryside,
my treasure, while I weep, is yours to hold.

A poem of separation, with the poet far from Laura. **1–2**: Ps. 101:8: "I have watched, and am become as a sparrow all alone on the housetop." **12–13**: Petrarch's usual way of describing the countryside around Vaucluse, where he likes to imagine her.

227 *Aura che quelle chiome bionde et crespe*

Breeze that embrace those blond curls airily,
stirring them, softly stirred by them in turn,
and having scattered supple gold, again
amass and knot it once more prettily,

you linger round those eyes from which love's wasps
so sting me that I feel it even here
and seek my treasure stumbling, like a poor
horse that because it shies at shadows trips;

for seeming now to find her, now aware
how far I am, my heart sinks or it soars,
perceiving what I wish or what is true.

Stay with her living radiance, happy air,
and clear swift-running river, as for you,
why can I not exchange my course for yours?

Like 226 a poem of separation that ends with the poet envying the area where Laura is. **1–4**: He addresses the breeze that comes from where she lives, as in 15 (Chiòrboli); for the breeze in her hair, see note to 90.1–2. **6–7**: *seek . . . stumbling*: mentally, as the following lines make clear. **13–14**: The river is running toward her, he travelling away.

228 *Amor col la man dextra il lato manco*

Love with his right hand opened my left side
and planted in my innermost heart's core
a laurel tree of so intense a shade
no emerald, pale by contrast, could compare.

The plow my pain, the breeze my heartfelt sighs,
the moisture falling from my eyes soft rain,
it flourished till its fragrance reached the skies,
something I think no other leaves attained.

Virtue, renown, honor and lively charm,
pure beauty clothed in a celestial form:
such are the roots of that most noble tree.

It fills my heart wherever I may be,
a welcome weight; and bowing in chaste prayer,
as if to something sacred, I adore.

Here the laurel is the image of Laura in the poet's heart (cf. Yeats, "your image that blossoms a rose in the deeps of my heart"). **1**: The left side is where the heart is. **5**: *pain (pena)*: so Contini and Santagata; some editors prefer *penna*, pen. **7**: *fragrance*: fame.

229 *Cantai, or piango, et non men di dolcezza*

I sang and now I weep, and yet to me
the tears bring no less pleasure than the songs;
because my heart is set on higher things,
the cause, not its effects, is all I see.

And so I bear a gentle or harsh tone,
attitudes that are humble, kind or cruel,
equably; no load bows me down at all
nor is my armor punctured by disdain.

Then let them treat me as they've always done
–Love and the world, my lady and my fate–
I think my future offers only joy.

Whether I live or die or pine away,
there is no nobler lot beneath the moon,
for what tastes bitter has so sweet a root.

1: The first line of 230 will form a contrast, but this does not imply thematic
or narrative continuity between the two poems (S).   4: *i.e.*, I concentrate on
Laura, not the songs or tears she inspires.

230 *I' piansi, or canto ché 'l celeste lume*

I wept and now I sing; that living sun
no longer hides her heavenly light from me,
in which chaste love reveals with clarity
its holiness and sweet power once again.

She used to draw from me a river of tears
to shorten my life's thread; I could not hope
feathers or wings would help me to escape,
much less a bridge or ford or sail or oars.

My copious flood of weeping had spread out
so widely and its shore looked so remote
I saw no way of reaching it at all.

Now Pity sends an olive branch (no palm
or laurel), makes the weather once more calm
and dries my tears to keep me living still.

1–2: *sun*: Laura; *light*: from her eyes.   5–11: The river of the poet's tears
becomes more like a sea that engulfs him (cf. the pool of Alice's tears in *Alice in
Wonderland*).   12: *Pity*: Laura.   12–13: *olive, palm, laurel*: She offers peace, not
victory; perhaps there is a suggestion of Noah's dove returning with the olive
branch to show that the flood had abated. Gen. 8:11.

231 *I' mi vivea di mia sorte content*

I lived content, with no cause to complain,
without tears, envying no happier state,
for if some lover is more fortunate,
his pleasures are not worth one of my pains.

Now the bright eyes I never will regret
being tormented by, nor wish it less,
are covered by a cloud so dark and close
the sun of all my days has almost set.

O Nature, mother merciful and cruel,
whence come such power and urges so opposed,
creating beauties you proceed to kill?

All power flows from one living fountainhead,
but highest Father, how can you allow
someone to rob us of your dear gift now?

7–8: Laura has an eye infection, occluding the splendor of the poet's sun. The situation will be taken up in 233.   **14**: *someone (altri)*: Nature (Ponte).

232 *Vincitore Alexandro l'ira vinse*

Wrath conquered Alexander; in that fault
the conqueror was inferior to his father,
no matter that Appelles and no other
had leave to paint him or Lysippus sculpt.

Tydeus was so transported by his wrath
that dying, he chewed Menalippus' head;
anger made Sulla not just bleary-eyed
but blind, and in the end it caused his death.

Valentinianus knows how wrath brings on
such punishment; and Ajax, whom it slew,
so cruel to many, then to himself too.

Wrath is brief madness and unless restrained,
a chronic madness that can lead a man
to his disgrace and sometimes to his end.

A moral sonnet with classical *exempla*; Petrarch's correspondence is full of such sententious passages. **1–2**: Petrarch translates the ancient writer Solinus: "the conqueror of all was conquered by wine and wrath" (D); *father*: Philip II of Macedon. **3–4**: By Alexander's order he could be portrayed only by certain artists. *Nat. Hist.* 7.37.125. **5–6**: Mortally wounded, Tydeus asked his companions for the head of his enemy and shocked them by chewing on it until he died. *Theb.* 7.716–66; *Inf.* 32.130–31. **7–8**: The dictator Sulla was said to have died in a fit of rage (S). **9–10**: The 4th century AD western emperor Valentinianus I was said to have died of a stroke brought on by anger (D). **10–11**: Ajax, who killed so many in the Trojan War, killed himself when the armor of the dead Achilles was awarded to Ulysses (*Metam.* 13.384–98).

233 *Qual ventura mi fu, quando da l'uno*

Fortune was with me that there came from one
of all of history's loveliest two eyes,
when I saw pain dim and disturb their gaze,
an influence that sickened and dimmed mine.

As I returned to satisfy my need
to see the only one for whom I care,
heaven and Love that day were more than fair,
beyond the sum of past gifts they bestowed;

for from my lady's right eye, her right sun
rather, the illness came to my right eye
that causes me delight instead of pain;

as if possessed of mind and power to fly,
it passed the way a star shoots through the sky,
nature and pity guiding it straight on.

This sonnet takes up the theme of *RVF* 231, but instead of being troubled by Laura's eye infection, the poet is glad it is contagious, so he can feel at one with her.

234 *O cameretta che già fosti un porto*

You were my refuge once, my little room,
during my daily storms that were so fierce;
you are a fountain now of nightly tears,
which I keep hidden all day long in shame.

You, little bed, a comfort once and rest
in so much trouble, from what doleful urns
Love bathes you now with those slim ivory hands,
cruel to no one but me – ah, how unjust!

And so I flee my rest and solitude,
but more myself and my sweet train of thought,
which as I chased it lifted me in flight;

and for my refuge now I seek the crowd
(who would have guessed?), that enemy of mine,
I fear so much to find myself alone.

Love has gone from difficult but rewarding to simply tormenting, and the poet
seeks to end it.   **6–7**: His eyes become jars of tears that Laura overturns.   **9**:
rest, solitude: his bed and his room.   **12–13**: Where Love made him shun the
crowd (*e.g.*, 129.15–16), he now sees joining it as a remedy for love. In *My Secret*,
74, St. Augustine reminds Petrarch that Ovid's remedy for love was to avoid
lonely places and mingle with people.

235 *Lasso, Amor mi trasporta ov'io non voglio*

Carried astray by Love against my will,
I cross a line I know well I should not,
which makes her, the sole monarch of my heart,
find me more troublesome than usual.

No expert helmsman ever kept from rocks
a vessel laden with a precious freight

with more skill than I've steered my leaky boat
around her obdurate pride's potential shocks.

But a downpour of tears and violent gales
of endless sighing now have driven it,
adrift in my sea's dreadful storm-tossed night,

to where it irritates her and brings pain
upon itself, already near stove in
by waves and stripped of rudder and of sails.

Apparently paired with *RVF* 236 as an incident in which the lover feels guilty
for having been too importunate.

236 *Amor, io fallo, et veggio il mio fallire*

Love, I am guilty and I see my fault,
but act like someone burning up inside;
my growing torment makes my judgment fade
until the pain has almost put it out.

In times past I controlled my hot desire
for fear of troubling her calm lovely face;
I can no more: you snatched the reins, now loose,
and my soul has grown reckless in despair.

You are the cause if suddenly it bolts:
you stoke its fire and prick it with your spurs,
until, to save itself, it tries rough ways;

but the main cause is those rare gifts of hers.
At least, Love, make her understand my case
and grant herself forgiveness for my faults.

5–11: The horse and rider metaphor has appeared in different ways before (see
notes to 6.1 and 147.1–2); here the horse is the poet's desire in line 5, but becomes
his soul (desire having been given free rein), in lines 8–11.

The sea has fewer creatures in its waves,
nor up above the circle of the moon
are stars so numerous gazed on by the night,
nor do as many birds nest in the woods,
nor so much grass abound in field or meadow   5
as are the cares that fill my heart each evening.

Day after day I hope the final evening
will separate my living earth from waves
of tears and leave me sleeping in some meadow;
for such distress no man beneath the moon   10
has suffered, as is known throughout the woods
where all alone I wander day and night.

I never yet have had a quiet night,
but sighing go from morning into evening,
since Love made me a citizen of the woods.   15
Before I rest, the sea will lose its waves,
the sun's light will be borrowed from the moon
and flowers in April die in every meadow.

Wasting away I trail from field to meadow,
anxious by day and weeping through the night,   20
my state as changeable as is the moon.
The moment I see dusk descend at evening,
sighs from my chest and from my eyes salt waves
issue to drench the grass and shake the woods.

Hostile are cities, welcoming are woods   25
to my cares, which I roam through this high meadow
venting aloud, accompanied by the waves'
murmur in the sweet silence of the night;
for this I wait all day until at evening
the sinking sun trades places with the moon.   30

If only with the lover of the moon
I now lay fast asleep in some green woods,
and she who in high day brings on my evening
would, with the moon and Love, visit that meadow
and stay there for the length of one whole night,   35
the sun and day forever beneath the waves!

Born in the night beneath the shining moon
upon rough waves, my Song, within the woods,
you'll reach tomorrow evening a lush meadow.

A sestina that sounds a good deal like poems early in the Laura sequence, especially another sestina, *RVF* 22.   **8**: *living earth*: the poet's body, *i.e.*, death will free him from his sufferings.   **25–36**: The scenery of the night-time walk suggests Vaucluse (and see note to 37).   **27**: *waves*: apparently of the river Durenza, see below.   **31–36**: The parallel with 22.31–36 is striking.   **31–32**: Seeing the beautiful shepherd Endymion asleep, the goddess of the moon fell in love and at her request Zeus made him sleep eternally.   **33**: Laura, who leads him to death before his time.   **37**: *rough waves (dure onde)*: apparently a punning reference to the Durenza, which joins the Rhone near Avignon.   **39**: *rich meadow*: where Laura lives.

238   *Real natura, angelico intelletto*

Royal temperament, unclouded spirit blessed
with angel's intellect, immediate
discernment, lynx-eyed vision, noble thought
such as in truth is worthy of that breast;

with many ladies chosen from the rest
to beautify that festive gathering,
his faultless judgment quickly saw among
those faces, all so fair, the loveliest.

Those more advanced in age or station he,
with a brief gesture, told to stand aside
and graciously received that one alone.

He kissed her eyes and brow most courteously,
which raised the others' spirits, every one,
but I felt envious of the rare sweet deed.

An eminent man pays a visit to Avignon and at a public reception bestows a
ceremonial kiss on the most beautiful local woman, who is of course Laura.
(Cf. the noble Italian mentioned by Dante (*Inf.* 16.37), who in a similar incident
with the emperor, said that only her future husband would kiss her.)   **1–4**: The
intelligence and good judgment of the great man prepare a foil for Laura.   **2**:
angel's intellect: Angels do not understand by reasoning, as we do, but know
directly and immediately. *ST* 1.54.5, 1.55.2.

239 *Là ver' l'aurora, che sì dolce l'aura*

Just before daybreak, when a fresh spring breeze
often, in the new season, stirs the flowers
and little birds begin to sing their verses,
sweetly I feel the memories in my soul
stirred by the one who holds them in her power,   5
so that I must once more take up my notes.

Ah, might I tune my sighs to such sweet notes
that they would soften Laura like the breeze,
persuading her who quells me with her power!
But winter will become the time of flowers   10
before love blossoms in that noble soul
that never yet has cared for rhymes nor verses.

How many tears, alas, how many verses
I've scattered in my time, and with what notes
have I attempted to subdue that soul!   15
She stands, though, like a stark crag in a breeze
that gently ruffles the new leaves and flowers
but fails against a more substantial power.

Both men and gods are conquered by the power
of Love, as can be read in tales and verses;   20

I felt it at the budding of the flowers.
But now my tears, my prayers and my lord's notes
fail to make Laura (who can bind the breeze?)
release from suffering or from life my soul.

To make a last attempt, my wretched soul,   25
marshal your native gifts, put forth your power
now while we still can breathe life's vital breeze.
There's nothing that's impossible for verses:
they can charm even serpents with their notes
and deck the winter's ice with budding flowers.   30

The meadows laugh now with new grass and flowers;
it cannot be that her angelic soul
will fail to hear the sound of amorous notes.
But if our ruthless fate holds greater power,
we shall go weeping as we sing our verses   35
and with a lame ox ride to hunt the breeze.

I net the breeze and from the ice pluck flowers,
wooing with verses a deaf, unmoved soul,
prone to ignore Love's power and all my notes.

1: *breeze*: One of the rhyme words in this sestina is "breeze (*l'aura*)", with the usual play on Laura's name (here the spring breeze reminds the poet of her). In stanzas 2 and 4, however, Petrarch substitutes "*Laura*," requiring paraphrase in translation to preserve the sestina form.   **6**: Among the rhyme words, "notes" is more or less interchangeable with "verses," the two representing the musical and verbal sides of poetry.   **16**: Now the breeze is assimilated to his wooing poetry; Laura is its obstacle.   **21**: He fell in love with Laura in the springtime (*RVF* 3).   **22**: *my lord's notes*: my verses inspired by Love (S).   **27**: Here *l'aura* has become the breath of life or the vital spirits.   **28–30**: Poetry has magical powers, whether to charm snakes or make flowers bloom.   **29**: *serpent*: Petrarch names the asp, which was believed to stop its ears against magicians' conjurations by putting one ear to the ground and plugging the other with its tail. *Li Livres dou Tresor* 1.138; ed. Francis J. Carmody (University of California Press 1948).   **36**: *lame ox*: as his hound (see 212.8).

I have implored Love and again I pray
that he will vindicate me to you, sweet
torment and bitter bliss, if with complete
faithfulness I depart from the straight way.

Lady, I won't deny that this is so:
reason, which should restrain a righteous soul,
gives way in me to passion, and its pull
forces me sometimes where I should not go.

You, with a heart the heavens illuminate
with intellect and virtue, both as bright
as any ever rained from favoring star,

should say, with pity and no scorn, "He's so
consumed by this face, what else can he do?
Why is he greedy – and why am I so fair?"

A variation on the theme of *RVF* 236.

241 *L'alto signor dinanzi a cui non vale*

The lord before whose power it does not pay
to run or hide, much less to make a stand,
started a blaze of pleasure in my mind,
sinking a flaming shaft of love in me.

Though by itself that blow from his first dart
was mortal, to complete his enterprise
a new one, barbed with pity, he then chose,
so now from both sides he attacks my heart.

The first wound burns and shouts out flames of fire;
the second drips with tears squeezed from my eyes
by sorrow for your pitiable state;

but those two springs do nothing to abate
one spark amid the fire in which I blaze;
pity instead increases my desire.

7, 11: Laura's condition is generally thought to be an illness (see her illness in *RVF* 31, 33).

242 — *Mira quel colle, o stanco mio cor vago*

"My weary restless heart, look at the hill
where we left lately her who cared for us
a little once and pitied us no less,
and now would have our eyes create a pool.

"Return there, I'm content to stay alone;
see if perhaps it may be time our grief,
which until now has grown, may find relief,
you who foresee as well as share my pain."

"You know yourself no longer and address
your heart as if he still were part of you,
wretch, full of empty thoughts and foolishness!

"When you and all you yearn for parted ways
and you went off, he stayed with her, not you,
and hid himself in her resplendent eyes."

The poet argues with himself (see *RVF* 68).   **1**: *hill*: near where Laura lives (see the companion poem, *RVF* 243). The poet is apparently on a journey, remembering their last meeting there.   From *RVF* 249 on there will be references to a final meeting they had.

243 *Fresco, ombroso, fiorito et verde colle*

Cool shady hillside, flowering and green,
where now in thought and now in song she walks,
showing us how a spirit of heaven looks,
she who in fame eclipses everyone,

my heart, who left me for her (being wise,
and more so if he never should come back),
counts places where your grass preserves the mark
of her slim foot and moisture from my eyes.

Close by her side, he murmurs with each pace,
"Could that wretch only stay a short while here,
who's tired of weeping and of living now!"

She smiles at that, but this match is not fair:
without a heart I am a stone, but you
a paradise, sweet sacred favored place.

This sonnet is addressed to the wooded hill that Laura frequents and where
the poet met with her before going abroad. *RVF* 242, which mentioned their
meeting, described how his heart remained with her there.

244 *Il mal mi preme, et mi spaventa il peggio*

Depressed by present evils, fearing worse,
for which I can foresee a wide clear road,
I feel like you that I've been driven mad
and so I rave, my thoughts obsessed like yours,

nor know if I should pray for war or peace,
for harm is grievous, but then so is shame.
Why wring our hands, though? All that is to come
has been determined in the highest place.

Though I do not deserve the high esteem
you offer me – for love inveigles you,
which often makes a sound eye see askew –

to raise your soul to the celestial realm
is what I would advise, and spur your heart,
because the road is long and time is short.

This occasional poem responds to a sonnet by Petrarch's friend Giovanni Dondi about a conflict between Venice and Padua that took place in Petrarch's old age and greatly troubled both men (Daniele, Ponte, S, D). **5–6**: *war . . . shame*: war brings harm, but surrender brings humiliating conditions.

245 *Due rose fresche, et colte in paradiso*

Two dewy roses, plucked the other day
at dawn on May the first in paradise,
made a fine gift a lover, old and wise,
shared between two young lovers equally;

at this, with his sweet words and with the way
he smiled, which would have made a savage love,
their faces brightened, with the radiance of
love's blush suffusing them like a new ray.

"There is no pair like this beneath the sun,"
he said as he both smiled and sighed; this done,
he hugged the two of them and turned away.

Roses and words he shared – my weary heart
rejoices still and fears, recalling that.
Oh happy eloquence, oh joyous day!

Commentators have speculated in vain about the identity of the old lover or the young couple; the likelihood is that the question is not meaningful. The poem parallels *RVF* 94 in that line 13 describes the poet's reaction to the scene based on his own experience. The weary heart and the alternate joy and fear are constants of Petrarch's poetic personality.

246 *L'aura che 'l verde lauro et l'aureo crine*

When the breeze stirs green laurel and gold hair
ever so gently as it softly sighs,
such are the grace and charm that it displays
entranced souls leave their bodies as they stare.

This white rose, born with cruel thorns all around,
when will we find her equal in the world,
the glory of our age? O living God,
let my last day arrive before her end

so that I may not see the great loss stun
the public, the world left without its sun
like my eyes, which have known no other light,

my soul, which wants to hold no other thought,
and my ears, which are deaf to empty noise
without those sweet and proper words of hers.

This is the first suggestion of Laura's death, which becomes a recurring premonition in poems that follow.   **1–4**: The poem opens with a triple pun: *L'aura*, the breeze, is Laura and her sigh stirs *lauro*, the laurel (her limbs), and golden (*l'aureo*) hair, a sight that ravishes souls from their bodies.   **6**: See Cant. 2:2, "As the lily among thorns, so is my love among the daughters."

247 *Parrà forse ad alcun che 'n lodar quella*

It may appear to some that when I praise
her I adore on earth, my style is forced,
making her far more noble than the rest,
holy, chaste, charming, beautiful and wise.

To me it seems the opposite; I fear
she will scorn common language of my sort,
who merits terms refined and erudite.
Let any skeptic catch a glimpse of her

and he will say, "What this man hopes to do
would weary Athens, Smyrna, Mantua too,
Arpinum and the Greek and Latin lyres."

No tongue of mortal could be adequate
to her divine worth; Love drives and inspires
my own not by my choice but by my fate.

: *the rest*: all other women.   **10–11**: The references indicate the ancient Greek and Latin masters of epic poetry (Homer, Virgil), lyric poetry (Pindar, Horace) and oratory (Demosthenes, Cicero).

248 *Chi vuol veder quantunque pò Natura*

One who would see where heaven and nature did
their finest work down here should come and gaze
on her, the sole sun not for just my eyes
but the blind world, where virtue is ignored.

Let him come quickly, though, for Death steals first
the best and lets the bad remain behind;
and she, awaited in the blessed land,
a passing mortal beauty, cannot last.

He will see wonders if he comes in time:
all virtues, beauties, every regal trait
joined in one body in harmony together;

then he will scorn my inarticulate rhymes,
my insight blinded by excess of light;
but if he comes too late, he'll weep forever.

249 *Qual paura ò, quando mi torna a mente*

I'm gripped with fear when I recall the day
I left my lady grave and full of care
(and left my heart with her); despite the fear
I let my mind return there constantly.

I see her standing modestly there still
with other beauties like a rose among
field flowers, neither glad nor sorrowing,
as if she dreaded some yet unknown ill.

She'd put her usual gaiety aside,
the garlands and the pearls and the bright clothes,
the laughter, song and sweetly courteous talk.

I left my life there, feeling great unease;
now sad forebodings, troubling dreams and dark
thoughts are attacking me – all false, please God..

The premonition of Laura's death that darkened *RVF* 248 will continue through
RVF 254.

250 *Solea lontana in sonno consolarme*

In dreams my lady used to bring relief
with her angelic look from far away;
she brings me sorrow now and frightens me,
and I have no defense from fear and grief;

for often in her face I seem to see
real pity mingled with deep-felt distress
and hear things that convince me to repress
all joy and any hope for what might be.

"Do you recall that last evening we met,"
she asks me, "when I left with your eyes wet,
as the late hour demanded I be gone?

"I could not tell you then, nor wanted to;
I tell you now as something known and true:
you must not hope to see me on earth again."

5: *often*: still in dreams.   9: *last evening*: See *RVF* 249.

251 *O misera et horribil visïone!*

A wretched, horrifying vision came!
Can it be true that her sustaining light,

which eased my life in its most heartsick state
and in high hope, is quenched before its time?

How could a crash so thunderous not be heard,
but she herself must bring the news to me?
May God and nature now not let it be
and my sad premonition prove absurd.

My only recourse lies in hoping still
for the sweet sight of her resplendent face,
my sustenance and the glory of our time.

If, to ascend to her eternal home,
she's left the place in which she used to dwell,
I pray that my last day may now be close.

1: *vision*: the dream in *RVF* 250.   5–6: Petrarch is in Italy, while Laura has remained in Provence.   13: *place*: her body.

252 *In dubbio di mio stato, or piango or canto*

Not knowing where I stand, I weep then sing,
I fear and hope; I vent in rhymes and sighs
my pressing pain, while roughly Love applies
his file to cause my tortured heart to sting.

Ah, will her sainted face some day again
give my eyes back the light they used to see
(I cannot guess what will become of me)
or sentence them to weeping from now on?

And gaining heaven, which her merits won,
will she not care what happens to them here,
left in the dark without their only sun?

Living in dread amid this endless war,
I'm not the man I once was any more
and stumble down a doubtful path in fear.

253 *O dolci sguardi, o parolette accorte*

Sweet glances, observations laced with wit,
will I now see and hear you anymore?
Gleaming blond locks that Love employs to snare
my heart and once it's trapped dispatches it;

beautiful face that this hard fate of mine
gave me to bring me tears and never joy;
hidden deception, cheating amorous ploy,
to give me pleasure that brings only pain!

Even if sometimes from those gentle eyes,
the shelter where my life and my thoughts thrive,
a chaste but tender glance may come to me,

quickly, to scatter any good I have,
Fortune, alert to do me harm, supplies
horses or ships to send me far away.

Given this poem's place in the sequence, the first two lines appear to allude to the poet's uncertainty about Laura's death. The rest of the sonnet, however, merges that dilemma into the continuing story of his difficulties in love, including his frequent travels.

254 *I' pur ascolto, et non odo novella*

I still am listening but I do not hear
news of my sweet beloved enemy,
nor know what I should think of it or say,
my heart is so transfixed by hope and fear.

Beauty has hurt the beautiful before;
she is more beautiful than anyone,

more chaste; God wants to take this paragon,
perhaps, to light the sky with a new star,

or rather sun. If this is so my life,
its troubles lasting long, its respites brief,
is over now. O cruel departure, why

compound my loss by sending me away?
My little drama's final scene is done
and in my middle years my time has run.

The last of the premonition sonnets: Petrarch in Italy fears Laura may be dying in Provence; he was in fact in Italy when he heard of her death. In the following poems, however, definite knowledge of her death will be long postponed and the sequence will return to earlier themes. **5**: Perhaps Callisto (Greek: "most beautiful") for whom see 33.3n. **11–12**: *departure*: See *RVF* 249–50. **14**: When Laura died in 1348, Petrarch was 44.

255 *La sera desiare, odiar l'aurora*

To long for evening, hate for dawn to come
belongs to lovers who are fortunate;
my tearful sorrow only grows at night
and morning is for me a happier time,

for often one and the other sun come forth
at the same time, as if two orients broke,
in beauty and in splendor so alike
that heaven falls in love again with earth,

as happened when the new boughs first were green
that have become so rooted in my heart,
more than myself I hold another dear.

What these hours do to me, so opposite,
means that I welcome dawn, which eases pain,
night with its suffering I both I hate and fear.

: One sun is Laura, one east her window (see 100.1–2, 219.10–14).   **8**: *again (anco)*: for this meaning, see *ED* 1.253 and Ponte.   **9**: When Apollo the sun god loved Daphne and she became a laurel.

256 *Far potess'io vendetta di colei*

> Ah, could I take revenge on her in full,
> whose words and glances are destroying me,
> and who to hurt me further runs away,
> hiding from me those eyes so sweet and cruel!
>
> So bit by bit she sucks out and devours
> my vital forces, which, exhausted, droop;
> and then at night when I should be asleep,
> over my heart like a fierce lion she roars.
>
> My soul then, which Death chases from its home,
> leaves me and, liberated from that knot,
> to her, although she menaces it, hastens.
>
> I would be quite surprised if at some time,
> with tears, words and embraces, it did not
> disturb her slumber if she ever listens.

6: For the vital spirits, see note to 17.9.   **9–12**: Petrarch contaminates the motif of death from love with that of the lover's heart leaving him for the beloved (S).   **9**: *then . . . home*: in dreams his tortured state appears as death, chasing his soul from its body.

257 *In quel bel viso ch'i' sospiro et bramo*

> My eyes were fixed, intent and passionate,
> upon the face that makes me sigh and yearn,
> which she, as if to say, "Where have you gone?"
> screened with her hand, my second favorite.

My heart, still caught – a fish upon a hook
or on a lime twig an unwary bird –
upon that living model of the good,
ignored the gesture, too engrossed to look.

My vision, now deprived of its first view,
as in a dream created a new route,
so its enjoyment still would be complete.

My soul, suspended between glorious sights,
felt I know not what heavenly delight,
a sweetness inexpressible and new.

Reproving the poet's rapt gaze, Laura breaks it; but his mind's eye still gazes
on her hidden face, while his physical eyes see her hand. This double vision,
superimposing imagination on reality, transports him.   **3**: *she (Amor)*: as in
108.2 and 129.36, Love is here a personification of Laura.

258 *Vive faville uscian de' duo bei lumi*

Live sparks leapt out from two resplendent eyes
that sweetly flashed at me at the same time
as noble language in a gentle stream
flowed from a wise heart, interspersed with sighs.

I'm still consumed by the mere memory
each time that day returns and I recall
how I could feel my vital forces fail
seeing her stern look change so graciously.

My soul, so used to sorrow as its food
(the power of long-time habit holds great sway)
before this double pleasure felt so weak

the unexpected taste of something good
made it, now hoping and now fearing, quake,
uncertain whether to abandon me.

7: For the vital spirits, see note to 17.9.

259 *Cercato ò sempre solitaria vita*

I've found a solitary life the best
(as known to riverbanks, woods, meadowlands),
so as to flee those deaf and squinting minds
for whom the road to heaven has been lost.

If I could live this life where I belong,
it would, if not in my sweet Tuscan air,
be in the shady hills of Vaucluse, where
the Sorgue facilitates my tears and song.

But fortune, which has always been my foe,
drives me again where anger makes me brood,
seeing my precious treasure in the mud;

for once, however, it has been a friend,
and not unjustly, to my writing-hand,
as Love saw and my lady and I know.

1–8: Petrarch loves solitude this time (as opposed to, *e.g.*, *RVF* 129) to escape the intrigue and vice of papal Avignon (for which see *RVF* 136–38).   **9–14**: Fortune, however, drives him to Avignon, where Laura lives, and he is indignant to see his jewel in such a setting. Nonetheless, he is thankful for something known only to Laura and him – likely that he got to clasp her hand while there (Daniello).

260 *In tale stella duo belli occhi vidi*

Beneath a favoring star I saw two eyes
so ravishingly lovely, pure and sweet,
beside those charming nests Love occupies
my weary heart scorns any other sight.

None can compare, not those who won all praise
in any age or any far-flung place;
not she whose beauty caused the dying cries
of Troy and brought such long travail to Greece;

nor the fair Roman who with a steel blade
opened her own chaste outraged breast, and not
Polyxena, Argia nor Hypsipyle.

In truth her clear superiority
is nature's glory and my great delight,
except that it comes late and quickly fades.

3: *nests*: still Laura's eyes (see 71.7).   **7–8**: Helen, most beautiful of women and
cause of the Trojan War.   **9–10**: Lucretia, who committed suicide after being
raped by the king's son.   **11**: Polyxena: Trojan princess loved by Achilles. Argia:
daughter of King Adrastus, wife of Oedipus's son Polynices. Hypsipyle: queen
of Lemnos, loved and abandoned by Jason.   **14**: *late*: in this last degenerate age
of the world; *quickly fades*: likely another premonition of her death, given the
position of this poem in the sequence (see 248.8, 14).

261 *Qual donna attende a glorïosa fama*

If any woman aspires to be hailed
as truly worthy, courteous and wise,
let her look steadily in my foe's eyes,
she who is called my lady by the world.

How to love God, how honor should be won,
how a light heart accords with chastity,
can all be learned there, and the straightest way
to heaven, which waits and longs for her to come.

There learn the speech unmatched by any style,
the lovely silences and winning ways
of which no writing can convey a part;

the boundless beauty, though, that dazzles all
cannot be learned there, for those splendid eyes
are gifts of fortune, not acquired by art.

"Life's the most precious thing, it seems to me,
chastity in a lovely lady second."
"Reverse them, mother; nothing can be reckoned
precious or lovely without chastity.

"She who gives up her honor is no more
a lady nor is she alive; though she
may look the same, her life is bound to be
more cruel than death, with bitter pains to bear.

"I never wondered at Lucretia's fate
except that for her death she needed steel
and that her grief was not enough alone."

Let the world's great philosophers opine
on this point; we shall see their maxims crawl,
while her opinion rises up in flight.

A dialogue between Laura and an older woman, addressed respectfully as
"mother," with a final comment by the poet.   **9**: *Lucretia*: see 260.9n.

263 *Arbor victorïosa triumphale*

Victorious and triumphal tree, the crown
honoring the general's and the poet's head,
how sorrowful you've made me and how glad
during this fleeting mortal life of mine!

Great lady, you who only care about
honor, which you have such a harvest of,
you do not fear the snares or nets of Love
nor is your good sense conquered by deceit.

Nobility of blood and things that we
hold precious, whether rubies, pearls or gold,
you think base burdens worthy of your scorn.

Your beauty, with no equal in the world,
would irritate you did it not adorn
the precious treasure of your chastity.

This sonnet, which closes Part 1 of the collection, resumes the laurel theme, but now the pain of the poet's unrequited love is sublimated into praise of Laura's chastity, also the theme of *RVF* 262 (S).   **1**: *tree*: the laurel, here a term of address to Laura parallel to "lady" in line 5 (see "column" in 10.1).

PART TWO

264 *I' vo pensando, et nel penser m'assale*

    Thinking about my life, I am attacked
by such intense compassion for myself
it often forces me
to weep for reasons other than I used to;
    for seeing day by day my end draw near,   5
a thousand times I've begged God for the wings
by which our intellect
can rise to heaven from this mortal jail.
    But so far this has been to no avail,
despite my sighs, my prayers, the tears I've shed;   10
and that it should be so is only just:
one who can stand yet falls beside the road
deserves to lie in dirt against his will.
Those arms in which I trust,
so merciful, I see are open still,   15
yet tales of others' failures
dishearten me; I tremble for my state,
still spurred by passions near my final date.

    One thought that echoes in my mind repeats,
"What do you want? What are you waiting for?   20
Wretch, can you really not
see how it shames you that time slips away?
    "Decide now on a prudent course, decide
to rip out from your heart each clinging root
of pleasure that can never   25
bring happiness and does not let you breathe.
    "If, sick and tired of it now, you loathe
that cheating sweetness, ever fugitive,

the only kind this traitorous world can give,
why base your hope on that foundation still,   30
where there is nothing firm to rest upon?
Now while your body lives
the reins on loose thought are in your control:
tighten them while you can,
for to delay is dangerous, as you know;   35
it would be none too soon if you start now.

   "You're well aware of all the heady sweetness
your eyes imbibed with their first sight of her
whose birth I wish were still
waiting to happen, leaving us in peace;   40
   "and you remember, as indeed you should,
how instantaneously her image ran
straight to your heart, which might
not have caught fire from any other torch.
   "She lit it, and if the deceptive heat   45
lasted for years, still hoping for a time
that has, for our salvation, never come,
raise yourself now to a more blessed hope
by gazing at the heavens wheeling round you,
beautiful and eternal.   50
If your desire is satisfied down here
by a glance, a word, a song
whose pleasure turns to harm, what joy awaits
you there, if here these trifles seem so great?

   On the other side a sweet yet arduous thought,   55
settled within my soul with wearisome
and yet delightful weight,
feeds hope and stirs up longing in my heart,
   which, filled with love for glorious renown,
pays no attention if I freeze or burn   60
or if I'm pale or thin;
and if I kill the thought, it comes back stronger.

Since I was sleeping swaddled, this desire
has day by day been growing up with me
and now I fear one tomb will shut us in.   65
After my soul, stripped of its limbs, is bare,
the longing finally will be left behind;
but then, if Greek and Latin
speak of me after death, it will be wind;
and I, because I fear   70
I'm gathering what will scatter in an hour,
want to abandon shadows, grasp what's sure.

But that first passion fills me so completely
its shade blights any others born nearby;
while the years slip away,   75
writing about her I neglect myself;
    and the clear light of her resplendent eyes
that melts me tenderly in its warm splendor
restrains me with a rein
against which strength and cunning cannot win.   80
    How does it help then that my little boat
is smeared with pitch if it is still held back
by moorings like these two among the rocks?
Lord, you have freed me from the other knots
that in their different ways bind the world fast; 85
ah, why then do you not
take from my face this lingering shame at last?
For like a man who dreams
I have my death before my eyes, it seems,
and would defend myself but have no arms.   90

I see what I am doing, not deceived
by lack of knowledge but coerced by Love,
who makes those who believe
too strongly in him stray from honor's road;
    and often I feel rising in my heart   95
noble disdain that harshly censures me,

making my hidden thoughts
show in my face for everyone to see,
    for loving a mortal creature with the faith
that ought to be reserved for God alone   100
least becomes those who long for virtue's crown.
With a loud voice this scorn calls back again
my reason, which my senses led astray;
but when it would obey
the call it hears, bad habit drives it on,   105
painting before my eyes
her who was born only to make me die,
pleasing too greatly both herself and me.

    I do not know what span the heavens assigned
my tenure when I first arrived on earth   110
to bear the bitter war
I have contrived to wage against myself,
    nor through the mortal body's heavy veil
can I foresee what day will close my life;
but I can see my hair   115
changing and my desires within as well.
    Now that I feel the time for my departure
approaches or at least cannot be far,
like one schooled by past loss and put on guard
I'm pondering where I left the right-hand road,   120
the route by which one reaches the good port;
and on one side the goad
urging me back is sorrow barbed with shame,
while on the other still
I'm held by pleasure grown so strong with time   125
it dares with death itself to strike a deal.

    Song, this is how I am: my heart has now
become as cold from fear as frozen snow,
sensing myself expire beyond all doubt;
for while deliberating, I have wound   130

upon the beam much of my little cloth.
No more oppressive weight
than what I bear in this state could be found –
my elbow rubbed by death,
I seek a new direction for my course   135
and see the better but pursue the worse.

Part Two of *Scattered Rhymes* begins with a canzone that offers the most detailed poetic exploration yet (more than *RVF* 142) of Petrarch's spiritual dilemma, paralleled at even greater length in prose in *My Secret*. In the poem Petrarch debates with himself; in the prose work one side is taken by St. Augustine. (In *RVF* 360, the debaters will be Petrarch and Love.) The poet's love for Laura and his thirst for poetic glory are both impediments on the road to salvation, as St. Augustine explains to him.   **4**: *other*: not for unhappy love.   **6**: *wings*: grace.   **8**: *jail*: as usual, the body.   **14**: the arms of the crucified Christ.   **18**: *passions (altrui)*: the double impediment mentioned above (S).   **19**: *one thought*: the voice of morality.   **39**: *I*: the thought.   **55**: *thought*: the thirst for literary glory.   **60–61**: *freeze . . . thin*: symptoms of love in erotic poetry; here effects of arduous study.   **73–80**: The two quatrains explain in parallel how his amorous passion keeps him from the goal of grasping eternal truth (72).   **81–87**: Despite preparations, his voyage to salvation is held back by these two: love for Laura and hunger for fame.   **84–85**: *My Secret* proclaims that Petrarch's vices are limited to those two.   **97–98**: His self-contempt makes him blush (see 87).   **103**: By pleasing herself too much (as he thinks), Laura scorned the poet's love; by pleasing him too much, she made him forget God.   **126**: *dares . . . deal*: seeking to maximize its remaining time and leave as little as possible for repentance (Zingarelli). Cf. Augustine's "Lord, make me chaste, but not yet." *Conf.* 8._.   **130**: *beam*: the part of the loom on which the woven cloth is wound.

265 *Aspro core et selvaggio, et cruda voglia*

A hard and savage heart, a ruthless will
clothed in a humble, sweet, angelic shape
will, if the rigor she's embraced keeps up,
gain little honor from my corpse as spoil;

for in the times when flower and grass and leaf
are born and die, in bright day and dark night,

247

I weep continually because my fate,
Love and my lady give me cause for grief.

A memory helps me live on hope alone:
I saw how trickling water had consumed,
through sheer persistence, marble and hard stone.

There is no heart so hard that tears and love
and prayers in time's slow process cannot move,
no will so cold that it cannot be warmed.

In this sonnet and the next, Laura is still alive. Santagata opines that it was important for Petrarch not to make the penitential theme, which will be predominant in Part Two, depend on external biographical fact, but rather result from a psychological process of maturation. 4: *i.e.,* killing an unarmed enemy brings no glory.

266 *Signor mio caro, ogni pensier mi tira*

My dear lord, always present in my mind,
devoted thoughts draw me to visit you,
but my bad fortune (what worse could it do?)
pulls back the reins, turns me and wheels me round.

What's more, the yearning Love breathes into me
drives me toward death without my being aware;
calling on my two lights no matter where
I find myself, by day and night I sigh.

Love for my lady, reverence for my lord:
these are the chains in which I've long been bound,
whose heavy weight I willingly assumed.

A noble column, laurel ever green,
one fifteen years, the other now eighteen,
I've carried in my heart and never shed.

Addressed to Petrarch's patron Cardinal Giovanni Colonna.   **3–4**: Petrarch's excuse is his need to travel in Italy, far from the cardinal in Provence.   **7**: *two lights*: Laura's eyes (Ponte).   **12–13**: *laurel . . . 18 years*: Laura, met in 1327 (so this is 1345, three years before her death); *column . . . 15 years*: the cardinal (Petrarch's patron since 1330).   **12**: *column*: the same pun on Colonna as in 10.1.

267 *Oimè il bel viso, oimè il soave sguardo*

Ah gone, the lovely face, the gentle glance,
the proud and carefree way she used to move!
All gone, the words that made the coward brave
and taught the wild rough spirit deference!

Ah, gone the smile that struck me with the dart
from which I now expect no good but death!
Royal soul, the worthiest to rule on earth
had you not come among us here so late!

In you I still must breathe, for you still burn,
being always yours; and if I am deprived
of you, all other pain is less in kind.

You filled me with desire and hope again
when I last left the greatest beauty alive;
but all our words were scattered by the wind.

The first notice of Laura's death. Petrarch wrote that she died in Avignon on April 6, 1348 (the year of the Black Death) and he learned of it the following month in Italy.   **8**: *late*: see 260.14n.   **9**: *you*: the face, glance, etc. lamented in the octet.   **12–14**: He refers to their last meeting, some six months before her death, recounted in *RVF* 249–250.

268 *Che debb'io far? che mi consigli, Amore?*

What should I do? What is your counsel, Love?
It is high time to die
and I have lingered longer than I wish.

Dying, my lady took my heart with her;
wanting to follow it   5
I now must interrupt these evil years,
    since I can never hope
to see her here and waiting is for me
a torment: her departure
changed into weeping every joy of mine   10
and all the sweetness of my life is gone.

    Love, I lament with you, for you can feel
how bitter is the loss;
I know that you are saddened by my grief,
    or rather ours, for on the same cruel reef   15
our ship became a wreck;
for both of us at once the sun went dark.
    With what words could I ever
give adequate expression to my sorrow?
Ah, blind, ungrateful world,   20
you have good cause to weep with me: you lost
with her whatever beauty you possessed.

    Your glory is fallen and you do not see it,
nor were you ever worthy
to know her while she lived down here among us   25
    or feel the pressure of her sainted feet,
for such a lovely creature
should have made heaven brighter with her presence.
    But I, who have no love,
now that she's gone, for this life or myself,   30
weep and call out for her;
this is what's left of all my hopes, no more,
and all that now sustains my life down here.

    It has become earth now, the lovely face
that gave us evidence   35
of heaven and what its happiness must be;
    now her invisible form in paradise

has laid aside the veil
that cast a shadow on her flowering years,
    to be put on again,   40
never to be divested any more,
when we shall see her changed,
all the more beautiful, as everlasting
beauty surpasses beauty that is passing.

    More beautiful than ever now, my lady   45
visits my mind once more
like one who knows where she will be most welcome.
    This is one pillar holding up my life,
the other her illustrious
name, which resounds so sweetly in my heart.   50
    But when I recollect
that my hope, which lived on while she still flourished,
past question now is dead,
Love understands well what becomes of me
and she, I hope, so close to truth, can see.   55

    Ladies who gazed in wonder at her beauty
and her angelic life,
the way she walked on earth like one from heaven,
    lament for me, let pity overcome you,
but not for her, now risen   60
into great peace while leaving me in war;
    and if the path is blocked
much longer that would let me follow her,
only Love's words to me
can hold me back from severing the knot.   65
But speaking within my mind, he plants this thought:

    "Rein in the grief that carries you away,
for your excessive passion
will lose the heaven to which your heart aspires
    "where she, thought dead by many, is alive   70
and seeing her remains

smiles to herself – you alone make her sigh.
  "She begs that you will not
extinguish her renown, which through your tongue
still lives in many lands,   75
but if her eyes were dear to you, bid fame
illuminate the glory of her name."

  Avoid bright sky, green places,
do not approach where there is song or laughter,
my Song, no, my lament;   80
you have no business among cheerful crowds,
desolate widow, dressed in your black weeds.

The lament for Laura. Commentators point to the influence of Dante's *Li occhi dolenti*, lamenting the death of Beatrice (for text and translation, see Barolini/Lansing, 252–53). Teodolinda Barolini notes that lyrics on the death of the beloved, popularized by Petrarch, begin with Dante. *Id.*, 243. Despite the disconsolate congedo, the stanza form – 11 lines with lines 2, 5, 7 and 9 short – imparts a light cadence consistent with the final stanza's mitigation of the poet's grief through knowledge of Laura's beatitude and his continuing mission of praise. **1**: *Love*: as usual, the god. **5–6**: The poet contemplates suicide (again at 62–65). **37–44**: Her invisible soul (the form that animates the body) is now separated from it (the veil). But after the Last Judgment it will be joined in heaven by her body in its glorified form. **55**: *close to truth*: near God, who is eternal truth. **65**: *knot*: of body and soul. **67–77**: Love points out that suicide will bar the poet from heaven, where he is hoping to join her. He needs to go on living because she wants him to maintain her fame through his poetry. **71–72**: She smiles at her corpse as at a memory of childhood; but she sighs for the poet's spiritual danger, like Beatrice in *Inf.* 2.103–16.

269 *Rotta è l'alta colonna e 'l verde lauro*

  Shattered the column and the laurel tree
  that soothed with their cool shade my weary mind;
  I've lost what I can hope no more to find,
  from north to south, eastern to western sea.

Death, you have robbed me of my double treasure
that made me live in joy and walk with pride;
no land or power could make me whole in trade,
nor orient gems nor gold beyond all measure.

And yet if this is destiny's decree
what can I do except possess my soul
in grief, eyes always wet and face bent down?

Ah, how our life appears so beautiful,
but in a morning we lose easily
what took long years and much toil to obtain!

1: *column, laurel*: Cardinal Giovanni Colonna (see *RVF* 266) died three months
after Laura in the great plague of 1348.

270 *Amor, se vuo' ch'i' torni al giogo antico*

Love, if you want me back beneath your yoke,
as you appear to, you must manage first
to pass a strange new test
before I yield to you and bend my neck.
 Go find my dearest treasure in the earth,   5
which, hidden from me, leaves me destitute,
and find the wise pure heart
in which my life once took up residence;
 and if it's true your power is as great
in heaven and the abyss as they report   10
(for I believe among us here the sense
of your power over all
is deeply lodged in every noble soul)
take back from Death the one he took from us,
display your banner once more in her face.   15

Restore the living light to those bright eyes
that guided me, rekindle the soft flame
that's spent, yet all the same

253

sets me afire. (What did it do ablaze?)

    No stag has panted for a spring of water   20
more eagerly than I for her sweet ways,
whose loss now makes me bitter,
a feeling that – I know myself – will grow,
    for in my wild desire the very thought
of her can spark a frenzy and I go   25
where even a faint beaten track gives out
and, wearied in my mind,
chase after what I cannot hope to find.
And so I scorn to come now when you call:
beyond your realm you have no power at all.   30

    Ah, make me hear that soft breath in my ear
the way I still can hear it now within,
which, raised in song, had power
to calm my anger and resentment down,
    leave my tempestuous mind once more serene   35
and cause its dark base fogs to disappear;
it raised my style to soar
where it no longer reaches on its own.
    Strengthen my hope to equal my desire
and help my sense perceive her like my soul;   40
restore a presence I can see and hear,
without which eye and ear
are useless to me and my life is death.
The power you use against me now will fail
with my first love still covered by the earth.   45

    Let me see once again that glance, a sun
upon the ice in which I was encased,
and find you at the pass
my heart crossed over never to return.
    Take up your golden arrows and your bow,   50
and let me hear the twanging I once heard,
which was the sound of words

that taught me everything of love I know.
    Loosen her tongue again, in which were set
the hooks that always caught me with the bait   55
I long for still; and once more hide your snare
in her blond curling hair,
for nothing else entangles my desire,
and spread it with your hands upon the breeze,
bind me with it and I will be well pleased.   60

    No one will free me from that golden snare,
artfully loose, braided, or dressed up high,
nor from the piercing gaze
she turned upon me, sweet and yet severe,
    which night and day kept my desire green,   65
more even than the laurel or the myrtle
both when the woodlands dress
in leaves and shed them, and the fields in grass.
    But since Death snapped the knot with scornful pride
from which I feared release and you cannot,   70
although you search the world, find what you need
to tie a second one,
how does it help you, Love, to press your plot?
What can you do to me? You now have lost:
the arms that made me quake. Your time has passed.   75

    Your weapons were her eyes, from which shot out
arrows alight with an invisible fire
that had no cause to fear
reason, for man has no defense from fate;
    her pensive silence, laughter, gaiety,   80
virtuous behavior, gracious conversation,
words that if understood
would have made base souls gain nobility;
    her angel's countenance, reserved and meek,
for which she heard on all sides such great praise;   85
her sitting and her standing, which would make

one who observed her doubt
which of them more deserved to take the prize.
The hardest heart you conquered with these arms;
with you disarmed now, I am safe from harm.   90

You bind with one knot now and then another
souls that the stars incline to accept your sway,
but only with one tie
could you bind me, for heaven ordained no other.
That one is cut and I have not rejoiced   95
in freedom. "Noble pilgrim," I still cry,
"what heavenly decree
bound me to this life first but loosed you first?
"God, who retrieved you from the world so soon
displayed such eminent virtue to us here   100
only to make our zeal for heaven burn."
I surely do not fear
more wounds from your hand, Love, for now in vain
you bend your bow, whose shots do not go straight;
it lost its power the moment her eyes shut.   105

Death has now freed me, Love, from all your laws,
for she who was my lady went away
to heaven and now my life is sad and free.

The entire canzone is addressed to the god of Love, including the short congedo,
usually addressed to the poem itself. The exception is lines 96–101, addressed to
Laura in heaven.   **1–15**: As in *RVF* 271, Petrarch is apparently tempted to love
another woman after Laura's death; but he tells Love that only by resurrecting
Laura could he gain power over him again.   **17**: *flame*: in her cheeks (S).   **20**:
stag: see Ps. 41.2 (with Laura substituted for God).   **33**: *breath (l'aura)*: her breath
issues in a singing voice, but *l'aura* also means herself through the usual play
on her name.   **36**: *dark base fogs*: his physical passion.   **40–43**: My paraphrase
here simplifies a passage dense with philosophical terms.   **46–47**: Her glance
melted his youthful indifference to love (Ponte; see 23.24–25).   **48–49**: He
met Love in her eyes, where his heart passed over into hers (S).   **50–53**: Her
words were the twang of Love's bow shooting the golden arrows of desire
(Moschetti).   **54–60** *et seq.*: The poet asks Love to recreate images that won his

heart in earlier poems.   **66**: *myrtle, laurel*: evergreens, one sacred to Venus, the other the image of Laura.   **69–75**: *i.e.,* why continue vainly scheming, Love, to entice me with new feminine beauty?   **96**: *pilgrim*: on earth, like all of us

271   *L'ardente nodo ov'io fui d'ora in hora*

Death loosed the burning knot that bound my life
for twenty-one whole years from hour to hour;
anguish like that I'd never felt before
and now I think that no one dies of grief.

But Love, unwilling to let go of me,
had hidden in the grass another snare
and with new tinder lit another fire,
making it hard for me to break away.

And had I not experienced the pain
from first love, I would surely have been caught
and blazed up higher, being less green wood.

So Death has liberated me again,
scattered and snuffed the fire and snapped the knot –
against him strength and cunning are no good.

1–2: Petrarch counts 21 years from the date he met Laura to the date of her death.   **5–8**: He suggests that he was tempted to love another woman after Laura's death (reminiscent of Dante and the *gentile donna* in the *Vita Nova*).   **12**: The pain of first love (see 1–3) convinced him not to fall in love again. Others (Ponte, Chiòrboli) see a reference to the premature death of the second woman. Although the grammar is ambiguous, this reading seems inconsistent with the first tercet.

272   *La vita fugge, et non s'arresta una hora*

Without an hour's halt life runs away
and by forced marches death comes on behind;
the past and present weigh upon my mind,
as does the future, all three troubling me.

Remembering times that were torments my heart,
as does awaiting those to come; to tell
the truth, had I no pity on my soul
by now I'd now be beyond both trains of thought.

What sweetness my sad heart may once have known
comes back to me, but then I also see
my voyage harried by a violent gale;

I see storms even in the port and he
that steered me nods, while mast and rigging fall;
the stars on which I used to gaze are gone.

7–8: If the poet did not fear damnation, he would have committed suicide by now.   **12–13**: *he that steered*: reason.   **14**: *stars*: Laura's eyes.

273 *Che fai? che pensi? che pur dietro guardi*

What are you thinking? Why the backward turn
to look for times that never can come back?
Desolate soul, why do you always stack
more wood upon the fire in which you burn?

The sweet looks and the gentle words that were,
which you depicted and described in full,
have left the earth and you know all too well
that it's too late to look for them down here.

Ah, don't renew the memory killing us
nor dwell on a delusive, shifting thought,
but one that's firm, to reach an end that's sure.

Turn now to heaven since nothing pleases here;
seeing that beauty was most unfortunate
if both in life and death it steals our peace.

As in *RVF* 150, the poet addresses his soul.   **6**: *depicted and described*: in verse.

274 *Datemi pace, o duri miei pensieri*

Leave me in peace, cruel stubborn thoughts of mine!
Do I not bear enough, when Love and Fate
and Death besiege my walls and storm my gate?
Must I find other enemies within?

And you, are you still what you were, my heart,
disloyal to me alone, receiving spies,
willing accomplice of the enemies
so quick and eager to procure my hurt?

Love's coded messages get through to you,
in you Fate flaunts the victory she has won
and Death renews the memory of the stroke

beneath which what is left of me must break.
Stray thoughts are armed with fantasies in you,
and all my ills I blame on you alone.

6: *disloyal . . . alone*: as during Laura's life, when the poet's heart was Love's
accomplice. **9**: *you*: still his heart; *coded messages*: enticements that elude reason
(Ponte). **10, 11**: *victory, stroke*: Laura's death. **13**: *fantasies (errore)*: In his heart
his restless thoughts still turn into hopeless yearnings.

275 *Occhi miei, oscurato è 'l nostro sole*

My eyes, our sun is darkened in broad day –
no, risen up to heaven, where she is shining;
we'll see her there, where she awaits our coming,
saddened, perhaps, because of our delay.

My ears, the sound of her angelic words
is heard by those who better understand.
My feet, your competence does not extend
where she who drew you to her now resides.

Why do you cause me so much heartache then?
It's not my fault you cannot as before
see, hear or find her in her former places.

Blame death instead; or rather praise the One
who at once locks and opens, binds then looses,
and after sorrow gives us joy once more.

6: *those . . . understand*: Heaven's inhabitants understand Laura better than the
world, which was never worthy of her.   13: *locks and opens*: the gates of heaven;
binds then looses: soul to body.   14: *joy*: in heaven.

276 *Poi che la viſta angelica, serena*

Now that her form, angelic and serene,
has vanished suddenly and left my soul,
brushed by dark horror, deeply sorrowful,
I try with words to mitigate my pain.

As he who was its cause and Love know well,
it's only natural I mourn for her
because my heart possessed no other cure
for all the troubles of which life is full;

that comfort you have taken from me, Death.
And you who now have custody and enclose
that beautiful meek face, most happy earth,

where have you left me, blind, disconsolate,
now that my tranquil, sweet and love-filled light
has gone out and no longer strikes my eyes?

5: *he*: Death.

277 *S'Amor novo consiglio non n'apporta*

Unless Love offers counsel not yet heard,
there is no doubt I must exchange my life;
my soul is suffering so from fear and grief,
for my desire still lives and hope is dead.

This leaves my life bewildered and dismayed,
reduced to bitter weeping night and day,
without a rudder on a choppy sea
or dangerous path without a trusted guide.

My guide's an image in my memory,
the real one under ground, or rather high
above me, shining brighter in my heart;

not in my eyes, for this sad mortal veil
shuts out from them the light they long for still
and makes my hair before its time turn white.

1: *counsel*: advice that would free the poet from hopeless desire (S).   2: *exchange my life ('l viver cange)*: i.e., for death.   12: *veil*: the body.

278 *Ne l'età sua più bella et più fiorita*

During her lovely flowering time, her May,
when Love exerts on us his greatest strength,
abandoning in earth her earthly sheath,
my life's breath parted from me suddenly;

alive, she climbed to heaven, lovely and bare;
from there she rules me, holds my thoughts on her.
Why has my last day, the next life's first hour,
not stripped away the mortal husk I wear?

Then as my thoughts ascend with her in flight,
my soul would follow, joyful, free and light,
and I would be relieved of all this pain.

Nothing but harm can come from this delay:
I burden myself more as time goes on.
Ah, to have died three years ago today!

1–8: At first it is sad that Laura died in the flower of her age, but it becomes apparent that she experienced a spiritual spring, shedding her body as a plant bursts from its seed or a butterfly from its chrysalis. **4**: *breath*: perhaps the most poignant use of the Laura/*l'aura* pun. **6**: *holds . . . her (mi sforza)*: *mi fa forza*, i.e., she compels me always to think of her (S); makes me want to join her (Fenzi). **14**: This turns out to be an anniversary poem.

279 *Se lamentar augelli, o verdi fronde*

When I hear birds lamenting or green leaves
stirred by a soft breeze in the summer air
or the low murmuring of limpid waves
between cool shady flowering banks, as here

I sit and write, preoccupied by love,
I see and hear the one earth hides today,
whom heaven once showed us and who, still alive,
responds to my deep sighs from far away:

"Why do you waste away before your time?"
pitying me she asks. "Why does a stream
of sorrow still pour forth from your sad eyes?

"Ah, weep no more for me: dying, my days
became eternal; when I seemed to shut
my eyes, they opened on the inner light."

1–5: Petrarch is back in his rural retreat in Vaucluse, sitting beside the river Sorgue.

280 *Mai non fui in parte ove sì chiar vedessi*

Nowhere I've been could I so clearly see
the sight I long for but can see no more

as here, nor have I elsewhere felt so free
to let a lover's grieving fill the air.

I have not found a valley that possessed
such hidden nooks for sighing as are here,
nor do I think Love ever had a nest
so soft on Cyprus or another shore.

The birds, the boughs, the flowers and grass, the river
all speak of love, as does the breeze's breath,
together urging me to love forever.

But you who call from heaven, most fortunate
soul, by the memory of your early death
beg me to scorn the world and its sweet bait.

1–2: In Vaucluse Petrarch's beloved countryside brings Laura back to him more strongly than he felt her in Italy.   **1**: *clearly see*: in imagination.   **7**: *Cyprus*: isle sacred to Venus.

281 *Quante fiate, al mio dolce ricetto*

How often I've sought out this private place,
fleeing the rest (and myself, as it were),
eyes moistening my chest, sprinkling the grass
and sighs disturbing the surrounding air!

How often, apprehensive and alone,
I've gone down pathways shadowy and dim,
chasing in thought the joy that once was mine,
taken by Death, which makes me call for him!

Sometimes, as if a goddess or a nymph
arising from the Sorgue's transparent depth,
I've seen her take a seat upon the bank;

across a glade I've sometimes seen her walk,
a living woman pressing the grass down,
her face expressing pity for my pain.

The third sonnet on returning to Vaucluse.   **9–14**: Visions of Laura in nature began during her lifetime; see especially *RVF* 129.

282   *Alma felice che sovente torni*

You who return so often, soul in bliss,
to comfort the long sorrow of my night
with eyes that Death has not extinguished but
enhanced with more than mortal loveliness,

what gratitude I feel that you consent,
by coming back, to bring my sad days cheer!
Seeing you, I begin to find once more
your beauty in this place you used to haunt,

where I went singing of you all those years;
now, as you see, instead I go in tears,
tears not for you, no, tears for my own loss.

I find one solace for my anguish here:
when you return I know you as you were,
the way you walk, your voice, your face, your dress.

In *RVF* 282–286 Laura returns in dreams to console and advise the poet.   **8**: *this place*: Vaucluse.

283   *Discolorato ài, Morte, il piú bel volto*

Death, you have quenched what were the loveliest eyes
ever yet seen and blanched the loveliest face;
and from the loveliest knot you have cut loose
the spirit that fervent virtue set ablaze.

One moment, and you took it all from me,
silenced the gentlest accents ever heard
and changed to lamentations all my words;
all I hear rubs me raw and all I see.

My lady does indeed at times return
to comfort me, for pity draws her here;
my life has known no other comfort since.

Could I convey her words, her radiance,
I would inflame with love not only men
but even the heart of a tiger or a bear.

3: *knot*: the living body, animated by the soul.

284 *Sí breve è 'l tempo e 'l penser sí veloce*

The vision comes then fades so suddenly
that gives me back my lady who is gone,
it offers scant narcotic for my pain;
but while I see her nothing troubles me.

My captor Love, who keeps me on this cross,
trembles on seeing her at my soul's door
where she slays me, still seeming as aware,
sweet-looking, gentle-voiced as she was once.

She proudly, like the mistress of the house,
enters and chases with her brightening face
the dismal thoughts from my dark, heavy heart.

My soul, which cannot bear so strong a light,
breathes on a sigh, "I bless the hour, the day
your bright glance opened this path into me!"

5–8: A difficult quatrain. How does the vision of Laura slay the poet (7) – with sweetness, with excess light (12)? Why does Love fear her coming (6) – does it prevent him from tormenting the poet (5)? **13–14**: On the day he first saw Laura her eyes opened the way to his heart that she still travels in death.

285 *Né mai pietosa madre al caro figlio*

Never did loving mother give her son
nor ardent woman her beloved spouse,
when in precarious straits, such good advice
mingled with sighs expressing her concern,

as she, from her high refuge in the skies,
seeing my grievous exile, gives to me.
Returning with her usual sympathy,
a double pity showing in her eyes,

mother's and lover's, she now fears, now burns
with a chaste flame, encourages and warns
what to shun on this journey, what to embrace,

numbers the perils of which life is full
and begs me not to wait to lift my soul;
and only while she speaks do I find peace.

286 *Se quell' aura soave de' sospiri*

Could I portray the gentle sighing breath
of her who was my lady, now in heaven,
although she still appears to live and even
to walk and feel and love as yet on earth,

what passionate desires my words would spark!
Kind and solicitous she comes to me
again, afraid that on the road I may
give out or go astray or else turn back.

She points me straight, and I, who understand
her chaste enticements and her cogent pleas
murmured in low, commiserating tones,

must, as she wishes, take myself in hand,
such sweetness comes to me from what she says,
which would be able to wring tears from stones.

1: "breath (*aura*)": *i.e.*, Laura's murmuring voice (9–11).

287 *Sennuccio mio, benché doglioso et solo*

Sennuccio, though you've left me here alone
grieving, I'm comforted to know how far,
escaping from the body where you were
held prisoner and dead, you now have flown.

You see both north and south celestial poles,
the wandering stars along their twisting route,
and realize how our view from here falls short;
your joy in this leaves me somewhat consoled.

I beg you, though, on reaching the third sphere:
greet Cino, Dante and Guittone for me,
our Franceschino and all that company.

And you can tell my lady of the tears
in which I live in, a beast who roam the woods,
remembering her life, her face, her words.

Sennuccio del Bene, the Florentine poet addressed or mentioned in *RVF* 108,
112, 113 and 144, died in 1349.   **3–7**: Sennuccio's soul is rising through the
spheres of heaven.   **5**: The stars of the northern and southern hemispheres
cannot be seen at the same time from earth.   **6**: *wandering . . . route*: the planets
moving within the zodiac.   **9–14**: *third sphere*: that of Venus, imagined as the
heaven of lovers and love poets.   **10**: Guittone was the leading Italian poet of
the generation before Dante; for Cino, see *RVF* 92.   **11**: *Franceschino*: a minor
poet and a friend of Petrarch.

288 *I' ò pien di sospir' quest'aere tutto*

Filling the air around with sighs, I gaze
from these steep hills upon the gentle plain
where she was born who held my heart within
her hand in flowering and in fruitful days

and now has gone to heaven, so stunning me
by her departure that my eyes, which tire
of vainly searching for her from afar,
leave no place anywhere around them dry.

Among these hills there is no brier or stone,
upon these bankside boughs no green leaf hangs,
no blade of grass is growing in these fields,

no drop of water rises from these springs,
no beast, however wild, roams in these woods
that does not know how bitter is my pain.

2: *hills*: of Vaucluse. **2–3**: *plain . . born*: the plain between Vaucluse and
Avignon, location of the village where Laura was born (see 4.9–13 and note). **4**:
in . . . days: the poet's youth and maturity (S). **12**: For the spring the river
Sorgue issues from, see note to 323.37–38.

289 *L'alma mia fiamma oltra le belle bella*

My quickening flame, fair beyond all the fair,
to whom heaven was so generous and kind,
has now returned – too early, to my mind –
to her own homeland and her proper star.

Now I awaken and I see she spurned
my ardor for my profit, not my loss,
adopting an expression sweet yet cross
to damp the youthful urge with which I burned.

I thank her now for that wise resolution,
that with her gentle yet unyielding gaze
made me, though burning, think of my salvation.

O gracious arts succeeding in their goals,
one working with the tongue and one the eyes:
I for her glory, she to heal my soul!

4: *proper star*: Venus; see note to 287.9–14. **5–8**: This is the poet's first recognition in *Scattered Rhymes* of Laura's motive in resisting him, developed at length in *Tr. Mort.* 2 (see Appendix). **12–14**: Enlightened by Laura's attitude, the poet comes to understand that the fulfillment of his love is to praise her through his art.

290 *Come va 'l mondo! or mi diletta e piace*

How the world goes! I now am pleased no less
by what most galled me once; now I know well
I lost a brief war to find lasting peace
and all that torment was to save my soul.

Always delusive, hope and longing both,
a hundredfold in any lover's case!
Had she who sits in heaven and lies in earth
contented me, it would have been far worse!

But then blind Love combined with my deaf mind
led me so far astray that by main force
I was compelled to go where death held sway.

Blessed be she who set me back on course
for port and with her gentle tact restrained
my guilty passion so I would not die.

11, 14: "For the wages of sin is death. . . ." Rom. 6:23.

291 *Quand'io veggio dal ciel scender l'aurora*

When I see Dawn descending from the sky
with rosy blush and hair of shining gold,
I turn pale, for I'm suddenly assailed
by Love and, "There is Laura now," I sigh.

"Happy Tithonus, knowing when you'll see
your dearest treasure come to you again,
but what of me and my sweet laurel then?
If I would once more see it I must die.

"Your partings cannot be so hard to bear,
for always in the evening she comes home
and is not bothered by your whitened hair.

"Dark are my days and desolate my nights,
bereft of her who carried off my thoughts
and left me nothing of her but her name."

1–2, 3–4, 9–11: Loving the mortal Tithonus, the dawn goddess obtained for him
the gift of immortality; but she forgot to ask for eternal youth, so he grew ever
older. 4: This is one of the few appearances of Laura's name. Petrarch varies
his usual pun: *l'aurora*, the dawn, morphs into *Laura ora*, Laura now.

292 *Gli occhi di ch'io parlai sì caldamente*

The eyes of which I spoke so ardently
once, and the arms, the hands, the feet, the face
that stole me from myself, enchanting me,
and islanded me from the human race,

the curling golden hair that used to gleam,
the lightning flash of that angelic smile
that made a paradise on earth one time
are a small pile of dust that cannot feel.

And still I live, which makes me chafe and grieve,
without the light I loved so ardently,
in a great storm on a dismasted ship.

This is the end of all my songs of love;
the vein of inspiration has run dry
and my lyre can do nothing now but weep.

In an earlier draft of *Scattered Rhymes* this was the last poem in the collection.

293 *S'io avesse pensato che sì care*

If I'd thought people would appreciate
my sighs as they expressed themselves in rhyme,
I would have captured, from their earliest time,
more of them in a style more exquisite.

Now that she's dead, who occupied the height
of every thought, compelling me to speak,
I cannot, with no file for such fine work,
make my dark, grating verses smooth and bright.

All I was aiming to accomplish then
was to afford my troubled heart some ease
by venting somewhat, not to acquire fame.

I wished to weep, not by my tears win praise;
now when I'd gladly please, that noble one
calls me to her, worn out and fallen dumb.

294 *Soleasi nel mio cor star bella et viva*

Alive and lovely, in my heart she stayed
like a great lady in a humble home;
now that she's gone, from mortal I've become
– while she is now a goddess – simply dead.

My soul, despoiled, with all its treasure gone,
and Love, stripped of his light, lost at one stroke,
would make a stone for very pity break
but there is none to tell or write their pain,

for they mourn inwardly, where ears are deaf
save mine; and I am burdened by such grief,
I can do nothing any more but weep.

We are no more than shadow and dust in truth,
our passion nothing else than a blind mouth
and only a delusion all our hope.

295 *Soleano i miei penser' soavemente*

Whispering long went on among my thoughts
as they discussed a favorite theme of theirs:
"Pity is near, and she regrets it's late;
perhaps she speaks of us, or hopes or fears."

Now that the last hours of her final day
have robbed this passing life on earth of her,
she sees and hears from heaven how we are;
no other hope of her remains for me.

Oh noble miracle, oh happy soul
and high rare beauty without parallel,
gone quickly to the place from which she came!

There her good life has earned a crown and palm,
she whom her own great virtue and my wild
passion made bright and famous in the world.

7: *we*: my thoughts and I.

296 *I' mi soglio accusare, et or mi scuso*

I used to blame myself, but now no more;
now I take pride in, even boast about
the honorable jail, the bittersweet
wound that I kept concealed year upon year.

Envious Fates, how soon you snapped in two
the spindle winding up the shining, soft
strand for my snare and broke the golden shaft
that had made death a pleasure strange and new!

For not a man alive during her day
was so in love with life, joy, liberty
he would not go against his natural bent

and choose, instead of singing songs about
another love, to groan for her, live caught
in that snare and from that wound die content.

5–8: The Fates spin the thread of Laura's life, which forms the snare in which the poet is caught. Instead of cutting it, they break the spindle on which it is being wound, apparently indicating her premature death. They also break the golden arrow with which Love wounded him, probably her glance (see 297.7–8, 10–11).

297 *Due gran nemiche inseme erano agiunte*

Two natural enemies once joined together,
Beauty and Chastity, so peacefully
her blessed soul felt no disharmony
since they first lived in her with one another;

but now through Death they have been wrenched apart:
one is the boast and glory of the skies,
the other in earth, which cloaks the splendid eyes
that shot so many love-inspiring darts.

The gentle ways, the wise and modest speech
sprung from a fine mind, glances that would each
transfix my heart (on which the scars still show)

have vanished; since I linger here below,
perhaps I may yet consecrate to fame
with this sad, weary pen her noble name.

6–7: Chastity is an attribute of her soul in heaven, beauty of her body in the ground.

298 *Quand'io mi volgo indietro a mirar gli anni*

When I look back at how the fleeing years
scattered the cares and hopes I long sustained,
put out the fire where cold as ice I burned,
ended my time of trouble-filled repose,

dispelled my faith in love's deceits at last,
and left in pieces what was all to me,
one part in earth, the other in the sky,
the compensation for my losses lost,

I shake myself and find myself so bare
that I am filled with heartache and dismay;
I envy the most miserable condition.

O Fate, O Death, O Fortune, O my star,
and O forever sweet and savage day,
how you have plunged me into desolation!

2–4: *scattered . . . repose*: three parallel images of the poet's ambivalent emotions toward Laura. **5**: *deceits*: illusory hopes. **8**: Laura's presence consoled the poet for his disappointment in love (D). **9**: *shake myself*: returning to reality (S). **13**: *day*: April 6, the date on which the poet met Laura and the date on which she died 21 years later.

299 *Ov'è la fronte, che con picciol cenno*

Where is the forehead now whose smallest sign
would turn my heart toward hope or else toward fear?
Where are the brows beneath which those twin stars
guided my life's course by the way they shone?

Where the good sense, the ready wit she had,
her wise and proper, sweet and modest speech,
the beauties gathered in her, which were such
they made of me for so long what they would?

Where is the noble look that kind face held,
which used to give my weary soul relief
and where my thoughts were written plain to see?

Where is the one whose hand once held my life?
How much is missing from this wretched world
and from my eyes, which never will be dry!

1: *sign*: changing between smooth and creased, indicating her mood
(Chiòrboli). **11**: in the sense that the poet's thoughts depended on the expressions on Laura's face; see 72.60, III.1.

300 *Quanta invidia io ti porto, avara terra*

How much I envy you, rapacious ground
that clasp her snatched from me in your embrace
and hide from me the look of that dear face
where refuge from my troubles could be found!

And how much heaven, which closes shut to keep,
after it gathered in so avidly,
the spirit that those lovely limbs set free,
and yet for others seldom opens up!

How much I envy fortunate souls whose fate
is now to share her holy company,
the joy I longed for every day and night!

And how much Death, who pitiless and cruel,
having snuffed out my life in her, now dwells
within her eyes and does not summon me!

8: *i.e.*, most people go to hell after death, the common medieval view. **14**:
Love used to live in Laura's eyes, whence he shot arrows that killed the poet in
a pleasing way. See, *e.g.*, 270.76–77, 296.7–8. Now Death lives there and though
he has taken the poet's true life, he will not deliver the coup de grâce.

301 *Valle che de' lamenti miei se' piena*

Valley resounding with my cries and groans
and river that my tears swell frequently,
you woodland creatures, you birds roaming free,
fish that the river's grassy banks confine,

clear air, warmed by the sighs that I exhale,
sweet path that finish now so bitterly,
hill that once gladdened and now sadden me
but up which Love by habit leads me still,

I see in you the way you looked before;
ah, not in me – from such a happy life
I have become the home of boundless grief.

From here I viewed my bliss, now come to see
the place where, rising naked to the sky,
she left in earth the beauty that she wore.

1: *Valley*: Vaucluse. **2**: *river*: the Sorgue. **6–7**: The path leads up the hill from
which he used to see Avignon, where Laura lived (see *RVF* 117).

302 *Levommi il mio penser in parte ov'era*

A vision raised me up to where she stayed,
the one I look for on this earth in vain;

among the spirits the third sphere contains
I saw her once more, lovelier, less proud.

She took my hand and said, "Within this sphere
you will rejoin me, if my wish comes true:
I am the one who caused such pain for you,
whose day was done before its evening hour.

"My bliss cannot be grasped by mortal mind.
I only wait for you and something which
you loved, now still below: my lovely veil."

Why did she stop then and release my hand?
For hearing her compassionate chaste speech,
I came close to remaining there as well.

3, 5: The heavens are concentric crystalline spheres in which the planets are embedded. The third is the heaven of Venus, the place of lovers. See 287.9–11; *Par.* 8–9.   **4**: *less proud*: In the poet's visions of Laura after her death, she is more openly affectionate than in life; in *TM* 2 (see Appendix) she will confess that she loved him (implied here in 6 and 10).   **11**: *veil*: her body, which will be reunited with her soul at the Last Judgment.

303 *Amor che meco al buon tempo ti stavi*

Love, in good times you kept me company
along these banks conducive to our thoughts
and strolled, to settle up our old accounts,
in conversation with the river and me;

and you leaves, flowers and grass, shadows and waves, soft breeze,
closed valleys, sunny slopes and towering hills
who were my refuge once in love's travails,
my harbor among often storm-wracked seas;

you wandering denizens of these green woods,
you nymphs, you that the cool and grassy floor
deep in the flowing crystal hides and feeds:

dark are my days that were so bright before,
as dark as Death, their cause; so on this earth
the destiny of each is sealed at birth.

In Vaucluse the poet calls on Love and the features of the landscape to witness his
sorrow (as in *RVF* 301). **2**: the banks of the Sorgue. **9**: birds. **10**: *nymphs*:
See 281.12. **10–11**: *you . . . feeds*: fish.

304 *Mentre che 'l cor dagli amorosi vermi*

As long as passion's worms still made a feast
out of my heart, which burned in passion's flame,
I tracked through lonely and remote terrain
the scattered footprints of a roaming beast.

I had the boldness to complain in song
of Love and her who seemed to me so hard;
my talent, though, was green, my technique crude,
my new thoughts not yet settled: I was young.

That fire is dead, marked by a small stone now;
had it been able over time to grow,
as others' have, until our age was ripe,

then armed with rhymes that I have laid aside,
my words, their style matured now, would have made
rocks break and overcome with sweetness weep.

1–2: Worms and fire appear together in scripture (*e.g.,* Ecclus. 7.19, Is. 66.24)
as the punishment of sinners (De Robertis). For the image of the worm, see
360.69–70. **9**: *fire*: now Laura as well as the poet's youthful passion (S).

305 *Anima bella da quel nodo sciolta*

Beautiful soul released now from the knot
that once was nature's loveliest piece of work,

look down from heaven upon my life turned dark,
my temper gone from joyful to distraught.

The former error of my heart is gone
that turned your gentle look at one time hard,
set against me; now wholly reassured,
turn your gaze this way, hear my sighs again.

Look at the cliff from which the Sorgue is born;
you'll see a lone man on the riverside,
whom sorrow and your memory sustain.

Do not look, though, at where your body lies
and where our love was born, and so avoid
seeing your townsmen's vice that you despised.

1: *knot*: of body and soul, *i.e.* her living body.   5: *error (falsa opinïon)*: the poet's sensual understanding of love (S).   9: The Sorgue gushes up from below a dramatic cliff at Vaucluse.   12–14: The poem suddenly turns political, urging Laura's spirit not to look at Avignon, where she lived and is buried, and attributing to her Petrarch's condemnation of its corruption (see *RVF* 136–38, 259).   12: *body*: understanding Petrarch's "dwelling" (*albergo*) as the earthly dwelling of her soul (S).

306 *Quel sol che mi mostrava il camin destroy*

The sun that lighted for me the straight path
that climbs by glorious steps to heaven's gate,
returning to the highest Sun, has shut
beneath a stone my light, her jail on earth;

bereft, I am reduced to a wild beast
wandering on solitary weary feet
with heavy heart and eyes downcast and wet
across the world, for me a rugged waste.

In this way I go searching all the places
I saw her in; you, Love, who torture me,
my only guide to show which trail to take.

Not finding her, I see her holy traces,
all pointing toward the highest-trending way,
far from the Styx and the Avernian lake.

1: *sun*: Laura   3: *Sun*: God.   3–4: Her body, now in the tomb, was the poet's
light and the prison of her soul.   14: The Styx was a river and marsh in Hades,
to which it was believed there was an entrance at Lake Avernus near Naples.

307 *I' pensava assai destro esser su l'ale*

I thought my wings were strong enough in flight,
the strength not mine but his who makes them spread,
to celebrate in fitting song the knot
Death loosed me from, though Love still keeps me tied.

I found by trial that I was weak and bent
like a slim bough on which a great weight lies.
"No one achieves what heaven does not grant,"
I said. "He courts a fall who mounts too high."

Never could wings of inspiration soar,
much less a weighty style or learned speech,
where Nature flew in weaving my sweet knot.

Love followed, exercising so much care
in beautifying her, I was not fit
even to see her; but my luck was such.

RVF 307–309 deal with the inability of art to convey Laura's unique glory.   2:
his: Love's.   3, 11: *knot*: Laura.   7: *heaven . . . grant*: in forming his natural
disposition (Neri).   10: *weighty style (stil grave)*: a play on words: this is the most
elevated poetic style but in terms of the metaphor weight is opposed to flight (S).

308 *Quella per cui con Sorga ò cangiato Arno*

She for whom I exchanged Arno for Sorgue
and servile riches for free poverty

turned saintly sweetness, which once nourished me,
so bitter that I now grow thin and sag.

Since then in song I've tried in vain to trace
her signal beauties, so the age to come
may cherish her and hold her in esteem;
my verse, though, cannot limn her living face.

But still, one here, two there, I dare to try
to sketch the beauties that were hers alone,
scattered in her like stars across the sky;

but when I come to her immortal soul,
which was on earth a brilliant but brief sun,
my intellect, my art, my courage fail.

1: For Laura's sake he preferred Provence to his native Florence; but as auto-
biography this is fiction (S).   2: He declined employment at the papal court
in Avignon for penurious retirement at Vaucluse (D).   3: *turned*: by dying.

309 *L'alto et novo miracol ch'a' dí nostri*

The startling miracle that in our time
appeared on earth but did not wish to stay,
whom heaven just let us glimpse, then took away
quickly to beautify its starry dome —

this is the theme on which Love bids me speak,
to picture her for those who have not seen;
he freed my tongue and put to work in vain
my time, my talent, paper, pen and ink.

Poetry has not reached perfection yet;
I see it in myself, and everyone
has felt it who has written about love.

Let wise men silently appreciate
truth that surpasses words and sigh, "Ah then,
blessed the eyes that saw her when alive."

An extended version of the ineffability topos: Laura was a miracle beyond the power of language to convey.

310 *Zephiro torna, e 'l bel tempo rimena*

Zephyr returns and ushers in the spring
with opening buds and grass, his tender brood,
Philomel's sobs and Procne's twittering,
the season's little bursts of white and red.

The meadows laugh, the sky once more is clear;
Jove gazes at his daughter with delight;
and love suffuses water, earth and air,
moving all creatures to desire a mate.

But as for me, the heaviest sighs return,
drawn from my heart's recesses by the one
who took with her to heaven the only key;

the singing birds, the fields where new flowers bloom,
fine ladies' gracious manners are for me
nothing but empty wastes where cruel beasts roam.

1: *Zephyr*: the fructifying west wind.   3: Philomel was turned into a nightingale and Procne into a swallow; although their legend is horrific, they appear to function here simply as the singing birds of the idyllic medieval spring.   6: Jupiter is close to his daughter Venus, patron of vernal regeneration, in the springtime sky.   9: *return*: because Laura died in the spring.

311 *Quel rossignuol, che sì soave piagne*

The nightingale that so melodiously
sobs for his young, perhaps, or his dear mate,
floods the dark fields with sweetness and the sky,
as skillful heartfelt notes keep pouring out;

all night it seems his sobs accompany
mine, stirring memories of my own hard fate;
for there is no one I can blame but me,
who thought no goddess subject to Death's might.

How easily he's fooled who feels secure!
Those splendid eyes that put the sun to shame,
who could have thought they would become dark loam?

Now I'm convinced that my cruel destiny
uses this life of tears to make me see
nothing down here that pleases can endure.

1–5: Petrarch echoes *Georg.* 4.511–15, where Orpheus weeps like a nightingale
whose nest has been robbed.   14: Cf. 1.14.

312 *Né per sereno ciel ir vaghe stelle*

No planets moving through a cloudless sky
nor armed knights passing in a cavalcade,
no frisky creatures scampering through a wood
nor pitch-smeared vessels crossing a calm sea,

no news of a good outcome happening
nor love poems in a high and gorgeous style
nor, amid lawns and fountains, beautiful
and modest ladies joining in sweet song

nor anything at all can touch my heart –
she took it to the grave with her, who was
the only light and mirror for my eyes.

Living is drawn-out pain, a weary weight;
I seek the end, to see her once again
whom it were better never to have seen.

1–8: a series of things expected to stir admiration or delight.   11: *mirror*: of
perfection (S); see *Purg.* 15.67–75 (people reflect God's love on each other as
mirrors reflect the sun).   14: *better*: to be spared suffering, as in 264.38–40.

313 *Passato è 'l tempo omai, lasso, che tanto*

Gone is the time and will not come again,
in which I lived refreshed in the fire's heat;
gone is the one who made me weep and write,
though she has left me with the tears and pen.

Gone now, that sainted face will not come back,
but going, left her eyes fixed in my heart –
mine once, for he was eager to depart,
following her who wrapped him in her cloak.

She took him underground and to the skies
where now she triumphs in the laurel crown
that her unconquered chastity has won.

If only I could leave behind these sighs,
freed from what holds me here, this mortal veil,
to be with them among the blessed souls!

2: *fire*: of his passion.   **7–8**: For the poet's heart leaving him to go to his lady, see *RVF* 22 and note.   **8**: *cloak*: Laura's body, a variant on the more common image of the mortal veil in line 12.   **9**: In the grave are his heart's memories of her beauty; in heaven his heart's devotion to her soul.   **14**: *them*: Laura and his heart.

314 *Mente mia, che presage de' tuoi damni*

Anxious already, you could dimly sense
your future loss, my mind, in the glad time,
intently searching that loved countenance
for comfort in the suffering to come;

from her words, her expression, her whole air
of pity tinged with sorrow, new to me,
you might have said, had you been more aware,
"The years of my contentment end today."

My wretched soul, what sweetness we felt then;
we burned so in that moment, seeing there
the eyes that I would never see again;

and leaving, I committed to their care
as though to faithful friends my noblest part:
my loving thoughts and my devoted heart.

Another version of Petrarch's last meeting with Laura before he left for Italy,
already evoked in *RVF* 249–50.   **2**: *glad time*: when she was still alive.   **6**:
pity . . . sorrow: She is worried about what will become of him when she is gone.
See *TM 2*, 73–75 (in Appendix).

315   *Tutta la mia fiorita et verde etade*

I now was past my green and flowering age;
the fire that burned my heart was cooling off
as I approached the point from which our life
begins to slope down toward its final stage.

Now my dear enemy began to see
her wariness could be relaxed somewhat
and her unswerving virtue, become sweet,
turned my old bitter suffering to joy.

The time was coming when Love makes his peace
with Chastity and lovers finally may
sit down together, talking candidly.

Then Death grew envious of my happiness,
rather my hope, and like an enemy
in arms leaped out of ambush on the way.

This poem and the next two form a group in which the poet, his passion cool-
ing in middle age, is on the verge of a satisfactory platonic relationship with
Laura, when her death intervenes. Compare the account in Petrarch's Letter to
Posterity: "In my youth I suffered from a love that was overwhelming yet unique

and honorable. I would perhaps have suffered from it longer except that when the fire was already cooling, a premature but opportune death extinguished it." *Sen.*18.1.   **9–11**: Petrarch stages such a frank discussion in *TM2*, where Laura's spirit visits the poet after her death and confesses her love for him, which her virtue required her to conceal (see Appendix).

316   *Tempo era omai da trovar pace o triegua*

The time had come to end my war with peace
and I was on the right track, so it seemed,
until my glad steps were turned back by him
who equalizes all disparities;

for as a mist disperses in the wind,
she whose eyes guided me upon my road
– whom I must follow now in thought instead –
passed through life swiftly, leaving it behind.

She had not long to wait, age and grey hair
so changing me she need have had no fear
of how I'd speak to her about my old

troubles, for with chaste sighs I would have told
of my long suffering, which she now can see
from heaven, I'm sure, and grieves for it with me.

1: *war*: the poet's struggles in love.   **3**: *him*: Death.   **9–13**: See 12.9–14, where the poet already took comfort in a time when this might happen.

317   *Tranquillo porto avea mostrato Amore*

Love had at last revealed a tranquil harbor,
out of my endless tempest's roiling surge,
during the years when prudent mature age
doffs youthful vices, donning virtue and honor.

Now the deep loyalty of my heart shone through
and her eyes held a troubled look no longer.
Ah Death, so quick to break off with cruel fingers
the fruit of long years in an hour or two!

Had she lived, we'd have come to a time when,
speaking in her chaste ear, I could lay down
the old weight of my sweet thoughts, at last heard.

and she perhaps would have replied to me,
while sighing, with some gentle holy word,
both of our faces lined, our hair gone gray.

9–14: See note to 316.9–13.

318 *Al cader d'una pianta che si svelse*

After one tree was rooted up and fell
as if an axe or wind had brought it down,
spreading its airborne leaves upon the soil,
exposing lifeless pale roots to the sun,

I saw a tree that Love chose as the goal
of my thoughts and the Muses as my theme;
as ivy creeps about a trunk or wall,
it bound my heart and made itself a home.

The living laurel where my soaring thoughts
once made their nest along with my warm sighs
that never stirred a leaf on any bough,

transplanted in the sky, left roots below
in that loyal home, where there's one who calls out
sadly, and there is no one who replies.

Per Santagata (contra the majority), the tree of the first quatrain is not the laurel but another tree whose fall reminds the poet of Laura's death. (If the first tree is Laura, the second quatrain could suggest she only became his love and the theme of his poetry after her death.)   **5**: *I saw*: in memory (S).

319 *I dì miei più leggier' che nesun cervo*

Swifter than deer my days have all sped by
like shadows, and the good times could be missed
by blinking, a few cloudless hours at best,
sweet and yet bitter in my memory.

Ah world, unstable arrogant and vain,
one must be blind to trust in you at all;
in you my heart was carried off, and still
is held by one now earth, not flesh and bone.

Her spirit, though, the better part of her,
living forever in the height of sky,
enchants me with her beauties all the more;

and I go lost in thought, my hair grown gray:
what is she is like today, where does she dwell,
what would it be to see her lovely veil.

4: *bitter*: because brief and rare.   7: *in you . . . off*: the poet's heart left him to
go to Laura, who was part of the passing world.   14: *veil*: her once beautiful
mortal part (like 311.11, a reflection of the unflinching preoccupation of the
time with death and decay).

320 *Sento l'aura mia anticha, e i dolci colli*

Once more I feel my old breeze; the sweet hills
appear before me where the light was born
that kept my eyes, while it was heaven's will,
eager and glad, and now wet and forlorn.

O fleeting hopes, mad thoughts of yesterday!
The grass bereaved, the stream a turbid flood;
the nest is cold and empty where she lay
and I live on who wished to lie here dead,

hoping at last the soft prints of her feet
and her eyes, which had made my heart ignite,
would bring relief from my long suffering.

I served a cruel and stingy lord, I learn:
while my fire was in front of me, I burned
and now I mourn its ashes scattering.

The poet returns from Italy to Provence, with its memories of Laura, and reflects
on the sorrowful change since he saw her here.   1–4: The sweet hills appear
to refer to those of her birthplace, between Avignon and Vaucluse (See *RVF*
4).   1: *breeze (l'aura)*: the usual pun.   2: *light*: Laura.   5–11: The landscape
is now Vaucluse, where he recalls the scene of *RVF* 126.   6–7: In 126.1–7 the
grass where she lounged was full of flowers and the waters of the Sorgue were
clear.   7–11: In 126.27–39 he wanted to be buried in this place so that her foot-
steps on his grave and her tears for him might bring him some comfort.   12:
lord: Love.   13: *fire*: Laura.

321 *È questo 'l nido in che la mia fenice*

Is this the nest in which my phoenix put
her plumes on, crimson glowing against gold,
beneath whose sheltering wings my heart was held
and who draws words and sighs from it as yet?

O first root of my welcome malady,
where is your face, from which the radiance came
that kept me happy while I lived in flames?
Unique on earth, in heaven you now have joy.

Here you have left me wretched and alone,
needing to come in sorrow to the ground
that as a shrine to you I venerate,

seeing night darkening on the hills around,
from which you soared to heaven in your last flight
and where your eyes once caused the day to dawn.

This continues the theme of *RVF* 320; the geographical references are elastic, sliding among Laura's birthplace, Avignon and perhaps Vaucluse.   **1–4**: For Laura as the phoenix, see *RVF* 185, the image continued in lines 8 and 13.   **1**: *nest*: Laura's birthplace; contrast 320.7.   **6**: *radiance*: of her glance.

322 *Mai non vedranno le mie luci asciutte*

> Never with dry eyes or a tranquil mind
> will I review the verses that you wrote,
> in which your warm affection sparkles yet
> and which were crafted by a generous hand.
>
> Spirit unvanquished in the strife of earth
> who now from heaven infuse such sweetness still,
> leading my rhymes that strayed back to the style
> from which they have been kept apart by Death,
>
> I hoped to show you work of greater weight
> among my tender leaves. What star so cruel
> it envied, noble friend, our fellowship?
>
> Who hides you prematurely from my sight,
> you who are in my heart and on my lips?
> But soft sighs in memoriam calm my soul.

Many years after the death in 1341 of his good friend Giacomo Colonna, Bishop of Lombez, Petrarch re-reads a sonnet from the bishop congratulating him on being crowned poet laureate earlier the same year. Moved, he writes this tribute to his friend.   **7–8**: The testament of friendship restores to his style the sweetness it lost at Laura's death (Ponchiroli).   **9–10**: The tender leaves allude to the laurel crown on which he was being congratulated for poetry then recent (S). He noted in a letter mourning the bishop's death (*Fam.* 4.13) that he had wanted to present his friend an early draft of his Latin epic *Africa*.

323 *Standomi un giorno solo a la fenestra*

> One day I stood alone before my window,
> from which I saw so many marvelous sights

that merely looking almost left me dazed.
   A graceful doe appeared upon the right
with a maiden's face that would have made Jove blaze,   5
chased by two hounds, one black, the other white;
   those two began to bite
the noble creature's flanks so savagely
that as I watched they drove her to the pass
where, shut within a tomb,   10
beauty was snuffed by death before its time.
I sighed to see her fate, so pitiless.

   And then I saw a ship on the high seas
with silken rigging and a golden sail,
fashioned of ivory and of ebony,   15
   bearing a cargo of precious merchandise.
The sky deep blue without a cloudy veil,
the breeze was gentle over a calm sea;
   then a storm suddenly
came from the east and stirred up winds and tides   20
so much they dashed the ship against a reef.
Oh what abysmal grief!
Sunk in an hour, lost irretrievably,
the peerless treasure that a small space hides.

   A straight young laurel tree was flourishing   25
(one of the trees, it seemed, of paradise)
within a tender grove, its sacred boughs
   enclosing shade from which came such sweet song
of gaily colored birds and other joys,
my senses felt the world begin to fade.   30
   And then before my eyes
the whole sky altered, growing dark with cloud;
a bolt of lightning struck the happy tree
and instantaneously
uprooted it; my life was saddened then   35
for there will never be such shade again.

A crystal spring gushed up in that same wood
below a cliff, and from it cool and sweet
water spread outward, softly murmuring;
    no countrymen or shepherds ever strayed   40
as far as that secluded shady seat,
but nymphs and muses matched the sound in song.
    While I sat marveling,
lost in the sweetness of that harmony
and spectacle, I saw the earth split wide   45
and swallow up the spring
and all around, which still brings grief to me;
the memory alone leaves me dismayed.

    Seeing a wondrous phoenix, its wings dressed
in crimson and its head in gold, fly through   50
the wood, alone and proud, I thought at first
    I saw a heavenly immortal shape,
until it reached the laurel, roots up-thrust,
and the clear spring the earth had swallowed up.
    Everything flies to its end;   55
seeing the leaves lie scattered on the ground,
the splintered trunk, the living water dry,
as if in scorn it turned
its beak against itself and instantly
vanished; with love and pity my heart burned.   60

    Finally I saw amid the flowers and grass
a graceful lady walking deep in thought
(the memory makes me burn and tremble now),
    humble herself but proud toward Love. The dress
she wore was a pure and dazzling white,   65
yet woven so it seemed both gold and snow;
    but I could see her head
appeared to be enclosed in a dark cloud.
A small snake pierced her heel then as she walked;
and as a flower when plucked   70

wilts, she departed, happy and secure.
Ah, nothing in this world but tears endures!

My song, you well may say,
"Now these six visions have, in passing by,
stirred in my lord a sweet desire to die." 75

The poet sees six visions that allegorically represent the death of Laura and the loss that brings. The first two visions are independent and straightforward; the remaining four, centered on the landscape of Vaucluse, are related and are less easy to interpret. **6–9**: *hounds*: a metaphor for time (night and day). **9**: *pass*: that leads to death, a frequent image of Petrarch's. **14–15**: The ship's colors are Laura's. **19–20**: The storm from the East is the great plague of 1348, which carried off between a third and half of Europe, including Laura. **24**: *small space*: i.e., the grave. **25–36**: The events that take place in Vaucluse have something of the impossible about them. Because the laurel was supposed to be immune to lightning, the vision suggests that Laura's death violated nature. **26**: *sacred*: to Apollo and the Muses. **26**: *paradise*: Eden. **37–48**: The spring is the source of the River Sorgue, which surges up from beneath a great cliff at Vaucluse. The image of muses harmonizing with the river's melody suggests that the spring is being conflated with Helicon, the Muses' spring in mythology. This vision thus symbolizes not so much Laura's death as a result of it, his loss of poetic inspiration. **49–60**: The mythological phoenix went up in flames and was reborn repeatedly; here its suicide is terminal and violates (mythical) nature. In Nos. 185 and 321 the phoenix was Laura; here, though the bird bears her traits, it is better to think of it as the image of poetry inspired by Laura, which the poet thought immortal, but is impotent before death (S). Otherwise Laura as phoenix would be committing suicide on seeing the death of herself as laurel. **61–72**: Laura appears (finally as a human) as Eurydice, fatally bitten by a snake while walking through a meadow (a natural death). *Metam.* 10.8–10. Like Orpheus, Petrarch cannot bring her back with his art; but Laura's future in heaven is assured. **66**: Laura's colors again. **71**: *secure*: in hope of heaven; i.e., the final vision ends more consolingly. **75**: *lord*: the poet, who wants to be with Laura.

324 *Amor, quando fioria*

   Love, when my hope still flowered
of recompense for my fidelity,
she who would grant the gift was snatched from me.

   Ah, death devoid of pity, ah, cruel life!
One thrust me deep in grief,
extinguishing my hope before it grew;
   the other holds me here against my will,
unable to pursue
her footprints, for it will not let me go.
   Yet, as she ever was,
my lady's seated in my heart's core still
and sees my life herself for what it is.

2: At this point in the collection, the recompense would appear to be the type
of relationship described in *RVF* 315–317.

325 *Tacer non posso, et temo non adopre*

   I must speak but I fear my tongue may not
effectuate the purpose in my heart,
which only wants to praise
its lady, who is listening from heaven.
   How can I, Love, unless you tutor me,   5
find mortal words to equal her divine
beauty and all the merits
hidden by her profound humility?
   In the rich prison from which now she's free
her noble soul had not remained for long,   10
that April day when first I saw her face;
and then I ran at once,
it being both the year's and my life's spring,
to gather wildflowers in the fields about,
hoping to please her eyes when all decked out.   15

The walls were alabaster, the roof gold,
the door was ivory and the windows sapphire;
these last caused the first sigh
to gain my heart, and will my final one.
  Love's messengers rode out from them, all armed   20
with flaming arrows; I can see them still,
advancing laurel-crowned,
and quake today as if they rode again.
  Inside there could be seen a lofty throne
made of a square-cut diamond with no flaw,   25
on which the beautiful lady sat alone;
before it was a crystal
column, and every thought inscribed within
would shine through on it so transparently
it brought me joy and often made me sigh.   30

  I saw confronting me the sharp and shining
weapons and their victorious green standard
which win the field against
Apollo, Jove and Mars and Polyphemus,
  where weeping is forever fresh and green.   35
Unable to find help, I let myself
be led away, a captive,
and now I see no hope of an escape.
  But as while you are weeping you may still
see something that attracts your eyes and heart,   40
the one who even now imprisons me
stood on a balcony,
the singular perfection of her time;
and with great longing I began to gaze,
forgetful of myself and all my woes.   45

  I was on earth, my heart in paradise,
distractions sunk in sweet oblivion,
my body, I could sense,
so filled with wonder it had turned to stone.

And then a lady, quick and confident,   50
ancient in years but youthful in her face,
seeing me so intent
from the expression of my brow and eyes,
    said to me, "Listen now to my advice,
for I have powers you do not understand: 55
I bring men in an instant sorrow or joy,
swifter than any wind,
and govern all the changing world you see.
Keep staring like an eagle at that sun
and meanwhile let your ears drink my words in.   60

  "The day when she was born, the stars that cause
among you mortals favorable effects
occupied places high
in heaven and faced each other lovingly.
    "Venus and Jupiter in benign aspect   65
were dominant in high auspicious stations,
and the cruel baleful planets
almost dispersed from the entire sky.
    "The sun had never dawned on such a day:
the earth and air rejoiced and in the sea   70
and rivers all the waters were at peace.
Among such favoring stars
there was a distant cloud that troubled me;
I am afraid it will dissolve in tears
if pity does not change the heavens' course.   75

    "Arrived amid the low life of this world,
which truthfully did not deserve her birth,
so wondrous to behold,
saintly and sweet already in first youth,
    "she seemed a gleaming pearl set in pure gold.   80
Crawling at first and then with tottering steps,
she touched the trees with green,
turned water clear and softened earth and stone;

296

"her palms and soles made grass grow fresh and lush
and her eyes caused the fields to burst with bloom;   85
she quieted the winds and rising storms
with words not yet quite formed
lisped by a tongue that scarcely had been weaned.
So to the blind deaf world these signs made clear
how much the light of heaven shone in her.   90

    "And when, her virtue growing with her years,
she reached her third age, her full flowering time,
beauty and grace like hers
the sun, I think, till then had never seen,
    "her eyes alight with innocence and joy,   95
and her speech sweet and healthful for the soul.
All tongues are dumb to say
of her what only you appreciate.
    "Celestial radiance makes her face too bright
for you to let your vision linger there;   100
and the great beauty of her earthly jail
so fills your heart with fire,
no other ever burned with sweeter pain.
But her abrupt departure will, I fear,
make life seem bitter to you all too soon."   105

    That said, once more to the revolving wheel
on which she spins our mortal thread she turned,
the sad and certain prophet of my loss:
for in a few short years
she who now makes me long to die, my song,   110
was snuffed before her time by Death most cruel,
who could find none more beautiful to kill.

9: *prison*: Petrarch's usual image for the body; but in the following stanza, what
seems an abrupt transition is an allegorical description of the prison.   **13**: The
poet met Laura in April 1327, when he was 23.   **14–15**: *wildflowers*: his early
poetry.   **16–17**: the features of the prison (see 9): *roof*: her hair; *walls*: her body;
door: her teeth; *windows*: her eyes.   **20**: *messengers*: glances inflaming love.   **22**:

The messengers are already victorious as they approach, hence crowned with laurel (also her emblem).   **26**: *lady*: her soul (see 10).   **28**: *column*: her forehead, on which her thoughts can be read because of her open nature.   **31–32**: *sharp . . . standard*: What seems an abrupt transition is a reference to Love's armed messengers of 20–23; the standard is the laurel.   **34**: all four conquered by love.   **46–49**: The poet's ecstasy repeats the experience of 126.56–65.   **50**: *lady*: Fortune, whom Petrarch regards as an agent of providence (as Dante does in *Inf.* 7).   **59**: *eagle*: believed to stare at the sun; see 19.1 and note; *sun*: Laura.   **61**: *stars*: planets ("wandering stars").   **67**: Mars and Saturn, considered unfavorable.   **73**: premonition of Laura's death.   **74–75**: Fortune is speaking to the poet before Laura's death.   **81–88**: Laura is paralleled with Jesus, stilling the storm (Luke 8:24) and performing other miracles that revivify earth – all while a toddler, no less.   **107–08**: Petrarch turns Fortune into one of the Fates; her wheel, the common medieval symbol of life's instability, becomes the wheel on which the thread of mortal life is spun.   **106–13**: In this largely narrative canzone, the congedo, in which the poet sends his song into the world, has been transformed into part of the story.

326   *Or ài fatto l'extremo di tua possa*

Now you have shown the utmost of your power,
cruel Death, and made Love's kingdom destitute;
now you have put the light of beauty out
and in a narrow grave interred its flower;

you have despoiled our age of what was once
its jewel, by which its honor was held high.
But merit and repute, which never die,
are not within your power; keep the bare bones,

for heaven now has the rest and fills with joy
to see her splendor, like a lovelier sun,
while good souls here will not forget her name.

New angel, now triumphant in the sky,
let pity for me up there overcome
your heart as here your beauty conquered mine.

327 *L'aura et l'odore e 'l refrigerio et l'ombra*

Gone now, the breath, the scent, the cooling shade
the laurel gave me and its thriving sight,
my weary life's refreshment and its light;
he took them who depopulates the world.

As the moon's shadow makes the sun go dark
for us, my light is gone from me; I must
ask Death himself for help against Death's worst,
the thoughts Love floods me with have turned so black.

My Lady, after sleeping a brief while,
among the blessed ones you wake again
where the soul plunges deep in the divine;

and if my rhymes have any power at all,
here among noble minds the memory
of your name will be kept eternally.

4: *he*: Death – this verse was terribly true in the great plague of 1348, in which
Laura died.   **7–8**: The poet's grief makes him ask Death to take him as well.   **9**:
"Our birth is but a sleep and a forgetting" (Wordsworth).

328 *L'ultimo, lasso, de' miei giorni allegri*

The last of all my happy days had come,
of which in this brief life I've seen but few,
and it had turned my heart to melting snow,
perhaps a presage of this sad dark time.

I felt myself grow numb in body and mind
as from malarial fever coming on,
but at the time I little knew how soon
my incomplete contentment was to end.

Her eyes, now bright in heaven with the divine
glory from which eternal life rains down,
leaving my own here, now forlorn and poor,

spoke with a chaste gleam I'd not seen to mine:
"Friends, do not be perturbed; though nevermore
on this earth, we shall meet again elsewhere."

This sonnet and the next two recall the poet's last meeting with Laura, already
the subject of *RVF* 249, 250 and 314; the theme will be developed in full detail
in the following canzone, *RVF* 331.   **8**: *incomplete*: because she did not return
his love.   **13–14**: Here and in *RVF* 330 he can read her eyes; in *RVF* 329 and
331 he laments not being able to.

329 *O giorno, o hora, o ultimo momento*

O day, O hour, O moment – our last one,
the stars conspiring to impoverish me!
Confiding glance, what did you wish to say
as I left, never to feel glad again?

My loss is all too clear now in my mind,
but then I thought (oh idle, baseless thought!)
by leaving I would lose not all, but part.
How many hopes are scattered by the wind!

For heaven had decreed the opposite:
the light on which I lived would be put out,
as her look, sweet and bitter both, revealed;

but there was then before my eyes a veil
preventing me from seeing what I saw
to make the sudden shock of sorrow raw.

See note to *RVF* 328.   **5**: *now*: after Laura's death.   **7**: *i.e.*, he did not think
he was saying goodbye forever.

330 *Quel vago, dolce, caro, honesto sguardo*

That lovely glance, so sweet, so chaste, so dear,
appeared to say, "Take of me what you can,

for you will never see this face again,
once with reluctant steps you go from here."

My mind, swift as a leopard you may be,
but not in making out your coming woes.
How could you not have noticed in her eyes
what you see now, when it's destroying me?

Silently and while sparkling more than ever,
they told mine, "Friendly lights that in a sweet
way for so long a time made us your mirror,

"heaven awaits us, you will think too soon;
but he who bound us here dissolves the knot
and yet to grieve you wants you to live on."

See note to *RVF* 328.   **1**: *glance*: see 329.3.   **10**: *lights*: the poet's eyes.   **13**:
knot: that ties soul to body.   **14**: *grieve*: God imposes a trial on the poet by
requiring him to live after Laura's death.

331 *Solea da la fontana di mia vita*

I used to leave the spring that fed my life
and travel widely across lands and seas,
following not my wishes but my star;
    always I went (Love in this helping me,
who saw the bitterness of those exiles),   5
feeding my heart on hope and memory.
    But now I raise my hands and I lay down
my arms before my cruel and violent fortune,
which has deprived me of a hope so sweet.
Memory alone remains,   10
so my desire must feed on that alone;
and weak with hunger now, my soul grows faint.

    A courier on the road, for lack of food
will of necessity slow down his pace

as the strength ebbs that has propelled his speed. 15
    So in my weary life, which lacks the precious
nourishment eaten up by him who leaves
all the world naked and my poor heart sad,
    sweet turns more bitter now from hour to hour,
pleasure more irksome; I both hope and fear 20
I will not see this short road to its end.
Mist or dust in the wind,
to be no more a pilgrim here I flee;
so be it, if that is my destiny.

    For me this mortal life has held no joys 25
(as Love, with whom I talk about it, knows)
except for her who was its light and mine;
    since dying here, she was reborn in heaven,
that spirit by whom I lived, to follow her
(were it allowed) has been my great desire. 30
    But always I come back to this regret:
I was unable to foresee my future,
which on that day Love showed me in her eyes,
counseling otherwise;
for many of those who died disconsolate 35
would earlier have ended fortunate.

    There in the eyes where my heart used to dwell
until my cruel fate, envious of its joy,
evicted it from such a splendid home,
    Love's own hand had inscribed for me to see 40
in pitying characters what would become
of my long yearning in a little while.
    Lovely and sweet it would have been to die
if when I died my life did not as well
because the noblest part of me would last. 45
Death has dispersed my hope
and now a little earth hides all my best,
yet I live; when I think of this I weep.

If my poor intellect had stayed with me
in time of need and not been pulled instead   50
by other longings, leading it astray,
    upon my lady's brow I might have read:
"This is the end of all your happiness
and the beginning of your deep distress."
    If I had understood this, gently freed   55
while in her presence from my mortal veil,
this flesh with all its trouble and its weight,
I could have gone before
to see a throne in heaven prepared for her;
now I will follow her with hair gone white.   60

    Song, if you find a man at peace in love,
say, "Die in happy days,
for timely death is a refuge, not a grief;
he who can die well should not seek delay."

1–3: The poet used to leave Laura to make his frequent trips from Provence into
Italy.   17: *nourishment*: hope; *him*: Death; see note to 327.4.   27: *its light*: of
mortal life in general.   31–60: The final meeting once more: by showing the
poet Laura's coming death in her eyes, Love was counseling him to die of grief
on the spot (55–57) instead of traveling to Italy, which would have precluded his
present misery.   36: *heart . . . dwell*: See III.1.   39: *evicted*: by her death.   44:
my life: Laura.   49–51: *i.e.*, had he not been distracted by her beauty (S).

332 *Mia benigna fortuna e 'l viver lieto*

With fortune kind to me, my life was happy;
but bright days giving way to quiet nights,
my sighs that quivered softly and the style
that sounded sweetly in my verse and rhymes
were suddenly reduced to grief and tears,   5
making me hate my life and long for death.

Cruel, premature, inexorable Death,
you give me reason never to be happy

but spend all my remaining life in tears,
with darkened days and brokenhearted nights.   10
My heavy sighs cannot be caught in rhymes
and my harsh suffering defeats all style.

What has it come to now, my amorous style?
To speak of anguish, to discourse on death.
Where have my verses gone now, where my rhymes   15
that noble hearts heard, troubled and yet happy,
the talk of love that whiled away the nights?
Now I can only think and speak of tears.

Mixed with desire, so sweet to me were tears
the sweetness of them flavored all sharp style   20
and kept me thinking of her through the nights;
tears are more bitter to me now than death,
who hope no more for that glance, chaste and happy,
the noble subject of my humble rhymes.

Love set a shining target for my rhymes   25
in fine eyes once and sets it now in tears,
reminding me in sorrow I was happy;
so with my sentiments I change my style,
and I am begging you again, pale Death:
deliver me from these tormented nights.   30

Sleep keeps its distance now from my cruel nights
and the old harmony from my hoarse rhymes,
which cannot speak of anything but death,
so that my singing has been changed to tears.
Love's realm has not so changeable a style,   35
which is as sad now as it once was happy.

No one who ever lived has felt more happy,
and no one now lives sadder days and nights;
this doubled sorrow calls for doubled style,
which draws forth from my heart tear-sodden rhymes.   40

I lived on hope, now only live on tears,
nor against Death have any hope but Death.

Death killed me and now nothing else but Death
can let me see once more that face, so happy,
that made a pleasure of my sighs and tears,   45
the showers and sweet breezes of my nights,
when I was weaving lofty thoughts in rhymes
while Love lent wings to lift my feeble style.

I wish I'd mastered such a piteous style
that I could snatch my Laura back from Death   50
as Orpheus his Eurydice with no rhymes;
then would my life be more than ever happy!
But failing that, one of these anguished nights
may soon, I hope, close these two springs of tears.

For many years, Love, I've been shedding tears   55
over my grievous loss in sorrowing style,
nor do I hope from you less savage nights;
and that has caused me to petition Death
to take me out of here and make me happy
where she is whom I sing and weep in rhymes.   60

Should they rise high enough, my weary rhymes,
to reach her, freed from passions now and tears
and with her beauties making heaven happy,
she'll recognize the changes in the style
that she perhaps found pleasing before Death   65
brought her bright day and darkened all my nights.

All you who sigh in hope of better nights,
who hear about or write of Love in rhymes,
pray my petition may be heard by Death,
refuge from miseries and end of tears: 70
to change for once his usual deaf style
that saddens men, so he could make me happy.

Happy in only one or a few nights;
so in a harsh style and tormented rhymes
I pray that Death will terminate my tears.   75

Petrarch says in line 55 that he has wept for Laura for many years, assigning
a late date to this poem. **1–4**: After Laura's death the poet's sufferings from
unrequited love recorded earlier in the sequence are remembered as joys, and
his lachrymose verses as glad songs. **19**: *desire*: to see her. **39**: *doubled style*: A
normal sestina would have ended with the previous stanza. Petrarch goes on to
double the form with the same rhyme-words. **42–43**: The only remedy for
Laura's death is his own (see 327.7, 300.12–14 and notes). **49–51**: Orpheus's
song moved the king and queen of the underworld to pity and they allowed
him to bring his wife Eurydice back to the world of the living. **51**: *with no
rhymes*: ancient poetry was not rhymed; (perhaps also a reference to sestina
form? S). **66**: Eternal day contrasts with successive nights in time. **71–72**:
Death's age-old policy is not to listen to people. Ordinarily they are begging
him not to come; now he can make the poet happy by changing the policy this
one time and coming when called. **73**: *you*: lovers.

333 *Ite, rime dolente, al duro sasso*

Go to the hard stone, my poor sorrowing rhyme,
that hides my precious treasure in the ground;
call on her there – from heaven she will respond
though her remains lie deep in the dark tomb.

Tell her I tire of living and would be done
with navigating through these treacherous waves;
but that I gather up her scattered leaves
and follow step by step where she has gone,

speaking of none but her, alive and dead
(no, living still, immortal now indeed),
so that the world may know and cherish her.

May she be watching for my final day,
so close now; may she come to summon me
and draw me up to be as she is there.

7: *leaves*: with reference to Laura/laurel, the leaves here being his recollections of her, the scattered rhymes of this collection.   **12–14**: Laura becomes the poet's patron saint, as Beatrice becomes Dante's in *Inf.* 2.

334 *S'onesto amor pò meritar mercede*

If chaste love can be worthy of reward
and pity's power endures, I'm sure to gain
the prize; my faithfulness outshines the sun,
obvious to my lady and the world.

She long mistrusted me but now has found
that what I want – she need no longer guess –
is what I always wanted; then my face
or words she read, but now my heart and mind.

I hope that even in heaven she may grieve
for all my sighs, as it seems she reveals
with pitying looks when she returns to me;

I hope she comes to meet me when I leave
this mortal wrapping, with those kindred souls
who are true friends of Christ and chastity.

4: The world knows his faithfulness through his poems.   **6–7**: *what I want . . . always wanted*: Laura mistrusted his love because she understood its sexual component; his current assertion that it never had one is inconsistent with many poems in Part One.   **11**: *returns*: in dreams.

335 *Vidi fra mille donne una già tale*

Once among many ladies I saw one
who stormed my heart with sudden love-struck fear,
observing – not imagining – she appeared
like a celestial spirit who'd come down.

She had no thought of earthly, passing things,
like one whom heaven and nothing else concerned.
My soul, which often froze for her and burned,
wishing to follow her, spread both its wings.

She flew too high, though, for my earth-bound weight
and shortly after disappeared from view;
remembering, I am numb and frozen still.

O windows shining once with inner light,
where he who saddens all but very few
found entrance to a frame so beautiful!

7: The typical alternation of love and fear echoes line 2.   **12–14**: *windows*:
her eyes; *he*: Death. The light goes out of a person's eyes at death (Chiòrboli).
Petrarch seems to have remembered the phrase "death enters through the win-
dows" from Jeremiah 9:21.

336 *Tornami a mente, anzi v'è dentro, quella*

She comes to mind (rather is always there,
for Lethe could not cause me to forget)
as in her flowering youth, the year we met,
resplendent in the radiance of her star.

I see her with that innocent sweet look,
so beautiful and so reserved and shy.
"It's really her, she's still alive!" I cry,
and beg that she will let me hear her speak.

Sometimes she answers, sometimes she is still.
Like someone who's confused, then sorts it out,
I say, "This was your mind's trick, nothing more.

"You know well that in thirteen forty-eight,
the sixth of April, in the day's first hour,
she left her body here, that blessed soul."

: *Lethe*: river in the classical underworld that induces oblivion.   **4**: *her star*: Venus (see 289.4).   **12–14**: *RVF* 211 ended by recording the date and time of his first meeting Laura, exactly 21 years before her death.

337 *Quel, che d'odore et di color vincea*

My sweet tree that for color and for scent
surpassed the fragrant and resplendent East
and all its fruits, flowers, leaves, grass (so the West
could boast it was uniquely excellent),

my laurel, where there used habitually
to dwell all beauty and all ardent good,
would often see my goddess and my lord
sitting beneath its shade companionably.

I built a nest of noble thoughts I'd culled
in that life-giving tree; in fire and ice,
burning and trembling, I was more than glad.

When her perfected virtues filled the world,
wanting to beautify his heaven, God
recalled her, who was worthy of his bliss.

1–8: Laura as the laurel looks down to see herself and the god of love sitting in conversation beneath her branches (see the similar doubling in 34.13–14). Petrarch in effect revises the Daphne/Apollo myth from attempted rape to companionship, because as the myth applies to Laura, she is always already the laurel.   **3**: *fruits . . . grass*: i.e., of the Orient (Leopardi); *West*: where Laura lived, which made it surpass the fabled Orient.

338 *Lasciato ài, Morte, senza sole il mondo*

Death, you have left the world without its sun,
darkened and cold, Love blinded and disarmed,
light-hearted grace stripped bare, beauty infirm,
courtliness banished, chastity cast down,

and me, a burden to myself, undone.
Only I mourn her yet the whole world should,
for you have ripped up virtue's noblest seed.
Who can replace her, now that she is gone?

Air, earth and sea should weep for humankind,
which lacking her is like a meadow bare
of flowers or like a ring without its jewel.

Nor did the world know her when she was here;
I knew her, who to mourn her stay behind,
and heaven, which the tears' source makes beautiful.

1: For Laura as the sun, see 9.11 note.   2: *Love . . . disarmed*: Laura's eyes were the love god's light and also his weapons.

339 *Conobbi, quanto il ciel li occhi m'aperse*

With heaven opening my eyes that far,
while Love and my own efforts spread my wings,
I saw most beautiful yet mortal things
rained on a single person by the stars.

Her many other exceptional and rare
beauties, of heavenly, immortal kind,
since they surpassed what I could understand
were more than my weak human sight could bear.

So everything I said of her or wrote,
praise now repaid in front of God with prayers,
was a mere droplet from a boundless sea;

the pen cannot outrun the poet's wit
and when you hold the sun in a fixed stare,
the brighter it becomes the less you see.

3: *most . . .things*: Laura's outstanding physical beauties, produced through nature with its astral influences.   5–6: *many . . . kind*: by contrast, the sublime qualities of her soul, created directly by God.

340 *Dolce mio caro et precïoso pegno*

My precious treasure, dear to me and sweet,
whom nature took and heaven now keeps for me,
why does your pity for me so delay,
you who supplied my life such staunch support?

At least in sleep you sometimes would appear
so I might see you; now instead I burn
without your comfort. Why let this go on?
Surely no scorn or anger lives up there,

feelings that down here sometimes make a heart,
though tender, feed upon a lover's pain,
defeating Love within his own domain.

You see within me and can feel my hurt
and you alone can make my sorrow ease:
appear to me again and still my cries.

This sonnet and the three that follow take up the theme of Laura's visits to
the sleeping poet, already developed in Nos. 283–86.   **11**: *domain*: the heart
(Leopardi).

341 *Deh qual pietà, qual angel fu sì presto*

Ah, what compassionate angel made such haste
to carry my lament beyond the sky?
For now I feel my lady come to me
just as she used to, looking sweetly chaste,

to soothe my desolate heart's misery,
seeming so humble, not remote or proud,
that I draw back from envying the dead.
I live and living does not trouble me.

Blessed is she who causes bliss as well
in those who see her or else hear a word
that only she and I can understand:

"I grieve for you, my dear and faithful friend,
but my severity was for our good."
What else she says would make the sun stand still.

1–8: This directly takes up the narrative of *RVF* 340.   **13**: *severity*: her refusal
in life to accept his passion (see *RVF* 264); this idea is developed in more detail
in *TM* 2.88–120 (see Appendix).

342 *Del cibo onde 'l signor mio sempre abonda*

With food my lord forever keeps on hand,
sorrow and tears, I feed my weary heart;
I turn pale often and my trembling starts
at the remembrance of its cruel deep wound.

But she who had no equal in our age
comes to the bed where grief has left me weak,
her aspect such that I dare hardly look,
and sits compassionately on the edge.

With that smooth hand that I desired so much
she dries my eyes and brings me with her speech
sweetness no mortal man has felt before:

"What good is knowledge when you feel despair?
Weep for me no more. If you only could
be as alive as I, who am not dead!"

1–4: This formula, typical of the poems of unrequited love, now refers to bereavement.   **4**: *its*: my heart's.   **13–14**: Laura is more alive than the poet because
death is the door to our real life, and he should grieve no more at her attaining it.

343 *Ripensando a quel, ch'oggi il cielo honora*

As I recall the soft glance that today
lights heaven, the bend of the blond head, the face,

the gentleness of the angelic voice,
once sweet, and now a piercing grief to me,

I'm filled with wonder that my life goes on;
and it would not, if she who made us doubt
if she were lovelier or more chaste were not
so prompt to come and help me toward the dawn.

Oh how she greets me, kind and sweet and pure!
And how she listens closely and notes well
the lengthy tale of suffering that I tell!

When dawning day shows through her, she goes back
to heaven, knowing all ways leading there;
her eyes are moistened, as are both her cheeks.

This completes the series on Laura's nightly visitations.   **8**: Dreams toward morning were believed more truthful. See *Inf.* 26.7 ("But if as morning nears we dream the truth"); *Purg.* 9.16–18.   **13**: *knowing all ways*: having possessed all the virtues in life (Chiòrboli).

344 *Fu forse un tempo dolce cosa amore*

There was a time, perhaps, when love was sweet,
not that I know when that was; but it's now
so bitter nothing's worse, a truth they know
who learn it as I have from grief's full weight.

She who was once the glory of our days,
who now adorns and brightens heaven, in life
made any comfort I found rare and brief;
now she has cut me off from all repose.

Cruel Death has taken from me all I had;
even the bliss that soul, now free, enjoys
provides no comfort for this misery.

I wept, then sang; now I cannot change mode,
but my soul's gathered sorrow night and day
vents through my tongue and spills out through my eyes.

10–11: In this mood, the poet's grief is not really for Laura but for himself.   12:
change mode: The poet can no longer alternate singing and weeping (for which,
see *RVF* 229 and 230).

345 *Spinse amor et dolor ove ir non debbe*

My love and sorrow forced my querulous tongue,
as it complained, to go where it should not,
saying of her I craved and sang about,
something that if correct would be a wrong:

her blessedness should make my pain abate,
console my heart and leave it feeling calm,
seeing she now has grown so close to Him
who while she lived was always in her heart.

In truth I am consoled and grow serene,
nor want to see her still here in this hell;
I'd rather live this living death alone.

My mind's eye sees her, still more beautiful,
ascending with the angels in their flight
to her and my eternal Master's feet.

3: *saying*: i.e., in 344.10–11.   11: *live. . . death (morire et viver)*: because to go
on living without her (Chiòrboli) or "in this hell" (Apollonio-Ferro) is death.

346 *Li angeli eleƈti et l'anime beate*

The blessed souls and angels, residents
of heaven, on the day my lady passed
beyond us, gathered round her from the first,
filled with surprise and tender reverence.

"What light is this, what beauty yet unknown?"
they asked each other. "No such lovely soul
has risen from the sinful world in all
the present age to this exalted zone."

And she, rejoicing at her change of home,
joins ranks with those of the most perfect sort
and yet turns back to see, from time to time,

if I am following her, and seems to wait.
I raise all my desires and thoughts to heaven,
because I hear her urging me to hasten.

347 *Donna che lieta col Principio nostro*

Lady who rest in our Beginning, full
of the gladness that your holy life has won,
seated upon a high and glorious throne,
arrayed in something more than purple or pearl,

O wonder among women, sublime, rare,
now in His face who sees all things you see
my steadfast love and pure fidelity
that made me spill much ink and many tears,

and know I felt for you on earth the same
as I now feel when heaven is your home,
wanting the splendor of your eyes, no more;

and so in recompense for our long war,
which turned me from the world toward you alone,
pray for me that I may come join you soon.

1: "I am the Alpha and the Omega, the beginning and the end, saith the Lord
God. . . ." Apoc. 1:8.   4: *something*: heavenly splendor.   6: See *TM* 2.77–78 in
Appendix.   9–11: As in 334.6–7, Petrarch becomes an unreliable narrator. His
assertion here is not consistent with many poems in Part One, *e.g.*, 22.31–36 (or,

for example, with 351.1–4, 10–11, let alone with Petrarch in penitential mode, as in *RVF* 355). **12–13**: In 341.13 Laura in a dream characterized their long war differently: "my severity was for our good." **14**: *you (voi)*: Petrarch switches to the plural form, apparently including Christ, as in 349.14, or the blessed souls.

348 *Da' più belli occchi, et dal più chiaro viso*

The loveliest eyes and the most radiant face
that ever shone, framed by the brightest hair,
whose splendor made the sun and gold appear
to dim, the body formed in paradise

revealing hands and arms that staying still
would have subdued the ones who most held out
against Love, and the lovely nimble feet,
the sweetest speech and the most melting smile

– these were the air I breathed, and now delight
the king of heaven and his winged messengers,
while blind and naked down here I remain.

I look toward just one comfort for my pain:
that she who understands my every thought
may gain for me the grace to be with her.

9: "the air I breathed (*prendean vita i miei spiriti*)": literally, [from these] "my [vital] spirits drew life." In Galenic physiology the air we breathe (like Laura's beauties for the poet here) nourished the vital spirits, for which see note to 17.9. **11**: *blind and naked*: deprived of her and her light.

349 *E' mi par d'or in hora udire il messo*

Always that messenger I seem to hear,
the one my lady sends to summon me,
so that my mind and body steadily
change, and I'm so worn out these last few years

I hardly recognize myself by now;
I've put the life I used to lead away.
I would be glad to learn my destined day,
and yet the end must not be far, I know.

Happy the day I flee this earth-bound jail,
leaving dispersed in torn scraps that I shed
my mortal dress, so heavy yet so frail,

and rising from these thronging shadows fly
until I soar so far in the clear sky
that I can see my lady and my Lord.

1: The tenor of the poem suggests that the messenger is the angel of death, whom the poet eagerly awaits. 3: *so that (così)*: in that expectation (Chiòrboli). 4: *last few years*: since Laura's death.

350 *Questo nostro caduco et fragil bene*

This frail and fleeting quality that men
call beauty, made of shadow and of wind,
except in this age never was confined
to just one body, source of all my pain;

for Nature does not choose, nor is it fair
to make one rich while beggaring the rest;
yet here on one she lavished all her best
(pardon me, beauties, or who think you are).

Such beauty never, now or in old days,
was or will be, but it was too concealed
to gain attention from the foolish world.

Quickly it vanished, but it gladdens me
to trade the sight heaven offered fleetingly
only so I might please her holy gaze.

12–14: The poet is consoled for Laura's early death because heaven has exchanged his sight of her beauty on earth for the eternal vision of her only so that he might live in a way that will please her as she looks down (Ponte).

351 *Dolci durezze, et placide repulse*

> The sweet severity and calm rejection
> born of chaste love and sympathy as well,
> the charming anger that knew how to cool
> my daft (as I now see) and flaming passion;
>
> the noble words, resplendent with her bright
> honesty that was highest courtesy;
> the spring of beauty, flower of purity
> that plucked all base desires from my heart;
>
> and that divine glance, a man's happiness,
> now flashing, to restrain my daring mood
> from any conduct rightly disallowed,
>
> now quick to solace me in my distress:
> this studied back-and-forth became the first
> root why my soul's salvation was not lost.

In *TM* 2.88–120 (see Appendix), Laura, appearing to the poet after her death, explains that her behavior toward him in life was carefully balanced for both their sakes: stern when he became too ardent and kind without undue encouragement when her severity made him despondent.

352 *Spirto felice che sí dolcemente*

> Spirit in bliss who once so tenderly
> caused eyes far brighter than the sun to move,
> who formed the sighs and phrases, still alive,
> reverberating in my memory,

I saw you once, alight with a chaste fire,
moving, among the violets in the grass,
not with a lady's but an angel's grace,
her feet who's more than ever with me here,

and whom, returning to your maker then,
you left here as the splendid veil you'd worn,
allotted to you by the highest fate.

At your departure, Love and courtesy
left the whole world, the sun fell from the sky,
and Death began to make himself seem sweet.

8: *her feet*: objective complement of "moving" (6). (The poem is addressed to Laura's spirit, in lines 1–8 as the animator of her living body.) **9**: *whom (la qual)*: no longer the living Laura but her corpse. **14**: *sweet*: by sending Laura to heaven (D).

353 *Vago augelletto che cantando vai*

Wandering warbler, singing on and on
or sobbing, maybe, at your good times' end,
seeing the night and winter close at hand,
while day and the glad season now are gone,

if you could know, the way you know your own
grievous affliction, how I match your state,
you might come down to this disconsolate
breast to make common cause in heartfelt groans.

My share of them might overpower yours:
the mate you weep for may be living yet,
which heaven and Death deny me stingily;

but the unwelcome season, the dark hour
and memories of the bitter years and sweet
move me to speak with you in sympathy.

The second sonnet addressed to a bird, presumably a nightingale, as in *RVF* 311.

354 *Deh porgi mano a l'affannato ingegno*

Ah, lend my flagging faculties a hand,
Love, and assist my feeble, halting pen
to speak of her who is a citizen,
immortal now, of the celestial land;

help my poor verses hit the target, lord,
of her praise, on their own too high a reach,
for the unworthy world has now no match
in virtue or beauty, and it never had.

"Everything heaven and I could give," he says,
"was hers, with forthright speech and wise advice.
Death has despoiled us now of all of these.

"Since Adam's eyes first opened, there has not
been beauty such as hers: let that suffice.
Weeping I say it, weeping you must write."

355 *O tempo, o ciel volubil, che fuggendo*

O time, O wheeling heavens, how you flee,
deceiving wretched mortals who are blind;
O days more swift than arrows or the wind,
experience has revealed your tricks to me;

but I excuse you and myself I blame,
for Nature furnished you with wings to fly,
and me with eyes, which I held steadily
on what harmed me; I now feel grief and shame.

It is high time, indeed by now past time
to turn my eyes to something far more firm
and put an end to my unending woe;

not from your yoke, Love, does my soul depart,
but from its harm – an effort, as you know:
virtue's not random but a strenuous art.

356 *L'aura mia sacra al mio stanco riposo*

My sacred breeze blows through my troubled sleep
so frequently that I make bold to tell
her all the hurt I've felt and I still feel,
which while she lived I never dared bring up.

I mention first that fetching glance, the start
of all the years that have tormented me,
then tell how joy mingled with misery
as by the day and hour Love gnawed my heart.

Silent she stands while pity paints her pale
and staring straight at me she breathes a sigh
as tears enhance the beauty of her face.

Then overcome by sorrow suddenly,
weeping and angry with itself, my soul,
shaken from sleep, returns to consciousness.

357 *Ogni giorno mi par piú di mill'anni*

To me each day seems a millennium
until I follow my dear faithful guide
who led me in this world, while now she leads
me up to the untroubled life to come.

The world's tricks cannot hold me back from this
because I know them all; now so much light

is shining down from heaven into my heart,
I start to count each day I live a loss.

Nothing that death can do strikes fear in me,
for our king suffered it in greater pain
to make me resolute in following now;

and recently death entered every vein
of her who was my gift from destiny
and did not agitate her tranquil brow.

2: *guide*: Laura.   10: *king*: Christ, with reference to his crucifixion.   13: *gift*:
as a guide, emphasizing the parallel with the death of Christ (D).

358   *Non pò far Morte il dolce viso amaro*

Death cannot give her face a bitter cast
yet her sweet face can sweeten Death. What guides
to dying well besides these do I need?
She points the way, who shows me what is best,

and He who came so generously to spend
his blood and broke down hell's gates with his foot
comforts me by his death and gives me heart.
Then come, Death, for I greet you as a friend.

It is high time now, so do not delay;
were it not so, in truth the time came when
my lady passed from this life and went on.

Since then I have not lived a single day;
with her I travelled, and my journey's end
came when her final footstep touched the ground.

2: *sweet . . . Death*: See *TM* 1.172: "In her face even death looked beautiful."   3:
besides these (altre): Laura and Christ.   5–6: Christ redeemed mankind by dying,
after which he descended to hell, smashing its gates and leading to heaven the
just souls of the Old Testament.   10: *the time came when*: that is, when the poet
really died, as explained in the second tercet (S).

When my most gentle, faithful comfort comes
and sits upon the left side of my bed,
speaking in her sweet reasonable way
to give some respite to my weary life,
    I ask, my face grown pale from fear and grief,   5
"Where are you coming from now, blessed soul?"
She draws out from her breast
a sprig of laurel and a frond of palm
and says, "The empyreal
heaven's blest precincts I have left behind   10
and only come to ease your troubled mind."

    Humble in my expression and my words,
I thank her, then ask, "How were you aware
of my condition?" She: "The woeful waves
of tears, of which you never have your fill,   15
    "with gales of sighs pass far through space until
they come to heaven, where they trouble me.
It so distresses you
that I have left earth's misery behind
and reached a better life,   20
which should delight you if you loved me so
as in your words and looks you say you do.

    "I weep for nothing but myself," I say,
"that I remain in darkness and in torment,
because I've always been as sure you'd risen   25
to heaven as of a thing seen close at hand.
    "Why else would God and Nature ever send
virtue so richly down on a young heart
if everlasting life
had not been destined for the good you'd do,   30
you, one of the rare souls
who lived among us nobly here until
you soared to heaven after a brief while.

"But what can I do except weep, alone
and wretched, who am nothing without you?   35
I wish I'd died unweaned and in the cradle
and not have suffered love's cruel injuries."
    She: "Why torment yourself, why flood your eyes?
Far better to have raised your wings from earth
and weighed on a true scale   40
your sweet deceptive chatter of complaint
and perishable things.
Follow me, if it's true you love me best,
and pluck the laurel or the palm at last."

    "I meant to ask you earlier," I reply,   45
"what is the meaning of those leafy branches?"
And she then: "You should answer that yourself,
for one of them you celebrate with your pen.
    "The palm is victory; I was still young when
I conquered my desires and the world's lures;   50
and laurel is the triumph
I earned because the Lord gave me the strength.
Turn to Him now and seek
succor from Him when enemies harass,
so we are with Him when you've run your race."   55

    "Is this the blond hair in its golden knot,"
I say, "that binds me still, are those the eyes
that were my sun?" She: "Do not make the blunders
common to fools, nor think nor talk their way.
    "I am bare spirit, rapt in heaven's joy;   60
what you seek has been dust for many years.
To free you from distress
I am allowed to look like this, as I
shall be again, but more
dear to you, lovelier than when, cruel and kind,   65
I gained salvation for us in the end."

I weep, and with her hands
she dries my face; I hear her softly sigh;
she vents her anger then
in words that have the power to break stones up;   70
and after that she leaves, and so does sleep.

The visitation of Laura's spirit in a dream (see *RVF* 340–43, 356) is dramatized
in a dialogue in Petrarch's penitential mode that echoes his prose work *My
Secret*. **38**: From here on, Laura's spirit rebukes Petrarch's feelings for her and
his poetry about her. Her stern figure recalls Beatrice rebuking Dante when
she meets him at the end of the *Purgatorio*. Both poets are accused, though in
different terms, of loving false images of good. **47–48**: *celebrate . . . pen*: the
laurel in its connection with poetry in Petrarch's verse. **49–52**: She equates
the palm with victory, specifically her spiritual victory over herself and the
world, and the laurel with triumph, the celebration of victory. **54**: *enemies
(altri)*: the world, the flesh and the devil (but Petrarch's diction is typically
indeterminate). **63–64**: After the Last Judgment Laura's spirit will be reunited
with her glorified body. **65–66**: *cruel and kind*: see *RVF* 351. In Santagata and
Dotti's reading she will still be harsh to him in heaven – why she would need to
do that is hard to understand. **69–70**: *anger*: She is exasperated that his tears
show her failure to reform his attitude.

360 *Quel'antiquo mio dolce empio signore*

Having brought suit against my long-time sweet
cruel lord in the tribunal of the queen
who governs the divine
part of our nature, sitting in its summit,
I state my case there, as if I were gold   5
refined in fire, and show how I am burdened
with sorrow, fear and horror,
a man afraid of death and seeking justice.
And I begin: "My Lady, when quite young
I put my left foot into this one's realm   10
where, except scorn and anger,
I met with nothing; and so many strange
torments I suffered there

my endless patience finally was exhausted
and I conceived a hatred for my life.   15

    "And so until today I've passed my days
suffering in flames – what honorable, useful
paths I have scorned, what pleasures,
and all to serve this ruthless flatterer!
    "What quick wit could come up with ready words   20
to put before you my unhappy state
and all my just complaints,
many and grave, against this ingrate here?
    "How little honey and, ah, how much gall!
How he has trained my life to bitterness   25
with his deceiving sweetness,
which lured me into his enamored flock!
For if I'm not deceived
I had it in me to rise very high;
he took my peace and plunged me into war.   30

    "Moreover, this one made me love my God
less than I should and care less for myself;
so, doting on a lady,
I have neglected what should most concern me.
    "In this he's been my only counselor,   35
forever sharpening my youthful longing
on his cruel stone, which gave me
hope for some easing of his ruthless yoke.
    "Wretch that I am, why were high intellect
and other gifts bestowed on me by heaven?   40
For my hair changes, yet
I cannot change my obstinate desire;
so has the heartless one
whom I accuse stripped me of liberty
and made a bitter life a sweet dependence.   45

    "He drove me to explore deep wilderness –
wild beasts, rapacious bandits, prickly brambles,

peoples with barbarous customs,
the difficulties travelers endure,
   "mountains and valleys, swamps and seas and rivers,   50
a thousand snares spread everywhere I went,
winter's cold out of season
danger always imminent and exhaustion.
   "Nor did he nor the other enemy
I fled from ever leave me for a moment;   55
so if I have not met
a premature harsh death before my time,
it is that heaven's mercy
cares about my salvation, not this tyrant,
who feeds upon my sorrow and my loss.   60

   "Since serving him, I've had no hour of peace,
nor hope to have; my nights have banished sleep
and cannot call it back
with spells or soporifics. By deceit
   "and violence he has managed to control   65
my vital functions; and since then, no night-time
bell in a town I may be in has rung
but I have heard. He knows I speak the truth,
   "for no worm ever gnawed through old dry wood
as he my heart, in which he's burrowed deep,
threatening it with death.   70
From this arise my suffering and my tears
and all the words and sighs
with which I tire myself and maybe others.
Render your judgment, you who know us both."   75

   My adversary then with harsh reproaches
begins: "Now, Madam, hear the other side.
I will explain in full
the truth from which this ingrate strays so far.
   "In youth he was apprenticed to the trade   80
of selling lawyer's phrases – that is, lies –

and he is not ashamed,
though brought to my delights from this dry boredom,
   "to lodge complaints against me, me who kept him
free from the greed that often works its harm,   85
of which he now complains,
gave him the sweet life – he says misery –
where he rose to some fame
through me alone, who raised his intellect
to heights he never could have reached himself.   90

 "He knows that Agamemnon and Achilles
and Hannibal, a scourge upon your land,
and he who both by fortune
and merit was the most illustrious,
   "stooped, with my acquiescence, to love slaves,   95
as their stars had decreed when they were born;
and yet for him I chose
out of a thousand worthy women, one
   "whose like will not be seen again on earth,
not if Lucretia should return to Rome.   100
Such a sweet way of speaking
I gave her, and so soft a singing voice
that in her presence never
could vulgar or improper thoughts survive.   105

   "This was the gall and these the scorn and anger,
sweeter than any other lady's all.
Good seed can yield bad fruit:
that's my reward for serving such an ingrate.
   "The way I guided him beneath my wing   110
his poems soon charmed the ears of knights and ladies.
I made him mount so high
his name shines among those who ardently
   "love poetry, and with great delight they make
collections of his verse in many places,   115
he who might now be only

one of the mob that mutters in the courts.
I've raised him up and made him
famous through all he's learned while in my school
and through her who was matchless in the world.   120

  "And finally, to explain my greatest service,
I held him back from many shameful actions,
knowing that base behavior
could bring no satisfaction to a youth
  "as modest and reserved as he'd become   125
in thought and deed since he had pledged allegiance
to her who stamped her mark
deep in his heart and formed him in her image.
  "All his exceptional and noble traits
have come from her and me, whom he accuses.   130
No nightmare ever was
as unreal as his charges against us,
he that has, since he's known us,
enjoyed the favor of people and of God.
That is what this proud man complains about.   135

  "Further, and most significant of all,
I gave him wings to soar above the skies
through mortal things – perceived
truly, a ladder up to the creator;
  "for gazing on the wealth and the perfection   140
of virtues she possessed who was his hope,
he could have risen from
one likeness to the next to the First Cause.
  "He said so more than once himself in verse,
but now forgets me as he does the lady   145
I gave him to support
his feeble life." On hearing that, I raise
a tearful wail and cry,
"He gave her to me but soon took her back!"
"Not I, but He who wants her for himself."   150

At last, both turning to the judge's bench,
each of us rests his case, I quavering
and he in angry tones:
"Most noble Lady, I await your judgment."
And smiling, she replies,   155
"I have been pleased to hear your arguments,
but such a complex case requires more time."

2, 4: *lord (and defendant)*: Love; *queen (and judge)*: Reason, whose seat is in the brain (*summit*).   **5–6**: *gold . . . fire*: purified by harrowing trial (to emphasize his good faith in making his plea).   **10**: *left foot*: making the wrong choice of sensuality (see 264.120–21), but his youth implies innocent mistake.   **31–34**: The poet charges Love with having made him love the creature more than the creator, the charge St. Augustine makes against Petrarch in *My Secret*.   **36–38**: *(whet) stone*: traditionally understood as the poet's hope of love, because the cruelty of Love's yoke would be relieved if his passion were reciprocated.   **54**: *other enemy*: Laura; the poet claims that his frequent travels were undertaken to escape her, which is at best special pleading.   **66**: *vital functions (spirti)*: the vital spirits, for which see note to 17.9.   **80–90**: At his father's urging, Petrarch initially trained as a lawyer, which he regards as a debased trade because lawyers take money for their services (unlike the ancient orators, who represented clients gratis). See Fam. 20.4. Love claims he freed the poet from this low desire for money and turned him to the liberal study of poetry.   **93–94**: Scipio Africanus, Petrarch's personal hero among the ancients and the subject of his Latin epic.   **100**: For Lucretia, see 260.9–10 and note.   **106**: *gall, scorn, anger*: that the poet complained about at lines 11 (scorn and anger) and 24 (gall).   **121–28**: Far from inspiring the sensual passion whose frustration tortured the poet, Love (he claims) arranged a chaste romance (of the sort suitable to stilnovist poetry).   **139–43**: Love refutes the argument that he made the poet forget God (31–34). The poet should have understood that by beginning with human love and virtue the mind can rise to contemplate God, the first cause of all things. This argument is made to Petrarch by St. Augustine *My Secret*.   **144**: *said . . . in verse*: see, *e.g.*, 72.5–8, 306.1–2.   **157**: In the same way, the discussion in *My Secret* ends without being resolved.

361 *Dicemi spesso il mio fidato speglio*

My truthful mirror frequently has told
me all that waning strength, soul-weariness,

stiff joints and wrinkled skin proclaim no less:
"It's time to face the truth now – you are old.

"Obedience to nature's course is best;
the power to stand against it ebbs with time."
Suddenly then, as water quenches flame,
I waken from a long deep sleep at last.

I see our life, how rapidly it runs
and how we cannot be here but the once.
Something she said wakes echoes in my heart,

she who is free now from her lovely knot
but who was such a wonder in her time
she's stolen every other lady's fame.

11: What she said is left to intrigue the reader, but it is likely to be comforting,
like what she says to the poet in the next sonnet.   12: *knot*: the union of body
and soul that was her mortal self.

362   *Volo con l'ali di pensieri al cielo*

I fly to heaven on the wings of thought
so often that I feel as if I were
one of those who possess their treasure there,
leaving their veils on earth, now torn apart.

Sometimes my heart will shiver from sweet chill
when I hear her who turns my face pale say,
"My friend, I love and honor you today
for as your hair changed, your life did as well."

She leads me to her Lord, to whom I bow,
and I beseech her humbly to allow
my staying here to see them face to face.

She answers, "You are destined for this place;
twenty or thirty years' delay seems long
to you and yet is but a little thing."

4: The body is torn by the soul's departure.   **10–12**: The colloquy is not with God but with Laura as the poet's intercessor, as indicated by her reassuring and comforting tone (Chiòrboli).

363 *Morte à spento quel sol ch'abagliar suolmi*

Death made the sun that dazzled me go dark;
darkened the eyes that were secure and chaste;
the one who made me freeze and burn is dust,
my laurels withered up, now elms or oaks.

I see my gain from this and yet I mourn:
nobody now can make my thoughts both bold
and timorous, or turn them hot and cold,
fill them with hope and make them droop forlorn;

no longer ruled by him who wounds and heals,
who held me for so long in torment once,
I learn how bittersweet my freedom feels.

I turn, with adoration and thanksgiving,
to Him who rules the heavens with a glance,
not merely surfeited but tired of living.

1: *sun*: Laura.   **4**: *laurels withered*: death has made the poet's loving thoughts turn despondent (oak and elm not being evergreen like laurel).   **9**: *him*: Love.

364 *Tennemi Amor anni ventuno ardendo*

For twenty-one long years Love held me burning,
joyful in fire, in sorrow full of hope;
after my lady and my heart rose up
to heaven together, ten years more in mourning.

Now I am tired and blame my life for that
long failing, which came near to kill the seed

of virtue in me; and to you, great God,
my last years I devoutly dedicate,

repenting for the years I spent so ill,
years that I should have put to better use,
avoiding passion's troubles, seeking peace.

Lord, who has shut me in this prison cell,
free me and save me from eternal loss,
for I admit my fault without excuse.

The first of two penitential sonnets that close the Laura cycle and lead back to
the opening poem in the collection.　**1–4**: Petrarch met Laura in 1327 and she
died in 1348.　**12**: *prison cell*: his body.

365 *I' vo piangendo i miei passati tempi*

I grieve for all the time that I've run through
loving immoderately a mortal thing,
not taking to the air despite my wings
fit for a flight not altogether low.

You see my vile and shameful sinfulness,
invisible, immortal king of heaven;
succor my feeble soul, which has been driven
astray, make up its deficit with your grace;

so that if I have lived in storm and war
I die in port and peace; so if my stay
was useless, with some honor I may go.

In the brief span of living left to me
and in my dying, let your hand be near.
I hope in no one else, as well you know.

2: *mortal thing*: Laura; see 360.31–34 and note.

Beautiful Virgin, clothed in the sun's rays
and crowned with stars, who pleased the highest Sun
so much that he concealed his light in you,
   love moves me to write verses in your praise,
but I cannot begin without your help   5
and His whose love changed him to flesh within you.
   I call on her who answers everyone
who calls on her with faith.
Virgin, if the extreme
misery of our human lot has ever   10
moved you to pity, deign to hear my prayer,
support me in my war,
though I am dust and you the queen of heaven.

   Wise Virgin, one among the happy number
of the five blessed prudent virgins – rather   15
the first among them, with the brightest lamp;
   O firm shield over people in distress
against the ravages of death and fortune,
affording us not just escape but triumph;
   O refuge from blind passion that flares up   20
here among foolish mortals;
Virgin, now turn your splendid
eyes, which in sorrow saw the savage wounds
impressed upon the limbs of your dear son,
to my imperiled state,   25
who come to you in doubt and seeking counsel.

   Virgin immaculate in body and soul,
daughter and mother of your noble child,
you who light this life and adorn the next,
   through you the highest Father's son and yours,   30
O high clear window through which heaven shone,
 came down to save us in the last of days.

Among all habitations on the earth
none except you was chosen,
Virgin most highly blessed,   35
who have transformed the tears of Eve to joy.
You who are able, deign to make me worthy
of His grace, O forever
blessed one, crowned in the celestial realm.

Virgin most holy, full of every grace,   40
who through your high and true humility
mounted to heaven where you hear my prayers,
    you gave birth to the fountainhead of pity,
the sun of justice, who irradiates
the world that's darkened with thick clouds of error.   45
    You in yourself embrace the cherished names
of mother, daughter and bride,
Virgin most glorious,
spouse of the King who freed us from our bonds,
leaving the world in joyous liberty.   50
Now in his sacred wounds,
assuage my heart, I pray, you who bring joy.

Virgin whose peer the world has never seen
and with whose beauties heaven fell in love,
whom no one ever equaled or approached,   55
    your holy thoughts and pious actions served
to consecrate your fruitful virgin womb
as a living temple fit for the true God.
    Your patronage could fill my life with joy,
Mary, if through your prayers,   60
Virgin most merciful,
where sin abounded grace may more abound.
I pray, as I kneel suppliant in my mind,
that you will be my guide
and lead my crooked path to a good end.   65

Radiant Virgin, star forever shining
steadfast above this stormy sea, the one
trustworthy guide for a devoted steersman,
　　look down and see in what a fearsome tempest
I find myself, alone and rudderless　　　　　　　　70
and closing in upon my final scream.
　　But nonetheless my soul relies on you –
sinful, I won't deny,
Virgin, but I implore you
not to allow your foe to laugh at me.　　　　　　　75
Remember that our sin was what made God
assume, to rescue us,
our human flesh within your virgin cloister.

　　Virgin, how many tears I've strewn, how many
pleadings and honeyed praises, all in vain,　　　　80
only for my own pain and grievous harm!
　　Since I was born upon the banks of Arno,
travelling now through one land, now another,
my whole life has been one long time of troubles.
　　Beauty that dies and fleeting words and gestures　85
have crushed my soul completely.
Life-giving holy Virgin,
do not delay, this year may be my last;
between my sufferings and my sins, my days
have all gone by, more swift　　　　　　　　　　90
than arrows, and now only death awaits me.

　　Virgin, that one is dust and keeps my heart
grieving, who kept it weeping while alive
and had no sense of all my sufferings;
　　but had she known, what happened would have happened

95
anyway, for if her desires were other
it would have meant my death and her dishonor.
　　Now you, the queen of heaven and our goddess

(if saying that is proper),
most understanding Virgin,   100
can see the whole and what she could not do
would not be difficult for your great power:
to terminate my sorrow,
for your own honor and for my salvation.

   Virgin in whom alone I place my hope   105
for help that meets my desperate situation,
do not desert me at the final pass.
   Look not at me, but rather Him who made me;
let not my worth but his high image in me
move you to care about a man so wretched.   110
   Medusa and my fault have made me a stone
dripping with useless moisture;
Virgin, now fill my weary
heart with repentant holy tears, and let
at least my final weeping be devout,   115
without the earthly mud
the first contained, which was not free of madness.

   Kind Virgin, enemy of pride, allow
the love of our shared origin to move you
to pity a contrite and humble heart.   120
   If I could love a transitory bit
of mortal clay with such intense devotion,
how shall I love you, noblest of all creatures?
   If with your helping hand I rise again
from my low wretched state,   125
Virgin, I swear to cleanse
and consecrate to you my thoughts, my talent,
my style, my tongue and heart, my tears and sighs.
Conduct me to the better
crossing and welcome my reformed desires.   130

   The day approaches and cannot be far,
the way time hurtles on,

Virgin who has no peer,
while fear of death and conscience pierce my heart.
Commend me to your son, true man, true God;   135
entreat him that he may
on my last day receive my soul in peace.

1–3: This hymn to the Virgin Mary begins as it will go on, weaving a tissue of Marian devotion from scripture, scriptural commentary and hymns. A Marian hymn also begins the final canto of Dante's *Paradiso*. **1–2**: "And a great sign appeared in heaven: a woman clothed with the sun . . .and on her head a crown of twelve stars. . ." Apoc. 12:1. **2–3**: The Sun is God and the verses refer to the incarnation of the Word in Jesus Christ, as does line 6. **14–16**: In a parable of Jesus the five wise virgins bring oil for their lamps and when the bridegroom comes at midnight go in to the marriage, while the five foolish virgins must go buy oil. Matt. 25:1–13. **27**: *immaculate . . . soul (d'ogni parte intera)*: because of her virginity and sinlessness, but also perhaps a reference to the immaculate conception (Contini). **28**: "daughter" because her son is her creator. **31**: *window*: Chiòrboli quotes Fulgentius: "Mary became the window of heaven, because through her God transmitted the true light to the ages." **32**: *last of days*: the last age of the world, inaugurated by Jesus. **36**: *turned the tears*: by giving birth to Jesus, who saved us from the consequences of Adam and Eve's sin. **47**: *bride*: Mary is the bride of the Holy Spirit. See Matt. 1:20; *Purg.* 20.96–97. **49**: *mother, daughter, bride*: i.e., of Christ. For "daughter," see line 28 and note; Christ is Mary's spouse through his participation in the generative power of the Holy Spirit in the unity of the Godhead. **62**: This verse translates Rom. 5:20. **75**: *foe*: the devil. **79–81, 85–86, 92–97**: The ratio of petition to praise has been gradually increasing; now Petrarch becomes more confessional about his sexual passion for Laura and his present repentance. **109**: *image*: Gen. 1:27. **111**: *Medusa*: Laura's beauty, like Medusa, could leave one who saw it stunned immobile; see 179.9–11. **115–17**: His devout weeping will not be soiled, like his weeping over Laura, with the madness of carnal passion.

Appendix

TRIUMPH OF DEATH II

The night that followed the catastrophe
   that quenched the sun, or placed it back in heaven,
   and left me stranded here like a blind man
spread through the air the sweet spring morning chill
   that with the whitening of Tithonus' lover   5
   lifts up the veil that leaves our dreams confused.
I saw a lady looking like the dawn,
   wearing a crown of oriental gems,
   move toward me from a host of spirits with crowns.
She spoke to me with sighs, held out to me   10
   the hand that in the past I'd so desired,
   which sowed eternal sweetness in my heart:
"Can you now recognize the one who first
   made you depart from the well-traveled way?"
   Thoughtful she seemed, with a wise gentle look,   15
as when my heart in youth was first aware
   of her; she sat and made me sit upon
   a bank well shaded by a beech and laurel.
"How could I fail to recognize the goddess
   who gave me life?" I answered through my tears;   20
   "but tell me, please, are you alive or dead?"
"I am alive and you are still dead now,
   and will remain so till your final hour
   comes, which will raise you from the earth," she said.
"But the time we have is briefer than our wish;   25
   be careful, therefore, to restrain your speech

before the dawn, already close, is on us."
And I: "At the ending of this sunlit other,
   what men call life, ah, tell me, you who know
   by tasting it, if dying is such pain."   30
"As long as you keep following the crowd,"
   she said, "in its blind, obstinate opinion,
   you have no chance of ever being happy.
For noble spirits death is just the end
   of a dark prison, but it brings great pain   35
   to those concerned with nothing but the mud.
And now my death, which brings you so much grief,
   would make you celebrate, if you could feel
   a thousandth portion of my present joy."
She said this with her eyes devoutly raised   40
   to heaven. Then she moved those rosy lips
   silently till I said, "Atrocities
like those wreaked by Caligula and Nero,
   the onset of sharp pains and burning fevers
   make death appear more bitter far than wormwood."   45
"True, I cannot deny," she said, "the anguish
   that leads to death is difficult to bear,
   more so the fear of being damned forever;
but if the soul turns for support to God
   and the heart too, which in itself perhaps   50
   is weary, what is death but a brief sigh?
I was already near the final crossing,
   worn out in body but alert in spirit,
   when I heard someone speak, a deep sad voice:
'Unhappy he who counts the days, for each   55
   will seem a thousand years! In vain he lives,
   never to see her face to face on earth.
He travels through the sea and all its shores,
   but everywhere he goes, it is the same:
   he thinks and speaks and writes of her alone.'   60
I turned my drooping eyes then where the voice

came from and saw the one who for our sakes
  moved me to pity you and check your ardor.
I knew her by her face and by her speech,
  which oftentimes had comforted my heart,   65
  first chaste and beautiful, then grave and wise.
Even when I was at my loveliest,
  in my green age, which was your favorite
  (something that many thought and talked about),
my life was little less to me than bitter   70
  compared to the sweet, gentle kind of death
  I later felt, though mortals rarely do;
all through my passing I was happier
  than one returning home from banishment,
  except that I was gripped by pity for you."   75
"My lady, by the faithfulness," I said,
  "that I believe was clear to you back then,
  confirmed now in his face who sees all things,
did Love at any time inspire the thought
  that you take pity on my lengthy suffering   80
  without infringing on your chaste resolve?
For your sweet anger and sweet indignation
  and the sweet concord written in your eyes
  kept my desire in doubt for many years."
I'd hardly said these words when I could see   85
  the sweet smile flash that at one time had been
  a sun reviving my depleted forces.
Then she said, sighing, "Never was my heart
  parted from you, nor will it ever be,
  but I used stern expressions to damp down   90
your fire, because there was no other way
  to save us both and our young reputations;
  a mother with a whip is no less kind.
I told myself so often, 'This one loves,
  no, burns; now I must find a remedy,   95
  which one who fears or craves can hardly do;

341

let him see sternness, not the way I feel."
    This is what often turned you and restrained you
    the way a bit does with a horse that shies.
Innumerable times my face was painted   100
    with anger, while within Love burned my heart;
    desire, though, always yielded to my reason.
Then, if I saw you overcome by sorrow
    I'd turn my gaze upon you tenderly,
    saving your life while I preserved our honor.   105
If your distress was overpowering
    I'd greet you kindly with my glance and voice,
    sorry for you but wary of giving hope.
These were my arts with you, my strategems;
    now a kind welcome, now a show of anger.   110
    You know it, for you sang about it often.
Sometimes I saw your eyes so full of tears
    I murmured to myself, 'Without some help,
    this one is finished, if I know the signs.'
Then I'd provide what comfort would be proper.   115
    Sometimes I saw your ardor so spurred on
    I said, 'This time a tighter bit is needed.'
So, hot and flushed at times, then cold and pale
    now sad, now glad, I've led you up to here
    still safe though tired, and I rejoice for it."   120
"My lady, this would be full recompense
    for all my faithfulness, could I believe it,"
    trembling I said, and not with a dry face.
"O you of little faith! Unless I knew it
    to be the very truth, why would I say it?"   125
    she answered, and her face appeared to blaze.
"Whether you pleased my eyes while I was living,
    I will not say, but I was greatly pleased
    by the sweet knot I saw around your heart;
and am pleased by the good name, if I hear   130
    truly, your poems have brought me near and far.

In your love I sought only moderation.
That was your only lack, and while you hinted,
  with downcast looks, at what I always knew,
  you opened your heart's secrets to the world.   135
This is what made me cold, which still disturbs you,
  for in all else we shared the kind of concord
  Love brings so long as virtue governs it.
In us the flames of love were almost equal,
  at least when I had recognized your fire;   140
  but one revealed them while the other hid them.
You were already hoarse calling for pity
  while I was silent, for my shame and fear
  made my great longing seem inconsequential.
Grief is no less because you smother it,   145
  nor greater when you go about lamenting.
  Truth does not grow or shrink from being expressed.
But were all veils at least not torn asunder
  when I accepted in your presence only
  your poems and sang, 'Does our love dare no more?'   150
My heart was with you though my eyes were lowered.
  You grieve at this as though your share were worse,
  when I gave you the best and kept the least!
And you ignore that though my glance was taken
  a thousand times from you, it was restored   155
  thousands and thousands and was turned to you
with pity; it would always have remained
  gentle toward you had I not been afraid
  of your sparks, which were dangerous for us.
I want to tell you more, as I am now   160
  about to part from you, to leave you with
  a final word you may perhaps find welcome.
Happy enough with most things life provided,
  with one alone I was not satisfied:
  that I was born in such a humble place.   165
I still regret my birthplace was not nearer,

at least somewhat, to your own flowering nest.
But it was lovely because there I pleased you
for if I was unknown to you, your heart,
    the only one that I can trust, might well   170
    have turned elsewhere and left me with less fame."
"Not so," I said, "the sphere of the third heaven,
    with its unchanging influence, would have raised me
    to such great love wherever we were born."
"Let it be so," she said, "I have received   175
    honor that still is mine. But in your pleasure
    you are not keeping track of the time's flight.
Aurora now has left her gilded bed
    to bring back day to mortals, with the sun
    already risen chest-high from the ocean.   180
She comes to bid me leave and I am sorry.
    If you have more to say, try to be brief
    and match your words to the remaining time."
"You've made my years of suffering easy, even
    welcome," I said, "with your compassionate words;   185
    but life without you will be hard for me.
Therefore I wish to know, my lady, whether
    it is my fate to join you late or soon."
    She said, already leaving, "I believe,
your time on earth without me will be long."   190

1: *catastrophe*: The immediately preceding *Triumph of Death I* described Laura's death in detail. 2: *sun*: As throughout *Scattered Rhymes*, Laura is the sun; she has returned to heaven, where she was born, and left the world dark. 5: *Tithonus' lover*: Aurora, goddess of the dawn. 6: *dreams confused*: The early morning traditionally brings truthful dreams; this is always when Laura appears to the poet. 14: *depart . . . way*: the power of love raises the poet above the common herd. 54: *someone speak*: Petrarch leaves the speaker mysterious. The following passage will show only that it is a real woman well known to Laura in life, now presumably in heaven with the extensive knowledge of the blessed of events on earth. 55–60: As Laura dies, the voice tells her how the poet will grieve for her. 148–50: a probably fictional episode when he presented her with poems in public and she, accepting the gift, sang or recited one of them.   **165**: *humble place*: the village near Avignon referred to in *RVF* 4.   **167**: *flowering nest*: Florence, with a pun on the name. 172: *the third heaven*: that of Venus, which inspires love.

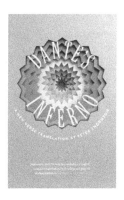

A new verse translation of Dante's *Inferno*.

'Thornton's new translation of Dante's *Inferno* immediately joins ranks with the very best available in English. Opting for unrhymed blank verse, the translator succeeds in capturing the poet's first-person narrative voice with unusual accuracy, spontaneity, and vividness, rendering the otherworld journey with vigor and a flare for the dramatic without ever sounding either strained or unduly creative. Succinct and balanced end-of-canto notes adeptly elucidate historical, classical, and theological references, making this volume a choice contender for both college and general reading audiences.'

Professor Richard Lansing, Brandeis University

'Peter Thornton's eminently readable *Inferno* combines accuracy, elegance, and vitality, while its accompanying notes situate the poem effectively in its critical and wider cultural contexts.'

Dr Tristan Kay, University of Bristol

'Thornton's very readable and accurate verse translation of *The Inferno* captures much of the drama and psychological nuances of Dante's poem. The extensive notes provide a wealth of critical insights, as well as an especially good guide to the poem's historical and literary references and to the centuries-long commentary tradition.'

Professor Christopher Kleinhenz, University of Wisconsin-Madison